HER BEST FRIEND'S SECRET

DEIRDRE PALMER

Storm
PUBLISHING

Ebook ISBN: 978-1-80508-348-1
Paperback ISBN: 978-1-80508-350-4

Cover design: Lisa Horton
Cover images: Alamy, Shutterstock

Published by Storm Publishing.
For further information, visit:
www.stormpublishing.co

ALSO BY DEIRDRE PALMER

The Wife's Revenge
The Girl in the Dark
The Night She Died

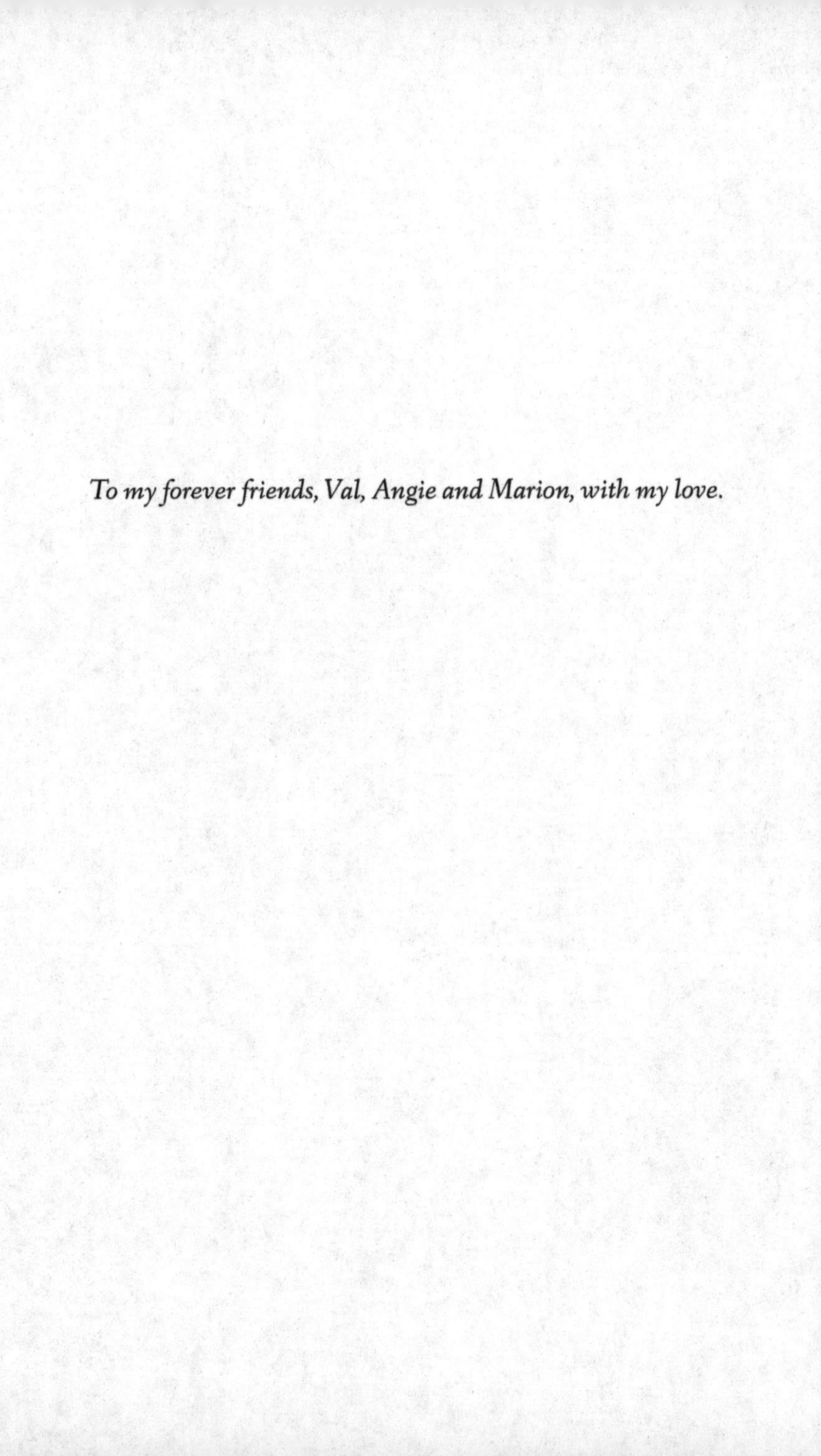

To my forever friends, Val, Angie and Marion, with my love.

ONE
BRIONY

'It's true what they say about you, then? Sweet sixteen and never been kissed. That's what I heard.'

I wanted to stare him out, lock my gaze to his, my head held high. Brazen, like Samantha, quietly confident, like Molly. But as I was neither of those things, I couldn't do it. Instead, my eyes traced the key-shaped lines in the pattern of the Axminster carpet until they found his long, pale feet and ludicrously hairy toes. He was barefoot, as he often was around the house.

'Ah, I see it is true then.' He laughed, a manic ripple of sound that ran around the room, then stopped abruptly, as if someone had sliced it off with a knife.

Now I did look up, sharply. It wasn't true, but my private life wasn't up for discussion, not with Jeremy, anyway.

'Who said? Nobody *said.* You've heard nothing about me. You're making it up. Anyway, what's it got to do with you?'

'Everything that goes on in this house is to do with me,' Jeremy said. 'And since you're a part of this house, for now, anyway, that includes you. Haven't you worked that out yet, Briony?'

I didn't reply. I'd understood the grim truth of his statement almost from the hour I pitched up here.

Jeremy was Alice's only child, the golden boy. I was the lodger, deposited in rural Gloucestershire at fourteen years of age by my father when he'd moved to Australia to set up a branch of his IT business in a shiny tower overlooking Sydney Harbour.

My mother died when I was four. Alice Church had been a neighbour and close friend of my maternal grandmother, and later became my godmother. I don't suppose she'd envisaged her duties stretching as far as giving me a home, although the generous dollops of cash my father paid into her account each month must have sweetened the pill a little. Without this incentive, Summerdene would have succumbed to years of neglect and collapsed to the ground in a wood-wormed heap.

Jeremy held on to both sides of the doorway, swinging back and forth while he examined my face forensically to check if he'd managed to embarrass me. The backs of my knees had started to itch. I imagined the skin; dry, scaly, flaring to red-raw. I resisted the urge to scratch. Unsticking my feet from the carpet, I launched myself towards the doorway, preparing to duck beneath his arm if needs be. But he moved aside just in time.

'Where do you think you're going?' He smiled, his tone playful, as if he was joshing with me. As if this whole conversation had been a joke.

'School. As if it's any of your...' I tailed off. It was never worth trying to rile Jeremy. I would only have come off worst.

'School? On a Saturday?'

'The library. To revise.' I stalked into the hall, remembering to grab my school rucksack from the coat hooks as I passed.

Slamming the front door as hard as I dared, I crossed the gravel drive towards the gate, sensing Jeremy watching me from the sitting-room window.

I shivered, even though it was a warm, sunny day.

TWO

BRIONY

Flinging my rucksack down, I dropped onto the ground beside Samantha. Molly immediately moved across to sit on my other side. There we sat, the three of us, our backs against the scratchy bark of the beech tree which was as familiar to us as our own skin.

Samantha – she was always Samantha, never Sam, or, God forbid, Sammie – had once said we were like the three witches from *Macbeth*. Molly had objected to this on the grounds that the witches sat around a cauldron, so they must have sat in a circle facing one another, whereas we, of necessity because of the backrest, were fanned out, shoulder to shoulder, in a semi-circle.

Samantha had countered this with an acidic comment: 'Why do you have to be so *literal*?'

I was with Samantha. We'd spent enough time at the Kissing Tree, planning and scheming and whispering secrets, for the witchy analogy to be spot on. The seating arrangements didn't come into it. I didn't say so, though.

Samantha nudged me. 'How's the creep today?'

'Still creepy.'

She made a sicky sound in her throat. Molly pulled a face and began nibbling the quick of her thumbnail.

Jeremy was a joke to them, nothing more, because that was how I presented him. A joke with enough of a sinister side to lend an edge to our conversations, and make me feel I had allies, even though they didn't know the half of it.

'Where is he now?' Molly's exaggerated throwaway tone seemed fake, as if it wasn't a casual enquiry but a question she really wanted to know the answer to.

'Jeremy? Skulking around the house, like he does.'

'You'd think he'd have something better to do at his age. What is he? At least twenty, surely?'

'Twenty-one. He's doing a college course in Oxford. Not the *actual* Oxford, of course. He's too dim.'

Jeremy was supposedly taking a business course at a far lesser establishment than Oxford University. From what I'd gathered, he'd clocked up half a degree from a midlands polytechnic before deciding it wasn't for him. Which, roughly translated, meant he'd dropped out with no academic qualification at all. Or – I favoured this option – he'd been kicked out. Apparently, he'd had a few jobs since then: working at an estate agency, being a rep for a stationery firm, and temping in various offices. I couldn't help wondering why none of these jobs had come to anything. Too idle to put in the effort was my theory.

'He's too old to be faffing about with college courses,' Samantha said. 'Oxford's miles away. Plus it costs an arm and a leg to get there. Who pays for that, then? Or does he hitchhike?'

'He only goes in about three days a week, by train,' I said. 'He never seems short of dosh. I reckon he came into some money when his father died. Alice probably subs him as well.'

Samantha smirked. 'I expect she hoped he'd become a doctor, like his father. As if.'

We all laughed.

'If she did, she's never said. Anyway, no med school would have him,' I said. 'Can you *imagine?*'

And imagine we did, for the next few minutes. Silently, each in our individual ways, with the hum of the spring woods around us, the sun burning down through a canopy of bright new leaves, the air sweet with the scent of bluebells, and tangy with wild garlic.

'What's in the bag?' Molly nodded at my rucksack.

'Books and stuff.'

'No sweets?'

'No, just books. You have to pass the shop on the way here. You could've bought sweets.'

'No money,' Molly said.

'Me neither.' Samantha sighed regretfully. 'The books, though?'

'I told the creep I was going to school, to revise in the library.'

'Why you have to lie to him I'll never know.' Samantha turned on me, eyes ablaze with indignation on my behalf. 'Why do you need to tell him anything at all? What's it to him where you go and what you do?'

I'd given up wondering that myself, long ago. I shrugged. 'It's just easiest.'

Easiest, when Alice was engaged in her endless village community activities, leaving me and Jeremy in the house, to lever myself out of an uncomfortable situation as fast as possible, and by any means.

'I wonder how many girls have actually popped their cherries right here, where we're sitting now?' Samantha said, after a while, narrowing her eyes as she gazed upwards through the branches.

'Annabel in the lower sixth said she did it with the captain of the rugby team from that posh school in Cheltenham,' I said. 'You know that. We spoke about it before.'

'Annabel Healy is a liar,' Molly chipped in. 'We said that, too. It was all in her head. Nowhere south of that.'

We all giggled.

'Would you, though? Do it here, out in the open where anyone could see? There are plenty of pathways through the woods,' Samantha said. 'People take shortcuts, all the time.'

I didn't reply. Neither did Molly. We'd had this conversation before, too, more than once. It had become boring, ages ago. Samantha was obsessed with losing her virginity, that's what it was. God knows why.

'Jeremy might have done,' Molly suddenly said. 'I can't imagine him forking out for somewhere special to do the deed.'

We were back to Jeremy. I sighed inwardly.

'Never mind forking out for some*where* to do it. He'd have to pay some*one* to do it *with*,' I said. 'Anyway, why are we talking about him again? Isn't it enough I have to live with the creep?'

'Mind you,' Molly said, 'he's not that bad looking. For a creep, I mean.'

Samantha peeled away from the tree trunk. We both looked at Molly, aghast.

'Really truly?' Samantha said. Then, thoughtfully, addressed me. 'She's got a point, Bri. Even you can see he's not exactly Quasimodo when the wind's in the right direction.'

The way she spoke made it sound as if she was challenging me to disagree. Molly was looking at me questioningly. I felt ganged up against.

Truthfully, if you were pushed to describe Jeremy to a stranger, you might lean towards almost handsome. Around five-eleven in height, he had glossy, mid-brown hair, regular facial features and deep-set grey eyes that on another bloke might have been considered sexy.

On another bloke; I have to emphasise that.

Jeremy's physical attributes weren't exactly lacking. But if you saw beneath the surface dressing and witnessed the supercilious expression and the Jekyll and Hyde personality I was treated to on a daily basis, he became the most unfanciable bloke on the planet.

'Has he got a girlfriend?' Molly asked, in that same fake-casual way of hers.

'If he has, he's never said. Not to me, anyway. He goes out though, in the evenings, sometimes at weekends. Never says where.'

'Up to no good,' Samantha said, with a firm nod. 'That's where.'

Molly and I just looked at her and shook our heads.

'I don't want to know where he goes, or who with,' I said. 'If there is a girlfriend, she won't last long, guaranteed. Now can we drop the subject of my weirdo housemate and talk about something more interesting before I lose the will to live?'

'There's a new carving,' Molly said after a moment, jabbing the air with her thumb. 'Round the other side.'

Molly liked to keep track of these things. Some loved-up couple's initials would have been added to the generations of hopeful hieroglyphics defacing the pewter grey bark. We all got up to look. Molly was right. A new carving was always obvious, the letters dark, raw and open, like wounds, from the recent use of somebody's penknife.

'G loves L forever,' Samantha said, running her finger along the wonky letters. 'Or is it O loves C?'

I turned away. 'Who cares. Let's not get into all that again. Whoever they are, they want their bumps felt.'

'You do believe in love, though?' Molly said. 'Life would be too depressing otherwise.'

'Yeah, I suppose,' I said, without much conviction. I ran my gaze across the myriad amorous carvings stretching back across the decades. 'But I bet you hardly any of this lot made a go of it. I mean, a first kiss at the Kissing Tree? So what? We've all done that, and none of us have a boyfriend.'

We fell about laughing at this. It didn't take much.

I felt better now. The talk of Jeremy had disturbed me, which was stupid. Nobody should have that much power over another person. I skirted the fat trunk of the beech tree and resumed my seat between its twisted roots. The others did the same.

'We have to get tickets for the end-of-term disco before they sell out,' I said. 'Don't forget to bring the money on Monday.'

'It's always about bloody money.' Samantha brushed twiggy bits off her trousers with an irritated hand. 'We'll have to get summer jobs or we'll never get to go anywhere or do anything.'

'Where, though?' Molly said. 'There's nowhere in Mistlecombe. We could try Stroud, I suppose. Not very exciting, though, is it?'

'Or Cheltenham,' Samantha said, 'which means getting the bus or train to Stroud station, then changing. Too much bother, too much money.'

Samantha and Molly sighed in unison.

I kept quiet. If there was one positive thing about being dumped in the middle of the Cotswolds – apart from having these two as my best friends – it was that my father made me a generous monthly allowance. I didn't need to find a job to tide me over till sixth form, although working would give me something to do and get me away from the house, and Jeremy. I didn't dismiss the idea.

'Something will turn up,' I said. 'Let's not even think about it till after O levels.'

There was more sighing at the mention of the dreaded exams before we fell into our usual round of trying to outdo each other on the revision stakes, each of us claiming we were so far behind we might as well walk away from school right now without troubling the treacly floorboards of the examination hall.

It wasn't genuine, of course. I'd been working my socks off, and I suspected the others had, too. Qualifications were a means of escape. We had at least worked that out if we knew nothing else about life.

THREE
BRIONY

'How did the revision go? Get a lot done, did you?' Jeremy beamed at me across the table.

'Were you revising today? Good for you.' Alice reached for the salad bowl and helped herself to another wedge of tomato. 'You'll go far, working hard like you do. Won't she, Jeremy?'

Jeremy nodded. 'Yep, and going to the school library to study, that's real dedication.'

Alice turned to me, surprised. 'Did you go to school? I'd have thought it was quiet enough here.' She didn't wait for my reply. 'It's the atmosphere, I expect. The right atmosphere works wonders, for most things.'

'You do talk twaddle, Mother,' Jeremy said, winking at me. 'As it happens, I went for a long run today. Briony would've had the house entirely to herself. Quiet as the grave. No disturbances.'

I quailed inwardly. Jeremy knew full well I hadn't gone to school today, either from some ridiculous sixth sense he seemed to possess, or because he'd followed me. My money was on the second.

'Alice is right,' I said. 'Studying in the library focuses my mind. Keeps me on track. Anyway, I do mostly revise here. I just felt like going to the library today.'

I heard the trace of *so-there* in my voice. I hoped they hadn't noticed, although in Jeremy's case I didn't care.

Dinner, as always, was delicious. The chicken was roasted to perfection, the potatoes sliced and baked with cream and garlic, Dauphinoise style, the salad crisp and fresh.

Alice was an excellent cook, for which I was eternally grateful. The meals my father used to serve up were carelessly thrown together and tasteless, until the girlfriends – there had been several over the years – had got involved. And even then, dinner had been more about being loaded into a taxi and whizzed to a fancy restaurant than the homely domestic catering a growing girl might have expected.

The restaurants were chosen to impress, of course. They hadn't impressed me. I would sit there playing gooseberry, yawning, bored out of my brain and wishing I was at home with *The Waltons* and cheese on toast.

Consequently, the only cookery skills I'd learned had come from home economics lessons at school but never had the chance to put into practice. Alice occasionally accepted my genuine offers of help but mostly she waved me away. She preferred to get on with it without me under her feet.

Now, I concentrated on my food and let Jeremy and his sly comments float past me. I'd become practised in distancing myself inside my head. It was the only route to a reasonably happy existence.

But Jeremy wasn't finished with me yet.

'By the way, Briony, I see there's an end-of-term disco at your school, after the Os. You'll be going, I expect?'

How did he know about the disco? The same way he knew about everything, I thought.

'Yes, I'll be going.' I turned to Alice. 'If that's all right?'

'Of course it is. You know you don't have to ask, Briony. It'll be good for you to have some fun after your exams. Do you need money for the ticket? Or for something to wear?'

Alice's small brown eyes peered eagerly at me, reminding me of a rabbit. I felt a tug of affection for her and had a sudden urge to get up and give her a hug. Except Alice didn't do hugs, and anyway it would only earn me a snide comment from Jeremy later.

'No, I'll be all right, thanks. It's not that expensive, and I've already got a dress I haven't had the chance to wear.'

'Well, I hope the boys behave themselves.' Jeremy brandished his fork. It had a bit of chicken skin stuck to it. 'I know those comprehensive school oicks. One-track minds.' He chuckled. 'Mind you, some of the girls aren't backward in coming forward either, so I heard.'

Mistlecombe Lane High School had been fortunate enough to avoid contact with Jeremy, who'd been sent to a minor public boys' school outside of the village. Some of the stories I'd heard about that school would make your hair stand on end. How *dare* he look down on the comprehensive kids?

'Jeremy! What a thing to say,' Alice said. 'Briony's is a very good school, *very* good. And I'm sure she knows how to conduct herself.'

'Just kidding.' Jeremy smiled across at me. Or rather, leered. 'Young Briony here will be the epitome of good behaviour. Set an example to the rest of them, I wouldn't wonder.'

I screamed inside, and bit down hard on a bit of radish, catching the side of my tongue.

'I'll be fine,' I said, nursing the pain in my tongue and looking at nobody in particular. It was all the defence I was prepared to put up. Not that I should have needed any.

Alice got up from the table, cleared the dinner plates and fetched the rhubarb crumble. Jeremy picked up the spoon and served himself a portion. Thinking today's undercover taunting was over, I let my shoulders subside. But Jeremy, it appeared, had more to say.

'Seriously, though,' he said, through a mouthful of crumble. 'I could walk down to the school with you, Briony, when you go to the disco. See you safely there. And I'll meet you when it's over and walk you home afterwards.'

'I do go out on my own, you know,' I said, trying not to sound snappy for Alice's sake. 'I'm not a child. I don't need chaperoning. And I can find my way home in the dark, surprisingly enough.'

'Well, the offer stands,' Jeremy said evenly. 'It'll be no trouble.'

Alice paused, the cream jug in mid-air. 'Actually, Briony, it might not be a bad idea to have Jeremy see you home, at least. Just in case.'

In case of what? Now Alice was at it, treating me like a child. Or not a child, in Jeremy's case.

I screwed my napkin into a tight ball in my lap. 'The disco's ages off. Exams first.'

'Even so, let's remember Jeremy's offer when the time comes, shall we?'

There was no answer to that. Not one that wouldn't upset Alice, anyway. I let the napkin fall to the floor and began eating my crumble. Jeremy, I knew without looking, would have a triumphant look on his smug face.

The school disco loomed ahead, the shine having been rubbed off it somewhat. But I would go, and I would have a fab time; I'd make sure of that. Jeremy could just go and boil his head.

FOUR
BRIONY

2022

'Now then, Alice Church's will.'

Callum West's kindly face loomed closer to the screen. Behind him I saw not the expected trappings of a solicitor's office, but a clutter of saucepans and bowls artfully arranged on plain wooden shelves. In the bottom right-hand corner of the screen sat a chunky white pottery mug with 'The World's Best Grandad' in red lettering. A dog yapped in the background and was urgently shushed by a female voice.

'Yes, Alice. My godmother.' I nodded and smiled, wishing he would get on with it. The first five minutes had been spent in general chat, which was all very friendly and nice, but I had a Year 5 class waiting for their dose of Tudor history at the school where I taught, ten minutes away. I'd only nipped home in the lunch break to take this prearranged call. The solicitor, on the other hand, seemed in no hurry at all; the calming effects of working from home, maybe. I wouldn't know, my own experience having been the very opposite of calm.

'Yes, your godmother. As executor, I have to tell you that

everyone's in the will, and I mean everyone. Including the milk-man's horse.' He chuckled, as if he hoped to soften the blow by making a joke of it.

It was no surprise to me, and therefore not a disappoint-ment, to find that I was one among dozens of beneficiaries. I hadn't even thought about it in those terms since I learned of Alice's death. She and I had virtually lost touch years ago. I didn't plan it that way and, no doubt, neither did she. But Life, with a capital L, had other ideas.

I would have gone to the funeral, and been glad to, but as it turned out, there hadn't been one. Straight to the crematorium, on her own, with no fuss, had been Alice's fervent wish. And that, apparently, was exactly how it had been.

I'd half-expected a letter, or an email, at most. Instead, I'd received a phone call from a secretary, and now here we sat, me in my flat in Brighton, Alice's solicitor somewhere in the north Cotswolds. The suggested timing of the meeting hadn't been convenient, but curiosity had won out and I'd gone ahead and arranged my day accordingly.

A thin wodge of twenty-pound notes danced before my eyes. No, make that tens. Or fives. I didn't want Alice's money, but I couldn't help thinking there must be some point to this personal meeting. Maybe it wasn't money, but something from the house; a painting, hopefully one of the watercolour land-scapes from the hall, not the lugubrious still life with the dead pheasant that had hung above the dining room fireplace.

Callum was talking. I brought myself back to the moment, with one eye on the kitchen clock.

'Alice was involved with a number of charities. Local ones, mainly. The hospice near Mistlecombe, the Woodland Trust, that sort of thing.'

'I remember,' I said, thinking fondly of Alice always rushing off to some committee meeting or other, or to sit behind a stall at a summer fair. 'Good causes were her thing. I imagine they'll all benefit.'

'Some, certainly.' Callum looked down, presumably at the paperwork. 'As well as the people who'd helped her in her later years. Cleaner, gardener, the local shopkeeper who delivered groceries to her door, the taxi driver from the village.'

'Yes. Well, good for her.' I waited.

'Mark you, we're not talking large sums here. Not at all. The rest home wasn't cheap. Are they ever?' He chuckled. 'No, these are just... *considerations*, shall we say. For those she wanted to show her appreciation to.'

Do I need to know all this? I shifted impatiently on my seat. Callum must have noticed.

'Right, then, Briony. Moving on to Alice's bequest to you.' He smiled. 'It's the house. Summerdene. The property goes to you in its entirety, plus what remains of the contents, and Alice's personal effects. There's also a cash sum of several thousands. It's not a fortune, but I'll let you know the exact figure when I have it.'

My heart stuttered. I felt hot, all over. Adrenaline spiked my stomach and shot through my limbs like poison darts. '*Summerdene?* I'm to inherit Alice's *house?* Are you sure?'

Callum's face receded from the screen as he leaned back in his seat and stretched his arms in front of him. 'Absolutely. We spoke about it, of course, Alice and I, when she made the will.'

'But...'

'Mrs Church's only child – her son, Jeremy – unfortunately passed away just over a year before her own death. Well, you know that, of course. She had no other relatives. Jeremy himself wasn't married, neither did he have any children.'

I still couldn't quite believe what I'd heard. 'But we never really kept in touch. I hadn't heard from her recently.'

Neither had she heard from me, I thought guiltily. I had

replied to her letter telling me about Jeremy, but that exchange had been our first in a long time.

'I'll write to you formally, of course. Probate's taking its time but it'll be through any day now. So they say.' Callum appeared to be gathering his papers together. 'I'll just double-check your details, if I may.'

Minutes later, our business at an end and polite thank-yous and goodbyes exchanged, I watched the solicitor's face slide away as the screen went dark.

I wanted to laugh, cry, jump up and down for joy, sob my heart out. In the end, I did none of those things. Instead, I quietly closed the front door behind me and walked back to school, scarcely feeling the ground beneath my feet.

FIVE
BRIONY

'Are you sure this is right, Mum?' Faye leaned forward and peered through the windscreen. 'Shouldn't you have let the satnav do it?'

'Oh ye of little faith.' As if I needed satnav to show me the way to Summerdene. It may have been years since my last visit, but I could have driven here blindfolded.

'Satnav wouldn't help. It would get confused where the lane peters out and you'd end up in the farmyard.'

I guided the car slowly around another twist in the narrow, tree-fringed lane and stopped beside a shoulder-high brick wall.

'Yes, this is it! I recognise it from the photos,' Faye said.

I refrained from telling her she should have trusted me on this.

'Jump out and open the gates, will you?'

Faye got out of the car and pushed open the black, wrought-iron gates, bubbled with rust. I drove carefully through and parked on the gravel forecourt, which was big enough for three cars, four at a pinch.

Summerdene was built of creamy Cotswold stone that reminded me of Madeira cake. A stone portico supported by two columns added grandeur to the sea-green front door, and decorative brick insets framed the leaded light windows. The grey stone tiled roof, studded with soft mounds of moss, supported a chimney at each end. The house's pleasing proportions were marred only by a flat-roofed extension to its right-hand side, its entrance now almost obscured by overgrown shrubs.

'When was it built?' Faye said, wandering around the forecourt and staring up at the house, hands on hips, like a professional brought in to inspect the place.

'I think it was 1820, or thereabouts.'

'Georgian, then. I thought so.' Faye pointed towards the extension. 'Shame about the ugly add-on. I don't like that.'

Neither did I.

'That was Alice's husband's surgery. Edward was the village GP. Come on, let's get inside.'

I walked up to the front door, keys in hand. My head was full of conflicting emotions at being back at Summerdene, and all this hanging about was making me jumpy.

The door creaked open reluctantly, from age, and because of the heap of letters and stuff behind it. I gathered up the envelopes and leaflets, quickly flicking through in case there was anything important. There wasn't. I shuffled the lot into the space where a half-moon table used to stand.

There were two reception rooms, one each side of the hallway. Faye had already wandered into the larger one, to the left.

'Cool. I love the high ceiling and the cornices. I bet this was a really elegant room in its heyday.'

My mind flew back to the times I'd spent in here, watching TV with Alice, and sometimes Jeremy, or reading, curled up in one of the squashy, cretonne-covered armchairs that used to furnish it. They were gone now, along with the two sofas. Only a large sideboard remained, its mahogany surface dulled with age and neglect, a couple of high-backed wooden chairs and the faded and worn Axminster carpet with the key design.

'I imagine it would have been, once,' I said, remembering the homely, bordering almost on shabby, look this room had when I'd lived here. Faye was right, though; its proportions would excite any potential buyer. But it wasn't something a teenage girl would notice, nor care about. I certainly hadn't.

Potential buyer. This, after all, was why I'd come, to give Summerdene the once-over, alert the local property agent, and hightail it back to Brighton. There was no reason to drag this out.

Faye and I toured the rest of the downstairs. Behind the smaller reception room was the dining room with French windows overlooking the back garden, then the large, square kitchen with a larder and a utility room.

Apart from the sideboard and chairs in the first reception room, all the furniture had been removed from downstairs, including the rosewood dining table and six carved chairs, leaving an oblong of brighter carpet where they'd stood. A few ornaments and pictures were scattered about, as well as some of the crockery and kitchen utensils, as if whoever had cleared the house – on Alice's instructions once she'd entered the rest home, I understood – had done so in a rush and not bothered to make sure everything had gone. No money in any of it, obviously. Well, there wouldn't be.

We moved upstairs. There were five good-sized bedrooms, and a white-tiled bathroom big enough to hold a barn dance. The upstairs was mainly empty, apart from the curtains, carpets and a vast wooden cupboard on the landing which used to hold the linen. Too awkward and heavy for the clearance people to move, obviously. I peeped inside and caught a whiff of lavender. Apart from a cardboard box at the bottom, seemingly full of junk, it was empty. I felt relieved. Furniture and ornaments I could deal with; sheets, towels and bedding were too personal, and reminiscent of stuffy, restless nights spent in the back bedroom that had been mine for the four years I'd lived here.

Faye had been remarking on this and that as we'd walked around. I'd hardly listened, enmeshed as I was in my own complicated thoughts and feelings. Back downstairs, she stood by the door halfway along the passage that led to the kitchen.

'This must lead to the surgery.'

'Yes, it was Edward's private access.'

'Can we see?'

She tried the handle but it wouldn't budge. I knew it wouldn't. It was always kept locked when I'd lived here, apart from the occasional intrusion I didn't want to think about right now.

'There's nothing to see. It'll have been emptied out. It's just a shell.'

I had no idea whether this was the case or not, although I hoped fervently that it was. Whatever, I wasn't about to investigate.

'Okay.' Faye moved away from the door. 'Mum?'

'What?'

'This house is amazing. I can't believe it's all yours.'

'I know. Neither can I.' I smiled.

I could sense my daughter's mind turning – I wasn't sure in which direction. Faye would never ask me for money so it couldn't be that. She'd always been independent, hell-bent on making her own way in the world, however hard it was. If – when – I had money to give, I knew it would take all my powers of persuasion to get her to accept it.

We wandered back into the larger living room. Faye perched herself on the deep window ledge.

'It's a good, solid house,' I said. 'Somebody will bring it back to its former glory.'

Faye lifted her chin. Her blue eyes focused on me intently.

'So why don't you?'

'*Me?* You mean, keep Summerdene? Do it up and rent it out? Why would I want the bother?'

'No, Mum. I mean, why don't you live in it yourself? It's perfect. It kind of suits you.'

I laughed. 'Right. And what would I do, stuck in the middle of the Cotswolds? Behave.'

Faye was silent. The intense look was still in place.

'You're serious, aren't you?' I said. A hundred conflicting emotions raced around my system. I couldn't catch hold of any of them.

'Deadly. Mum, this could be a fresh start. You could turn Summerdene into a guest house, a B&B. People would pay a premium to stay somewhere so romantic.'

I laughed. It echoed around the almost empty room. Where did my daughter get these ideas? 'B&B? Have strangers in the house? That's *crazy.*'

'Only a few at a time. There'd still be heaps of space for your private quarters. Think what fun it would be!'

I made a sound like a snort. 'Fun? Would it? You mean give up teaching to play host to a procession of tourists?'

'You said yourself you were tired of teaching.'

'I didn't quite say that, Faye. I said I'd had enough of moving from school to school every few months.'

Since the small private school I'd taught at for years had closed down with, literally, a day's notice, a permanent post – the right one – had eluded me. Educational funding was heading down the Swannee, taking me with it. Was I in need of a complete change? Possibly. But maybe not one as drastic as Faye was suggesting.

'Also, Mum,' Faye continued, as if I hadn't spoken, 'it would be good for you to be away from Dad, geographically speaking. Living in the same town as him, even though he's remarried, is like a comfort blanket that's got old and smelly but you refuse to get rid of it. You've been divorced for *three years*, Mum.'

I started. Faye's words were penetrating parts of my mind I had forcibly shut off. I hadn't realised she knew me so well, understood my innermost thoughts, my fears, my anxieties. But I guess I'd lost the knack of hiding my feelings from her.

I was silent for a moment. Then I nodded, my hand covering my mouth. Faye smiled. She obviously took this as a sign that I'd acknowledged the truth: I was scared to leave the town where we'd been so happy as a family.

The separation and eventual divorce had been amicable in the end, and painstakingly civilised. We weren't working as a couple any more and no matter how hard we'd tried, we couldn't fix it. So I'd wished Tony well, as he did me, and we'd gone our separate ways.

There'd been sadness, yes, and guilt that I hadn't managed to make a success of my marriage. The feeling of failure rolled constantly beneath me, like mild waves on a benign sea. But I didn't regret marrying him. We'd had our moments, Tony and I, and of course, we had Faye.

'I know, and I am moving on. The smelly old blanket's in the bin.' I laughed. 'Anyway, you're forgetting one vital point with this crackpot idea of yours,' I said, deliberately changing the subject. 'I can't cook.'

'This is true,' she said. 'It's not insurmountable.'

'Isn't it?'

A pause, then we both laughed.

'Come on,' I said, walking out of the room, 'let's go into the village and find a café. I could murder a cup of tea.'

SIX

BRIONY

1986

'Can I kiss you?' Daniel Wilson's face was already inches from mine. It seemed a done deal.

He was in my year and in some of the same sets as me. Honestly, if I'd wanted a snog that desperately – I hadn't – I'd have chosen a sixth-former, preferably one who was leaving, so I wouldn't have to face him again. At least there was a tiny element of mystery surrounding the sixth form boys whereas our lot were under our feet, all day, every day. We knew all their failings, and their horrible habits.

Daniel Wilson had made a beeline for me from the minute I walked into the hall with Molly and Samantha, all three of us displaying neon smiles and laughing loudly to mask our self-consciousness. I'd turned my back on Daniel at first. I'd rather have watched from the sidelines while I sussed out the lie of the land, as Molly put it. But I supposed it was flattering to have a boy to dance with straight away – I use the term 'dance' loosely, and 'with' looser still – and I'd caved in without too much effort on Daniel's part.

We'd bopped about to Bananarama, Bucks Fizz, and similar chart-toppers the teachers in charge mistakenly thought were cool, several feet apart from each other, not making eye contact, and constantly being elbowed in the back by others dancing around us.

Twenty minutes in and I was bored silly as well as roasting hot, and looking for a means of escape. But as I danced closer and closer to the edge of the floor, Daniel moved with me, and I hadn't managed to lose him by the time I was sucking flat lemonade through a paper straw in the refectory.

I had at least managed to lose Jeremy. I'd successfully kiboshed his plan to escort me to the disco by casually announcing at dinner that I'd arranged to meet Samantha and Molly by the postbox at the end of Back Lane, which, on this occasion, happened to be the truth.

'There, Jeremy,' Alice had said. 'Briony won't be walking to school on her own, and it's not even dark.'

''Course,' Jeremy had muttered into his lamb casserole. Then he'd looked up and given me a narrow-eyed stare. 'I'll be at the school gate at ten. That's what time it ends, I believe. I'll see you home safely.' He attempted a smile. It didn't work fully. I attempted one back – peace at any price. Even worse. I turned to Alice instead, and complimented her on the food.

Daniel was fair-to-middling good-looking, if a touch on the pasty side. The Head had issued a warning that there was to be no 'extreme' dressing, and jeans were not to be worn. Like most of the boys, Daniel had opted for the safe, American preppy look. He wore pressed khaki trousers, a bright green polo shirt, and smelled of chewing gum, overlaid with the woody scent of aftershave, probably borrowed from his dad.

I felt my nostrils start to shrivel as he closed in on me. Let him have his kiss, I thought, as I allowed his lips to press inexpertly against mine, then we'd be done. I felt I'd be missing out on the fun if I had Daniel Wilson by my side for the whole evening. Besides, I was dying to catch up with Molly and Samantha.

Daniel and I were standing in the darkened corridor leading away from the hall. We weren't the only ones. Every so often a teacher or prefect would stroll past, heads down, looking but not looking. Sentry duty, Samantha called it.

One kiss turned into several. It wasn't exactly an unpleasant experience, but I began to feel claustrophobic as the need to get away became more imperative.

'Always fancied snogging you, Briony,' Daniel growled, as we broke apart one more time.

'Well, now you have,' I said. 'Gotta go. I'll catch up with you later.' Easing myself from his grip, I half ran, half walked, along the corridor, back to the hall where Madonna was giving her all.

'What do I do?' I wailed. 'What do I flippin' well *do*? Come on. You're usually the ones with all the answers.'

The disco was winding down. Mrs Peachy, the deputy head, was imploring the two DJs from the sixth form to stop the music for the fourth time. The dance floor was almost empty and people stood about in chattering groups or trailed through doorways. Molly, Samantha and I had gravitated to the arch that opened onto the science quad to debrief and take some much-needed air.

Meanwhile, at the main school gate, a mere fifty yards away, Jeremy waited. I hadn't actually seen him but I knew he was there; I could feel his evil vibes striking through the brickwork of Mistlecombe Lane High. Knowing how his mind worked, he'd have arrived before ten in case he missed me. It was nearly a quarter past now. He'd be getting impatient. I had no intention of walking home with him; there was absolutely no possibility of that. For one thing, I'd feel stupid, being led away like a child in front of the rest of the upper school. For another, I wasn't going to let him control me when, for once, I had the power to stop it. I didn't care what Alice would think, or say. I had to give Jeremy the slip.

We couldn't hang about outside school for too long because the staff would be policing the grounds, and in any case, we couldn't be too late getting home. A decision would have to be made, and soon.

'The back way?' Samantha said.

Leaving the back way meant trekking miles across the sports pitches to the gate that was reserved for delivery vans, sports team buses, and the occasional fire engine if someone had set off the alarm. It was bound to be locked at this time of night, and there was no chance of scaling it in my pink dress with the short, flouncy skirt. And even if I could, I'd then have to walk home the long way round, and who was to say I wouldn't run into Jeremy anyway as I reached Back Lane?

I gave Samantha a hard look.

'Yeah, right,' she said. 'Not the back way.'

'I saw you getting off with Daniel Wilson,' Molly suddenly said, as if we hadn't been in the middle of trying to solve a massive problem.

I raised my eyes. 'He wouldn't take no for an answer.'

'You did say *no*, then, to a snogging session in the top corridor?' Samantha said.

'Tried to.' I grinned. 'No, I didn't, actually. Anyway, what's the harm? At it happens, it was quite nice.'

'Quite nice,' Molly said, putting on a posh, mocking voice. 'Is that it?'

'Yep. That just about covers it. What about you, then? I saw you slow-dancing with Mike Thingy. Any action there?'

'Not so's you notice,' Molly said, her voice flat with disinterest. 'We were standing next to each other when "Lady in Red" started. Anyway, we're friends. He goes to art club. You don't get it on with your friends, do you?'

'Definitely not,' Samantha said. 'That would be seriously weird.'

I nodded knowingly. None of us really knew what we were talking about. Even at sixteen, our combined experience of boys was as flimsy as a Kleenex. Truthfully, we didn't have a clue. But we could act wordly-wise with the best of them. Everyone acted, everyone. It was what you did to get along.

'Well, I got a snog,' Samantha said proudly.

'Who?' Molly and I said together. Clearly, neither of us had spotted that, to our shame.

Samantha shrugged. 'Malcolm Phillips. Sixth form.'

Molly and I exchanged a look. 'Blond Malcolm? Plays football? Leaving this year?' I said, just to check.

'Yep.'

'He's shorter than you,' Molly said.

'Not by much,' countered Samantha. 'A slight drawback, admittedly. But I'm not going out with him so it doesn't matter, does it?' She sighed melodramatically. 'He's an excellent kisser. He'd be all right for you, Moll. You match his height.'

'Err, no thanks.' Molly pulled a face. 'I know where he's been. I don't want your leftovers, thanks very much.'

We dissolved into giggles. Behind us, somebody turned off a light or two. Time to go. Which brought me back to my current predicament.

In the end, we decided I would leave school by the main entrance with everyone else; hide in plain sight, as it were. Molly and Samantha would stay right by my side, and then I'd make a run for it.

My break for freedom was so successful, I wondered why I'd made such a fuss about it in the first place. In fact, it was so successful that I didn't clap eyes on Jeremy at all – surprising since, with all the running he apparently did, he could easily have outrun me if he'd tried.

Reaching home, breathless and in a sweat, I forced myself to stand outside the house while I caught my breath and re-tied my ponytail before letting myself in and strolling nonchalantly into the hall.

'Hello, love. Did you have a good time?' Alice said, coming out of the sitting room.

Then, without waiting for my answer – I doubt she was interested in the goings-on at a school disco – she said she was making cocoa and did I want some. I didn't, but my gut instinct told me it would look odd to dash straight upstairs, so I said yes, please.

Jeremy didn't seem to be home, and I began to think that maybe I should have taken the line of least resistance and let him walk me home. Instead, he'd presumably wasted his time looking for me and I would surely pay for that over the coming days. But as Alice and I were finishing our cocoa at the kitchen table, I heard the front door open and close and, a moment later, he strolled into the kitchen.

'There you are, Briony,' he said. 'I must have been waiting in the wrong place. Still, you're home now. That's all that matters.'

I kept quiet. What could I say?

Jeremy offered me a smile. If I hadn't known otherwise, I would have said it was an ordinary, friendly smile. Brotherly. Was he acting for Alice's sake, pretending he wasn't furious with me for giving him the slip? Had he even gone to the school at all?

Alice didn't contradict him, so she must have thought he'd gone to meet me, as arranged.

I went to bed soon after. Alice followed me up. Half an hour later, I heard Jeremy going to his room. Everything normal, or as near as. Everything the same as always.

Except, somehow, it wasn't.

I lay awake for ages, thinking I was missing something and trying to work out what it was but my brain was too tired to make any sense of it. Dragged into sleep, I dreamed I was slow-dancing with Daniel Wilson, only it turned out it wasn't him at all; it was a giant stick of Wrigley's.

Jeremy was fine with me the next morning, if 'fine' could ever be applied to him. He seemed in a good mood and whistled a nameless tune as he made toast under the grill. He offered me some. I accepted, feeling surprised and wrong-footed. I'd expected a stern telling-off for bailing out on him last night; snide comments and low-level threats thinly disguised as jokes, at the very least. Instead, he slung two slices of toast onto a plate and pushed the butter dish towards me.

I was still marvelling over my lucky escape when Alice called from the sitting room where she was reading the daily paper with her coffee.

'Briony? Your friend's here. She's coming to the door.'

The bell sounded at that moment. I went to answer and found Samantha on the step.

'You're out early for a Saturday,' I said, through a mouthful of toast. 'I've only just got up.'

I held the door open but Samantha stayed where she was, inclining her head sideways, indicating that I should step outside. I did, pulling the door almost closed behind me. I didn't want Jeremy earwigging. Presumably, neither did Samantha.

'What's all the secrecy?'

Samantha pulled me further away from the door, as far as the huge rhododendron that almost blocked the path to the old surgery.

'I'm a bit worried, Bri,' she said.

'About me? Oh, you don't need to be. I'm fine.'

I started to tell her about Jeremy and my lucky escape but she interrupted me.

'No, not about you. Although that *is* good. When you ran

off last night, literally, I watched you go to make sure you were okay and weren't being chased – actually, where *was* Jeremy? I didn't see him at the school gate... oh, never mind that. It's Molly. One minute she was right next to me – well you know she was – and the next *poof!* Vanished, just like that.'

My tired brain couldn't cope with this. 'What d'you mean, *vanished?* Don't be daft.'

'I know, it sounds mad. There were tons of kids about and at first I thought she was in the crowd somewhere. Only I looked and she wasn't. There was no sign. Honestly, Bri, I was dead miffed. I mean, we'd agreed to walk home together. We always do, living so close, and it *was* after the disco...'

Definitely odd, I thought. And not like Molly at all. She and Samantha were as thick as thieves. They lived in the same part of the village, a couple of streets apart. Why would Molly not want to walk home with Samantha? It was unnatural.

I questioned Samantha further, and wondered if Molly had nipped back into school to use the loo or something. But she had been gone too long. Samantha had given up waiting and walked home on her own, and then she'd decided to nip round to Molly's house to see if she'd arrived home safely. But, according to Samantha, she wasn't there.

'Did you ring the bell?'

Samantha shook her head. 'I didn't like to. There was no light on in her room, or the bathroom, so I slipped round the side of their house and peeped through the downstairs window. Her mum and dad were there, and her sister, but Molly wasn't, and she couldn't have been in bed by that time. She obviously hadn't got home before me. I hung around for a while, then I went home.'

'So, did you phone, or go round this morning?'

'Oh no, she left me to walk home on my own and never said a dicky bird. I wasn't chasing after her this morning. Why, would you have done?'

Yes, I would. This was typical Samantha. Worried about Molly one minute, not doing the obvious and calling on her the next.

'That's why I came round here,' Samantha continued, letting out a long sigh as if I was stupid. 'To ask if you saw her last night, or if she's rung you this morning, or anything.'

I hadn't seen Molly, or anyone else, last night. I'd been too desperate to outrun Jeremy.

'Nope. Nobody's rung this morning. I'd have heard the phone from upstairs.'

'Well, I'm sure she'll come up with some plausible-sounding excuse. Forget it.' Samantha wagged a finger at me. 'If you see her, don't let on I was asking, will you? I shall play it cool when I do speak to her. *Dead* cool.'

'Yeah, dead cool,' I said.

Samantha turned to go, then: 'See you later? Twelvish? Usual place?'

'Okay, usual place.'

SEVEN

BRIONY

2022

I took my bags upstairs to the bedroom I'd earmarked as mine –
Alice's old bedroom, which made sense as it was the largest and
had an en suite bathroom, small and basic, but it would do –
and began making up the bed with the sheets, pillows and duvet
I'd brought from home the last time I was here.

This was my fourth visit to Summerdene in as many weeks
and I still couldn't believe I'd let Faye talk me into this. And
then she'd astonished me by announcing she was coming with
me, not just to stay for a while and see me settled in, but permanently. Or, as permanently as anyone could predict at this early
stage. I wasn't sure how she would cope away from the noise
and vibrancy of the city, but she seemed determined, and time
would tell.

I didn't know yet if my own move was permanent; it was too
early to know. I'd hung on to the Brighton flat, just in case. And
no, I'd assured Faye, it wasn't because I needed her father to be
within shouting distance. It made sense in every way, including
financially. I'd let the flat out through an agent to a young

couple on a six-month contract. Having the option of returning if things didn't work out made me feel slightly less at sea than if I'd cut myself off completely.

Faye wasn't with me today. She had loose ends to tie up regarding her house-share in Brixton, an in-office work meeting, and 'other things' to do, apparently. I'd wondered whether these 'other things' included seeing Nick, her ex-boyfriend, even though she'd declared she wanted nothing more to do with him – nobody was more pleased about that than I was, believe me. But I hadn't asked, and I wouldn't. If she wanted to tell me, she would, in her own time.

She'd accompanied me on my last three visits to Summerdene, when we'd been busy organising suppliers for gas, electricity and broadband and having furniture and kitchen equipment delivered, most of what I owned having stayed in the flat. I'd appreciated her eye for design and her *what-the-hell-just-order-it-Mum!* attitude, otherwise I might have prevaricated so much I'd have been moving into an empty shell today.

It wasn't that I couldn't decide in what style to furnish the house; Faye and I had agreed on an eclectic mix of vintage and contemporary rather than the obvious period design. It was more a case of watching my spending, and I'd concentrated on getting our bedrooms sorted, making the main living room comfortable, ordering a TV, and fitting out the kitchen with the essentials. The guest rooms I would deal with later. I had also exchanged the dark, heavy drapes throughout the house for lighter curtains in whites and creams, and the rooms already had a much airier feel.

The authorities had indicated they'd be in favour of granting me a licence to run Summerdene as a guest house, providing I met the legal requirements regarding fire safety and could comply with the other numerous regulations. I was optimistic about the success of my application, and had begun making plans for my embryonic business, with Faye's help.

But first, I wanted to make Summerdene our home.

I'd stuffed the car not only with clothes and other personal possessions but with a set of my mother's brown kitchen bowls, a pretty Minton tea set which had been a wedding present, a couple of pictures, cosy throws from my old sofa, and some colourful cushions I particularly liked. Other than that, and the few things Alice had left behind, everything in Summerdene would be new, or sourced from one of the antique or second-hand shops in the area.

I thought I'd done quite well, considering.

As I tucked the sheet into the sides of my bed, I dropped to my knees and peered underneath. No dust or fluff remained. I'd splashed out on a firm of cleaning specialists to give the house a thorough going-over, and thorough they had been as far as I could tell from my inspections. It had cost a small fortune, but the last thing I wanted to do was start scrubbing and washing down when I got here. I would probably have to employ some-body to keep the guest accommodation in order but I could think about that later.

So now, the windows shone, the cream-coloured woodwork gleamed, where it wasn't chipped, and even the walls looked brighter. Luckily, Alice had mostly favoured plain walls over patterned wallpaper, so I was saved that particular nightmare. Instead, the walls were painted in innocuous magnolia, pale blues and greens, and although they would need repainting at some stage, they were fine for now. The exception was the dining room, which had sage green wood panelling up to dado-rail height, and above that, a riotous, Oriental design wallpaper on which unlikely looking birds perched among even more unlikely-looking flowers and trees.

The dining room wallpaper had given me something to look at during mealtimes when I wanted to avoid looking at Jeremy. I was glad it was still here; it reminded me that everything that had happened in this house was real, and not conjured from the overheated brain of an imaginative teenager.

My new king-sized bed had that new, slightly rubbery smell about it. It wasn't unpleasant, but I opened the window wide to let in the fresh air. I'd encouraged Faye to take the room next to mine, the one I'd used when I'd lived here before. It didn't have an en suite, but it meant our two rooms would be together at one end of the house, leaving the other three further along the landing for the guests, so it made sense. Besides, I didn't want Faye in Jeremy's old room. I didn't tell her that, of course. She could use the family bathroom on this floor, which would be exclusively for our use; she'd seemed content with that.

The bathroom fitters had already made a tour of inspection with a view to ripping out the old-fashioned hand basins from the guest bedrooms and fitting small en suites with showers. It would mean using up all that remained of the money Alice had left me, but it had to be done, and I'd accepted the estimate with a rapidly beating heart.

It was half past one and I was starving. I'd been so intent on making sure I'd brought everything I needed from the flat, I hadn't given a thought to food or drink, apart from a large bottle of water, now half empty.

I gave my hair a quick brush and splashed my face with cold water, then locked up and set off for the village, on foot. I'd sat in the car for long enough today.

The nearest house to Summerdene was some way along Back Lane, on the same side. The two properties were separated from one another by a stand of trees and an overgrown plot containing stunted fruit trees, their branches white with lichen, the bases of their trunks swallowed up by long grass and weeds. I'd never known who had owned the old orchard, but whoever it was had clearly abandoned it to be reclaimed by nature.

The house on the other side of it was a small, white-walled thatched cottage, its name, Kestrels, scorched into a wooden plaque beside the porched front door. As I approached, I tried to remember who had lived there when I was at Summerdene before. The best I could come up with was that it had belonged to an old couple, as seen from a teenager's point of view, though they could have been forty or fifty.

Drawing level with the gate, I sensed movement. As my eyes were pulled towards the house, a figure rose from beyond the hedge and I found myself facing a man who I guessed was a few years younger than me. He was six feet tall or more and had jet black hair locked into chin-length spirals, a light brown complexion and ink-dark eyes. He looked incongruous against the quaint cottage backdrop, like an exotic bloom in a dandelion patch.

'Hi.' He smiled and moved a step closer to me. He was holding an earth-encrusted trowel with bent prongs. Another step, and he tripped over a tussock of grass, righting himself with a self-deprecating grin. '*Shit*. Damn garden. Ah, sorry, sorry.'

My turn to smile. 'It's fine. You've got your work cut out, by the looks of it.' I waved towards the hummocky grass and the riotous jumble of leggy plants and flowers surrounding it, threatening to take over the path completely. 'But I rather like it the way it is,' I added, truthfully.

'Me too. Who needs manicured lawns and poker straight borders?' He laughed. The corkscrew curls bobbed. 'If they do, they won't find them here, that's for sure. You should see the back. It's a bloody jungle. Oops, sorry, again.'

'How long have you lived here?'

'Too long, or not long enough.' He smiled ruefully. 'Five

months, actually. How about you? I haven't seen you before. Do you live around here?'

'I do, at Summerdene, along the road.' I smiled back. 'And if you're wondering how long I've been there, the answer is four years, or half a day, depending on how you look at it,' I said, matching his cryptic reply.

He looked puzzled, as well he might.

'I should explain,' I said.

And I did, briefly, telling him I'd lived at Summerdene as a teenager, and had now returned as the house's owner.

He didn't elaborate on his own response. Instead, he introduced himself.

'I'm Marcus,' he said. 'Marcus Schofield.'

'Briony Harrington. Alice Church was my godmother. Her late husband, Edward, was Mistlecombe's one and only GP. He ran the practice from Summerdene, in the little building tacked onto the side. There were no medical centres back then.'

'Before my time,' Marcus said.

'Of course. Mine, too,' I added, in case he thought I was that ancient. 'I'd better be going. I'm off to the shops for supplies.'

Marcus took a step sideways onto the wonky brick path, managing to stay upright this time. 'The shops are quite good for your basics.' He waved the trowel, releasing a lump of mud that narrowly missed his foot. The trainers he was wearing looked far too good for gardening, as did the smart indigo jeans. 'The White Hart does a good meal, if you ever have the need.'

I thanked him, raised my arm in a slightly awkward wave and set off smartly along Back Lane.

EIGHT
BRIONY

Faye arrived three days later, on Saturday. Although I'd enjoyed my brief time alone, it seemed so quiet here compared with Brighton, and I was glad to see her.

I eyed her giant case on wheels, its smaller companion standing on the front path, and the rear window of her cream Mini half-obscured with bags.

'You'll have to make do with the one wardrobe and the chest of drawers for now. Maybe we'll have some fitted at some stage.'

'It's fine,' Faye said airily, beginning to bump the large case up the stairs.

She may have been twenty-four, but her method of clothes storage hadn't progressed much beyond those of a twelve-year old – hang up the best stuff and fling the rest over any available surface, including the floor. But my daughter had matured in ways that really mattered and I looked forward to spending quality time with her.

Over dinner that evening, I gave Faye the good news that my application to run Summerdene as a guest house had been approved in principle, and it was just a matter of rubber-stamping by the appropriate committee.

'We need to start advertising,' Faye said. 'The summer season's almost here. Have you even thought about it, Mum?'

'Give me a chance. I've only just got here. There are no beds in any of the guest rooms, let alone anything else, but I'm not rushing. I want to enjoy living here for a while before I open the front door to all and sundry.'

Truthfully, I was nervous about taking the next step. I had no experience of the hospitality industry, unless you counted the waitressing, chambermaiding and bar jobs I'd had as a student, so far distant now as to be no help whatsoever. And I still hadn't got around to solving the problem of my being a rubbish cook.

I would need to be earning before long, but I would have the rent from the Brighton flat and my own savings to be going on with. Faye would be contributing to the household expenses; she would work from home in her PR consultancy role and go to London when she needed to.

'Yes, it'll be like a little holiday.' She was silent for a moment. She stood with her back to the butler sink, hands heeled against the rim, regarding me closely. 'Will you miss teaching?' she asked, as if it had only just occurred to her.

'Bound to, for a bit, but I'll be too busy to think about it.' I smiled brightly.

I'd already experienced more than one moment of panic and had started researching teaching jobs in the area. There were some, nothing I'd seriously consider, but it showed there were openings if I chose to look for them, and again I could always sign on as fill-in staff if push came to shove and the B&B idea didn't take off, or I hated it. I could also advertise my services as a private tutor.

But Faye didn't need to know all that. She needed to know I was determined to make a success of this new venture.

'You were right. I do need this change,' I said brightly. 'I expect I'll miss lots of things, not only teaching.'

Faye dropped her gaze. 'How d'you feel about being miles away from Dad?'

I sighed inwardly. I could do without this analysis of my feelings. But clearly Faye felt it was important and I didn't want her worrying about me. Perhaps she was feeling guilty that she'd been so persuasive in getting me to leave Brighton.

Well, she needn't have been.

'Faye, it's not an issue. I've not given him a thought since I got here.'

This wasn't entirely true, but I had shaken off my fear of leaving the area that still contained my ex-husband. Or, I was close to it, anyway. Besides memories are portable. The ones I hadn't discarded as being too painful were right here with me.

It came to me that Faye was really talking about herself and Nick.

'Did you speak to Nick again before you came away?' I dared to ask.

For an instant, my daughter's face coloured. It told me all I needed to know.

'He popped round for coffee, yes.'

'To the house?' The house Faye had shared in Brixton. Nick had never officially moved in but I'd had the impression he'd spent most of his time there before the split. His nights, anyway, I thought uncharitably.

'*Yes*. I asked him to come round, okay? I didn't have time to meet him anywhere else.'

I held up my hands. 'Okay, sorry. I'm only concerned for you, that's all.'

Faye let go of the sink she'd been clinging to, came to the table and put her arm around my shoulders. 'I know. Sorry, Mum. I probably shouldn't have asked to see him again. I guess I wanted the closure thing, you know? What with me moving so far away...'

I reached for Faye's hand and squeezed it. 'You don't have to explain yourself to me, lovey. As long as he was kind to you.'

'He was okay. We said goodbye and he wished me luck. He didn't stay long.' She let out a long sigh. 'So that's that then.'

I didn't reply.

She hasn't accepted it, I thought. My darling daughter still harboured hopes that Nick, with whom she'd conducted an intense, fiery relationship since university, had miraculously transformed from unfaithful, lying loser into loving, devoted boyfriend. As if that was ever going to happen.

But it wasn't for me to interfere. Faye would handle it in her own way. She was strong; she'd be fine. We both would.

'Dad said he'd meet me in London when I'm next there and take me out for lunch.'

'That'll be nice,' I said, meaning it. 'What shall we do this evening? A walk? Or telly? Or, we could go for a drink at the pub. I went there for lunch yesterday, just to see what it was like.'

'You went to the pub, on your own?'

I laughed. 'I am a grown-up now, and it's not 1950! It was only lunch. I wanted to check the place out.'

'Any good?'

'Yes, it was very good. The landlord and his wife – they're called Clive and Joan – were welcoming. We had a little chat. I expect they were pleased to see a new face, and a potentially new customer. The evening menu looked nice.'

'We should go there,' Faye said. 'Telly tonight, though, I think. I'm knackered from the drive. She picked up one of the dirty plates and gazed around the kitchen. 'Where's the dishwasher?'

'Still in the shop. I'll need to have the cupboards altered to fit one in. I'll get a carpenter to take a look.'

'Well, you don't want to hang about, Mum. Think of all those eggy breakfast plates.'

I was, but I couldn't worry about that now, nor the million and one other details I'd have to sort out, including having a coded smart lock fitted to the front door so my guests could let themselves in while I was out.

But there was time enough for all that, once I'd taken my first booking. It didn't always do to plan too far ahead.

Later, we curled up, each of us at one end of the new L-shaped turquoise velvet sofa, and watched TV. I must have drifted off to sleep because I woke with a start as the ten o'clock news began, having missed the end of the police drama we'd been watching, then realised Faye wasn't there. I was wondering if she'd gone up to bed when I heard the front door close and Faye came into the living room. She was holding a piece of paper.

'What's that?'

'Only junk. I went outside for some air and it was stuffed in the letter box.'

She passed me the piece of paper. I read the printed note aloud: '*Reliable local woman seeks position as domestic help. Cleaning, ironing, etc. Hours flexible to suit employer. Immediate start. Call Pippa Medhurst.*' A number followed.

'Somebody's enterprising,' I said, folding the paper and dropping it down by the side of the sofa among the magazines. 'Funny time of night to be leafleting though. It wasn't there when I went out to shut the gates just before nine.'

'Whoever it was must be keen to have flogged all the way down Back Lane,' Faye said disinterestedly. 'I'm off to bed. Night, Mum.'

'Night, darling,' I said. 'Faye?' She paused in the doorway. 'I'm so glad you're here. I'd have found it a bit daunting on my own.'

Faye laughed. 'Face it, Mum. If I hadn't come with you, you

wouldn't be here at all. This place would be on the market and you'd be back in your little cocoon in Brighton.'

At least she had the good sense not to mention Tony again. She'd made her thoughts clear on my apparent attachment to my ex-husband enough times already.

'I loved Brighton, and my little flat,' I said, feeling defensive. 'But you were right, I was rather stuck in the same old groove.'

'Telling me.' Faye grinned and swept out of the room before I could retaliate.

After Faye had gone upstairs, I switched the TV off, then went to the window. The gates were open again, just enough for somebody to pass through; whoever had dropped the leaflet, evidently. I ducked out into the hall, opened the front door and stood outside on the step for a minute, gazing up at the tiny crystal beads of stars strewn across a clear, blue-black sky, and breathing in the earthy scent of the air. Then I walked across the gravel to the gates, but before I closed them, I stepped out into the lane and looked around. There was no one about, unsurprisingly, and yet I felt the distinct sensation of a recent presence, a light disturbance in the air.

A shiver ran through me. Stepping back through the gates, I pulled them closed, sliding the latch across, and hurried indoors.

NINE
BRIONY

1986

As I walked through the village on my way to meet Samantha, I saw her coming towards me. Molly was with her. We converged outside the post office, greeted each other briefly, then set off along the high street, turning off at the lane which led to Mistlecombe Woods. It was our usual route; our feet seemed to take us there without any of us having made the decision.

'We bumped into each other on the corner of my road,' Samantha said, addressing me.

This, I gathered, was to let me know she hadn't called for Molly.

'Why are you telling her that?' Molly looked incredulous, as if Samantha had blurted out a secret.

'Well, we did, didn't we?' Samantha raised her eyes.

I sighed inwardly. If those two were going to be sniping at each other all day, we were in for a grim time.

'Yeah, we did,' Molly conceded, as we passed a row of three thatched cottages that backed onto the woods, each as familiar to us as our own faces. 'I bought sweets at the shop. Enough to share.'

Were the sweets meant to recompense Samantha for leaving her last night? I couldn't have said, but by the casual way Molly had mentioned the sweets, I decided not. I also decided I didn't care anyway.

We pushed open the old wooden gate to the woods and followed the narrow, uneven path to the infamous beech tree with its many carvings.

'It's damp,' I said, patting the mossy ground beneath its spreading branches.

'You've got jeans on. You'll be all right,' Samantha said, sitting down.

We sat in our usual arrangement, backs against the tree trunk, legs stretched out in front, and Molly produced a striped paper bag of penny sweets and passed it round. I took a candy banana. Samantha, I noticed, took two blackjacks and a fruit salad. We sucked and chewed in silence for a few minutes, until I couldn't resist any longer.

'Did you both get home okay last night?' I enquired casually, addressing the space in front of me.

Samantha nudged me in the ribs. I twisted irritably. Was I not supposed to ask? I wasn't going to tell Molly that Samantha had been round to mine this morning because I'd promised not to, but I was curious as to where Molly had got to after the disco. So, of course, was Samantha, only wild horses wouldn't have dragged it from her.

'Yes,' Samantha said, sharply. 'I was fine. On my own. In the dark.'

A heavy silence, then, 'Okay, I'm sorry,' Molly said. 'I got a bit sidetracked. We do walk home on our own sometimes. We're not joined at the hip. It's not a big deal, is it?'

'No, of course it's not,' Samantha said. I could feel the tension in her shoulders.

'Oh?' I said, all innocently. 'Didn't you walk home together, then?'

'I told you,' Molly said. 'I got sidetracked and we got separated. It's not as if there weren't millions of other kids going in the same direction.'

'Oh yes, millions. Just not you.'

Samantha's voice was all strung out. She was obviously still angry with Molly, which wasn't like her. Except, Samantha tended to get stroppy if her arrangements were messed up, so maybe it was.

Still buoyed up from Jeremy's decent treatment of me this morning, I decided it would be fun to add more fuel to the fire. I turned to look at Molly.

'Did you get off with someone last night?'

'No, of course not,' Molly said. I thought I saw her colour slightly, but it was hard to tell in the greenish light of the woods. Then she added, unnecessarily in my opinion, 'I don't know why you're asking me that.'

'Because you disappeared, that's why she's asking,' Samantha said. Then, realising too late she'd given herself away and now Molly would know the two of us had been discussing her, covered her tracks by turning the questioning on me. 'Are you going out with Daniel Wilson now, then?'

'Not as far as I know,' I said, reaching into the sweet bag on Samantha's lap and taking a fizzy strawberry strip.

'Either you are or you aren't.' Molly snatched the bag back and peered inside to see what was left.

'Aren't.' I unwrapped my fizzy strip and sucked it, feeling the burn on my tongue.

'Would you go out with him?' Samantha looked at me sideways. 'You must like him a bit to have snogged him all that time.'

'It wasn't *all that time*. It was five minutes tops. Anyway, you shouldn't have been watching.'

'Would you, though? Go out with Daniel?' Molly's voice

was lazy with half-interest. If I didn't know better, I'd have said her mind was busy elsewhere. In fact, I'd have sworn it was.

'I don't know,' I said, through a mouthful of popping sugar. 'If he asks me, which he won't, I'll decide then.'

'He's a bit of nerd but you could do worse.' Samantha took the sweet bag back off Molly and helped herself to the last blackjack.

'Thanks very much,' I said. 'You make it sound as if I'm desperate.'

'When we all know who *is* desperate.' Molly cocked her head towards Samantha. 'Desperate to get laid.'

Samantha pretended to be offended. Then all three of us burst into giggles and the last vestiges of tension vanished.

It occurred to me as I wandered home an hour later that Molly hadn't asked if I'd managed to evade Jeremy last night, which was odd, considering I'd made so much of it at the time. I wondered if Samantha had already told Molly that I'd managed to avoid him, but even if she had, Molly would have still mentioned it, under normal circumstances.

Molly still hadn't said where she'd got to last night, I realised, as I went through the gates of Summerdene. It probably wasn't anything interesting, anyway. She'd got talking to someone and then sloped off home without bothering to catch up with Samantha, that's all it was.

Molly was right, it wasn't a big deal. If she wanted to be all enigmatic about it, who were we to spoil her fun?

TEN
BRIONY

We all found summer jobs in the end. Samantha became a
junior assistant in a clothes shop in Cheltenham – she cadged a
lift with her father when he went to work in the morning, then
caught the train back to Mistlecombe at the end of the day.
Molly was taken on as a chambermaid in a country hotel a few
miles north of the village, riding her bike there and back if the
weather was fine, otherwise relying on the infrequent bus
service. I found a job in the village, shelf-filling and operating
the checkout at Pink's, the mini supermarket. We all worked
part-time; we weren't prepared to go as far as losing the whole
summer in the cause of netting a few quid.

As I said, I didn't so much need the money; it was more a
case of having something to do and getting out of the house
while Jeremy was in it. Although, he went out a fair bit, flogging
around the lanes in his running gear, or simply sloping off to
God knows where.

Alice, bless her, had a hand in my gainful employment.
Once she realised I was serious about getting a holiday job, she
did what she called 'putting a few feelers out'. Because of her
unrivalled interest in village affairs, especially the charitable

ones, and, probably, because she was the widow of the well-respected Doctor Church, she wasn't short of favours she could call in. I daresay there were a number of shopkeepers who would have found room for me, but the first call I got was from Mr Pink.

Alice pronounced me a heroine of sorts for taking on the job. This, with a wink at me and a pointed sideways nod at Jeremy, who I gathered was a whole lot fussier about the sort of thing he would or would not lower himself to do. I couldn't help smiling at Alice's half-serious comparison. Jeremy scowled and refused to speak to me for the rest of the day which suited me down to the ground. His juvenile behaviour astonished me at times.

In the second week of August, the nondescript, humid grey days turned to blue-skied scorchers, and Molly suggested river swimming. It wasn't something we did often, but at some point during the summer we had always enjoyed a dip in the river that meandered prettily between the meadows on the outskirts of the village.

Having managed to blag the same afternoon off from our respective workplaces, Molly, Samantha and I walked in single file along the path that led to the riverbank and crossed the rickety wooden bridge to our favourite spot, where the grass was smooth and the shallow bank made it easy to access the water. We'd put swimming costumes on under our shorts and T-shirts, and packed our bags with almost identical striped towels, our hairbrushes, and the makings of a picnic. Luckily, we had the place to ourselves, probably because it was a weekday. At weekends, the pub a mile or so upriver did a roaring trade in letting out rowing boats and punts, and the peace would be shattered by shouts and squeals and splashes.

'This is *heaven*,' Samantha said, turning onto her back and flapping her arms lazily in the water.

Her costume was bright emerald green, a colour only

Samantha, with her dark colouring, could get away with. It gleamed like silk beneath the water; she looked like an exotic fish. Mine and Molly's costumes were a modest navy blue with a white trim around the top, almost identical except Molly's had a halter neck while mine had straps that crossed over at the back and were the devil to tie single-handed. I reached round and checked the straps were secure before I slithered down the bank and slipped into the water. Molly followed me in, and we ducked, with a sharp intake of breath.

It *was* heaven. The cool water enfolded my overheated skin as I swam slowly towards the middle, the underwater plants stroking my thighs.

It wasn't a deep river by any means, as it was only a tributary to the main waterway some miles off, and neither was it especially wide. But it was *our* river, and we thought of this section of it as being entirely ours. The tangle of trees along the bank, the tips of their branches reaching to brush the water, the darting silver fishes, the velvet-coated water voles – if you were lucky enough to see one – and the intriguing dark holes in the muddy bank added a note of secrecy and reminded me of *The Wind in the Willows*. I kept this childish thought to myself, naturally.

After our swim, we spread our towels on the grass bank and lay there, shivering, but not wanting to get dressed yet. It was then that a strange sensation came over me, the feeling that we weren't alone after all. Yet, there was nobody that I could see. We'd passed a lone fisherman on the way, but he was hidden from our view by the bridge and the curve in the river.

I sat up, yanked the towel from under me and rubbed my hair. I'd had the sense to tie it up in a high ponytail, so only the ends were wet. Samantha had left hers loose. I think she liked the way it fanned out in the water. She always put on a show, even if there was nobody around except me and Molly. I watched her as I towelled my hair, then started on the rest of me. Even the way her limbs were arranged on the towel seemed studied; they were very slightly spread out, as if in invitation, but in a way that suggested that invitation could at any given moment be withdrawn.

Of the three of us, Samantha was the prettiest. Who am I kidding? Samantha was beautiful, from her glossy, black-brown hair which showed a tinge of red when the sun was on it, all the way down past her slender but curvy figure, her enviably jutting hip bones, to the peach-varnished tips of her perfect toes. In the words of most of the upper school, girls as well as boys, Samantha was drop-dead gorgeous, and she knew it. Which probably accounted for the look-at-me way she held herself. She'd perfected a walk which made her hair swing from side to side, a foot or so above her pert backside.

Molly was as pretty as Samantha, in my opinion, but in a quieter way. She wore her hair in a slightly messy pixie-cut, framing her heart-shaped face and enhancing her green eyes. Her colouring was fair to sandy, the sandy part revealing itself in a subtle sprinkling of freckles across her nose and along her forearms. Shorter than Samantha by a good few inches – and shorter than me by fewer – her well-proportioned figure had a tight, compact look about it, but at the same time there was a softness about her, a motherliness, almost.

Boys liked Molly, were drawn to her, you could tell, even if they did nothing about it. With Samantha, I suspected they were slightly intimidated by her rare beauty, her look-but-don't touch vibe which, of course, was entirely at odds with her flagrant wish not to be a virgin any longer than she had to.

As for me, I had enough self-esteem left, just, to allow myself to feel reasonably attractive. My hair was a darkish honey blonde, not very interesting in my opinion, but passable. Body-wise, I'd matured a little faster and a little too much in certain places than I'd have liked but as long as my boobs didn't decide to put on another growth spurt, I could live with that.

My eyes, an unusual green with gold flecks, I felt were my best
asset. The bits I hated most were my knees. Aside from what
went on, skin-wise, at the backs of them, they were pudgy; there
was no other word for it. So pudgy they even had dimples.

My perfunctory drying over, I automatically draped the
towel across to hide my knees, not from anyone else – there was
nobody there apart from Samantha and Molly – but from
myself.

'You'll catch your death,' I said to Samantha, as she sat up
and looked around. 'Your hair's soaking, you daft cow.'

'Daft cow,' Molly echoed, sitting up too and rubbing her
arms with her own towel.

The problem with one-piece costumes – bikinis didn't feel
right for river swimming – was the contortions required to get
the damn things off and ourselves back into dry clothes. Ever
one for the easiest, quickest option, I ducked behind a convenient tree trunk, peeled my costume off in one swift movement
without bothering to untie the straps, and was soon back in my
underwear, shorts and T-shirt. My clothes stuck to my still
damp skin but the hot sun would soon sort that out. Satisfied,
comfortable and feeling refreshed after my swim, I sat down on
the grass and gave myself up to watching the mesmerising,
languid flow of the river while the others entered the struggle.

Molly took my place behind the tree. Judging by the grunts
and swear words, she seemed to be having a fight to get her
costume off. Samantha nudged me and we started giggling.

'I can hear you two,' Molly said. 'This damn thing's too
tight, that's the trouble. I had it last year, when I wasn't so well
developed.'

This had Samantha and me in stitches again, especially as,
out of the three of us, Molly was the least developed. Behind
her tree, Molly sniffed a bit before she joined in the laughter,
eventually emerging with her costume under her arm and her
clothes on. I could see there'd been a fight there. She obviously

hadn't bothered to dry herself off at all, nor put on her bra. The top half of her would have won first prize in a wet T-shirt competition; her small, neat breasts suddenly seemed to have taken on a life of their own. She sat down next to me and began plucking at the T-shirt, pulling it away from her chest, which didn't help.

'Sod it, I'm not changing.' Samantha hoisted one strap of her costume back into place. 'I'll dry in the sun and put my clothes on after. Let's eat. I'm starving.'

And so we ate, demolishing crusty cheese rolls, jam doughnuts, cheese and onion crisps and melting Penguins as if we hadn't eaten for a month. As I drank orange squash from a flask, I heard a rustling noise and then a couple of light thuds coming from behind. I peered about. All was quiet again. A bird, I thought. Of course it was a bird. Or a rabbit. Birds don't thud, neither do rabbits. Maybe a branch got dislodged and fell to the ground.

The others didn't seem to have noticed anything. Had I imagined the sound? I didn't think so.

Molly scooched forward and perched on the rim of the bank, one leg stretched out, toes pointing towards the water but not quite reaching it. The way her back was arched made her breasts stand out further, if that was possible. She was smiling, a small, private smile. I wondered what was on her mind, but only for a second. It probably wasn't anything interesting.

Samantha sighed, and lay back on her towel, her elbow propping up her head, her hair dripping down the bony ridge of her back. I continued to watch and listen. But I heard nothing more except the faint hum of traffic from the distant A road, the occasional rustle from the riverbank and the plop of a fish.

And then, we all turned and looked behind us as a crackle of leaves and popping of twigs announced we had a visitor: Jeremy.

'What the...?' began Samantha, her face stiff with surprise and annoyance.

'Oh, it's you,' I said at the same time.

Molly stayed silent, but pulled herself back from the bank and sat cross-legged on her towel.

'It's rude to creep up on people,' Samantha said, grabbing her T-shirt and holding it protectively against her chest. 'What're you doing here?'

Jeremy took a step towards us, leaving the shelter of the trees. He was wearing a fitted white T-shirt and tight black cycling shorts. He stood with legs akimbo and hands on his hips, his gaze on all three of us at once. Or maybe just on Molly, who, I had noticed, didn't seem fazed by her lack of body coverage.

'I can be here if I like. It's a public place. I don't need your permission.'

'That's not the point,' I said. 'You scared the living daylights out of us, springing out like that.'

'Yeah,' added Molly. 'You shouldn't do that. It's not polite.'

Not polite? It didn't sound like Molly at all. Samantha and I grinned at one another. She'd thought the same.

'Yes, well, it's not, is it?' Molly scowled at both me and Samantha.

Jeremy just stood there staring at us, then relaxed his stance and dropped down onto the grass a few feet away. Instinctively, I gathered my picnic bag onto my lap.

'Yes, sorry. I apologise for giving you girls a fright. I should've called out.' He smiled. 'Did you enjoy your swim? If you have been swimming, of course?'

'We aren't wearing these for nothing,' Samantha snapped, gesturing at her swimming costume. Clearly she'd forgotten she was the only one of us still wearing one.

But Samantha's costume, and our wet hair and towels, weren't Jeremy's only clue to our activities. He'd been watching, I was sure of it. He'd been hiding away in the bushes like the sneaky little pervert he was, and snooping on us the whole time. My earlier gut feeling that there was somebody around had been right.

I swallowed and looked away, not wanting to meet his eye.

'Does my mother know you swim in the river, Briony?' he said suddenly.

I looked at him, lifting my chin. 'If you're asking whether I had permission, I didn't need it. Alice is fine with whatever I choose to do in my own time. She doesn't keep watch on my every move.'

Not like you.

Jeremy's face told me he understood my meaning.

I snapped round to face the river again, blocking him out. If I was to pay for it later on, I didn't care.

I wondered how he'd known we were here. Okay, he may have been on the river path, running, or cycling. But I'd never seen him take that route before, and this part of the riverbank wasn't visible from the path. It seemed rather too much of a coincidence. I thought back to this morning, trying to remember if I'd mentioned our proposed swim to Alice, either in front of Jeremy, or anywhere he might have been within earshot. I didn't think I'd said anything. I'd been running late for work, Alice had somewhere to be as well. Breakfast had been rushed, the three of us eating in relays rather than together.

But what did it matter how he'd known about the swimming? He'd found us, and now I wished with every cell of my being that he would just go.

My wish was granted.

'I'll be off then.' He got to his feet. 'Bye, girls. Enjoy the rest of your afternoon.'

He was gone, plunging through the trees from whence he came.

'He's got a sodding *cheek*,' Samantha said.

'Sodding cheek,' echoed Molly, sounding rather uncon-
vincing to my ears.

I kept quiet. I knew it was stupid but I felt that Jeremy's
unwanted appearance was somehow my fault.

'Jeremy told me he saw you at the river today, swimming with
your friends,' Alice said conversationally, as I chopped carrots
while she browned the casserole steak for our evening meal.

Chopping carrots I could manage, which was probably why
I was allowed to help. Little to go wrong there, unless I chopped
my finger by mistake.

'Did he?' I said, pausing in my chopping as I wondered
what ulterior motive Jeremy had for passing on this information.
It was hardly front-page news. 'Yes, I had the afternoon off. I
went with Molly and Samantha. Our first time this summer.'

Alice tucked the forward-facing ends of her grey-blonde
bob behind her ears and carried on turning the meat. A blue
haze rose from the frying pan. 'As long as you're careful, Briony,
and you keep away from the overhanging trees.'

'I do, don't worry. Molly and Samantha have swum in the
river since they were kids. They showed me, the first time.'

'It's an age-old tradition for the locals to take a river dip in
summer. Not that I ever did. Edward wasn't keen on me strip-
ping off in front of what he called the whole village. For a doctor
he could be surprisingly prudish.' Alice sighed. It sounded
somehow regretful, which puzzled me. I was reminded of
Alice's almost-silence on the subject of her husband. There
were no photos of him on display in the house, no anecdotes
she'd felt like sharing with me, no fond memories to surface at
given moments, as I might have expected. It made me feel as if I
couldn't ask her about Edward, so I never did. This sudden
mention of him today was all the more poignant for its rarity,

and I could only nod and smile, and wonder what the secret was, because I felt there was one.

Alice brightened. 'Was anyone else there today?'

Only Jeremy, I thought. Alice must have known that since he'd told his mother he'd seen me.

'There was nobody else swimming,' I said truthfully. 'It was dead quiet. We liked it. I took food for a picnic. I hope you don't mind.'

Alice began transferring the sizzling cubes of meat from the frying pan to the casserole pot with a slotted spoon. 'Of course not. You never have to ask about helping yourself to food, you know that. This is your home.' She gave a little laugh. 'Funny girl.'

I laughed too. I liked these times, when it was just Alice and me. If it was only the two of us living at Summerdene, my life would not be shadowed at all.

Jeremy was late coming to dinner. We heard him thumping down the stairs and as he took his place at the table, Alice smiled indulgently and shook her head. I'd fully expected him to make a barbed remark about the swimming, something designed to embarrass or humiliate me. After all, we hadn't exactly made him welcome when he'd pitched up this afternoon. But he didn't mention it during the meal. In fact, he barely spoke at all. All I got was a pointed look as we passed each other on the upstairs landing later, and the same leery smile he saved for me, as if he knew something I didn't.

ELEVEN

BRIONY

2022

If cooking wasn't my forte, it was ten times worse if I had to do it under pressure. Which was why, after much debate between myself and my daughter, I decided to bow to my weaknesses and offer my guests breakfast Continental style.

'It's fine, Mum,' Faye had said. 'People are into healthier eating these days. I expect they'd welcome something other than a fry-up and if not, they needn't come. Stop worrying.'

So I did. I stopped worrying, and between us, Faye and I drew up what we considered to be an acceptable and varied breakfast menu in advance of the arrival of our first guests.

We began by listing the various types of bread, croissants and muffins we thought we could offer – the village bakery would be our main source of supply for those, and apparently they were able to deliver – and we'd provide locally-made butter. By the time we'd added yoghurt, fruit, cereal, ham, tomatoes, and a range of jams and spreads, the breakfast thing looked in pretty good shape. Faye added a menu page to the website she'd made. It looked so pretty and appealing I didn't know why

I'd been so worried. As long as the silver monster of a toaster didn't decide to cremate six slices of bread simultaneously, there'd be no problem.

Even so, my heart was in my mouth as my first guests, a kindly couple in their sixties and the wife's older sister, trooped downstairs to the dining room on their first morning and sat themselves at the table with looks of anticipation. But again, I needn't have fretted. It was all fine; they tucked into their breakfasts with obvious enjoyment and seemed perfectly relaxed.

A modern beechwood table stood in the space where Alice's rosewood table had been. Against the wall stood a long, narrow oak table with chunky legs, acquired from a second-hand shop. Mixing modern furniture with antique worked well against the Oriental wallpaper background and I was pleased with the overall effect.

We used the side table to set out the food for guests to help themselves, so all we had to do was smile and chat, and make toast, tea and coffee to order. As so much of the preparation could be done in advance, we were streets ahead of the game.

I suspected that 'we' in time would become 'I' and I was fully prepared for that. Enthusiastic though she was about this venture, Faye had her own job and her own life. Mistlecombe was hellishly quiet compared with the capital; I didn't know how long she'd put up with it. But it was no good second-guessing. What would happen would happen, in its own good time. Meanwhile, having Faye alongside me from the start gave me a confidence boost, and I began to wake up earlier and earlier, eager for the day to begin.

To say I felt completely settled in my new environment may be overstating things a bit. I missed the buzz of Brighton and my cosy flat, and I missed school and teaching, too, though not as much as I'd thought I would. But I was getting there, and not a day went past when I didn't silently thank Alice for giving me lovely Summerdene, and the opportunities that came with it.

. . .

One thing I did need was domestic help, somebody to keep the dust under control, change the guest beds and scrub the bathrooms. I wasn't afraid of the hard work that went along with running a guest house, but I wanted to be free to do other things alongside, and enjoy my country life. I had considered using an agency, but I thought I should look locally first in case there was somebody wanting work.

One morning I set out for the village, intent on the old-fashioned method of putting a postcard in the post office window where such things still existed. I hadn't walked far along Back Lane when I heard my name being called, and Marcus caught up with me.

'Village?' He fell into step beside me.

'How did you guess?' I told him the purpose of my mission.

'I need to go to the post office myself,' he said. 'I could put your card in for you, if you like? Save you the trip.'

'No, thanks. I'll enjoy the walk, and I need to put my order in at the bakery while I'm there. Good of you to offer, though.'

'How's it going?' Marcus said. 'The bed and breakfast thing?'

Very well, I told him. 'The guests have been a mixed bunch so far. All ages, some here for the hiking and sightseeing. A woman moving to the area came to check out properties and schools for her son, and we had an author researching the location for his latest book. So far we've only had two of the three guest bedrooms occupied at the same time but that's okay. I don't need...' I was going to say I didn't need to rake in a fortune, but that would be too much personal information to share, so I smiled instead. 'It's all new and exciting at the moment, although if I can call running a small B&B in the Cotswolds exciting it probably shows I need to get out more.'

Marcus laughed. We walked on, and as we reached the

bakery and prepared to go our separate ways, he said: 'I don't suppose you're free tonight?'

'Free?'

'Yes, you know. Free, as in nothing planned. For this evening.'

I smiled, realising how stupid I must have sounded. It was so long since anyone had asked me that question I'd forgotten what it meant. If it meant what I was thinking it might...

'No, no plans. Except a quiet night in with the box.'

Like every other night.

We stepped aside to make room for a customer coming out of the bakery and wanting to cross the street.

'It's just that I was thinking...' Marcus said, looking as if he wished he'd never started this conversation, 'I was thinking about going for a meal at the White Hart, if you fancy coming with me?'

'The White Hart?' I repeated, sounding even more stupid than before.

Immediately, Faye sprang to mind. Marcus had meant just me, hadn't he? How was it possible to know without asking directly? My feet performed a fidgety dance on the pavement. I was getting this *so* wrong. A simple invitation – no more than a suggestion, really – and I was all over the place. I hadn't realised how inept I'd become at being normally social. I hadn't been a hermit in Brighton by any means, but I had let things slide socially, ducked invitations in favour of a quiet night in, alone. It had seemed easier that way.

But this was my new life. I wasn't in Brighton anymore. I was living in the north Cotswolds, with a new house and a new occupation. I needed to find my feet, fast, and make new friends before I became a withered up, embittered divorcee with no life of her own. Okay, that was over-egging it, but the general idea was there.

'I went in there for lunch one day. It's a nice pub. I'd love to join you. Thanks.'

I thought of something else. Assuming Faye wasn't coming with Marcus and me, she might well be heading for the White Hart herself. Never one to let the grass grow, my daughter had spent several evenings at the pub already. Not something I'd have done at her age or even beyond, pitching up at a strange pub in a strange village among people she didn't know. But plucky Faye had gone ahead and done just that, and had made a fistful of new acquaintances who no doubt would become friends, in time. I was pleased for her and full of admiration, after the Nick debacle.

'Okay?' Marcus looked at me. 'You're looking dubious.'

'Oh, no. It's only that Faye, my daughter, goes to the pub some nights. I wouldn't want to cramp her style.'

'I wouldn't worry. It's a small village. You can't keep clear of each other entirely. We'll sit in the corner, eat our dinner and mind our own business. How does that sound?'

I laughed. 'It sounds perfect.'

Faye wasn't going to the White Hart that evening as she wanted to finish some work. I elicited this information with a casual-sounding question and received the expected 'Why?' in return. I explained as rapidly and vaguely as I could that I would be there myself, and who I was going with. Luckily, Faye didn't get overexcited about my proposed outing, as she might well have done. In fact, she seemed preoccupied, which I supposed was to do with the work thing she was keen to get on with.

'I didn't know we had any neighbours,' she said, as I came downstairs in clean jeans and a white embroidered shirt, hoping to escape without further questioning.

'Well, we do,' I said. 'One, anyway. His name's Marcus

Schofield and he lives at Kestrels, the thatched cottage past the old orchard.'

'Oh, that cottage is *so* gorgeous,' Faye said dreamily. Then added, 'Not as gorgeous as Summerdene, of course. I love this house.'

'I do, too,' I said, relieved we'd moved on to the subject of houses and away from my dinner engagement, which I was suddenly, unaccountably, nervous about.

I needn't have worried. Marcus was waiting at his front door as I arrived – we'd decided I would call for him rather than the other way round, as he lived nearer the village end of Back Lane. We chatted companionably as we walked to the pub and continued in the same vein throughout, being seated at a window table in the pub and ordering our meals. Although I hardly knew him, I felt at ease and the talk flowed naturally.

It was only after we'd ordered pudding that I decided a little judicious questioning wouldn't be out of place. Marcus had already told me he'd only lived in Mistlecombe for five months, so I asked him where he'd lived before.

'Ashford,' he said. 'Busy place and getting busier by the day.'

'Is that why you left? For a more rural lifestyle? Although the Kent countryside is lovely...'

'So why didn't I just move out of town?' Marcus gave me a knowing look.

'I'm *so* predictable.' I laughed and raised my eyes.

'I wanted to get right away. Well, we did. Hannah and me. It was meant to be a fresh start. A sort of reboot.'

'A reboot. Yes, I get that.' I wanted to say I'd felt the same about my move, but I didn't want the conversation to turn to me before I'd found out more about him.

'Moving away didn't work. I hadn't expected it to. But you do your best, don't you?'

'You do,' I said, unsure what we were doing our best at.

'We rushed at it, like the proverbial bull at a gate. Or bulls at gates. Can you say that? Anyway, Hannah went online, earmarked the Cotswolds and the part she liked the most, and I found her what her little heart desired, a picture-book thatched cottage with roses round the door. Which I'm only renting, by the way. I don't have the megabucks you'd need to buy one.' He chuckled. 'I'm still working on the roses. Might not bother now.' He took a spoonful of chocolate brownie dessert. 'It's a common enough story. We were over. We'd tried to make it work, or I had. Not sure about Han. I suspected she had another bloke on the go, though she never admitted it, and I didn't press her because I didn't care enough. One day we had one row too many and she packed up her old kitbag and went back to Kent. I stayed put, so here we are.' He grinned. 'Here *I* am, I mean.'

I laughed; I couldn't help it. He had a wry turn of phrase and a gentle, self-deprecating manner that I couldn't help but find appealing.

Marcus went on to tell me he now worked at Gloucester University as a lecturer in Education, as he had at Kent University before the move. His new campus being in Cheltenham, the commute was easy. And then, with teaching being our common ground, although with very different experiences, we swapped notes happily for the rest of the evening.

We wandered home through the soft, summery night. Marcus insisted on seeing me to my front door. Not that I needed seeing, but it was sweet of him and it seemed churlish to argue.

Lots of things were sweet about Marcus, I was beginning to discover. I pushed that thought into touch right away. I didn't need the complication.

Only one small thing cast a shadow over the evening. I arrived home to find that Faye had gone out after all. She hadn't said she was going out, and I hadn't seen her at the pub, although it had been almost closing time when Marcus and I left and the crowd had thinned out. I didn't wait up for her; I was tired, and I knew I mustn't crowd her. My daughter and I hadn't lived together for years; we were sailing in uncharted waters.

I went to bed but didn't fall asleep until I heard her come in. Even though it was almost midnight, I hoped she might pop her head round my bedroom door and I flicked on the bedside light, just in case, then felt stupidly disappointed when she went straight to her own room. Resisting the impulse to go and check on her wasn't easy, but I managed it. I listened to the muted sound of movements from her room for a few minutes, then switched off the light and settled down to sleep.

TWELVE
BRIONY

1986

Jeremy, thankfully, had gone out. Alice and I were having what she called a quiet night in, of which there were many, and not so far and few between.

I could have gone round to Samantha's but as neither of us had much money after a shopping trip to Cheltenham, it would have meant spending another evening sitting on her bed, listening to tapes. It wasn't as if Molly would have been there; she had gone out somewhere. If Samantha knew where, she wasn't sharing it with me.

The three of us were changing, the dynamic shifting like scree on a rock face. I wasn't sure I liked it.

An American tennis player, Chuck somebody or other, had died of a brain tumour, aged only forty-five. I'd caught the report on the TV news earlier. It reminded me of my mother, Helena, who'd suffered the same fate at thirty-four.

I didn't think about her very often. If that sounds harsh, it wasn't. It was a coping mechanism I'd learned early on and it had become so ingrained into the workings of my mind, I didn't know how to be any other way. Besides, there wasn't much to think about. I only had a paltry store of memories of my mother, most of which had been conjured up from old photos and snatches of conversation that had come my way over the years, and were probably false.

My father had taken the same approach as me. At least, I imagined he had, as he'd rarely spoken about Mum, except during the raw, teary aftermath of her death, and I don't recall gleaning much comfort from his words then. I didn't blame him for that – he wouldn't have known what to do, what to say or how to be, any more than I did at four years old. Perhaps he should have known; after all, he was the adult. This thought had occurred to me much later on. But who was I to judge?

'Can I look at the album?' I said to Alice, tucking my magazine into the crevice of the armchair.

She looked up from the table mat she was crocheting. At least, I thought it was a table mat but it could have been anything. A confusion of cream-coloured yarn coiled hopelessly across her lap.

'Of course. You don't have to ask.'

I felt Alice's eyes following me as I crossed the room to where the album I was after lived a dusty life on the bottom shelf of the bookcase.

'Are you all right, Briony?' she said, as I returned, clutching the dark green volume.

I brushed on a smile. 'Yep, fine.' It was what Alice wanted to hear.

I opened the stiff pages of the album and thumbed to the place where the photos of my christening were ensnared at the corners by peeling cardboard fixers. There were no pictures of the actual ceremony inside the church. I wished there were, only I don't suppose it was allowed. There were just the two photos of everyone standing on the church steps afterwards.

'You weren't smiling,' I said, tapping at the photo. I'd said it before. I knew what Alice's response would be, but I found it comforting to hear these stories again.

'You were such a wriggly little thing, I was scared of dropping you.' Alice's face took on a faraway look. 'Once the service was over, I'd expected to hand you over to one of the family but somehow I got stuck with you till we got back to your nan's for tea.'

I laughed. I knew she was joking.

Over the page in the album were two more photos, this time of the christening tea party in Nan's front room, a square, white-iced cake taking centre stage beside a mountain of sandwiches; sundry friends and relatives squashed onto the tapestry three-piece suite clutching old-fashioned sherry glasses. Family parties and Christmases were always held at my grandmother's house in Worthing, the coastal Sussex town where we'd lived at the time. My parents' flat was too small for get-togethers, apparently. Or maybe that was just an excuse.

Alice had become my godmother almost by default. My parents had wanted me to be christened – goodness knows why; they weren't churchgoers – but with one week to go, they still hadn't got around to choosing godparents. Nan had swiftly stepped in and press-ganged Alice, her next-door neighbour and friend, to be godmother. A male cousin of my father's, whom I have never met since, was godfather. But Alice knew my mother and was fond of her, so it wasn't so far-fetched an idea for her to stand for me.

'I was so pleased Nora asked me, and of course, I said yes,' Alice said. 'It was a proud moment.'

I had heard this before, too, but I liked hearing it again.

'Jeremy wasn't there, of course,' Alice continued, looking back at her crochet. 'He'd never have stood still in church so we sent him to play at a friend's house.' She looked up. 'That's why he's not in the photos.'

'I know. You said before.' Jeremy's absence from a significant event in my life was a finger of warmth in an otherwise chilly climate.

Alice laid her crochet down on the sofa beside her. 'Briony?'

'Mmm?'

Alice paused, closing her eyes for a second, as if she needed to prepare herself for what came next.

'If you find Jeremy not quite as... accommodating as he ought to be – and I have judged that to be the case on occasions – try not to take it to heart. It's just how he is. He can be quite sharp sometimes, and he can be overly critical. If he's ever said anything out of place to you, then I can only apologise on his behalf.'

Apologise?

I drew in breath and held it. How much did Alice know? How much had she seen, or heard? Anger curdled low down in my gut, rising rapidly to my throat, rendering me speechless. If she knew how her son behaved towards me, how he slyly bullied me under the cover of so-called jokiness, why had she done nothing about it? Unofficially, I was Alice's ward. Surely, she should protect me, even if it meant siding with me against her son?

Letting my breath out in a rush, I pressed down hard on my anger, moulding it, reshaping it into something like resentment, which was still uncomfortable but easier to handle. Alice may have admitted that her darling son wasn't perfect, but I had the feeling that what she had said was, genuinely, all she knew.

When I opened my eyes, she was looking at me with such concern that I almost blurted it all out: the innocent remarks infused with meaning, the insinuations, the cross-questioning, all of it, including the voyeurism on the riverbank. It came to me then that perhaps he'd been watching me and my friends at the Kissing Tree, too. A couple of times I'd felt we were being watched in the woods and brushed it off as imagination. Now, I wasn't so sure.

But even if I'd wanted to confide in Alice, I didn't have the vocabulary.

I swallowed hard. 'It's all right.' Saying something and nothing seemed the only response.

It had to be all right, didn't it? I was sixteen, and powerless. Summerdene was the only home I had until I was old enough to strike out on my own. With any luck, Jeremy would leave before I did, although he seemed pretty much dug in to me.

Which was, I realised with a jolt, just the way Alice liked it.

She was thoughtful for a few minutes, her eyes unseeing as she gazed towards the window. I wondered if anything else was to come, any revelations about Jeremy that would confirm Alice's true understanding of the situation, that she knew how bloody awful her son really was. But there was nothing.

Instead, she picked up her crochet work and held it up by her fingertips. 'What do you think? Honestly, I wish I hadn't offered now.'

'Is it a table mat?'

'A mat, certainly. I suppose it could be a table mat, or a mat for a dressing table. It has to be a mat of some sort. I can only crochet round in circles. This is only the first. I'll have to do a couple more, make it a set. It's for the Townswomen's Guild craft fair, Saturday week.'

'Well, then, I think it's lovely,' I lied, wondering whoever would want such things. 'They'll be dead pleased with your contribution, I bet.'

Alice gave a short, sharp laugh. 'I'm not so sure about that. Shall we pull the curtains? August, and the nights are already drawing in.'

I got up to oblige. I wondered when Jeremy would be home, or where he'd gone. To the pub, maybe. He went there sometimes; he never said but I'd occasionally noticed the smell of beer on his breath. Not that I cared where he went.

I made us cocoa and took mine upstairs. The church clock

struck midnight before I heard Jeremy come in, by which time I'd been in bed for ages. As he came up the stairs and passed my door with a light tread, he was whistling softly, as if he was happy about something. Even that, a casual whistling, seemed aimed at me, as if it conveyed a message of some sort.

I punched my pillow into shape and pulled the duvet over my head. If I was getting paranoia, I needed a good night's sleep.

THIRTEEN

BRIONY

2022

Marcus pulled out a chair and settled himself at the kitchen table. Around us, the detritus of the guests' breakfast awaited my attention. Upstairs, there were beds to be made and bathrooms to scrub and replenish. I'd had no response from my postcard advertising for domestic help, and I could really do with it now I was getting busy.

I'd passed the post office last week and couldn't see my card in the window. I was sure I'd paid for three weeks, which hadn't expired, so it should still have been on display. There were new guests due at Summerdene and I'd been in a hurry to get home, so I hadn't had time to go in and renew my ad if necessary. I'd made a mental note to pop back at some point, but the days swanned past and I forgot all about it.

Perhaps Mistlecombe had a community web page or newsletter where I could post my enquiry, I thought. I should probably have thought of that in the first place. My laptop was beside me, charging on the kitchen counter, but Marcus was here now. I'd check it out later.

I switched the kettle on again. Faye usually helped clear up after breakfast before she started work, but she'd left for London yesterday afternoon to spend a few days checking in at her office and seeing friends. And no, Nick wouldn't be one of them, she assured me, as if I had asked the question. I hadn't, but her eagerness to put my mind at rest was as sweet as it was welcome.

Marcus looked very much at home in my kitchen. Since the university summer term had ended, he'd taken to calling in at this time of day, no longer pretending he was just passing, as he had the first time. I hadn't believed him – unless he'd intended to wander around the farmyard at the end of Back Lane, there was nowhere he could be passing to.

Today, though, there was a purpose to his visit. Would I like to go with him to Blenheim Palace on Saturday? I would. It was years since I'd been there and seeing the grand house and magnificent grounds through Marcus's eyes – it would be his first visit – was doubly attractive. I accepted without pretending to consult the calendar with its blank white squares staring at us from the larder door.

'I've got vouchers for afternoon tea,' he said, then laughed. 'Now I sound like a right cheapskate.'

I laughed too. 'I like a bargain. It'd be a shame not to take advantage.'

'Champagne is included,' he added, as if I needed any further enticement. 'You'll have to drink my share as I'll be driving.'

'That won't be a problem,' I said.

Were we dating, Marcus and I? I can honestly say I had no idea. I'd lost the knack of sussing out exactly what was what, or rather who was who, on the relationship front. I only knew I was enjoying Marcus's company, our casual meals out – mainly at the White Hart because it was handy and the food was superb – and our walks around the lanes, and up and down the sugarloaf hills around Mistlecombe.

I liked it, too, that he lived so close. I loved being the owner of Summerdene, but the responsibility weighed a little heavy at times. Even so, I wouldn't call on Marcus for assistance unless something drastic happened. But knowing he was nearby gave me a sense of security I didn't realise I'd needed.

I thought about Tony, and how Faye had suggested I'd been using him as a comfort blanket. Was I really so pathetic that I couldn't cope without a man within shouting distance?

In Brighton, my ex-husband had been my first port of call when a bathroom pipe sprung a leak, three months back. I'd reached out to him streets ahead of any thoughts of emergency plumbers. He'd fixed the leak, no problem. He was the best handyman I knew. And, no, of course he hadn't minded turning out, even if he and his wife had been about to have dinner. Cherie was fine about it, he'd assured me, and I'd believed him. In fact, she'd been the one to answer the phone to me in the first place. Cherie had been amenable to me throughout our limited contact, and she was much more suited to Tony than I was – or had become, in our later married years. I felt almost smug at how civilised we all were.

I wasn't in Brighton now, and not in range of Tony and his cheerful willingness to advise me on this or that, with or without a toolbox. But I wasn't looking for a substitute. I was strong and independent, as I kept telling myself. Hadn't I uprooted my entire life and moved across the country to set up as a B&B host without so much as a niggle of a doubt? Well, not quite. But I'd definitely made progress.

I was thinking about this and allowing myself a little congratulatory moment as I folded clean, fluffy pale blue towels over the rail in one of the guest bathrooms. And then, as I staggered downstairs with a pile of used towels, my mind looped round again and snagged on my current little problem: domestic help. Or rather, lack of. It was then that I remembered the flyer that had been pushed through my letter box. I should have looked ahead at the time, joined up the dots and rung the number, but I hadn't taken my first guests then, and it hadn't occurred to me.

I bundled the towels into the washing machine and, while it was fresh in my mind, went through to the living room and searched among the magazines beside the sofa. There, among other bits of junk mail I should have thrown out weeks ago, was the piece of paper. I smoothed out the creases and reached for my phone. Whoever it was would probably have found a job by now, but there was no harm in trying.

'Hi, Pippa Medhurst,' said a tired female voice on the fourth ring.

The voice brightened considerably when I explained why I was calling. Yes, she was free for a chat tomorrow morning, she told me. We set a time for her to come to Summerdene, and I ended the call feeling extremely hopeful.

I didn't feel quite so optimistic when, the following morning, I noticed it was almost half an hour after the time Pippa and I had agreed for her visit. I hoped she wasn't a time-waster, leaving me back at square one. But soon after, the doorbell sounded and a young woman, early twenties, stood on the step, holding out a hand to me and apologising profusely for her lateness.

'No problem,' I said, ushering her through to the living room and inviting her to sit in one of the armchairs. 'Back Lane is longer than you think.'

I shouldn't have made excuses for her, but I was relieved she'd shown up at all.

'Oh, I didn't walk. I rode my bike over. I propped it up against your hedge. Don't mind, do you?'

'No, of course not. It's handy to have a bike,' I said. 'Especially around here.'

'Yeah. Saves time.' Pippa flashed a smile.

I was tempted to remark that it hadn't saved her much time this morning, but I bit it back.

She was about five foot five, slender to the point of thinness, but she had a strength about her. Wiry, I suppose was the term. She had long, poker-straight black hair. Her narrow face was pale, made paler still by the black hair and the all-black outfit she wore: a loose-fitting black T-shirt, over black leggings. A tattoo of a bird with a hooked beak – eagle, perhaps? – spread its wings just above her collarbone, and a symbol of some sort graced one delicate wrist. She was too sharp-featured to be conventionally pretty, but she had a certain edgy attractiveness enhanced by large, hazel eyes.

Those eyes appraised me openly now, as Pippa slung one slender leg over the other and let her hands rest casually on the chair arms in a proprietorial way I didn't much like. But she wanted a job and I needed somebody, so I opened the conversation by asking her if she lived in the village, and if she'd always lived there.

'Not always. I was born in Mistlecombe. It was my home, till I grew up. Then I was away for a while, lived in a few places, trying stuff out, like you do. But I'm back now, living with my mum. I've got a little boy, Rory. He's four. Mum looks after him while I'm working or he goes to nursery. It won't be a problem.'

'That's good,' I said. 'Having your mum on hand, I mean.'

'Yeah.' Pippa gazed absently about the room. Then she looked back at me. 'Look, Mrs...'

'Harrington,' I supplied, feeling as old as the hills. 'But Briony's fine.'

'Briony. Right.' Pippa gave me a tight little smile. 'The thing is, I haven't got a reference, not a recent one at any rate. You'd be wanting one, I expect?'

'Well, yes. I was coming round to that.'

Actually, I'd forgotten all about references, having never employed anyone before, and I was grateful for the prompt.

'The lady I've been working for, well, she died. I hadn't been with her long but she was lovely. And then she was taken ill suddenly, and then she was gone. Just like that.'

Pippa cast her gaze downwards. When she looked up again, her eyes were misty.

'Oh, Pippa. How dreadful,' I said. 'You sound as if you were fond of her.'

'She was nice. She was ever so old, but still, it was a shock. Her house was big, not as big as this one but it took some cleaning, and I managed it. She always said I was a good worker. Best she'd had.'

'Ah, I can see the problem with the reference, then. What were you doing before you worked for the lady who died? I asked gently, not wanting to push this but feeling I should at least have a little more background.

'I worked in a shop but it shut down because of the pandemic and the owner moved away. Before that I stopped at home with Rory.'

'Oh, well, let's not worry about it any more,' I said, smiling to lighten the moment. 'I can see how things are.'

I'd have to overlook the lack of a reference. Faye would say I was too lax for my own good, and she'd probably be right. I wouldn't tell her, then.

'I thought you might have found a job by now,' I said. 'That flyer you put through my door came some while ago.'

'Flyer?' Pippa looked confused.

'Your advert,' I said. 'Offering your services.'

'Oh, that. Yes. We thought it was a good idea. Me and... Mum.' She uncrossed her legs, sitting forward on the chair. 'I really need this job. Rory grows out of his clothes as soon as they're on his back. You say what hours suit you and I'll fit in. Yes, totally.'

It sounded as if she was trying to convince herself as well as me. But she gave a bright smile that transformed her features and I felt myself warming to her. Pippa was a single mother – at least it sounded that way – living with her own mother, scratching a living with domestic work to fit in with her child's needs. It couldn't be easy.

I fell to practicalities about her hours, rate of pay, and the kind of duties I'd expect of her.

'Will it be cash in hand?' she asked, her mouth forming a little pout.

'Yes, I think that'll be fine,' I said.

I had thought about this beforehand and decided it wasn't worth getting involved in too many formalities at this stage; the easiest option all round. I passed Pippa a notepad and pen.

'Jot your address and phone number on there, if you would.'

She hesitated for a moment, her face clouded with doubt, and then began writing. She passed me back the notebook. I thanked her and put it down beside me without looking at it. Then we set out on a tour of Summerdene.

As we walked round the house, Pippa showed a real interest, asking me how old it was and seeming genuinely appreciative of Summerdene's charms. I decided I liked her. In any case, she was the only applicant.

As I showed her out after our tour, I handed her one of my little cards with the code for the front door security panel written on it. 'But do come in the back way. The door's always open when I'm home.'

'Ta.' She pocketed the card. 'See you Monday, then.'

She sounded resigned and I couldn't blame her for that. Another cleaning job couldn't be high on her list of ideal careers, but she was prepared to make the best of it. At least, I hoped she was. There was a chance that she wouldn't turn up on Monday. I'd just have to wait and see.

I gave her a cheerful wave as I closed the door.

It took until the middle of the following week for Faye to take an interest in my embryonic social life; I couldn't say I was sorry. She'd extended her London visit to a week, and had been out most evenings since. Now she'd finally got around to shining her spotlight on me.

'And what is this, Mother?' She peeled the magnet off the fridge and held it up, as if I'd never seen it before.

I stuffed the last pain au chocolat into my mouth and set the greasy plate aside for the next dishwasher run. 'It's a fridge magnet,' I said, through a mouthful of sweet flaky pastry. 'What does it look like? Scotch mist?'

Faye snapped the magnet back into place, crookedly. 'Since when did you collect fridge magnets?'

'I don't. It was a present. A joke, that's all.'

'A present from...?' Faye tipped her blonde head to one side and fixed me with a tell-all-or-else look.

'Blenheim Palace.'

'Ha ha, very funny.'

'Okay. I went there with Marcus Schofield, last Saturday. He bought it in the gift shop when I wasn't looking. Naff, isn't it?'

I smiled, remembering Marcus's insistence on buying me the magnet and presenting it to me, Blenheim Palace paper bag and all, with an ironic flourish.

'Yep, it's naff. But kinda cute. Are you two going out? I mean *properly* going out? Because if so, you have my blessing. It's about time you saw some action. You're only forty-nine, Mum.'

'No, I am *not* going out with Marcus, properly or otherwise.

We're just friends. And anyway, Marcus is only forty-five and I'm galloping hell for leather towards fifty.'

Suddenly I was certain there wasn't, and never would be, anything other than neighbourly friendship between Marcus and me. He'd never given any indication otherwise and neither, thankfully, had I. I'd treated him like any other new acquaintance because that was exactly what he was. It was a relief to finally have things straight in my head.

Faye wasn't having any of it. 'Fifty's nothing.' She bent to unload the dishwasher. 'He should be so lucky. He is pretty fit, though. Gorgeous eyes. And the rest.'

'I didn't think you'd noticed,' I said. I'd hurriedly introduced Faye to Marcus on the doorstep when he'd turned up one morning just as she was going out.

'Not the sort of thing that's easy to miss.' Faye laughed. 'Come on, Mum.'

'Come on, Mum, what? For heaven's sake, Faye, drop it, will you?'

Unconvinced, Faye grinned.

'Where've that lot gone anyway?' She pointed a finger at the ceiling.

'The guests? I don't know, do I? They don't hang about once they've eaten me out of house and home.'

Actually, I did know where this week's contingent were this morning – it was just the mention of Marcus that had made me forget for a moment. The two sixtyish couples, friends of one another, had set out for Bourton-on-the-Water, undeterred by the deadening, relentless heatwave that showed no signs of abating. The women were especially keen to see the model village. The retired vicar in the third room was continuing his tour of churches in the area. He was writing a book on church history, he'd told me, then happily confessed his doubt that the book would ever be finished. He'd stepped smartly towards his ancient hatchback, carrying an old-fashioned camera, a doorstep sized dog-eared notebook and a clutch of leaky biros.

'You don't think of vicars as retiring,' I mused. 'I always imagined they carried on vicaring till they dropped.'

'Well, let's hope he doesn't drop, literally. It's too hot to be racing around the countryside.' Faye laughed. 'Shall we sit in the garden after we've cleared up?'

'Definitely,' I said.

Now that I had help from Pippa who, to my relief, had turned out to be a hard worker, if a touch slapdash, Faye and I had taken to sitting outside whenever we could. It was too hot to do much else. There were trees at the end of the garden which provided welcome shade. Faye would bring her laptop, although I wasn't sure how much work she was doing. I would read and daydream until, inevitably, I slipped into a heat-soaked slumber.

This morning I made an effort to stay awake. I had food orders to place, the smaller sitting room I'd given over to the guests needed a going over, and the fridge needed cleaning out. Pippa couldn't do everything in the four hours a day I employed her, and in any case there was no reason why I shouldn't keep my own house in order. But the most urgent task on my agenda was the garden. It needed watering again. Thirsty flower heads drooped sulkily in the borders, and the shrubs, front and back, were on their knees for want of a drink. I had no idea what to do about the fruit trees with their shrivelled leaves. There was probably nothing I could do to chivvy them along to fruitfulness. Only a long, sustained downpour could do that. Faint hope, according to the forecast.

I yawned and stretched my arms above my head. 'Is there a hosepipe ban in force round here?'

Faye looked up from her screen. 'How should I know? Don't you keep tabs on these things?'

'Could you google it?'

'I'm in the middle of something. Ask our friendly neighbour, Marcus Wotsit, the one who looks like a poet. I bet he knows.'

Poet? I had to smile at that. Actually, I'd bet my last fiver Marcus had no more idea than I did and cared even less. Tony, however, could have recited all the hosepipe bans in place throughout the UK. I brushed aside the prickle of annoyance at this thought and turned my attention back to my desiccated garden. I would fetch the hosepipe in a while. Ban or not, there was no way I was dragging a heavy watering can around.

'Are you out tonight?' I said, disregarding Faye's tapping on her keyboard. 'Sorry, you're trying to work. Forget I'm here.'

She snapped the laptop lid shut. 'S'all right, I'm waiting for answers to stuff. I'll get back to it later.' She lay back in the deckchair, crooking one long, perfectly tanned and buffed leg over another. 'Yes, I'll be out, if that's okay with you.'

'Of course. Just asking because of dinner, that's all.'

'I won't need any, thanks.' She twisted her head to look at me, and I saw something in her expression, the way her mouth curved in a suppressed smile, and her blue-grey eyes shone.

'Faye?'

'Okay, I wasn't going to say anything until I was sure. But I *am* sure now.' She turned to me, the smile now at full beam, as if she couldn't hold it back. 'I've met someone. His name's Logan Worth and he's staying at the White Hart. They let out the rooms upstairs, you know.'

My heart quickened. My daughter had been up those stairs, seen those rooms. Well, one of them. It was obvious from the way her eyes flicked around, just missing mine.

'Tell me more,' I said, feigning a casual interest.

I had to know what we were dealing with here. This was my precious daughter, the one who'd had her heart trampled on so recently it still bore the tread marks of the dastardly Nick's size tens.

But Faye had drifted off into a world of her own.

'Who'd have thought a titchy little village like Mistlecombe could produce somebody as glorious as him?' she said dreamily.

Glorious? It wasn't a word I'd heard her use about anyone before. This sounded serious.

'How old is he? What does he do for a job? Why's he staying at the pub?' I counted off the questions on my fingers.

Faye laughed. 'Careful, Mum, you'll run out of fingers in a minute.'

I dropped my hands to my lap. 'It's fine. You don't have to tell me.'

'No, I want to tell you. It's just that it'll sound totally crazy. The last thing I expected to happen when I came here was to fall in love. Like, *really* in love.'

She was right; it did sound crazy.

'Faye, you could only have known him five minutes. It's too soon to know. Has he said how he feels about you?' I had a thought. 'He is free and single, isn't he?'

'Yep, free as a bird, and he feels the same as me. We're in love, Mum. Amazing, isn't it?'

She didn't want an answer to that, which was just as well.

This Logan – I could only think of him as *this Logan*; my mind refused to elevate him to anything more polite – had apparently swept my daughter off her feet, ambushed her with declarations of love, stolen her heart, and every other cliché you could apply.

He was thirty-five, eleven years older than her. She rushed out this information, presumably to give me no time to dwell on it. He was a quality assurance tester for a computer games company, she said. 'His home's in Stevenage but he can work anywhere,' she added brightly, as if I'd welcome this news.

He'd come to the village on a sort of pilgrimage, looking up old friends and family, although he'd never lived here himself. This seemed awfully vague, and implausible. Who were these friends and family? He must have strong ties to Mistlecombe for him to move halfway across the country. Faye didn't seem to know, when I asked. She said they hadn't talked about it much.

'We FaceTimed every day while I was in London, sometimes twice,' she said, as if it was the most important thing.

'When will I get to meet him?' I smiled, rubbing my hands together as if I was totally on board with this. Instead, I felt as if I'd been shocked by a defibrillator.

'Oh, some time,' Faye said airily. 'It's early days. We're getting to know one another first. Although it does feel as if I've known him all my life, and Logan feels the same.'

Does he really?

Realising how negative I was being, I scraped my brain for something more upbeat. Faye seemed happy; that had to be number one on my list of wishes for my daughter. Being with Nick had wearied her. Now she'd recovered that fresh-out-of-the-box sheen, which had to be a positive. Mistlecombe was a small village; it wasn't as if she'd been swallowed whole by a big city, as I'd sometimes felt when she'd lived in London. At least here I'd be able to keep an eye on her. Undercover, of course.

'Promise me you'll be careful,' I said. 'Take it slowly. There's no rush, is there?'

Faye's pretty face creased into a frown. 'He won't be staying in the village for ever. He'll have to go home some time.'

My wayward mind leapt ahead several stages. If Faye went home with him when the time came, Hertfordshire wasn't that far away. I tried to count it as a positive that Logan didn't come from Scotland. Or America. Or Australia. Though, I didn't feel very positive. But that was my failing, not hers.

I patted her arm, offered a motherly smile which made me feel about a hundred and two, and went indoors to make coffee. Hot day or not, I needed caffeine. It was too early for gin.

FOURTEEN

BRIONY

1986

It was Sunday afternoon, and I was bored. Summerdene, its walls brushed golden by the sun, slept like a well-fed cat. Jeremy was doing the same, sprawled in a deckchair on the lawn, although there was nothing cat-like about him, except perhaps the way he slunk about, suddenly appearing in the room when you hadn't noticed his arrival. Actually, that was more snake than cat.

Alice, never still if she could help it, was knee deep among the herbaceous borders, poking around with an ancient hand fork, wooden trug standing by. Not knowing what to do with myself, I was considering offering to help, without much heart, when I heard the phone ringing. I bolted indoors and grabbed it from the hall table just in time to hear Samantha's squeal at the other end.

'Oh, you *are* there. Good. I rang Molly. We thought we'd go to the river. You coming, Bri?'

'Swimming?' I said. 'No, I can't. Not today.'

'Oh, go on. It's more fun with three. Don't be a wet blanket.'

'I'm not. Wrong time of the month, that's all.'

'Come and watch, then. Meet you in twenty minutes. Phone box in the high street.'

Samantha had gone, giving me no choice in the matter. I was glad she'd rung, though. Sitting on the riverbank with my mates was infinitely preferable to hanging around here, and I wouldn't have to look at Jeremy.

Samantha was waiting at the phone box alone. Apparently, Molly said she had something she had to do first, and she'd see us there.

'Whoever *has* to do something on a Sunday afternoon?' Samantha moaned. 'Honestly, that girl gets more unreliable by the minute.'

'Will you call at her house on your way home?' I asked, already knowing the answer.

'God, no. If she can't be arsed, neither can I.'

As I'd suspected, Samantha's refusal to chase after Molly stood firm. I didn't blame her.

We set off for the river at a leisurely pace. It was Sunday afternoon; we were in no hurry.

'Aren't you going in, then?' I said to Samantha, after we'd claimed our usual pitch on the riverbank and had been there a while. 'It'd be a shame to miss out if you fancied a dip.'

She'd stripped down to her swimming costume and was laying half on her towel, half on the grass, one leg raised nonchalantly in the air, obviously for the benefit of the group of boys some yards further along the bank.

'Nah, shan't bother now.' Samantha lowered her leg, arched her back and stretched her arms high above her head. Her chest strained against the material of her costume.

'You'll pop out in a minute,' I said.

Lowering her arms, Samantha peered down at her chest as

she'd had no idea of the effect of her stretching. 'Oh well, they'd have copped an eyeful.' She waved towards the boys. 'Good luck to them.'

I hitched up the hem of my already short dress for my legs to catch the sun while the rest of me remained in the dappled shade of the trees. I remembered Jeremy's voyeurism when we were last here. I wished I hadn't remembered. There seemed to be hardly anything these days that didn't remind me of him, even when he wasn't present.

I scanned the group of boys to distract me. One of them was Daniel Wilson; I hadn't realised that earlier. After the school disco, I had gone on a date with him. If you could call ambling round the lanes of Mistlecombe and swigging Coke from cans, then perching uncomfortably on a subsiding park bench a date. He'd been quiet, not a lot to say for himself. The inevitable snogging session had been okay. Just okay. No fireworks.

We hadn't repeated the experience. Daniel, despite his declarations at the disco, clearly thought we had best leave it there, and we'd kind of called it quits, by unspoken agreement. Which was fine by me. I had no intention of beginning sixth form with a ready-made boyfriend by my side. I could do without the restriction.

The boys, including Daniel, were making a show of splashing in the water and calling loudly to one another whilst looking in our direction. Correction: in Samantha's direction.

'Bloody show-offs. Not a decent shag amongst them,' she announced.

I squealed with laughter. 'You should be so lucky. Or they should, more like it.'

Samantha effected a pose, one dramatic hand sweeping across her brow. 'I'm doomed. Destined to die wondering. Virginal until my last breath.'

'I still reckon you'll beat me and Molly to the finishing line,' I said. 'We said that, don't you remember?'

'Oh yeah. At the Kissing Tree. We said, me first, then you, then Molly.' Samantha looked round at me. 'Did you bring anything to eat?'

This sudden wild change of subject was typical.

'No, I didn't have time.' I'd had enough of the riverbank now. 'Molly's obviously not going to show up. Come back to mine. There's always heaps of cake and stuff.'

Samantha didn't need asking twice. She threw on her clothes and we trailed back to Summerdene.

On the grass near one of the flower borders stood the trug, heaped with weeds. No sign of Alice. And then I remembered she'd said something about going to tea with a friend. A note in the kitchen confirmed this: 'Bread in bin. Cake in larder. Ginger cake wants using. A.'

I made us a glass of orange squash each, then located the tin with the ginger cake and took out two plates.

'Where's the creep, then? Is he in?' Samantha said, looking around as if Jeremy might suddenly materialise from behind a cupboard.

'Doesn't look like it.' I'd noticed his deckchair was unoccupied as we passed, as well as the complete silence in the house. He must have gone out, too, thankfully.

As I sawed into the ginger cake with the bread knife, I wondered whether we'd been too hasty in leaving the river.

'You don't think we should ring Molly's house to see if she's at home?'

'What for?'

'In case she turned up after all. It would be a shame if she got all the way there and found us gone.'

Samantha hesitated. I could tell she was curious as to what had happened to Molly, only she would never have admitted it.

'Can do, if you like. We did wait ages, though.'

'Shall I or shan't I?'

'Yeah, go on then. If it makes you happy.'

We traipsed back along the hall and I picked up the tatty book containing addresses and phone numbers and flicked to the J's for Jones. Molly's mother answered the phone. No, Molly wasn't in, she said. 'Is that Samantha?'

'No, it's Briony. Samantha's with me, though.'

A pause, then, 'That's strange, because Mol said she was going river swimming with you two.' I heard the slight confusion in Mrs Jones's voice before she brightened. 'Oh well, I expect she got sidetracked. I'll let her know you were asking.'

'No, please don't bother. It wasn't anything important,' I said. 'Thanks anyway.'

I put the phone down and we returned to the kitchen, none the wiser.

It was only later, when we were up in my room, listening to *Pick of the Pops*, that I thought I heard a sound above the music, a clunk, like the sound of a door closing. Samantha, sitting on the floor beside my bed, tapping her fingers to the beat, didn't seem to have noticed. I didn't say anything. If Jeremy had come home, there was no point in spoiling the afternoon by drawing attention to it. I'd probably imagined it anyway.

FIFTEEN

BRIONY

2022

'That was really delicious. Thank you.' Replete with fragrant chicken curry, I picked up the last poppadum from my side plate and nibbled it.

'You can't go wrong with these dinner kit things, I find.' Marcus winked.

'Oh, I could, believe me.'

'I'm not sure I do believe you. You must have cooked a zillion dinners for your family, and I bet they were all perfectly edible.' He laughed. 'More than edible, I meant to say...'

I held up the hand holding the poppadum. 'Stop right there. I'll take edible, any time.'

We laughed. It came easily, laughing with Marcus. We were in his cottage, my first protracted visit to his home, and therefore the first chance I'd had to have a look around, although quite what I was looking for, I didn't know.

Or perhaps I did. Feminine touches, maybe? Photos? Something to indicate where his head was in relation to Hannah, his ex. Natural curiosity on my part, that was all.

There was nothing that I could see. The cottage was sparsely furnished, probably because it was a rental, but looked all the better for it. There were no paintings or photos displayed on the bumpy white walls. Propped on the wooden beam above the inglenook stood a large landscape watercolour in a worn gold frame. It looked as if it had been there forever. The big, squashy wine-coloured sofa – Marcus's, or had it come with the cottage? – held a variety of mismatched, colourful cushions. Other than that, the items in the living room, which ran front to back of the cottage, and those in the kitchen I'd seen, all had a practical purpose and were not purely for decoration.

It wasn't a lot to go on. I hadn't been upstairs, of course. The bathroom was downstairs, leading off the kitchen. Again, nothing significant was on view. I had stopped short of opening the bathroom cabinet; I was curious, but not obsessed. If Marcus wanted to tell me more about Hannah, and how he felt about her now, he would do so in his own time.

He confessed he hadn't planned dessert. 'I don't bother with them myself, so I didn't think, sorry. I think there's some ice cream in the freezer if you'd like some? Or shall I just make coffee?'

I was still full from the curry; coffee would be lovely, I told him.

We stayed at the table, chatting, while we drank it. Then Marcus surprised me by suggesting we head down to the White Hart for a late drink. I felt a dip of disappointment. This was my first invitation to his home and I'd looked forward to a cosy evening with just the two of us. But Marcus seemed keen to go out and, not long after, we were back in our usual haunt where I eyed my glass of white and hoped I'd be fit for breakfast duty in the morning. We'd had wine with the curry, a bottle I'd provided. I probably shouldn't be drinking any more tonight.

Oh well, too late now, I thought, as Marcus raised his own glass to me in a toast to nothing in particular.

'I'll be too squiffy to walk home at this rate,' I said happily, taking another sip.

'S'okay, I'll throw you over my shoulder.' Marcus winked at me. Or actually, he twinkled. Was that a thing? In my semi-inebriated state, I certainly thought so.

'You were telling me about before, when you lived at Summerdene with your godmother,' Marcus said, picking up the loose threads of a conversation we'd begun earlier. 'You went to school in Mistlecombe, then?'

'I did, from the age of fourteen, when Alice took me in.' I'd already explained how I'd come to be placed in my godmother's care without going into too much detail about my previous home life with my father. 'It was Mistlecombe Lane High School back then. I see it's called Mistlecombe Academy now. Plus it's twice the size.'

I'd passed my old school when I'd taken a walk around the village, reacquainting myself with familiar territory. Not much had changed, apart from the school. The original flat-roofed 1950s building had acquired several extensions that seemed to have been stuck on at random, and a gym and sports centre had sprung up in the grounds.

A vision came to me of the night of the school disco, and some boy I'd got off with. His kisses tasted of chewing gum, I remembered that, but I couldn't remember his name. Then outside afterwards, I'd virtually clung to Samantha and Molly at the gates before I made a run for it to avoid being walked home by Jeremy. It seemed out of all perspective now. But we were teens; we enjoyed a drama, and how easy it had been to conjure one up at will.

We never did find out what happened to Molly that night. After I'd run off, she'd apparently vanished, leaving Samantha to walk home alone.

And then, some weeks later, she'd disappeared completely.

Marcus was gazing quizzically at me. I shook myself back to the present.

'Sorry, I was just thinking back.' I picked up my glass. It was empty. 'I should be heading home. Early start tomorrow.'

'Yes, of course. I should have thought.' Marcus drained his own glass and stood up.

'It's fine.' I went to get up, and found myself facing my daughter.

'Mum! I didn't see you there,' she said. Her eyes flew to Marcus. 'Have you had a good evening?' Her voice was heavy with meaning I didn't have to guess at.

'Yes, thanks. I didn't see you either. We've not been here long.'

I looked past Faye. She knew exactly what I was looking for, or rather, who. I didn't have to look for long.

'Hey, there you are.' A tallish, slimly-built man with mid-brown hair, cut fashionably short at the sides and longer on top, came up to Faye and placed his hand on her shoulder in a possessive manner that set me on edge. He looked at me. 'Is this...?'

'My mother, yes.' Faye couldn't erase the peevishness from her voice. Clearly I wasn't supposed to be meeting Logan tonight, so unexpectedly – this was Logan, I assumed. Faye hadn't said.

'Briony,' I said, smiling. 'This is Marcus. We live near each other.'

'I'm Logan.' He began to reach out for a handshake, then changed his mind and made do with a nod and a smile. 'Pleased to meet you both.'

'And you,' I said stupidly.

I would have preferred to be completely sober for this introduction, but there was nothing I could do about that now. I hoped neither of them had noticed. But what the hell? I wasn't blind drunk, just a bit on the emotional side. In any case, why shouldn't I enjoy a few drinks on a night out? I was an adult, and we were in a pub, after all. The guilt that was roped around motherhood was never cut loose, no matter how old the child.

'Logan helps out here,' Faye said, at the same time I noticed the white apron tied loosely around his waist with the name of the pub embroidered on the pocket.

'I do the odd evening to supplement the day job,' he said, raising his eyes. 'It's how I get to keep the room. Could have got expensive otherwise.'

'I see,' I said, even more stupidly. I shuffled closer to Marcus, who had stood aside. 'Well, we're off home. See you later.' I touched my daughter on the arm, pointlessly staking my prior claim on her.

'Yeah. Don't wait up.' Faye widened her eyes fractionally.

'I wasn't going to. See you again I expect, Logan,' I said.

'You can count on it.'

He gave me a direct look which seemed to issue something of a challenge. At that moment, a tiny dot of recognition entered my brain. Something about the way his mouth twisted slightly when he smiled resonated with me. If he looked familiar – and I wasn't even sure he did, now – it would have been because I'd seen him in the pub before or passed him in the village without knowing who he was. Or, even more likely, my overheated, wine-befuddled brain just needed sleep.

SIXTEEN
LOGAN

2022

I had a miserable childhood, Briony, if you want to know. Social workers are meant to vet the adoptive families, I thought. A stupid assumption, as it turned out. Oh, I don't doubt that Joe and Kath were held up to the light and pronounced fit to be parents at the time. How they pulled that one off I haven't a clue. But appearances can be deceptive, as they say, and if any couple were expert deceivers, it was those two.

The house, a terraced job glued to a railway station yard, was adequate enough, I guess. Cramped, but clean. Well, it was until Joe brought a scruffy crossbreed dog home as a favour to a mate he owed and let it shit everywhere. That dog had an evil look in its eye. When she wasn't scraping crap off the floor, Kath dashed through her days in a cloud of cigarette smoke and chip fat from the chippy where she worked, hardly stopping long enough to notice she had a kid to look after – me. And then, they took in another waif and stray, a girl, no blood relation to me. Never did understand why they adopted her, unless it was to get the council to give them a bigger house, which never happened. Or to up the family allowance, which did.

Joe was a labourer on whatever building site would take him on. Okay, it was a fair old job and not that badly paid, except his idleness and permanent hangover saw him being laid off more times than the family budget could stand. And each time it happened, he and Kath argued and fought – physically fought, at times – and then they'd shake down and disappear into their respective, bleak little lives, until the next time.

Yep, lots of kids live that kind of life, and much worse. But as I say, half the time those two didn't even notice we were there, never mind take an interest. They fed us when they remembered, clothed us, and kept a roof over our heads. As for anything else, forget it.

It would have been sad if I wasn't so bloody angry all the time. I mean, they must have, at one point – well, two points – got their act together in order to become adoptive parents. But I guess they scrubbed up well, themselves and the house, when the occasion demanded it. Deceivers, as I said.

School was all right. I didn't mind school. I got the odd kicking – it was that sort of place – but I gave as good as I got. My sister – I got used to calling her that after a while – was well able to stand up for herself, too, which was just as well.

As soon as I left school, I left home. Always planned that, right from when I was a little kid. I could see the way the wind was blowing. My sister kept in touch, kept saying she missed me, begged me to take her away. So, as soon as she was old enough, I went back for her. She was bright. She could be useful, though I wasn't sure how at the time. As it turned out, I was right about that.

SEVENTEEN
BRIONY

'So, what did you think?' Faye ladled thick, creamy Greek yoghurt from the carton into a silver bowl, ready to take through to the dining room.

'Of Logan?' I layered two snowy napkins into the breadbasket, overlapping the points artistically – well, I thought it was artistic – then tipped in an assortment of rolls I'd warmed in the oven.

'*Yes*, Mum.'

'Faye, I hardly had time to take him in. I didn't even get a proper look.' Okay, that wasn't the pure unsullied truth, but it was true the encounter had lasted no more than a couple of minutes. 'Good looking, though. I'll give you that. He seems nice.'

Faye seemed satisfied, and carried the yoghurt through, along with the bowl of sliced peaches, apricots, melon and strawberries. I heard her greeting the first guests to arrive at breakfast, a young couple with a nine-month-old baby girl who'd squawked all the way down the stairs. The same grating cry I'd heard at three in the morning. And at four, and then again at five, accompanied by the loudly placating voices of her parents.

I went through with the rolls and took their drinks orders, noting that Sarah, the mother, didn't apologise for the noise. For some reason I hadn't factored babies and small children into my projected view of potential guests, although I had specified on the website that well-behaved dogs were welcome. Perhaps I should have added that grisly tots were not, given that this one must have woken up the whole house.

Was I turning into a miserable, child-hating old witch? Probably. But then I was tired and a bit hungover, so I could be excused.

Sarah stuffed the baby into the high chair I'd rushed out and bought when I'd taken the booking, and gave her a roll to chew on. Thankfully, the noise subsided. I felt sorry then for my mean thoughts; no doubt the couple were knackered from their broken night, and the child, with her big blue eyes and chestnut curls, was such a cutie, now she'd stopped crying. I smiled nicely, remarked on the sunny day, and fetched their pot of tea.

Back in the kitchen, the breakfast buffet fully loaded and the other guests now at the table, I made yet more tea, this time for Faye and me. Hopefully the subject of my daughter's new boyfriend had been parked for now. For some unaccountable reason, I didn't want to talk about it.

I was out of luck.

'I'm glad you liked Logan,' Faye said, sipping her tea whilst standing at the sink.

I didn't quite say that, but Faye heard what she wanted to hear.

'He's coming to London with me at the weekend. We'll leave on Sunday and probably stay till Wednesday at least,' she said flatly, as if she expected me to object.

How could I object to anything Faye did? She was her own woman and I was glad about that. I was also pleased she had at last accepted that Nick was history. We hadn't talked about it, but Faye had moved on, and I took that as hard evidence. What else could I do?

And now, so worryingly soon, she was head-over-heels in love with somebody else.

Oh God.

'Won't they need Logan at the pub?' I said.

'Oh, no, it's fine. He's a casual. He's not on a contract or anything.'

So that made it okay, did it? For Logan to walk off the job as and when he saw fit? *Bite your tongue, Briony.*

'It's all worked out really well,' Faye continued brightly, clattering her empty mug onto the draining board. 'Joan and Clive needed an extra pair of hands so they came to an arrangement about the room. It's his for as long as he wants.'

I decided to ignore this. It sounded too much like a permanent arrangement to me.

'How is Logan getting on with tracking down his family and friends? Has he found the people he wanted to see in the village?' I asked, sounding more upbeat than I felt.

Faye seemed puzzled for a moment. Then her face cleared. 'Oh, that. Yes, I think so. Some of them. He doesn't talk about it much.'

Which clearly meant she didn't have a clue and hadn't bothered to ask. Again, I thought how implausible Logan's given reasons for being in the village sounded.

But I knew nothing about him. Who was I to judge? Except I was only too keen to judge him for sweeping my daughter off her feet in less time than it took to varnish a barn door. He'd better be careful with her, that was all. He'd better not break her already fragile heart or he'd find himself with me to deal with.

Walking home from the pub last night, I'd given Marcus a brief rundown of Faye's tempestuous relationship with Nick.

He'd understood why I was wary about Logan and, by my own admission, very protective of my daughter. I never had to over-explain things to Marcus. It was as if he could read the subtext of whatever I chose to tell him, and how refreshing that was. Tony had needed every little detail spelled out, in large print, before he came within a yard of getting where I was coming from on any given issue, especially in the latter years of our marriage. I pulled back the thought. It was wrong, and unfair, to compare the two men who, after all, held completely different statuses in my life.

When we'd reached Kestrels, I'd told Marcus I'd be fine to walk the next few hundred paces to Summerdene on my own. He hadn't needed much persuading. Deep down, I was disap-pointed he hadn't asked me in for coffee – genuine coffee, no euphemisms. Which was ridiculous, because I'd said I had to get up early in the morning, and we'd already had coffee before we'd gone to the pub.

Was I starting to like Marcus Schofield more than was good for me, given he was only a friendly neighbour who seemed to enjoy my company once in a while? I asked myself the question, several times. I didn't like the answer.

Faye duly left on Sunday morning, saying she was meeting Logan at the station. I couldn't help feeling that the two of them going to London together was too much, too soon. They were staying in a hotel, not with her former housemates or any other friend. I wasn't sure if that was better or worse. Either way, Faye would naturally introduce Logan to her friends, he'd be drawn into her circle and become an even greater part of her life than he already was, if that was possible.

I tried not to be negative about my daughter's new love. If he made her happy, I couldn't argue with that. And if it all went pear-shaped, I'd be there to hug and console and talk endlessly into the small hours. God knows, I'd had enough practice.

I also resisted the impulse to text her too many times. I didn't usually do that when she was away, so why should this trip be any different? Instead, I kept a low profile, an almost invisible one, barring the odd cheery WhatsApp message.

My imagination was in full flight as usual. I visualised Faye, who could work anywhere, any time, tapping away at her laptop at the hotel, or in a park, or a coffee shop on the embankment. Logan would be working on his own laptop – in my version of events, anyway – and periodically they would lift their heads to gaze longingly at one another.

Maybe that was why they'd gone to London in the first place, to spend time together, away from the village. Away from me. Actually, no, cancel that last thought. I was never that paranoid.

I tried to forget about Faye and concentrate on my own life. I had Summerdene, and the beautiful Cotswold countryside, and I loved both. I even loved being a B&B host. I hadn't been sure I would, but I looked forward to changeover days, when guests I'd enjoyed chatting to regretfully departed but there were new ones to welcome and get to know. These days, all three guest bedrooms were mostly fully occupied and I was getting bookings from personal recommendation, friends and relatives of previous guests, which was heartening.

I liked having Pippa around, too. She'd soon got to grips with what needed doing and would arrange her work around the movements of the B&B guests so as to cause the least inconvenience. She usually started upstairs, with the bedrooms and bathrooms if the guests were at breakfast, or had already gone out. If she couldn't gain access to the bedrooms, she would help me in the kitchen with the breakfast things, or whizz around the communal areas with the Dyson and duster. Pippa, in her uniform of black leggings, or denim shorts, and baggy T-shirt, her hair swept into a high ponytail, was a breath of fresh air, as well as a godsend, and we chatted non-stop when we found ourselves together.

On Tuesday evening, the day before Faye said she might be home, although I hadn't heard for certain, Tony rang my mobile. The last time we'd spoken was two weeks after I'd moved to Mistlecombe, when I'd finally got round to ringing to give him my new address. We'd had our usual civilised exchange, and he'd wished me the very best in my new life, as if I'd moved to the other side of the world – or it felt like that, anyway.

Turning down the sound on the TV, I answered the call. I wasn't expecting to hear from him, and he must have heard the slight puzzlement in my tone.

'It's all right, Bri. Nothing major.'

'That's good,' I said, sensing a *but* just around the corner.

'No really, I only wanted to tell you I had lunch with Faye today. I thought you might want to know.'

'Did you?' Faye would have told me soon enough. We didn't keep secrets like that.

And then I realised what it was Tony really wanted to tell me.

'You met Logan, I'm guessing?'

'Logan, yes. She seems... ever so keen. Well they both do. Did. You couldn't have got a fag paper between them.'

I sighed. 'And you wondered if I knew about him. Tony, Faye lives with me. It's a small village. Even if she hadn't told me, I'd have known anyway.'

'You've met him, I take it?'

'I have, but it was all over in five minutes flat. No, make that three. We ran into one another in the local pub.'

'Oh, right. So, you didn't get to form an impression then?'

'Not really.'

Actually, yes. I didn't like him. For some reason I couldn't explain, I didn't like Logan. There, I'd admitted it, though only to myself.

'Presumably you had plenty of time to form an opinion,' I said.

A pause, then. 'This is the thing. The guy was charm personified. Exceedingly polite, friendly, interested in everything I said to him. Which wasn't a lot, I might tell you. I talked mostly to Faye. It was good to see her.'

'It's great having her here with me,' I said. 'I was surprised she wanted to bury herself in the Cotswolds.' We were wandering away from what was presumably the main topic. 'You found Logan a decent sort, then?'

'Yes, yes, of course. Clean, smart, intelligent. What's not to like? As I said, he was charm itself. It was as if he was dead set on impressing me. A bit OTT, I thought.' Tony chuckled. 'He couldn't keep his eyes off Faye, kept plucking at her sleeve as if he was afraid she'd escape.'

'You weren't keen, then?'

'I didn't say that. No, he was... very nice. Couldn't fault him.'

And yet Tony had reservations, the same as I did, I could tell. Reservations he hadn't actually voiced, but we knew each other well enough for the subtext to stand out.

'Well, cheers for ringing. I'll say goodnight, then,' I said. 'Have to get up at the crack of dawn these days to feed the troops.' I laughed.

Tony laughed too. And with a cheery 'goodnight' he was gone.

EIGHTEEN
BRIONY

1986

I stood at the end of my bed and rubbed at my sopping hair with a threadbare striped towel. All the towels we had were worn out, and most of the bedding, too. It wasn't as if Alice couldn't afford to replace them. The money my father sent would have gone a good way towards it. But Alice considered it wasteful to replace stuff that had some life left in it.

I'd left Pink's, the mini-supermarket where I worked, at 3.30, and as I'd sauntered home, the sky had suddenly darkened as if somebody had turned off a switch, there was a rumble of thunder, and the clouds split open. I considered taking shelter under the trees from the biblical rainstorm but, thinking about lightning strikes, decided it was a bad idea. Anyway, I was already soaked. Back Lane was awash by the time I reached it, and I'd had to leap across a deep, muddy puddle outside our gates.

It was Alice's afternoon for the WI. I knew she wouldn't be back for another hour or so. The light was on in the kitchen, the radio playing softly, indicating that Jeremy was in. I'd have loved a cup of tea, but instead I'd bolted upstairs and grabbed a towel from the airing cupboard. Hopefully, Jeremy wouldn't have heard me come in. I wasn't in the mood for him.

There was a tap at my door, and without waiting for an answer, Jeremy pushed the door open. He was wearing grey cord jeans and a sage green T-shirt. He was barefoot, as usual. I tried not to look at his hairy toes but somehow my eyes found their way there of their own accord.

'Bad luck, getting caught in the storm,' he said, a concerned smile in place. 'Why don't you use the hairdryer? Shall I fetch it for you?'

I relaxed, or tried to. This was Jeremy being normal, and brotherly, and potentially helpful. At times like this I gave him the benefit of the doubt – I had to. Life would have been impossible otherwise.

'The dryer's packed up,' I said. 'When I tried to use it the other day it smelled funny and the handle got hot.'

'Ah. That's no good then.' His eyes travelled downwards from my hair to the rest of me. Instinctively I crossed my arms over my chest. 'The rest of you is pretty wet, too. You'd better get changed before you catch your death.' He laughed. 'I'm turning into my mother, if such a thing is possible.'

At that moment, there was an almighty *crack* and a flash of lightning lit up the room like a stage set. I jumped. Jeremy took a step towards me but came no closer.

'Not scared of thunderstorms, are you?' he said.

'No, of course not.'

I wasn't overly keen on them but he didn't need to know that. I wished he'd go and let me get out of my wet clothes. Instead, he just stood there, his gaze fixed on me.

'It'll pass over soon. The storm.'

'I know. I'll just get changed, then I'll be down,' I said pointedly.

'Yes, right. I'll leave you to it.'

He backed out of the doorway and closed the door behind him. I went to the door and listened. I wouldn't have put it past him to hang around outside my room, though for what purpose I couldn't imagine. The landing floorboards creaked, and I heard his tread on the stairs. But before I peeled off my wet clothes, I propped the wooden chair under the door handle, just in case Jeremy took it into his head to pop back. I'd never done that before – never felt the need. Today, now, felt different, somehow.

I considered staying in my room until Alice came home. But she might be a while yet, especially if she'd hung on because of the rain, and I really needed that cup of tea. Besides, this was my home; I should be free to do as I liked in it.

Dressed in fresh jeans and sweatshirt, I went downstairs. Jeremy had already made two mugs of tea. He passed one to me and sat down with his at the kitchen table. It would have seemed churlish for me not to do the same. The least ammunition I gave him, the better. I sat at the opposite end of the table, my fingers curled round the warm mug. Rain peppered the window. The sky was as dark as charcoal.

'Better?' Jeremy said, after a moment.

'Much. Thanks. I needed this.'

He pushed the biscuit tin towards me. 'Or shall we have flapjack? Mum made some this morning.'

Without waiting for my reply, he got up and went to the larder, returning with two squares of flapjack. He put one in front of me. No plate. The flapjack tasted of butter and golden syrup. It crumbled, sticky and delightful, on my tongue.

'Scrummy,' I said, half-smiling at Jeremy, who was watching me like the proverbial hawk.

'Ma's baking's the tops,' he said. 'Get her to teach you while you're here, I should.'

I shrugged. 'May do. She's always so busy. Always in a rush to be somewhere.'

'True,' Jeremy said, looking thoughtful. 'Very true.' A small silence, then, 'Got yourself a boyfriend yet, Briony?'

I started at the question, as if there'd been another lightning flash. I couldn't control my reaction, much as I'd wanted to. Jeremy smirked at my discomfort. The sudden change of topic was typical of him. I should have seen it coming, the switch from fairly normal guy to fully-paid up creep, but somehow he always managed to take me unawares. I could have got up and left the room but this was my home as much as his, and I wasn't going to be herded around it like a frightened sheep. Besides, I hadn't finished my tea.

'If I have, that's my business.' I scratched at the inside of my elbow.

'Been hanging about by the Kissing Tree, have you? You and your mates?' Jeremy chuckled. 'You know what happens there. You want to watch yourselves.'

I didn't answer. If he was trying to be funny, he'd missed the mark by a thousand miles.

'Oh yes,' he continued. 'It's got quite a reputation, that tree. So have the girls who go there.'

I made a snorting sound. Really, this conversation, if you could call it that, was getting more bizarre by the second.

'The Kissing Tree is just a tree with carvings on it,' I said firmly. 'It's part of the village folklore. If a couple had their first kiss there, then carved their initials in the trunk, it meant they'd be together for life. Nobody believes that now, if they ever did.' I fastened Jeremy with a hard look. Or as hard as I could make it. 'You know all this. You've lived in Mistlecombe all your life. I heard the story practically the first week I got here. I don't know why you're even talking about it, unless it's to wind me up. In which case, it hasn't worked. So, tough.'

'You sound pretty wound up to me.' Jeremy folded his arms and regarded me with a sardonic smile.

I got up from the table and turned my back on him to rinse

out my mug in the sink. I wouldn't let him get to me. I was stronger than that.

But Jeremy hadn't finished.

'You need to loosen up a bit. Those friends of yours from school have got it down to a fine art. Being *loose*, I mean. And I should know.' He laughed. 'Like the pun?'

I swung round. It was all I could do not to chuck the mug at his stupid head.

'Please don't talk about my friends like that. In fact, don't talk about them *at all*.'

Jeremy held up his hands. 'Okay, okay, no need to get a cob on. I'm only joshing, being friendly. You should try it some time. You take yourself too seriously, Briony, that's your trouble.'

Before I could come up with a suitable put-down, sounds from the hallway indicated Alice's return. She came into the kitchen.

'Ah, tea. Just what I need, too. I had about ten cups at the WI, but it's not the same as a cuppa in your own kitchen. I managed to miss the rain, though.'

I switched the kettle on. 'Sit down. I'll do it.' I realised my hands were shaking.

Alice sank into the chair I'd vacated. If she noticed anything wrong with me, she didn't comment.

Jeremy got up and put his mug on the draining board.

'I'm nipping out. Be back for dinner,' he said, addressing his mother.

He sidled out of the room, leaving me quietly fuming.

NINETEEN

BRIONY

2022

I was in an introspective mood, coupled with a touch of melancholy. It wasn't like me, and I wondered where on earth it had come from. It could have been because of Tony's phone call – I always felt a gentle tug backwards whenever I spoke to him. Or, more likely, it was because Pippa had prompted me to talk about my past life in Mistlecombe while we took our coffee break in the garden this morning.

She already knew how I came to be living at Summerdene for the second time. I'd shared as much of my story with her as I had with Marcus – the facts, in outline, leaving out the bleaker aspects of my early life. Pippa had returned to the subject today.

'Your godmother who left you the house, didn't she have any kids, then?' she'd asked suddenly, as if we'd been midway through a conversation.

'She did,' I'd said. 'She had a son, Jeremy, but he died from a brain tumour a year before Alice died. She wrote and told me.'

'That's sad.' Pippa pulled her face into a gloomy expression that seemed almost comical. 'She didn't have anyone else to leave the house to, then? No other family, sorta thing?'

'There had been a few, years back, but none that were still around,' I said, remembering Alice attending her cousin's funeral in Worthing, then the solicitor telling me there were no living relatives.

'Good news for you, then.' Pippa had held my gaze for a second.

I wasn't sure how to take this. It seemed to imply some kind of wrongdoing on my side, as if I'd engineered my inheritance. But the girl didn't mean anything by it, I decided. Her questions were intrusive, but she was just curious and somewhat lacking in the social barrier department, so I tried not to mind.

Her next questions were a lot easier to handle. She'd asked what it was like for me as a teenager living in a backwater like Mistlecombe.

'There can't have been many opportunities for living it up,' she'd remarked, making me laugh.

'It wasn't the Dark Ages,' I'd said. 'There were actual buses and trains. We weren't cut off entirely from civilisation.'

I told her about the trips to Cheltenham and Gloucester for shopping, the cinema and music gigs, and, later, the clubs and pubs, the frantic race for the last bus or train home. And the rides we cadged from total strangers when we'd been reduced to hitch-hiking.

'Our parents knew nothing about that, nor my godmother. Although she was pretty relaxed about that sort of thing,' I said. 'I had two best friends, Samantha Dean and Molly Jones. We were The Three Musketeers, or the three witches from *Macbeth*, depending on our mood. We used to sit under the Kissing Tree to chat and eat sweets.'

'The Kissing Tree? What's that?'

I explained about the tree. 'Every village has its legends. The Kissing Tree is Mistlecombe's.'

'That's sweet,' Pippa had said. 'All the carvings and that. Romantic, too.'

I'd laughed. 'I suppose it was. It was innocent stuff, although we made a lot more of it in our heads. We used to try and work out who the initials belonged to, and gossip about them. It was all made up, of course.'

'Where are they now, your besties? Are you still in touch?'

'No idea,' I said. 'We lost touch, as you do. After A levels I went on to teacher training in Brighton, got a job in the town and stayed there. Samantha went to university somewhere northerly, Durham, I think. The last I heard of Samantha, she was managing a health club somewhere in Yorkshire. That was years ago. I expect she got married at some point, had kids, maybe. Her family don't live in the village now.'

I'd checked out the Deans' house and found it almost unrecognisable, with new windows and a double-height extension to the side. A fleet of children's bikes and scooters littered the lawn. The evidence was fairly conclusive.

I'd had no need to check out the Jones's old house.

'What about Molly?' Pippa said.

'No.' I shook my head. 'She left school before we took our As.'

I didn't elaborate, although Pippa loved a good story. If only I had a story to give her.

After lunch, I considered going for a walk to shake myself out of my reflective mood, but knowing I would have to pass Kestrels, decided against it. Marcus hadn't called in at Summerdene for five days – not that I was counting – and we'd made no firm arrangements to meet at any other time. If I passed his cottage, I'd have been tempted to call. At least, I'd have noted the absence or presence of his car, and any signs of activity. I didn't want to do either. My pride, where Marcus was concerned, was more or less intact, and I intended it to stay that way.

But I felt restless and needed to do something, so I decided to take a look inside the old surgery extension. I'd organised a survey of the house when it became mine but only a basic one; the roof of the extension had been rapidly inspected, which was all I'd wanted at the time. I know I should have checked out the interior before, but I'd had my reasons for putting it off, and had almost managed to forget it existed.

With Faye not due back until tonight, it seemed the ideal opportunity. This was something I would rather do alone. I fetched the old Blue Bird toffee tin from the kitchen shelf and rooted among the supposedly once-useful items it contained for the key. I couldn't find it at first. I only knew it had been kept in the tin because I'd seen Jeremy putting it back. Of course that was years ago; it didn't mean the key hadn't ended up somewhere else. But it wasn't on the bunch of keys given to me by the solicitor; those had all been accounted for. If the key wasn't in the tin, I had no idea where else to look.

I was about to give up and tip all the old cigarette lighters, hooks and nails, and other objects I couldn't identify into the nearest bin when my fingers closed around a key. Before I could change my mind, I took it out to the passageway and tried it in the door to the surgery. It fitted. I took a deep breath, creaked open the stiff door and went inside.

The grubby windows were laced outside with overgrown greenery, the space inside eerily dim, as if it was underwater. I tried the light switch, but the strip light it operated had expired long ago. I smelled dust, and damp, and something indescribable with disinfectant overtones. As I'd imagined – or rather, hoped – the place had been cleared, probably years ago. The house clearance people couldn't have gone in there, otherwise the key would have been among those the solicitor had given me. All that was left was an upright metal chair with a ripped plastic padded seat, an old-fashioned black telephone, strangled by its own cable, on the floor in the corner, and also on the floor, a rotating card index holder, empty of cards. The wooden boards of the floor itself felt sticky beneath my plimsolls, and a gingery brown line marked the area where the reception desk had been.

The extension comprised just two rooms: the reception and patient waiting area, where I was now, and adjacent to it, Edward's former consulting room. The interconnecting door stood ajar, and I could see that it, too, was empty of furniture, apart from a large, square hand basin fitted to one wall. I marched through, wondering why I'd put off this inspection for so long. My overheated brain had coerced me into believing that the old doctor's surgery somehow epitomised Jeremy and the fear and misery he'd caused me, because of what happened in here. But I was young and impressionable then, and not so able to deal with life's horrors. I had long ago pushed the memory of that day into touch.

Nothing about that time could hurt me now.

I laughed, actually laughed out loud, as I stepped into the consulting room. The sound echoed through the space. A tiny shiver ran through me as I had a vision of what used to stand in the corner between the window and the now green-stained washbasin. But it was only muscle memory. A skeleton made out of bits of joined-together plastic had no power to frighten anyone, life-sized or not. Anyway, it was gone now. I brushed the image from my mind.

Gathering myself, I scanned the floors, walls and ceilings in both rooms for signs of damp and decay. After all, that was why I'd come in here. There was a grey jagged patch running from the ceiling to the wall in the waiting room which might have been wet at some stage, though it looked dry enough now. Other than that, the extension seemed sound. I would have to decide what to do with it at some point but it had waited all this time; it could wait a bit longer. Alice, bless her, had obviously felt the same.

Or had my godmother had deeper reasons for shutting off the surgery and leaving it to its fate? As Faye had pointed out, its boxy shape spoiled the look of Summerdene's exterior. It did seem odd that Alice had never turned the space into something useful or had it knocked down years ago. It couldn't have been out of sentimentality; Alice must have had plenty of other ways of remembering her husband, other mementoes.

Not that I could guess at what those might be. She'd been strangely taciturn on the subject of Edward, as I remembered. I'd asked her a few questions about him early on in my stay, to make conversation as much as anything, but she would either answer with a short, sharp response, or not at all. I'd taken my cue from that, and hadn't mentioned him again. Neither, as I recall, had Alice, except briefly a couple of times, in passing.

But it was pointless wondering about it now. The time had long gone.

My eyes had adjusted to the gloom, and I went back into the consulting room for a last look around. It wasn't entirely empty, I saw now. In the dimmest corner there were old newspapers and magazines, roughly stacked. I immediately thought of spiders and decided to leave clearing those for another day. A crumbling cork noticeboard, skewered with pinholes and studded with rusted drawing pins, was propped against the wall behind the rubbish. Poking out from behind it was something light. I looked closer. It was a white plastic carrier bag. I stooped down and gingerly opened the top. Inside was a rolled up multi-coloured striped towel of the kind that used to grace Summerdene's airing cupboard. Puzzled, I pulled out the towel and shook it out. Some kind of garment fell to the floor. I picked it up. My fingers recognised the feel of the thin, slippery material. I was holding a swimming costume, navy blue, white trim. *My* swimming costume, the only one I'd had when I lived here.

A vision of Jeremy edged its way into my head. Jeremy, with his sardonic smile, leaning close to me, daring me to enter the old surgery, telling me I was a scaredy-cat if I didn't.

But that was irrelevant and had no connection to my discovery. It didn't explain why my swimming costume was here, in this room. I hadn't been wearing it on the day Jeremy enticed me in here, and I didn't have it with me. Why would I? As far as I knew, I'd never mislaid it. It had always been in its rightful place, in my bedroom drawer.

A chill ran through me. I shook it away, annoyed with myself. I was making more of this than I should. I looked down at the garment in my hands. It was just an old swimming costume. But how had it got here?

Holding the costume up to the half-light of the window, I looked at it properly. And that was when I realised. My swimming costume used to have straps that crossed over and tied at the back. This one had a halter neck.

It wasn't my costume at all.

It was Molly's.

Without thinking too hard about it, I'd stuffed the swimming costume back in the bag with the towel, taken it upstairs to my bedroom and pushed it to the back of a drawer. My brain was still struggling to find a plausible reason for Molly's swimming stuff being in my house thirty-six years later, or, for that matter, why it had ever been here in the first place, when Faye arrived home. She had Logan with her.

My first instinct was to run and hide. I couldn't deal with him right now. Faye came bouncing into the sitting room, having dropped her luggage in the hall, and kissed me on the cheek before I could escape.

'You don't mind if Logan stays for dinner, Mum?' She smiled round at him.

'I can just as easily eat at the pub.' His eyes were focused on me as if he was watching for my reaction.

'No, it's fine. I haven't planned a meal, though. I wasn't sure what time you'd get here,' I said, pointedly addressing my daughter.

A text would have been nice, I thought. I felt a dip of depression as Faye and Logan caught hands with one another, as if they couldn't bear to be physically apart for a minute. I remembered Tony's take on this. But I needed to form my own opinion. My initial dislike of Logan may have been unfair, and unfounded. If Faye was in love with him – and that was certainly what I was reading on her face – I should give the man a chance. He deserved that, at least.

I rallied, and got up from the sofa. 'It's nice to see you, Logan,' I said. 'I take it the trip went well?'

'Brilliant,' Faye and Logan said together, then laughed. 'Logan met all my friends, and they got on really well,' Faye continued. 'And I took him into the office, so he could see the set-up.' She grinned at Logan. 'God knows why he wanted to see it.'

'Because I want to know all there is to know about you,' Logan said, his arm snaking around Faye's waist.

They were gazing at each other like a couple of lovesick teenagers. Feeling surplus to requirements, I headed for the kitchen to check what food I had that would stretch to three.

Faye came up behind me. 'Mum, don't worry. Let's have a takeaway, our treat.' She glanced behind her at Logan. 'That okay with you?'

'Great. I don't want you to go to any trouble, Mrs Harrington.'

'It's Briony,' I said.

'Briony, yes. I shouldn't have descended on you like this.' He smiled.

It was what you'd call a winning smile, I had to admit. It

reached all the way to his eyes. I relaxed, or tried to. It wasn't easy when my mind kept flitting to the old surgery, and what I'd found there. I needed time and space to think, but there'd be no chance of that until later.

I was happy to have Faye home, and an hour later, we were sitting in a cosy threesome at the kitchen table, a Greek banquet in foil containers before us.

Logan was charm personified, I couldn't say otherwise. He was as solicitous with me as he was with Faye, listening to all I had to say with real attention, passing me the last souvlaki, making sure I had my share of pittas. He asked questions and listened to the answers. He seemed especially interested in Summerdene. He loved old houses like this one, he said, which might have led me to ask about his own research of friends and family in the area. Only, somehow, the talk moved on to something else, and the moment passed.

I ate and talked and laughed, and, despite my earlier reservations, I enjoyed myself. I'd opened a bottle of Sauvignon Blanc for Faye and me, found a Peroni for Logan, and the meal took on a celebratory tone. Which was right and proper – this, after all, was Faye's homecoming.

Although, looking at the two of them making eyes at each other over the dolmades, I couldn't help but wonder what else we were celebrating.

TWENTY

BRIONY

1986

'I dare you,' Jeremy said, standing by the door in the passage that led to Edward's former surgery. 'I dare you to go in. You've not seen inside since you got here, have you? And that would make it, what, two years and counting? What are you scared of, young Briony?'

'Nothing,' I said, my eyes sliding to the hallway, the front door. But Alice had gone to watch some amateur dramatic thing at the village hall. She wouldn't be back till at least half past nine. 'I'm not scared.'

Not of the surgery, anyway.

'It's just an old room your mother doesn't use any more. I'm going to watch telly,' I said, not moving.

'*Rooms*, plural. The waiting room, and the inner sanctum where my father worked his medical miracles. Think about it, Briony. The whole of the village must have passed through those doors at one time or another. It's part of Mistlecombe's history. You ought to at least have a peek.'

'If it was so important I see it, Alice would have shown it to me,' I said, annoyed at the pressure Jeremy was putting on me, for absolutely no reason as far as I could tell.

What he got out of his nonsensical game-playing was anyone's guess. Telling myself that Jeremy was a saddo, which I frequently did, didn't sit well. He was Alice's son, after all.

'One minute of your time.' Jeremy threw up his hands. 'You might be surprised.'

Surprised? Why would I be?

'Oh, go on, then. If it'll stop you going on about it, although why you're bothering...'

Jeremy didn't seem to be listening. The key was in the door, the door was being pushed open, and I was being hustled into the room, its light dimmed by filthy windows and the bushes outside.

'Wait!'

'Now what?' I said, letting my annoyance shine through.

'Turn around, that way.' His hands were on my shoulders. 'Don't look at the other room.'

'Jeremy...' I began, but did as he said. The sooner I complied, the quicker I'd be free.

I stood facing what presumably was the reception desk, a gingery wooden slab, empty of everything except an empty wire filing rack, a rotary card holder, an old-fashioned black telephone and the fractured brown circles of a hundred cups of tea. There was no chair behind the desk, just a cork noticeboard with an old calendar and scraps of this and that, drawing-pinned on. Arranged in the centre of the room stood a double row of metal chairs with plastic padded seats, the sort that always felt sticky to sit on. Edward had clearly never felt the need to upgrade the facilities.

While I waited, hot with frustration and irritation, I heard Jeremy's footsteps, the slap of worn-down navy blue espadrilles; for once he wasn't barefoot. I recognised the rattle and scrape of a window blind being pulled down. The space around me grew a little bit darker. A scuffing sound, then, 'Right, you can turn round now.'

I turned, a scowl in place. And then I screamed. Jeremy was no longer in sight. In his place, framed in the doorway to what must have been the consulting room, stood a six-foot tall skeleton, rictus grin full of alarming teeth, eye sockets unfathomable black holes. The dirty-white bones of one arm clicked twice in a pendulum swing, then stopped dead.

My heart crashed. My breath rushed in, filling my chest to bursting point. The thing was still, yet at the same time it seemed to advance on me. I backed away, and felt the solidity of the reception desk behind me.

Two arms – real arms – circled the skeleton's ribcage and manoeuvred it further back into the room.

'I didn't scare you, did I?' Jeremy laughed, as if he hadn't intended exactly that.

He came across and stood before me. 'Sorry, Briony.' He didn't sound sorry. 'It's okay. It's only fake, a bit of kit my father used. He'd had it forever. It's always been a part of this place. Come here.'

He reached for me, resting his hands on my shoulders, as if he was going to hug me. I stepped sideways and his hands dropped away.

'You gave me a fright. What did you expect? Shoving that thing at me like that.'

'Lighten up. It was just a joke, that's all.' Jeremy gestured at the skeleton, which I could now see was standing on a plinth, supported by an upright wire. 'Cool, though, don't you think?'

'No, I *don't* think. It's creepy.'

I shuddered involuntarily. He noticed, and before I could duck out of the way, his arm snaked around my back as he tugged me towards him.

'Don't...' I tried to move, but somehow he made it impossible.

'You were scared. My fault. Here, let me make it better. A hug, yes? Everyone needs a hug sometimes.'

Not from you, I don't. But there it was again, the power Jeremy seemed to exert over me, freezing me to the spot at will. I forced myself to move.

'Get off!' I kicked out, made contact with his shin.

He let go of me and stepped back. 'Hey, there's no need to be like that. I'm not going to hurt you.'

He reached out again, and I felt the brush of his fingers on the skin just above my collarbone, as if I'd walked into a spider's web. I twisted away.

'I'm going now,' I said loudly. 'I've had enough of your stupid tricks.'

But before I could get to the door, he'd closed the space between us, blocking my way. Then, even closer. I felt the edge of the desk digging into my back. The door seemed a hundred miles away.

'Oh dear, Briony. You don't need to be afraid of me.' His finger found the tip of my chin, lifting, forcing me to look at him. 'Like I said before, you need to relax more. Let yourself go, and you might even start to enjoy yourself. I'm really not that bad, you know. Ask your friend. She'll tell you.'

He lowered his head. I thought he was going to kiss me. His breath was warm on the side of my face. It smelled of coffee, and something sweet. I was so caught up in trying to put some distance between us that I only just registered what he'd said.

'I told you before, don't talk about my friends!'

'*Friend*, singular. She's really something, and she knows it.'

Light dawned. He had a thing for one of my friends. *Samantha.* It had to be her. My mind winged back to the river, when Jeremy had sprung out from the bushes and surprised us. Samantha, sleek and gorgeous in her emerald costume, the flirty poses for anyone who happened to be looking. Which Jeremy had been, hidden away in the bushes.

It was all in his head, of course; his little fantasy. He'd never approached Samantha, I knew that because she would have told me. If he knew the things she said about him, what all three of us said about him... Not that he'd care. He was too arrogant, too full of his own self-importance.

'Mind you,' he said, rocking back and forth on his heels, 'you're a pretty girl, too, Briony, and I hope you know that. Self-esteem is a valuable asset.'

Anger boiled inside me. 'Shut *up*! Get out of my way!'

I balled my fist against his chest and shoved as hard as I could. He reeled back.

'Hey, steady on. I'm only having a laugh. *We're* only having a laugh, aren't we?'

Before I could move, he was back, closing in, his hand tracing a path downwards from my shoulder, and I felt his fingertip brush my nipple through the thin cotton of my blouse.

At least, I thought I did.

When I looked down, his hands were nowhere near me. I couldn't have imagined it, could I?

'Right, time we were out of here,' he said briskly. He was feet away from me now. I hadn't noticed him move. 'I apologise for old bony over there. He's just a heap of plastic. He doesn't mean any harm.'

But you do, I thought.

I stared at him, speechless. Chuckling softly, he went to the door and opened it. Light flooded in from the hallway. Only a door had separated me from the rest of Summerdene – it hadn't even been locked – yet I, dumb teenager that I was, had let him hold me prisoner in this dingy old room.

Once we were out of the old surgery and Jeremy had locked the door behind us, it was all I could do not to rush upstairs and barricade myself in my room. But if anything, Jeremy's assault on me – if that was what it was; I was far from certain – had instilled in me a greater sense of self-preservation and a steely determination not to let him break me, so I went to the sitting room and curled up in the armchair with the TV on.

Moments later, Jeremy came into the room. I sat up straight and fixed him with a cold stare.

'You do *not* go near any of my friends,' I said, recalling Jeremy's remarks earlier. 'Nor me. Do you understand?'

Jeremy threw out his hands. 'Oh dear, oh dear. We have got ourselves worked up over nothing, haven't we? Some people have no sense of fun.'

I went to reply but couldn't think of anything to say. Jeremy continued.

'By the way, best not mention to my mother we were mucking about with the skeleton, eh? She might not approve as it belonged to my father.'

I just sighed and turned my gaze to the TV. I had no intention of telling Alice what had happened with the skeleton, and certainly not the rest of it. It didn't bear thinking about. All I wanted was to be left in peace to get on with my life.

I kept my eyes glued to the TV screen, and after a minute or two, I heard Jeremy leave the room. Alice came home around twenty minutes later. We chatted, and Alice made me laugh with her description of the play and all that had, in her opinion, been wrong with it. As soon as I could without seeming rude, I said I had reading to do, and went upstairs to bed. But it was several hours before the tension left me and I fell into a troubled sleep.

TWENTY-ONE

BRIONY

2022

After Logan's visit I began to think I might have misjudged him. I couldn't call myself a fully paid-up member of his fan club, but it wasn't for me to decide who my daughter fell in love with. He seemed to be treating her well, and I couldn't ask for more than that. I found myself telling him to come again soon as Faye and I saw him out, and I meant it. As the door closed behind him, Faye said a quiet 'thank you' to me, presumably for making Logan welcome. I realised then that she must have picked up on my former negativity. I hoped she also realised my caution was only because I wanted to protect her.

The following week was extra busy and I didn't have much time to think about Logan, which was probably a good thing. I'd taken bookings for two and three nights for two of the rooms, meaning fast turnarounds and extra cleaning and laundry, but I didn't mind. As long as people kept on booking, I was happy and could manage the extra work with Pippa alongside.

Pippa took a somewhat slap-happy approach to her work but somehow it all got done, and I felt lucky to have found her.

She could seem a little forward at times in the questions she asked about the house and Alice, questions she would suddenly arrow at me out of context, but it was better than having no curiosity at all, I decided. She said little about her own life, and I didn't ask. Working at Summerdene and having a small child probably didn't leave much time for excitement, even with her mother on hand. I felt sad for her, in a way. But Faye mentioned she'd seen her in the pub and I was glad she managed to have some kind of social life.

One morning I was deadheading the pots of pelargoniums in front of the house when I happened to glance through the sitting room window and saw Pippa, standing beside the shelving unit with a cupboard below, with which I'd replaced Alice's bookcase.

I abandoned the wooden trug with its slurry of shrivelled flower heads and went indoors.

'Pippa? Are you okay?'

She turned, momentarily startled. The cupboard door was slightly ajar. She kicked it shut with her heel.

'Yeah, fine. I had the duster and polish in my hand from doing the guests' sitting room so I thought I might as well whisk round in here.'

I'd cleaned the room myself only yesterday, but no matter. I couldn't fault the girl's willingness.

'Come on. Time for our coffee break.'

We had our coffee and biscuits in the kitchen. Pippa looked tired. There were dark smudges below her eyes. Or was that leftover eyeliner? I wondered if I was working her too hard. I squashed the thought. She was here to do a job, and I paid her quite generously. I wasn't used to employing anyone, that was the trouble. Faye would say I was a soft touch.

'What was she like, your Alice?' Pippa asked.

'I wouldn't call her *my* Alice. She was my godmother, and she was kind, and very good to me, but I wouldn't say we were close.' I thought for a moment. 'She wasn't an easy person to get close to. She didn't show a lot of emotion. But some people find it hard to show their feelings, don't they? It's just the way they are. Why do you ask?'

'No reason. I was just wondering, with you living in her house and everything,' Pippa said, leaving me none the wiser.

I didn't want to talk about Alice, nor field any further questions about her – from Pippa's demeanour I sensed there were some waiting to be released. The girl didn't mean to be intrusive, I was sure. But that didn't mean I had to go along with it.

'Pippa, why don't you just finish off downstairs, then go?'

She looked surprised but pleased. 'There's still an hour left. You sure?'

'Yes. Just give the dining table a quick polish, if you would. That'll be fine for today.'

'Ta, then. I will.'

Springing up from the table, she rinsed out her coffee mug at the sink and left the kitchen, brandishing the can of polish like a weapon.

Being rushed off my feet in the daytime, I was too tired in the evenings to do anything except loll in front of the box, which was just as well as Marcus was in Kent, visiting family and friends. It was quite a relief not to have to change and put on make-up to go out. He hadn't said exactly how long he'd be gone, but I had the impression it wasn't an extended visit.

I'd felt slightly disappointed he hadn't called in person to tell me he was going away, but had texted a brief message instead, promising we would catch up when he got back. I decided to be satisfied with that.

I hadn't given any more thought to my discovery in the surgery. But now, with time to spare, my mind wandered back in that direction and one wet afternoon, I ventured inside again.

The dark skies made the place even more gloomy, but I made myself go into the consulting room where I stood and gazed at the rubbish in the corner, willing it to offer up some sort of explanation.

The swimming costume and towel were now in my bedroom, tucked away in a drawer of the chest. I had examined them again in the light of my room and seen how the material of the costume had deteriorated and the white trim had turned dirty grey. There were no signs of mould, as I would have expected had the items been damp. Other than that, I'd had no useful thoughts about them at all.

Now, I stood with my arms wrapped around myself and thought, hard. Why was the costume here, in the surgery, let alone in the house at all? If Molly had come here and left it behind, I would have returned it to her, or she would have come back for it, but I had no memory at all of that happening. I wandered back into the waiting area, putting my face close to the window and peering out through the overgrown greenery festooning the glass on the outside. Did it matter why the costume was here? It was just one of those random things, lost in my fragmented memories from that time. And yet other things I remembered so clearly, they might have happened yesterday.

Especially that day, when Jeremy got me in here and... No. I pulled back from the image.

I thought instead about river swimming with Samantha and Molly, Jeremy making an unwanted appearance, and my disgust at his obvious drooling over us in our costumes. Well, maybe not me. Samantha, certainly, all showy and flirty. I always thought Jeremy had a thing for Samantha; he'd dropped enough hints.

Another memory surfaced, of the Sunday afternoon when Samantha and I had gone to the river. Molly had been delayed and said she'd meet us there, but she never showed. Eventually, Samantha and I had given up on her and we'd come back to

Summerdene. I'd worried that Molly might have gone to the river after all and we'd missed her. Either Samantha or I had rung her mother – it was me, I remembered now – but the call had left us none the wiser.

Molly never did tell us where she'd got to that day, no more than she'd told us what happened to her the night of the school disco, when Samantha had expected to walk home with her and been disappointed.

Thinking about it, none of this was particularly noteworthy – we were excitable teenagers; we all had secrets, and were entitled to keep them, even if they weren't that mind-blowing.

The biggest secret of all, mammoth, in comparison to these other non-incidents, belonged to Molly. The kind of secret that actually hurt rather than just causing puzzlement and annoyance.

But that was still to come.

I crossed the old waiting area and opened the door. As I emerged into the hall, the clunk as I closed the door behind me sewed another stitch into my mental picture. Samantha hadn't left Summerdene straight away. We'd gravitated upstairs to my room to listen to *Pick of the Pops* on my radio. We'd been alone in the house, I was sure of it. But I'd heard a sound, like a door being carefully closed.

After Samantha had gone home, I had walked around the house, and even bravely opened Jeremy's bedroom door and peeped inside. Nobody. The house was indeed empty. Not long after, Jeremy himself came home and marched through to the kitchen without a word to me. He'd seemed preoccupied, as if he hadn't realised I was there. It wasn't unusual, and I was happy to be ignored by him if it meant I was left in peace.

But something wasn't right about that afternoon. I felt it then, and I felt it now.

TWENTY-TWO
LOGAN

2022

In case you were wondering, Briony, the trail that led me to you began when I finally got to read the letter the social worker had written to me.

Three weeks after I finished school, I'd sorted out a place for myself in a hostel in London, and a job as a waiter. Time to go. When I left home – or what passed for home – I only had half an hour before I knew they'd be back. Ended up grabbing things at random, including a big old envelope full of papers and stuff they kept in a drawer. My name was on the envelope, so I reckoned it had something to do with me. I thought my birth certificate might be in there, which it was. I knew I'd need it at some point, so I took the whole thing.

Apart from my birth certificate, which I'd seen before, the rest was just stuff about my adoption, lists of kit my foster parents had passed on to my adoptive parents, that sort of thing. Nothing interesting. I nearly binned the lot.

And then I found the letter I was supposed to have been given when I was old enough, only they'd never bothered.

That letter, now, that *was* interesting. I already knew my birth mother's name – somebody must have told me, or I'd read it on the certificate. Anyway, the letter gave me *his* name as well, and it got me thinking.

My superior computer skills helped, along with a basic knowledge of how to find someone, even if they don't want to be found, but it still took me a while to track him down. I had a lot of wasted online chats with the wrong people before I hit the jackpot.

He didn't want to know at first. Not sure I would have done either. I had to use all my expertise in the persuasion department until he agreed to a meeting, to get me off his back, basically.

We met in a pub in Islington, his choice. Once I'd got him talking, he was surprisingly open to handing me all the information I never knew I needed, especially as he hadn't even known I existed. It was the shock of hearing from me out of the blue that loosened his tongue, I reckon, as well as wanting to get it all off his chest. There was definitely an element of that, like he'd bottled it all up and couldn't wait to let it out, although I did notice he was knocking back the Scotch.

So then I had your name, Briony. You got top billing in his story, like he had an axe to grind, and no wonder.

I only met him that one time. There were no promises to keep in touch. I didn't want that any more than he did. Not that there'd have been much chance because, as it turned out, the poor bugger had a brain tumour, inoperable. He dropped that in at the end of our meeting, like it meant nothing. Give the bloke his due, he didn't show any signs of feeling sorry for himself. I did, though. I mean, I felt sorry for him. He was my father, after all.

Five months later he was gone. I got a message from some doctor or other. Turned out he'd arranged it before he went. I guess that meant there was something there, some kind of attachment, and I was grateful for it. Can't pretend otherwise. It made me feel I owed it to him to put things right on his behalf, if you know what I mean.

His story was my story, and I kept looking without knowing what I was looking for – I guess I got a bit obsessed. I was reading the village newsletter online when I hit on Alice Church's obituary. So, the old dear had gone, but who got the house? I had to know, had to follow through what I'd started – I was doing this for him, not just for myself. So I decided to relocate to Mistlecombe and work from the inside out instead of the other way around.

A good plan, as it turned out, because there you were, Briony, all set up in Summerdene. (I'm slow-hand-clapping now.) It's not always what you know that counts in this life, it's who. In this case *mine host* the pub landlady. She knew Summerdene, and who lived there, as probably half the village did. Finding you had a daughter was a bonus. It gave me something to work with.

I believe in justice, Briony. That's all I want.

TWENTY-THREE
BRIONY

Logan paid me two visits in as many days. I'd mentioned when he came to pick up Faye one day that the back lawn needed cutting and I'd not had the time, but it was only in the form of casual chat while we waited for Faye to appear.

One mid-morning, I opened the front door, expecting to greet my next B&B guests, when I found him on the step, all smiles. Faye was in London and wasn't due back until this evening, which he must have known, and I felt wrong-footed by the unscheduled visit.

'Hello, Briony,' he said, stepping into the hall as I held back the door. 'Is your grass still in need of a trim? Only I had a bit of time so I thought I'd pop by and sort it for you.'

'Really?' I said, hesitating.

I don't know why I was hesitant. I'd say I'd got used to him rather than having taken to him completely, and I'd relaxed about him being around, but without Faye in tow he seemed different somehow. Too close, too familiar.

'Unless you've already done it,' he added, seeing the doubt on my face.

'I did give it a quick once-over,' I said. He looked almost

crestfallen, and I was being ungrateful. 'But since the rain, it's sprung up again. That would be great, Logan, if you're sure. Come through.'

I led the way to the kitchen and opened the back door. 'The mower's in the shed. It's old and not very sharp but it does the job. You'll find the extension lead with it. Plug it in here.' I indicated the power point next to the freezer.

The doorbell sounded again.

'Excuse me. That'll be my guests.' I headed for the front door, leaving Logan to it.

A seventy-something man, mostly bald, blue eyes twinkling in a pink face, beamed at me. His wife, similar age, with silver-blonde hair, came up behind him. The couple were similarly dressed, in neat jeans, shirts and gilets. I saw a green vintage Morris Minor Traveller on the forecourt.

'The Hollises,' the woman offered. 'Tom and Marion.'

'Hello,' I said. 'Come right in.' Then, when they'd piled into the hall with a heavy, old-fashioned suitcase and a large, floral-patterned tote bag, I added, 'Love the car, by the way.'

'That's Shirley,' Marion said. 'She goes like a dream. We named her after an aunt of mine. She was reliable, too.'

We laughed. I led the way upstairs, showed them to their room and invited them to come down to the guests' sitting room when they were ready, and I'd bring them some coffee.

I liked this type of guest. They were always polite and friendly, and kept the room tidy. Actually, I liked them all, and I'd had quite an assortment through the doors of Summerdene since I opened the business. Coming downstairs again, I had a warm feeling inside. Not for the first time, I congratulated myself on having made the right decision as regards my future. My immediate future, anyway – I never let myself get too complacent. Life had a way of reeling out a tripwire when you were least expecting it.

But for now, Summerdene was home, the business was

thriving, and I felt happier and more settled than I had in a long time.

My buoyant mood took a dive as I trundled through to the kitchen and heard the mower in full throttle. Logan was whipping the machine up and down the lawn as if his life depended on it. Suddenly, I resented the intrusion, and had to give myself a sharp talking-to. This man was Faye's boyfriend, and I had no reason not to think positively about him. Why I couldn't seem to do that was a mystery.

Taking myself in hand, I waved from the kitchen doorway to draw his attention. He switched off the mower and came to the door.

'Would you like coffee? Or a cold drink? I've got Cokes, or there are some cans of beer in the fridge.'

'Coffee's fine, thanks, Briony. Never touch Coke and it's a bit early for beer, even for me.'

'Right. Kettle's on. It won't be a minute,' I said.

My new guests had come downstairs, and I hurried along the hall to make sure they were comfortable in the sitting room before returning to the kitchen to fetch their coffee. Logan had come inside and was gazing at the shiny new coffee machine that, quite frankly, scared the living daylights out of me.

'Are we using this?' he asked. 'I know how it works. I can do it, if you like.'

'No, we're not. I use it for the breakfasts. In between it's instant.' I heard the snap in my tone, and winced inwardly.

'Fine. I just wondered.' Logan smiled and took down the jar of granules from the shelf above the counter.

'Sit down. I'll do it,' I said, almost pushing my way into the space he occupied and lining up four coffee mugs, the best local pottery ones for the Hollises, the everyday ones for Logan and me.

The kettle boiled and the coffee made, I made up a tray for my guests, including cream for their coffee and two scones with butter and jam, then put two mugs of coffee on the table for Logan and me. No scones.

Honestly, how juvenile I was! Begrudging Faye's boyfriend a measly scone with his coffee just because I resented his over-familiarity. Back again from the sitting room, I relented, and put the biscuit tin in front of him, the small compromise giving me a twinge of satisfaction.

'Ta.' He lifted the lid and took out a chocolate digestive. 'My favourites.'

'Faye's, too,' I said.

'Yes, I know. We've got so much in common, even down to our taste in biscuits.' He smiled. It seemed self-satisfied to me.

Again, I urged myself to stop looking for bad things about Logan when, on the face of it, there weren't any. I reminded myself how much she loved him, and I owed it to her to make the effort.

'That's lovely,' I said. 'It's good Faye's found somebody like you.'

Did I mean that? I had no idea.

'I'm very lucky, I know that,' Logan said, helping himself to another digestive. 'Faye's a great girl, and having a mum like you, well, that's a bonus.'

He winked, and I cringed. Okay, he was trying hard, maybe too hard.

'Do you have family?' I asked. 'Do they live near you? In Hertfordshire, I mean.'

'Ah, now you're asking,' Logan said, tilting his head to one side and smiling ruefully. 'My parents are in Bedfordshire,' he said, after a pause. 'Milton-Bloody-Keynes. Excuse my French. They're my adoptive parents. I'm adopted.'

I wondered at the repetition, and at the slightly sour note I detected in Logan's tone, the sudden steeliness in his expression.

'Oh, right, I see.'

There seemed nothing else to say. In any case, Logan had got up from the table, leaving his mug with coffee still in it.

'I'll go and finish off out there,' he said. 'How about I do some pruning or weeding or something after I've done the grass? Just point me in the right direction.'

His face softened, the smile as warm as toast. He was a funny one, this Logan. The sudden switches of mood were most disconcerting. I hoped I hadn't upset him by asking about his family. But it was a fair enough question, I thought.

'No, honestly,' I said. 'Don't do any more. But thank you. It's a relief to have the grass neat again.'

'No problem, Briony,' Logan said, placing a peculiar emphasis on my name. 'I'll leave you in peace in a while.'

And leave me in peace he did, having swung the mower around the last quarter of the lawn and nipped back to the kitchen to yank out the plug, giving me a cheerful goodbye at the same time.

The following day, he was back. He wasn't empty-handed. He held out a bunch of flowers to me, loosely wrapped in shop paper. They were stocks and pinks, and smelt delicious.

'For me?' I said stupidly, since he'd already thrust the bunch at me.

He shrugged. 'They had a load outside the greengrocer's. I thought you might like them.'

'I do,' I said truthfully. 'I'm not sure I deserve them, but thank you, Logan.'

'You're Faye's mother. Don't need any other reason,' he said, widening his eyes at me.

This was all a bit full-on, I thought, and quite unnecessary. If he thought he was edging his way into my good books, he was going the wrong way about it. It was too gushy, too much.

And then I realised how uncharitable that was of me, and I asked him in.

'No, I won't, ta,' he said. 'I'm on shift in the pub at twelve.'

'No rest for the wicked,' I quipped.

Pippa came up behind me, presumably curious as to who my visitor was. She hadn't been around yesterday when Logan was here as she'd left early to take her son to the dentist.

'This is Pippa,' I said. 'She comes to help out.' I nodded at Logan, and looked at Pippa. 'Logan,' I said. 'Faye's boyfriend.'

'Logan. Right,' Pippa said, as the two of them faced each other.

'Hi, Pippa,' Logan said, his face a blank.

'Of course, you've probably seen one another at the White Hart, as Logan works there,' I said, feeling a little awkward without knowing why.

I knew Pippa went to the pub because Faye had told me. But she looked as blank as he did.

'Dunno,' she said, and disappeared back into the hallway.

'Well, thanks ever so much for the gorgeous flowers,' I said brightly. 'I'll put them in water right away. You have a good day now.'

I smiled, remembering I was supposed to be making an effort with this man.

'I might see you later,' he said, stepping back onto the gravel. 'When Faye comes home.'

'Okay. Bye then.' I gave a quick wave and shut the door.

I didn't see Logan later; Faye, back from her work jaunt, only stayed long enough to unpack and have a cup of tea and a sandwich before she went off to the pub to meet him. I bit back the comment that it would have been nice if she'd spent an evening at home for once. Around eleven, I got a text from her telling me she'd be staying over and not to wait up. I hadn't; I was already in bed by then.

The following morning, while I was ferrying pots of tea and

coffee to the guests in the dining room, I heard the front door close and Faye hurried along the hallway.

'Sorry, Mum, I meant to get here earlier and help with the breakfasts,' she said breathlessly. 'Here, let me.'

She took the tray from my hands, and I heard her chatting to the guests about the weather as she gave them their drinks. I felt a rush of affection for her. I had the breakfasts down to a fine art and could manage on my own, but it was easier with two, and more fun.

Shortly afterwards, Faye and I sat at the kitchen table, drinking tea and picking at leftover pastries and fruit, our usual piecemeal breakfast. I had my ear trained to the doorbell, in case Marcus came. Then, when he didn't, I felt dejected. He must still be away, and I missed him. I wished I didn't, but I couldn't help my feelings.

'You okay, Mum?' Faye was studying me intently over the top of her mug.

'What? Yes, of course.' I smiled, bringing myself back to the present. 'Did you have a good trip to London? You didn't say last night.'

'Yes, fine. The usual.'

There was something on my daughter's mind; I could always tell. She kept looking at me, then averting her gaze, as if she was trying to weigh up something.

Then it came.

'Mum?'

'Yes, love?'

I stood up, preparing to clear the breakfast things away.

'No, sit down a minute,' Faye said.

I obeyed, feeling a twinge of anxiety. Whatever was coming, I wasn't going to like it.

'Logan and I had a long talk last night,' Faye continued. 'And we decided we want to be together, all the time. So...'

Oh God. She hadn't asked him to move into Summerdene,

had she? Not without checking with me first. What came next wasn't as bad as that, but it wasn't good news either.

'... we're moving in together. Logan's renting a cottage in Candle Street. It's tiny, but it's cute. It belongs to one of the customers Logan's friendly with. He's going travelling and doesn't want to leave it empty. Lucky, isn't it?'

'But you've not known each other that long, Faye,' I said. 'Isn't it all moving rather fast?'

Faster than light. I foresaw disaster. Maybe I shouldn't have but as Faye's mother, witness to her heartaches, listener of woes, drier of tears – those she let me see – that was my automatic reaction.

Faye put her mug down, rather hard. 'I knew you'd say that.'

'You weren't disappointed then, were you?' I retorted.

I was handling this all wrong but I was genuinely worried. And then it came to me that Logan's grass cutting, flower giving and compliments had all been in the cause of buttering me up, and I felt my shoulders stiffen in annoyance.

'I'm sorry,' Faye said, fiddling with her teaspoon. 'I know you're only looking out for me. But I am twenty-four, not eighteen. You can't wrap me up in cotton wool.'

'No, lovey,' I said, thinking if I'd been able to do that, I might have prevented her from the last disaster, courtesy of the awful Nick. But that was wishful thinking. Faye had to make her own mistakes, and I had to let her. 'I just want you to be happy, that's all.'

'I am. I will be.' Faye's eyes were alight, her expression button-bright. 'Please say you're okay with it, Mum. I'm not abandoning you altogether. I'll still come over and give you a hand with the B&B, and I'll still do the website.'

Faye had made up her mind, and there was nothing I could say that would change it.

'As long as you know you can come back here if it doesn't work out,' I said. I had another thought. 'Didn't Logan only come to Mistlecombe to look up friends and family? You said he'd be going home some time.'

'I know, but this is the thing – he really likes living in the village, and he can work anywhere, like I can.'

Yep, I thought. He can work anywhere, like millions of other people. Of course he can. I blamed the pandemic for throwing this fact into focus.

I stood up and picked up our mugs. 'Well, then, as long as it's truly what you want, and Logan treats you well, I shan't raise any more objections.'

I smiled at Faye. I felt like a fraud.

TWENTY-FOUR
LOGAN

I had to get her away from you, Briony. Divide and conquer. Easier for you to press the worry buttons when your daughter's not living in your pocket. Easier to get all kinds of ideas into your head, and not always pretty ones.

It's what mothers do, isn't it? Worry endlessly about their offspring. Most mothers, anyway.

You weren't too sure about me at the start, that was pretty obvious. The fixed smile, the sheer effort you had to make just to be civil. God knows why. I mean, blokes don't get more personable than me. A shame you couldn't see what your daughter saw in me from the outset. Good as gold, she was. But that was okay. It just meant I'd have to work a bit harder with you. I was prepared for that.

You were about to send me away when I turned up with my kind offer to cut the grass, I could tell. But I got to work with the facial expressions, and before long my feet were under your table, literally.

I had a good look at the house while I was pushing that damn mower around. The old place seems to have stood up well to the passing of time. Worth a bloody fortune. Character

Cotswold houses don't come cheap, as you well know, Briony. But don't get too settled. You might be as dug in as a pig in the proverbial but that's an illusion, a lie, as you'll find out soon enough.

After I'd sweated buckets mowing your lawn, I nearly dumped the idea of going back with flowers, but as it turned out it was worth it to see the look on your face, the grateful smile. Bit confused, too, I'd say. Didn't quite know what to do me with me, did you?

Funny, that.

TWENTY-FIVE
BRIONY

1986

August tipped over into September and the new school term would begin in a few days. One part of me wished that summer and freedom could go on for ever, while another part looked forward to becoming a sixth-former, with its inherent promise of life moving on, as well as the sense of superiority at school it would bring.

I had given up my weekday job at Pink's, although I was continuing to work on Saturdays, and was enjoying a leisurely breakfast in the sunny kitchen – alone, as Jeremy had gone to college and Alice to the village – while I considered the day ahead and how to make the most of it, when the phone rang in the hall.

It was Samantha. 'Meet me at the Kissing Tree,' she said, her voice sounding weirdly shrill. 'And don't be all day.'

'Now?' I asked. I wasn't in the mood to hurry anywhere. 'I've only just got up. Can't it wait?'

'No, it can't.' Samantha's voice changed down an octave. 'See you in fifteen. Please, Bri?'

'Yes, all right,' I said. 'Is Molly coming?'

'That, my dear Briony, is a very good question,' Samantha said, and put the phone down.

I trailed upstairs to my room feeling slightly anxious, as well as intrigued as to why I'd been summoned so early in the day. Well, half past ten, anyway. But knowing Samantha, it wouldn't be about anything desperate. She'd probably put a rinse on her hair and turned it ginger. Or, more likely, it was about some boy she liked, and the inevitable accompanying complications.

The weather was still warm, but I pulled a sweatshirt over my jeans and T-shirt. It could be cool in the woods, whatever the season. Deliberately not hurrying, I strolled along Back Lane, reaching the village just within my allotted fifteen minutes. It took me ten minutes more to wander along the high street and cut through the lane that led to the woods, by which time Samantha was virtually airborne with frustration.

'At last!' she said, jerking away from the tree trunk where she'd been standing as I plunged through the undergrowth, into the clearing.

'Okay, let's not break into a sweat about it,' I said calmly, sitting down on the mossy cushion beneath the tree. 'What's up, anyway?'

Noting the absence of ginger hair and anything else different about Samantha's person, my money was on boy trouble. Samantha hesitated, seemingly undecided about sitting down. I patted the space next to me.

'Sit down, you're making the place untidy,' I said, quoting one of Alice's sayings.

Samantha sat, pulling her knees up to her chin. 'She's gone, Bri. Molly's gone. Upped and left, not a word!'

'Gone? How d'you mean?'

This wasn't what I'd expected at all. Samantha looked dead serious, though. Her cheeks showed two bright pink spots of colour.

'What I *said*. Molly's gone away, and she didn't tell me she was going, or where, or why, or if she's coming back. Nothing. Presumably she said nothing to you, either?'

'Of course not,' I said. 'I would have told you. How do you know she's gone, anyway?'

Samantha looked at me as if I was stupid. 'Well, do you know where she is? Because I don't.'

'Not right this minute, no,' I said uncertainly. 'She can't have just *gone*,' I said. 'It doesn't make sense.'

'Lots of things don't make sense. Doesn't stop them happening,' Samantha said.

We sat in thoughtful silence for a minute or two.

'When did you last see her?' I asked.

It had to be at least three weeks since I'd seen Molly myself, which wasn't surprising as we had holiday jobs. She'd come into Pink's one day when I'd been working and we'd chatted behind the fruit and veg stand. I thought Samantha might have run into her more often as they lived so close.

'Can't remember. Not for ages, though. Of course, I *would* have seen her at the river – *we* would – if she'd bothered to show up.'

That Sunday afternoon was over two weeks ago; I didn't know why Samantha had to bring it up now. Clearly she was still annoyed with Molly over that. But it hardly mattered now; there were more important things at stake, apparently.

'I think you'd better start at the beginning,' I said.

'Well, I tried to phone her at home to see if she wanted to go shopping in Cheltenham,' Samantha began. 'I needed to get some stuff for school. I was going to ring you next but nobody answered. When I tried again, it sounded like somebody picked up the phone and put it straight down again.'

'Did you dial it properly? Sure you got the number right?'

'Of course I got it right. I'm not daft.' Samantha elbowed me in the ribs. 'I thought she might have been at work anyway, so I rang the hotel and some woman said she'd left.'

'Okay,' I said slowly. 'Well, she'd have left her job because school's starting, wouldn't she?'

'I know, but I thought it was worth double-checking. So, then I went round to her house.'

I wondered why it hadn't occurred to Samantha to go to Molly's before she rang the hotel. But that was Samantha; her logic was her own.

'And?' I asked.

'I knocked but there was no answer. The house had a closed up look about it and the downstairs curtains were drawn across so I couldn't see in. I looked through the letter box but it was too low and all I could see was the hall carpet.'

I had to smile at this. The letter box in Molly's front door was almost at ground level. I had a vision of Samantha almost lying on her stomach in order to peek through.

'Maybe they've gone on holiday,' I said. 'A last-minute thing. They'll have to be back for Thursday, when school starts. Why are you making such a drama out of it?'

'Because she never told me! She didn't say she was going on holiday, and she would have, wouldn't she? Anyway, it's hardly likely, is it? Not this close to term starting. They've already had a holiday. They went to Yorkshire when we broke up in July. And what was going on with the phone?'

Samantha had a point, but again I imagined there was some perfectly innocent explanation.

'Don't know about the phone, but maybe there was a family emergency,' I ventured. 'They could've gone to see some rellie or other.'

'Maybe.' Samantha brightened at this. 'Yeah, that could be it.'

Of course, the main reason Samantha was so put out was the absence of any contact from Molly, I realised that, and I kind of understood. We were a threesome, we told each other everything – in theory. Molly's failure to explain her disappearance on the night of the disco, and her no-show at the river swimming were just blips. Not typical.

As I thought this, I felt a rush of guilt that I'd said nothing to my friends about my experience with Jeremy in the old surgery. I wasn't sure why I hadn't, except that, deep down, lurked a faint feeling of shame. At least this current melodrama was taking my mind off it.

A light breeze swept through the shady clearing, rustling the leaves above our heads and setting the long grasses dancing. I felt chilled, despite the sweatshirt. I got to my feet.

'Come on.' I held out my hand to Samantha. It was time I took charge.

'Where're we going?' She looked up at me. I saw fearfulness in her eyes, and I realised how Samantha liked her life to follow a smooth path without wrinkles, nothing unexpected. It went against the gung-ho approach she displayed in public. But weren't we all a mass of contradictions in one way or another?

'Molly's house,' I said.

I wanted to see for myself. Samantha scrambled to her feet, and we left the Kissing Tree and its stories behind, and went in search of our own story, or rather, Molly's.

TWENTY-SIX

BRIONY

2022

Faye had only been gone from Summerdene for three days and I missed her, which was inevitable and would soon lessen, I knew. But I still had concerns about Logan I couldn't explain, and this pitched me into a constant low-level state of nerviness and apprehension. It was only my current guests, a lively family of two fifty-something couples and an older woman – somebody's cousin – filling the house with laughter and life, and the company of Pippa, that saved me from descending into gloom.

I'd known Faye wasn't likely to stay with me for ever, but I had hoped she'd have hung on a bit longer. I had seen her – she'd stopped by yesterday to help with breakfast – but she hadn't come this morning. This was how it should be, I accepted that. It didn't mean to say I liked it.

She'd talked about the cottage and how she loved living there, despite the ominous banging sound the pipes made when the hot water was on, but she'd said little about Logan. All she'd said was that he'd given up working at the White Hart, now that he no longer needed the accommodation.

Perhaps she'd picked up on my disapproval and didn't want to stoke any arguments. Not that there would be any; I'd resolved to stay positive, be happy for my daughter and not look for problems that didn't exist.

I realised I needed to start treating Faye and Logan as a couple, so I invited them to lunch on Sunday, promising a roast. I used to produce a decent enough roast dinner in my days with Tony, even if he had been on hand to rescue the potatoes, check the temperature of the meat and generally watch over me, which led to more mistakes than I'd have made if left alone.

'I'll have to check with Logan,' Faye said, sounding doubtful. 'Can I let you know?'

'Of course,' I said, feeling abjectly disappointed. If she was going to check every little thing with Logan, it didn't bode well, in my opinion. 'As long as I know before I do the shop on Friday,' I added.

I didn't have to wait that long. Pippa and I had just finished the beds when Faye rang my mobile.

'Sorry, Mum. We can't make lunch on Sunday. We're having a quiet day, spending some quality time together.' She sounded as if she was reciting from a crib sheet.

'Okay, another time,' I said lightly. 'I've got plenty to do anyway.'

It wasn't true, but it ought to be, I said to myself after Faye had ended the call. My resolve to make a new life for myself had waned rather, mostly because I'd been so busy playing host, and happily. All I wanted to do in my free time was curl up with a glass of wine and a book. But outside the walls of Summerdene, the golden days of late summer waited and I should make the effort to do something different. There were plenty of sights in the Cotswolds I should revisit. So much loveliness practically on the doorstep; I'd not seen a fraction of it yet. Remembering our walks, and our trip to Blenheim Palace, I thought about Marcus, and when Pippa had left for the day, her bike wobbling perilously among the ruts in Back Lane, I set out for Kestrels.

It was probably a waste of time, I thought. If he was back from Kent, he'd have come to see me, or at least phoned, so I was surprised to see his car parked on the spare bit of ground beside the cottage.

'Hello, Briony,' Marcus said, answering my knock almost immediately.

He was smiling, but his smile had a touch of embarrassment about it.

'You're back,' I said pointlessly, wondering if he was going to invite me in.

'Yep. Look...'

'Sorry. You're busy,' I said, backing away from the door. 'I'll see you another time.'

'No, no. Come in.' He held the door wide for me and I followed him through to the sitting room. 'Can I get you a drink? Coffee? Or a glass of wine?'

He sounded strangely formal, and I was beginning to wish I hadn't come now.

'No, thanks, I won't stop. Things to do, you know?' I didn't know, but I wasn't going to impose if I wasn't wanted. 'I saw the car and thought I'd stop to say hello, and ask if you had a good trip,' I said. Then I added, 'I didn't know you were back,' and immediately regretted it.

We stood facing one another; I hadn't been invited to sit down. Marcus steepled his hands to his mouth and shook his head slowly. He looked at me directly for the first time since I'd arrived, those dark, dark eyes locking with mine. My stomach did a little swimmy thing.

After what seemed like an age, Marcus broke his gaze and looked down at his feet.

'Marcus, what is it?' I said, stepping up to him. 'What's the matter? Do you want me to go?'

He seemed to gather himself. 'No, of course not. Sit down. I'll bring us drinks.'

I sat on the sofa and Marcus disappeared to the kitchen, leaving me feeling... well, weird, and confused. What was going on here? I had a sudden thought: Hannah was back. They'd made it up and she'd come back with him. That must be it. I glanced up at the beamed ceiling. Was she upstairs? Or had she gone to the village and was due back any minute?

Mentally, I prepared myself to meet her, be introduced as the woman who ran the guest house along the road. I even practised a friendly-neighbour smile while my treacherous heart squeezed down to prune-size.

Marcus came back with two glasses of white wine, and I couldn't help but be pleased he hadn't gone for the coffee option. He handed me a glass and sat down on the chair opposite.

'Thanks.' I took several sips, grateful for the alcohol spike.

Marcus put his glass of wine down on the coffee table without drinking any.

'I've got a confession to make,' he said. 'I got back from Kent three days ago, on Sunday evening.'

I waited. Clearly there was more to come.

'I should have come to see you right away. I wanted to, but I wasn't sure if I should.'

I frowned. We were just friends, weren't we? No more than that, despite my fantasies. So why did he feel guilty about not rushing along to Summerdene, and why had he been uncertain about seeing me? And then a tiny light switched on in my brain. I extinguished it, fast.

'It's fine. I didn't know when you were coming back anyway, so I wasn't expecting you. But, Marcus, if you wanted to see me, what stopped you?'

He picked up his glass and took a sip of wine. 'While I was

away I did a lot of thinking. There were things I needed to straighten out in my mind.'

It wasn't a direct answer; no answer at all, really.

'About Hannah?' I ventured.

'Oh, no, not about her. Okay, there are memories that pop up now and again, when I'm least expecting them. And then I start to wonder, what if I'd handled things differently, done this or that, whether we might have made a go of it.'

'I know that feeling all too well,' I said, smiling ruefully.

'I'm sure you do,' Marcus said gently. 'More so. You and your husband had been together a long time.'

'The feelings are the same,' I said, not wanting to belittle Marcus's experience.

He drank some more wine and put the glass down again. I kept hold of mine. I seemed to need something to hold on to.

'Anyway, that's all beside the point,' Marcus said. 'The truth is I missed you while I was away, Briony. I thought about you a lot. I surprised myself. I hadn't realised how much you'd come to mean to me, and not just as a friend.' He held up a hand as I went to speak. 'Yeah, I know that sounds nuts when we've only just got to know one another.'

Was I going to say I'd missed him, too, that I felt the same? If so, I was glad he'd stopped me blurting it out. Something inside, some little part of me that by some miracle was halfway sensible, urged me to keep quiet, keep my thoughts to myself.

'Is that why you didn't get in touch when you got home?' I asked.

Marcus nodded. 'I was confused about... about us, about the way I felt about you. I needed time to straighten things out in my mind, that's why I stayed away. I had to be sure that what I was feeling was real. And it is, I'm absolutely sure now. I'm sorry if this isn't what you want to hear, but I had to tell you, in case... in case there's a chance we could be more than just friends.' He smiled, and the warmth and hope in his eyes almost broke me.

But I had to stay strong. It couldn't happen – *shouldn't* happen – for a whole flotilla of reasons.

I looked at Marcus, so young and good-looking, and I thought about myself, almost five years older than him, and counting. I kept myself in good shape and could pass for pretty in a low light. But it wasn't only about looks. I couldn't handle a serious relationship, not now. I'd just changed my entire life and the emotional toll had been greater than I'd realised. Besides, I may be what Marcus wanted, or thought he did. But for how long? He could have any woman he wanted, and no doubt there was a queue forming around the university campus as we spoke.

I formed my next words carefully.

'I love spending time with you, Marcus. It's nice to have a friend to go to the pub with and go on walks and things. In that way, you mean a lot to me, too.'

'In *that* way.' Marcus smiled ruefully. 'It's okay, Briony. I get it. And you're quite right, we are friends and I would hate to do anything to spoil that.'

Oh, please do, my inner devil whispered.

Was I about to confess my own feelings, fall into Marcus's arms and throw caution off the nearest high cliff? I can't say I wasn't tempted. But then, a few months down the line, reality would kick in, Marcus would see me as the rebound relationship I surely would be, and he'd be off in pursuit of somebody much more suited to him, a young, super-intelligent, fresh-faced girl he had much more in common with, and I wasn't about to be cast off like last week's laundry. I didn't want that, I didn't deserve the heartache that would inevitably arise from getting tangled up with Marcus, not to mention the potential awkwardness of running into him all the time once it was over, since he lived so close.

No, I was fine on my own, happy to have him around for

chats and outings, but otherwise content to be single. It was better that way. One day I hoped I would meet someone – I didn't plan to spend the rest of my life alone – but that was for the future, when the time was right.

'I should go.' I stood up. 'Always so much to do. I love having the guests but they do make work.' I raised my eyes, trying to lighten the mood.

'I can imagine,' Marcus said, standing up too. 'I'll see you out.'

We traipsed to the front door and Marcus opened it.

'I'm sorry, Briony,' he said, as I stood on the step. 'Can we forget what I said? Go back to how we were before?'

'That's quite a big ask. Not easy to forget something like that. There's no need to be sorry, though. I'm very flattered.' I thought for a moment. 'Of course we can still be friends. I'd hate it if we weren't.'

We smiled at each other. I seemed unable to move off the step. Marcus stooped slightly towards me. For a second I thought he was going to kiss me. Instead, he put a hand on my arm then drew it away, but not until I'd felt the warmth of his skin against mine.

'Shall we grab a bite at the White Hart, Friday night?' he asked. 'If you're free, that is.'

'That would be lovely. I'll come by here around seven?'

'Great. I'll book a table to make sure.'

When Marcus had closed the door and I was out in the lane, I thought about what Faye would have made of it all. She'd have said I'd finally lost my mind completely. So, that was something else I wouldn't be telling her. I walked back to Summerdene with a determined stride. I'd take the car and go exploring this afternoon, which is what I'd intended in the first place.

I may have thrown away the opportunity for a new, exciting romance but I had kept hold of my self respect, my sense of self preservation and my independence. I would drink to that on Friday night.

TWENTY-SEVEN
BRIONY

1986

I saw what Samantha meant about Molly's house. It did look closed up and had a sort of abandoned air. I knocked the door and got no reply. We stood on the pavement outside the garden gate, gazing at the windows which showed no signs of life whatsoever. But it was mid-morning on a weekday. Her dad would be at work and the rest of them – Molly's mother, her sister, Molly herself – had probably gone out somewhere.

Obviously, we were overthinking this, letting our imaginations run away with us. Or Samantha was. So what if Molly hadn't been in touch lately? Perhaps she was just busy, and she did have other friends, we all did, although they tended to be confined to school and its related activities.

Actually, I did feel annoyed to think that Molly might have dropped Samantha and me in favour of another friend, or group of friends; I couldn't help it. Molly was entitled to do what she liked, with whom she liked, but it didn't stop me feeling she'd been somehow disloyal. We'd never gone this long without getting together or at least talking on the phone.

'Shall we go next door and see if they know if the family have gone on holiday?' I suggested, for want of a better idea.

'Can do.'

Samantha shrugged, as if she'd already lost interest, but she followed me round to the house next door anyway. I rang the bell. A dog barked from inside but nobody came. There was no close neighbour on the other side, as the Jones's house was on the corner of the street.

We'd crossed the road and started to walk away when a red post office van swung round the corner and stopped right outside the house. The postman got out of the van and marched up to Molly's front door, holding a large brown parcel.

'He'll be lucky.' Samantha made a snorting sound and carried on walking.

'Hang on,' I said, my hand on her arm. 'Look!'

She stopped, and we both watched as the front door opened a crack, just wide enough to see who was there: Molly's mother. She accepted the parcel and disappeared back inside, closing the door shut behind her.

'There you are,' I said, hating the note of triumph in my voice. 'Nobody's gone away. We've made it all up, like we always do.'

Samantha flounced her shoulders. 'Right, I'm going back to find out what's going on.'

She was halfway across the road, striding towards the Jones's house, before I could stop her. This wasn't a good idea. I wasn't sure why it wasn't, it was just a feeling. If all was not well in the Jones's household, they might not appreciate us butting in. But I was worried about Molly, even more so now, as well as curious, and I skipped across the street and caught up with Samantha on the doorstep.

She knocked hard, twice. We waited. She knocked again with the knocker, and rapped on the glass part of the door for good measure.

'We know her Mum's in. Why the hell doesn't she come to the door?' Samantha's voice shrill with frustration and annoyance.

I shushed her with a firm shake of my head. 'If there's anything wrong, we'll know soon enough. Molly'll find a way to let us know.'

Samantha nodded, but just as we turned to go, I saw a corner of the downstairs curtain drop suddenly, as if somebody had been looking out.

Samantha had noticed, too. 'Did you see that? Did you see, Bri? Bloody cheek! What's so wrong with us that she leaves us standing on the step like a couple of Jehovah's Witnesses?'

'I know.' I was puzzled as to why Mrs Jones hadn't opened the door to us when she knew we were Molly's best friends. We had to keep a sense of perspective, though. 'Like I said, Molly will be in touch with one of us soon and it'll all have been something and nothing.'

'Oh, you think so, do you?' Samantha sounded as disheartened as I felt.

'Well, I don't know, do I? But there's no point hanging around here.'

Back on the pavement, we looked up at the windows to check for any further movement, but there was none. Was Molly hiding inside with her mother, and hadn't wanted to see us? Had she spotted us, and asked her mother not to answer the door? It seemed unlikely. What possible reason could she have?

We dithered for a few minutes, neither of us knowing what to think, then walked back to the high street and treated ourselves to lemonade and cake in the café by way of consolation. Afterwards, we went to Samantha's house and played tapes in her room until we got bored and switched off the machine, letting the silence flood in.

'If Molly really is missing, or something awful's happened to her,' I said, dropping onto Samantha's bed, 'we'll find out soon enough. Word will get around the village. There'll be police about, asking questions. News reports and stuff.'

My own words stalled my breathing for a moment. Supposing some dreadful fate had befallen our friend? Here we were, treating her disappearance as a slight against the two of us, a minor inconvenience, when something unimaginably dire might have happened to her.

Now who was over-dramatising? I lay back on the bed and threw one arm nonchalantly over the side. I didn't want to alarm Samantha with my wild imaginings, although she probably had enough of her own.

Sitting down at her dressing table, she leaned into the mirror and plucked a stray eyebrow hair with the tweezers. 'I still keep thinking about the disco,' she said into the mirror. 'It was weird, the way she disappeared afterwards, and she never did say why. And the river thing, that was odd, when you think about it.'

'I know. We said so at the time.' I sat up.

We had put those incidents behind us, almost forgotten them. But they were very much on our minds now that we were faced with something much bigger.

Samantha got up from the dressing table and bowed theatrically, making a sweeping gesture with her arm.

'And here we have for your delight and entertainment, the Incredible Vanishing Molly Jones!'

We burst into laughter. I felt instantly better.

Thursday came, and we went back to school, swaggering in front of the fifth-year girls in our pared down version of the uniform – navy blue skirt but plain A line, no awful pleats, same blue-and-white striped shirt but with a royal blue sweatshirt instead of a scratchy navy blue V-neck jumper, and shoes of our choice, as long as they were black or brown, and flat.

Despite all evidence to the contrary, Samantha and I still expected Molly to come bouncing up to us, all smiles, ready to embrace the pain and pleasure of starting our sixth form studies. We shared a consoling hug when she didn't.

Among the A level subjects Molly had selected last term was one of Samantha's, Geography, and one of mine, English Lit. We swapped notes at lunch break.

'Any sign?' Samantha asked, hopefully.

'Nope,' I said. 'But I had a peek at the register for English Lit and her name's still down.'

'Same with Geography. There is some hope, then.'

Samantha's gaze swept the dining hall fruitlessly. We were clutching at the proverbial straw, and we knew it.

We used the last fifteen minutes of the lunch break searching out likely candidates for information on Molly's whereabouts.

'Dunno,' was the usual disinterested reply, until a spectacled girl called Belinda looked up from her plate of greasy spotted dick and anaemic custard and said: 'Seeing anyone, was she? Perhaps she's eloped with some boy.'

Samantha and I exchanged a look. Leaving Belinda to her pudding, we left the dining hall and went and sat on the grass bank outside. The possibility of a boyfriend being involved in Molly's disappearance hadn't occurred to us. Now we had a whole new angle to discuss.

'She wasn't seeing anyone, was she?' Samantha's brow wrinkled, her brown eyes narrowing as she looked at me.

'You know she wasn't,' I said, when truly, we knew no such thing.

'A secret boyfriend?'

I hesitated. 'No. Couldn't have. We'd have known.'

'Not if she kept it secret.' Samantha gave me a sideways look.

Another pause. Then I shook my head. 'She'd never have been able to keep it up. Not with us.'

'No, you're right, she couldn't have,' Samantha said. 'Not Molly. I mean, who would it have been, anyway? All the boys we know are here, at school.'

'Yeah.' The dinner break was over. We got to our feet. 'Look, she's not here right now, but she'll turn up sooner or later.' I crossed my fingers behind my back at this point. 'Even if she doesn't, let's make the most of sixth form. It'll be a blast anyway.'

'Will it?' Samantha looked doubtful.

'*Yes*,' I said forcefully. 'We've still got each other, haven't we?'

At the top of the bank, we parted to head for our separate classes. We had been three. Now, suddenly, we were two, and there was nothing we could do about it.

There was, however, something I could do about Jeremy, I was thinking, as I made my way home at the end of afternoon school. Maybe not directly, but I had to find a way of taking control.

Since the incident in the old surgery, I'd run it all through my mind, loads of times, mostly in the dead of night when sleep wouldn't come and all I could think about was Jeremy sleeping just yards away from me. I wished him all kinds of dreadful fates, prayed for them, but it didn't help because, firstly, wishing and praying never achieved anything in my experience, and secondly, because of what it would do to Alice if anything awful happened to her precious son.

What he did to me in the surgery was still unclear in my mind. His hand could have brushed against my breast purely by accident. Of course, he should never have been that close to me in the first place, so that was hardly an excuse. But the way he'd made me feel – threatened, controlled, frightened – was unacceptable, leaving out the possible assault.

Since that day, Jeremy had resorted to being his usual self. He dropped random supposedly innocent remarks full of innuendo and threw me personal comments as if they were sweets, as if I should be pleased to receive his back-handed compliments on the length of my skirt, the suntan on my legs, the way I did my hair. Each one stung me with implied criticism, and I felt as if I lived under a permanent spotlight. He never said these things in front of his mother, which only intensified the feeling of wrongness.

Jeremy's weirdness was one reason I was grateful to be back at school. His college course didn't start again until later in September, which meant he was mostly around when I got home in the afternoons, and all weekend. He was home most evenings, too, which hadn't happened before, but if Alice was out, I would go to Samantha's house so I didn't have to spend time alone in the house with him.

And then, suddenly, I noticed a change in him. The comments on my physical appearance stopped abruptly and were replaced by long looks that roved from the top of my head to my toes, followed by a twisted-mouth sneer. He only spoke to me when he had to, and Alice was present. Otherwise, I got the silent treatment. That, in itself, wasn't unusual, but it made me think there was something going on with him, other than his usual grievances against me, and against the world in general.

Even so, I wondered if I had offended him in some way, although I couldn't think how. And then I remembered it was Jeremy who had offended me, not the other way round, and I stopped wondering.

But all the time, my mind worked away in the background, replaying that day in the surgery, as if there was something I'd missed and needed to catch hold of. I felt on constant alert, waiting for the next thing to happen. It wasn't fair that I should live in fear of him, because that's what it was, fear. I knew I would never get any peace of mind unless I took matters into my own hands.

It was a case of self-preservation, I told myself, as I nipped out of school during a free period and went to the medical centre. Disregarding Alice's pragmatic approach to my care, if I didn't look after myself, nobody else would.

'Is there a doctor free?' I asked, reaching the front of the queue at the desk. 'It'll only take a minute.' It wouldn't, but I wasn't leaving now I'd made up my mind.

The receptionist on duty smiled warmly, and adjusted the name-badge which had worked its way loose from her blouse. *Ava Winters, Senior Receptionist*, it read.

'You haven't got an appointment, have you?' Ava said apologetically, after I'd given my name.

I hadn't had time to make one. Once I'd decided to come, I couldn't have afforded any delay, although it would have been nice to have seen a female doctor. I'd have to take my chance on that.

'Sorry, no. I didn't think,' I said.

Ava nodded kindly. 'Your eczema troubling you, dear? You know you can always drop in a note for a repeat prescription.'

'I know,' I said, 'but I just wanted a word, if that's all right.'

Ava tapped at her keyboard. 'Doctor Roberts should have a gap in around twenty minutes, if you could wait?'

I was due in class before then, but I doubted I would have had the courage to repeat this performance.

'Fine, thanks,' I said. I went and sat down.

When I finally gained entry to the hallowed portals of Doctor Roberts' consulting room, he gave me a fatherly smile over the top of his rimless glasses. One of the older GPs, he was gentle and kindly, and I'd seen him several times before. But on this occasion I'd rather have seen someone a bit less familiar, someone younger. Still, I was here now, and I duly stretched out my arms, palms uppermost, as he'd asked.

'Ah, yes. Inner elbows are a prime spot for you, as are the backs of your knees. Those the same, are they?'

'They are,' I said.

'Has it flared up anywhere else?' Doctor Roberts let go of my hands.

'No, just the two places,' I said.

'Well, it's the same old advice, I'm afraid.' He reached for a prescription pad. 'This stuff is still the best. Keep the areas cool if you can and try not to scratch. Come back if it troubles you further.'

'Thank you,' I said, pocketing the prescription and resisting the urge to scratch the inside of my elbow.

I sat on in the chair. Doctor Roberts took off his glasses, gave them a perfunctory polish on a bit of tissue, and replaced them. He regarded me with concern.

'Was there anything else?'

'Well...' I began, my mouth drying. Courage drained away. I couldn't say it, not to him, maybe not to anybody. 'No, that's all.' I stood up, thanked him, and left the consulting room.

I could do this. I could live my life at Summerdene the way I wanted. Jeremy wasn't going to spoil my life. I wouldn't let him near enough to do that.

TWENTY-EIGHT
BRIONY

2022

The White Hart was heaving on Friday night, more so than usual. It was the bank holiday weekend, though, so it wasn't surprising.

'Sorry,' Marcus said, as we pressed our way to the window at the back where our table awaited us, surrounded by other diners. 'I should have asked if you'd prefer to go somewhere less crowded. I didn't think.'

'Here's fine,' I said truthfully. 'Good thing you booked, though.'

After our last encounter, I wasn't sure I could handle sitting in a cosy nook with Marcus, relatively undisturbed.

We chatted amiably over our fish and chips and there was no awkwardness; I should have known there wouldn't be. It would be hard to be anything other than relaxed in Marcus's easy company.

I'd missed his flying visits to Summerdene in the mornings; I hoped they would resume and said so.

'I don't want to get under your feet, Briony,' he said.

I laughed. 'As if. Anyway, now Faye isn't living with me, it'd be good to have your company, somebody other than the guests and Pippa.'

'Okay, I'll pop along when I can, if you're sure. I can give you a hand with the breakfasts, now Faye isn't around so much.'

'She's hardly around at all these days,' I said gloomily. 'I invited the pair of them to lunch on Sunday but they can't make it. Apparently they're spending "quality time" together.' Aware of how sceptical I sounded, I tempered it with a laugh. 'But she works hard. She's entitled to spend her free time as she wants, and that doesn't mean hanging around her mother all the time.'

'But you miss her,' Marcus said, offering a knowing smile.

'I do,' I admitted. 'I'm getting used to it, though. It's not as if I saw a great deal of her when she lived in London, before we came down here. I just wish...' Marcus waited. 'I wish she wasn't so completely in thrall to Logan, that's all. It feels as if he's captured her, body and soul, in no time at all.'

'She's fallen head over heels in love, simple as that. Time has nothing to do with it. You can't always control these things,' Marcus said.

Oh but you can, I thought. At least you can give it a damn good try.

I sensed the heat of Marcus's gaze. I couldn't look at him. Perhaps I shouldn't have been so quick to accept his invitation tonight, nor to encourage his early morning visits to Summerdene. But I'd made it plain where I stood. I welcomed his friendship, and that's all it could be.

I spotted two of my B&B guests at a table across the room and waved at them to break the moment. When I dared to look back at Marcus he was studying the dessert menu. He passed it to me with a smile, and I had the distinct sensation of having escaped from something.

· · ·

To my surprise and delight, Faye arrived just before nine the following morning and immediately took over dining room duty.

'You don't have to, Faye,' I said, as she came back to the kitchen. with a stack of used cereal bowls. 'I can do it.'

'I know. I want to. Sweet couple.' She nodded towards the dining room.

'Honeymooners,' I said. 'They're touring the Cotswolds. This is their first stop.'

'Honeymooners? Bit long in the tooth I'd have thought.'

She giggled, and I shushed her.

'They can't be more than late fifties. Anyway, who says romance is only for the young?' I said.

'Fair point. One I made myself, not so long ago.' Faye winked comically.

Oh God. We were back to Marcus again. I was starting to feel besieged. Turning my back on Faye, I plunged my hands into the sink and began carefully washing the crystal tumblers I used for the breakfast juice, as they couldn't go in the dishwasher. They had been Alice's, and I experienced a moment of nostalgia as I handled them. We'd only used them at Christmas, otherwise they'd lived a pristine, sparkling life in the sideboard. I wondered if Alice would approve of them being used every day and, for that matter, what she would think of all the changes I'd made to Summerdene. So much was different about it now. But also, so much was the same.

'Mum? You okay?'

Faye was beside me, peering round at my face that I realised was tracked with tears. I hadn't realised I was crying. I wiped the tears away with a soapy hand, then had to dab my face with the tea towel to get rid of the suds.

'I'm fine.' I smiled. 'Just having a funny moment, that's all. I was thinking about Alice.'

'I'd liked to have met her,' Faye said. 'I could have asked her all about your teenage years and what you got up to.'

I laughed. 'She wouldn't have had much to tell – I made sure of that. Not that I got up to anything too awful. Actually, you did meet her once, when you were four, or five. Dad and I brought you here on the way back from our holiday in Somerset.'

Alice had met Tony once before that occasion, and she had been happy to meet my daughter in her own matter-of-fact way. My godmother had kept her emotions reined in, her innermost feelings ring-fenced. I never knew whether she'd always been like that or whether she'd learned it from experience.

Once she'd met Faye, I'd made subsequent visits to Summerdene, such as they were, alone. It had seemed best to keep that part of my life separate. I didn't really understand why I felt like that at the time, but I guess Jeremy and the memories he left me with had something to do with it.

Faye drew me into a hug and we stood for a minute, arms around each other.

'Are you all right, lovey?' I asked, as we broke apart.

She certainly looked all right. Her blue eyes were clear and bright, her complexion warm with a faint blush to her otherwise pale skin. She'd lost a little weight, I thought, but looked healthy and fit. Clearly I had no need to worry about her.

'I'm more than all right, Mum,' she said, picking up the tea towel and slowly drying a glass. 'Logan is...well, he's wonderful, and I'm so glad I met him.'

'That's all right, then. If you're happy, I'm happy. I'm glad living together is working out.'

Faye looked surprised. She'd probably never considered that her new living arrangements would be anything but blissful.

'It's brilliant, being together day and night.' She laughed. 'Well, except right now. Logan went to the bakery and I sneaked out and drove over here. Oh, don't worry,' she continued, obviously misreading my expression completely. 'I left him a note. I'll get back in minute, if that's okay?'

'Of course.'

I felt a dip of disappointment. I had imagined the two of us having coffee and a cosy chat after the guests had finished breakfast and the honeymooners had departed. The other couple and the young woman in the single room were staying on.

'Come round for dinner, the two of you,' I said, as Faye was leaving. 'How about Tuesday?'

She thought for a moment. 'Okay. Thanks, Mum. Logan'll be pleased.' She kissed me on the cheek.

I saw Faye out, then made a coffee and sat on the old iron bench outside the back door. I didn't like the idea of Faye having to sneak out, as she'd put it, the moment Logan's back was turned. Why hadn't she waited for him and the two of them come over together? Maybe she'd been joking, and there'd been no sneaking about it. But still...

I heard light footsteps and Pippa appeared around the side of the house. I smiled up at her, pleased to see her. I'd become quite fond of her as the weeks passed.

'Hello, Pippa. I was sitting here dreaming. I'd forgotten you were coming today.'

She sometimes put in an hour or two on Saturday mornings, which was useful as it was usually a changeover day.

'I nearly didn't make it. Rory kicked up a fuss about me going out but Mum soon sorted him out.'

'Well, you mustn't stay too long,' I said. 'If you could do the changeover room that would be great. I'll do the rest.'

'Yeah, no problem.' Pippa looked distracted. She leaned in the kitchen doorway, her hand moving slowly up and down the wooden frame. Three silver rings glinted in the sunshine. 'Mind if I have a word?'

My stomach flipped as my mind galloped ahead. She was

about to tell me she'd found a better job and was leaving. It had to be that.

'Of course. Come and sit down.' I slid along the bench to make space.

My mind had already reached the point where I needed to place an ad for Pippa's replacement. I never did find out what happened to the card I'd put in the post office window before. It had vanished before its time was up, but then I'd found Pippa, so it hadn't mattered.

'Pippa? What is it?' I asked, when she'd stayed silent for a minute.

If she was about to give her notice, I'd rather she got on with it.

She swivelled round on the bench to face me.

'I found out something. I didn't know what to do and whether to tell you or not. And then I thought if it was me I'd want to know and I knew I couldn't keep it a secret. It wouldn't be right.'

'Keep what a secret?'

This clearly wasn't about her leaving at all. Relief mingled with nervous anticipation. It wasn't like Pippa to be so hesitant. Normally, she said whatever was on her mind, straight out.

'You're not going to like it.' She turned towards the garden again, bowing her head slightly so that her hair fell forward across her face.

'Let me be the judge of that,' I said.

She sat up straight. 'Okay. That guy, Logan, he's dating your daughter, right?'

'More than dating,' I said. 'They've moved in together. They're renting a cottage in Candle Street.'

Pippa already knew that, surely?

'It's serious, then?' she said.

'Certainly looks that way. Pippa, what's this about?'

She took a deep breath. 'Logan's seeing somebody else. I

reckon it's been going on a while, probably all the time he's been with your Faye.' She gave me a look that seemed almost challenging as I did a minor double-take, my back thrusting painfully against the unforgiving iron framework of the bench. 'There, I said you wouldn't like it.'

'Pippa, how do you know this? Are you sure? Who is she?'

The questions rattled out. There were more piling up behind them, and not just for Pippa.

'I don't know her name,' Pippa continued. 'I know what she looks like. She's got reddish hair, auburn you'd call it. Has it piled up on top in a messy bun. Full in the figure, plenty of cleavage on show, if you get my meaning. She's a bit older than your Faye, I'd say. But then, he's older, isn't he?'

'A bit,' I said, not wanting to give out too much personal information.

But it didn't get much more personal than this.

'It's not just me. Other people have noticed them hanging around together,' Pippa said. 'Holding hands and that. Kissing goodnight down the alleyway by the pub, when they thought nobody was looking.'

'There isn't an alleyway by the pub,' I said. 'Unless you mean the paved area by the garden where they keep the barrels.'

'Not the White Hart. They aren't that stupid. The Duck and Hare, other side of the village. Well, hardly in the village. On the road out. You must know it.'

I knew of it, but only from driving by. It was a small place, old-fashioned, a bit run-down if the outside was anything to go by. I had never been inside, never had cause to.

'Pippa, are you sure this isn't just village gossip? Somebody out to cause trouble, for whatever reason?'

'Totally sure,' Pippa said, hazel eyes wide. 'I'd never have said anything otherwise. I saw them again the other day, talking outside the bakery in broad daylight. They were standing dead close and you could tell they knew each other pretty well. I was watching from the other side of the street. He touched her hand, like, really gave it a squeeze, and then they walked off, separately.'

She rattled the words out, almost as if she'd learned them by heart.

'That's hardly evidence,' I said.

The goodnight kisses and the rest might have been a case of mistaken identity. On the other hand, practically the whole village must recognise Logan from his stint at the White Hart.

I realised I was making excuses for him, for Faye's sake. If it was true, I couldn't bear it. But Pippa seemed so certain, and I didn't think she would have told me if there was any doubt. She wasn't a gossipmonger. I decided to push for a bit more information.

'Where does she live, this mystery woman?'

'I'm not sure.' Pippa looked doubtful for the first time. 'The new houses, I think. At the back of the school playing fields. It'll be more than kisses, deffo. He's playing away, properly. You get my drift.'

I did, and I didn't like it.

'Will you tell Faye?' Pippa asked.

'I don't know,' I said truthfully.

'You should. I'd want to know, if it was me.'

'There's not much to tell. It could all be a misunderstanding.'

Pippa sighed. 'I bet it's not. Men like that are the absolute pits, aren't they? Sorry, Briony. I did right to say something, though, didn't I?'

There was no easy answer to that so I kept quiet.

We sat on for a few minutes, Pippa nibbling at a green-painted thumbnail while a thrush serenaded us from a nearby bush. And then I realised the time, and carefully suggested we got on with our morning's work.

'Bedroom two. Changeover. I'm on it,' Pippa said.

Seeming relieved to be released, she sprung up off the bench and went indoors.

Faye and Logan came round on Tuesday evening, as arranged. I kept the dining room permanently laid up for the guests' breakfast but didn't want us to eat in the kitchen tonight. A while ago, I'd bought a second-hand folding gateleg table for just such an occasion, along with four stacking chairs, and I'd hauled them out from the understairs cupboard and set them up in the sitting room.

'Great idea, Mum,' Faye said approvingly, as she and Logan took their places. 'Can I smell roast dinner?'

'You can,' I said. 'You couldn't come on Sunday so I thought I'd push the boat out tonight instead.'

'I thought you said your mum couldn't cook,' remarked Logan when his plate of roast lamb and vegetables was put in front of him.

He looked up at me and grinned. 'Obviously, I wasn't meant to believe that. I didn't, of course. This looks wonderful.'

I laughed. 'Oh, I think you were meant to believe it, but I'd hold back on the praise until you've tasted it if I were you.'

Faye stabbed a crispy golden roast potato. 'What I *actually* said was that cooking made you nervous, not that you weren't any good at it.'

I realised the truth of this – it was Tony who had watched over me with a critical eye, making me doubt my capabilities, in cooking, in most things really. I'd never noticed in the early years, or if I had, I didn't mind. Sometimes Faye was more astute than I gave her credit for.

'Maybe,' I said, not wanting to bring Tony into the conversation. 'I'm still better off not offering cooked breakfasts, though, just in case.'

'It's a matter of confidence, isn't it?' Faye said, reaching for the mint sauce. 'Or lack of.'

'Yes, all right, Faye.' I smiled and raised my eyes.

I'd had enough of this topic. Instead, I asked about the cottage, and how the two of them found living in the centre of the village.

'I don't care where I live as long Faye's with me,' Logan said.

He gave her a full-on smile, then swiftly turned his gaze on me, as if he wanted to test my reaction. I'd sensed this about him before, his overt proprietorial manner with my daughter when he was in my company.

Pippa's revelation simmered at the back of my mind. Was Logan really sleeping with somebody else while acting the part of the devoted boyfriend? I watched him slyly, trying to discern the slightest nuance of behaviour that might point to his betrayal, and found nothing. I'd already decided not to say anything to Faye. I couldn't watch her crumble again, I just couldn't.

'We love our little cottage,' Faye said now. 'It's just the best, having a home of our own. Well, rented off Logan's mate, but ours for now.'

'I'll have to come and see it some time,' I said, smiling.

'Of course. Any time,' Logan said, and kissed Faye on the cheek, apropos of nothing at all as far as I could tell.

I brought in the lemon meringue pie – shop bought, I know my limitations – then Faye helped me make coffee, and we moved to the comfortable seats.

Logan offered to help me fold away the table and chairs, almost springing up from the sofa in his eagerness. When I politely declined his help, telling him I'd do it in the morning, he seemed displeased. He narrowed his eyes at me, and I felt a flash of déjà vu I couldn't quite catch hold of, as if there was something I should see or know, just beyond my reach.

TWENTY-NINE
BRIONY

1986

'Why didn't you tell me before?' Samantha demanded, her face a picture of outrage.

It was Sunday afternoon, and the two of us were sitting beneath the Kissing Tree. We'd been talking about Molly again, wondering for the millionth time where she was, and why she hadn't been in touch, when suddenly the words came out of my mouth of their own accord and I'd described how Jeremy lured me into the old surgery, and what had taken place there. But, typical of me, I'd overlaid the story with a heavy quilt of doubt that anything awful had actually happened.

'I'm not even sure he meant to touch me.' I cupped my breast automatically. 'It could have been accidental.'

'His hands shouldn't have been anywhere near you in the first place!' Samantha said. 'There shouldn't be any room for doubt.'

'I know. But I didn't want you to think I was a wimp and couldn't stand up for myself. That's why I didn't tell you.'

'I would *never* think that. Jeremy's a weirdo, we've always known that. He never gets the message, does he?'

'That's one way of putting it,' I said. 'But even if he does, it makes no difference. He sees me as an easy target for his tormenting. It's something I have to live with.'

'Is it?' Samantha gave me a sideways look. 'Really?'

'Yes, if I want to stay at Summerdene. Any trouble like that and Alice would send me away. My life's here now, until after sixth form, anyway. I'm not going to Australia even if Dad would let me, and anyway, why should I change my life and lose my friends, just because of *him*?'

'That's true,' Samantha said, nodding firmly. 'I've already lost one friend. I don't want to lose you as well. My life would be *totally* unbearable.'

Samantha drew a hand across her brow. I had to smile. She looked so stricken, her voice expansive with drama. That was one reason I'd not said anything before. Samantha never owned up to worrying about anything, and yet I knew she did. There was nothing she could do to help, anyway.

'Have you told anyone else what happened?' Samantha asked.

'No. I couldn't tell Alice, could I? She's his mother. She wouldn't believe me, and even if she did, she'd be mortified. I couldn't do that to her. I thought I might tell Dr Roberts. I went to see him to get my eczema meds and I nearly said something then, but I couldn't do it. I couldn't face all the trouble that would come afterwards. Anyway, he might have thought it was my fault.'

'Yeah, I can see how that might go.' Samantha flounced her shoulders. 'Oh, I wish there was something we could *do* to that bloody little perv! Make him suffer some awful fate. Castration would be top of my list,' Samantha said, her eyes blazing.

'Me too,' I said, pretending to consider this seriously. 'Poison might be easier. Or drowning. Or...'

'...paying a hit man,' Samantha said. 'I bet there's one in the village, if we knew where to look.'

'Yeah, maybe there's a card in the post office window, advertising that service,' I said, my tone mock-serious.

'I'll look when I go in for chewing gum,' Samantha said, playing along.

I had a vision of the two of us knocking on the door of some remote cottage in the dead of night with pockets full of cash.

'Life doesn't run like clockwork,' I said, properly serious now. 'If you expect it to, you're heading for a shedload of disappointment.'

Samantha looked at me in surprise. 'That's a bit deep, Bri.'

'Well, it's true. Take the Molly thing, for a start. People aren't always what they seem, don't act the way you think they should.'

Samantha made a snorting sound. 'She certainly didn't. We didn't know her as well as we thought. That's what you're saying.'

I nodded, as Molly's disappearance claimed pole position in my mind; it was never far from it. I was afraid for her, more afraid than I had been before in the face of no information whatsoever, no clues at all as to where she might be. I tortured myself daily with the idea of her being out in the world somewhere, alone and scared, having run away over some disaster; about kidnap, even murder – all of which would have come to light by now but I took no comfort from that. Terrible crimes might be kept under wraps if the investigations could be compromised otherwise. Teenagers ran away from home all the time, for all sorts of reasons, and dreadful things happened to them as a result.

Whatever it was, it can't have been nothing. Why else would Molly's family have battened down the proverbial hatches and her mother refused to speak to us?

Would we ever have the answers we needed?

My thoughts returned to Jeremy. He had seemed perfectly ordinary and harmless, if somewhat bossy and high-handed, when I'd first arrived at Summerdene – until his dark side began to seep through the cracks in his outwardly congenial appearance.

'I believe people get their comeuppance, in the end,' I said. Then, seeing Samantha's puzzled frown, 'Jeremy, I mean, not Molly. Molly's okay, deep down. We couldn't have got her that wrong. I'm sure she would have come and said goodbye to us, if she'd had the chance. Maybe she didn't want to say goodbye, couldn't handle it. But that evil little toad, well, he'd better watch out, that's all.'

I had no idea what I meant by that; I wished I did.

We sat back against the tree trunk, silent for a while, deep in thought. A twig fell from above, circling as it fell to land by my feet, dislodged by a bird or squirrel, probably. And then I heard a crunching noise, like footsteps; not loud, but in the quiet of the woods, unmistakable. I glanced at Samantha but she was deep in thought and didn't seem to have noticed anything.

I hoped we weren't about to be disturbed. I scanned the perimeter of the clearing for signs of movement and saw none. But there was something intangible about the stillness of the trees and undergrowth, as if the air around them had shifted.

Jeremy was in a strange mood when I arrived home later, even stranger than usual. He seemed not only angry with me – his default, these days – but with his mother as well. He snapped at Alice at the dinner table, over nothing at all as far as I could make out, which she gamely ignored in her inimitable way, making me wonder, not for the first time, why she was always so easy on him. After the meal, when she asked him to do the washing up, not that she should have had to ask, he carried the dirty crocks to the kitchen with a heavy sigh and an even heavier tread, despite the bare feet.

I stole at look at Alice but if she'd noticed anything amiss, her face gave nothing away.

'That was lovely,' I told her, in my small attempt to make up for Jeremy's grumpiness. 'Roast lamb's my favourite.'

Alice smiled. 'Yes, it was a good cut, nice and tender. You can always rely on our butcher.'

Hearing the noise of heavy-handed crockery washing coming from the kitchen, I felt I ought to go and help, for Alice's sake. I got up from the table, picked up the mint sauce jug and went through.

Jeremy turned from the sink and gave me a venomous look. What I'd done to annoy him today was anyone's guess. His ill temper was obviously directed at me; Alice had just caught some of the fallout. Deciding it was best to ignore him – anyone who could fathom what went on in Jeremy's head must be some kind of genius psychologist – I picked up the tea towel and began to dry the cutlery he'd angrily fished from the washing-up water and crashed onto the draining board.

We worked together in this haphazard way for five minutes, Jeremy's hands flailing about in the sink, splashing water in all directions, while I tried in vain to keep up the flow of carelessly washed china that found its way onto the corrugated metal.

Eventually, he gave a big, hopeless sigh.

'If you must get under my feet, the least you can do is keep up,' he snarled.

'*Shut up*,' I hissed under my breath, fearful of Alice overhearing. 'Just shut up, will you?'

He turned, fixing me with a look that was both ice and fire. 'Who are you telling to shut up? You want to watch it or you'll find yourself out on your ear, out of this house. What would become of you then, I wonder?' He paused. 'Oh yes, you'd be homeless, like the little misfit that you are. The cuckoo in the nest.'

This was new. Oh, I knew what Jeremy thought of me, and thought of his mother for having the gall to take me in, he'd made no secret of that. But saying the words aloud was a first, and to my shame, I felt my face heat up as tears pricked the backs of my eyelids. I wouldn't normally have reacted like that but I was tired and stressed, and my period was due.

I gulped in air. It sounded like a kind of sob. 'Do you want me to tell Alice how you treat me, the nasty things you say? Because I will, you know.'

A hollow threat, and Jeremy knew it. His lips curled in a sardonic half smile, half sneer.

'Ha, as if my mother would ever believe you.' Yanking out the plug from the sink, he jabbed a finger towards me. 'Tell what lies you like, Briony. It makes no difference to me. Oh, let me see. You've already done that, haven't you? A nice way to behave, I must say. Alice would definitely chuck you out if she found out you'd been spreading stories about me, little tell-tale you are.'

'I haven't...'

I stopped. Had Samantha and I been alone in the woods this afternoon, or had the noises I'd heard come from Jeremy? Had he been hiding, sneakily listening to our conversation? It wasn't beyond him, by any means. Nothing was beyond him; I'd begun to realise that.

He was drying his hands. I couldn't let him have the last word, I just couldn't.

I rounded on him as he reached the door. 'You call me the cuckoo but isn't it time you started being a grown-up and fled the nest yourself?'

Jeremy thrust his face towards me. His voice became a hiss. 'Oh, I won't be going anywhere until it suits me. I'll be staying put to keep an eye on you. You might have lost... other people... but you won't be losing me in a hurry. Oh no.'

Lost other people? What had he meant by that? It seemed all out of context...

My heart jumped. My brain took an even bigger leap.

'Who are you talking about? Who have I lost? Oh my God, Jeremy. Are you talking about Molly? Have you done something to her?'

'*Molly?*' He almost spat the name. 'Who's she? I don't know anyone called Molly. What could I have done? You're delusional. I always knew it.'

He slammed out of the kitchen.

My legs seemed about to give way. I hung on to the back of a chair for support. Had I linked Jeremy to Molly's disappearance, and actually voiced the words? Had I really thought he was talking about Molly being 'lost', or had the stress of the argument and my worry over my missing friend finally caught up with me and pitched me closer to the edge of reason?

I listened for Jeremy's tread on the staircase. When I heard it, I took several deep breaths, left the kitchen and went to the sitting room. I needed to be away from my own thoughts, if that was possible. I needed Alice, and calm.

She looked up as I entered the room. 'Thank you for helping,' she said levelly. If she'd caught any of the argument, she wasn't letting on. 'It wouldn't have hurt my son to have done the lot on his own, though.'

She smiled indulgently, as if she was talking about a recalcitrant teenager, which was exactly how he acted. I could hear him banging about upstairs, still in a fury. No doubt Alice could, too, but she said nothing.

She waved at the chair. 'Sit down, dear. Unless you're going out?'

'No, not tonight. Shall I make tea?'

'Yes, please, if you would.'

Alice had put the TV on by the time I returned with the tea, and we sat in companionable silence while Paul Daniels hosted a game show. I had some reading to do for school, and after a while I went upstairs to find the book. While I was in my room, I heard Jeremy going downstairs. I listened and waited, not wanting to bump into him, and then I heard him telling his mother he was going for a run.

'Be careful, then. It'll be dark soon,' I heard Alice say.

I rooted among the ever-growing pile of books I had for English Lit. Finding the one I needed, I went to the window and looked out before I went downstairs. The light was already fading fast, and a pinkish glow streaked the sky above the dark hummocks of the hills. I looked along the lane towards the farm and there was Jeremy, not running, not even walking. He was just standing there beneath a tree, statue-still, a tall, black shape hardly visible against the shadow, and I began to wonder if he ever did go running – I'd never witnessed it. Or was it an excuse to cover up what he'd really been doing?

THIRTY
BRIONY

2022

One morning, I fancied a walk to the village and I texted Faye to ask if she wanted to meet me for coffee. I hadn't seen her since she and Logan came for dinner last week. Presumably she hadn't had time to make an early morning visit, but that was fine. Faye was working, and she worked hard. She also had Logan to consider now, and I had to respect that.

Faye texted back straight away, telling me she'd see me in the café at eleven. Having finished my errands, I arrived ten minutes early, bagged a window table in the almost full café and awaited Faye's arrival. While I waited, I thought about what Pippa had said about Logan, again questioning my decision not to pass the news on to Faye.

Was that the right thing to do? I wasn't so sure now. I was her mother, after all. Adult though she was, it was still my job to protect her in any way I could. But Faye might not see it that way, and I'd hate us to fall out over what may well be idle gossip.

I was even less sure by the time she had greeted me with a

kiss on the cheek and taken her seat. She always seemed happy and full of life, especially since she'd met Logan, but this morning there was a kind of pent-up energy about her, and a rosy glow to her normally pale complexion.

'Shall we have cake?' I said, my eyes flicking towards the delectable display in the glass case on the counter. The café did the best coffee and walnut cake I'd ever tasted.

'I'm already spilling out of my jeans,' Faye said doubtfully, laying a hand on her almost concave midriff where a muffin top would be, if she had one.

'My treat. One piece isn't going to ruin your figure.'

'No, it's not, is it? Logan would say that, too. Go on, then. I'll have some if it makes you happy,' Faye said.

Oh well, as long as we have Logan's approval, that's okay, I thought, uncharitably. Somehow, the shine had been rubbed off our little mother-daughter tête-à-tête, although I wasn't sure why.

'How is Logan, by the way?' I asked, when our coffee and cake had arrived.

'Same as he was when you saw him last week.' Faye grinned.

'Ah, well, that's good. He seems... you both seem very settled.'

'After such a short time, you mean.' Faye widened her eyes at me.

'Maybe.' I couldn't deny it. There'd be no point anyway. Faye would see straight through me. 'It seems to be working out for you, and I'm pleased about that, for your sake. After what you went through with Nick, well...'

'Yeah, I know, Mum, and I know what I'm doing, honestly.'

Faye was obviously aware I still needed convincing. Perhaps she was trying to convince herself, too. I thought of Pippa and the news she'd been so eager to share with me, and I suddenly felt breathless and hot. Had I been right to withhold something that big, or potentially so?

I looked across at Faye as the words began to form themselves in my brain, saw her private smile as she toyed with her cake fork. She looked up, the fork still in her hand. And that was when I saw the ring. It had three tiny white stones, sparkly enough to be diamonds, set in gold shoulders on a narrow gold band. It was on her right hand, but still my stomach wavered a little.

'Oh, is that new? I've not seen you wear it before,' I said. 'It's so pretty.'

'I wondered if you'd notice.' Faye smiled, put the cake fork down and held out her hand for my inspection. 'Logan bought it for me in an antique jewellers' when we were in Cheltenham. Gorgeous, isn't it?'

'Are those diamonds?'

'Yep, they are.' The secret smile was back, as if she couldn't rein it in. 'I didn't want him to spend that much but he insisted. Sweet, isn't it?'

Sweet. Right. 'Faye...'

She laughed. 'Don't worry, Mum. It's not an engagement ring. Wrong hand, anyway. It's a sort of pre-engagement ring, a token of our love. Like, we may do it some time, for real.'

Somehow, I'd gone off coffee and walnut cake. I pushed aside my plate with some of the cake left. Faye had moved in with Logan after an indecently short amount of time, and now this. A 'pre-engagement' ring. I took a deep breath. If I didn't share my concerns with her, I'd be doing my daughter a disservice.

'Mum, what is it?' Faye peered across at me. 'You don't approve, do you? I just wish you could see how right Logan is for me, and me for him. Couldn't you try, just a bit?'

'Faye, don't,' I said. 'Don't get all narky. It's not that I don't *approve*. It's your life, not mine, and you know I've got your best interests at heart, always.'

Faye's expression softened. 'I know. Sorry. You were going to say something, though, I could tell. What was it? Go on, you might as well say it.'

I clasped my hands together, resting them on the table in front of me, leaning in to avoid being overheard by people at nearby tables.

'I heard a rumour about Logan. I heard that he was... *close* to somebody, another woman. Closer than he should be for someone who's in a relationship.'

I tried to keep my voice level, wringing the emotion out of it. But Faye looked appalled, as well she might.

'Who? What woman? Mum, you shouldn't listen to rumours. This is a small village. It runs on gossip. Who's spreading that sort of nonsense around?'

'Just somebody I know,' I said. 'It doesn't matter who.' I didn't want to drop Pippa in it. 'Faye, he's been seen, several times, being very friendly with a woman. It seems to be common knowledge that he's sleeping with her.'

I felt the sharp edge of Faye's pain as if it was my own. But it was no use fudging the issue, not now I'd come this far.

Faye's face was a study in fury and disbelief. I reached for her hand. She allowed the merest touch before she snatched it away.

'No. Logan isn't out of the house long enough for anything to be going on. We're together practically the whole time. He loves me. He'd never cheat on me, *never*.'

'Darling, I'm so sorry. I wasn't going to tell you but I thought you had the right to know what was being said, even if it isn't true. But if there's the slightest shadow of a doubt... Please, Faye, just think...'

'No,' Faye repeated. 'You want this to go wrong, don't you?

You've been down on Logan right from the start, and now you're trying to split us up by repeating this… this *crap*!'

I began to refute her declaration that I'd never liked Logan. Except, of course, she was spot on. I had tried so hard to take him to my heart, because Faye loved him, but somehow it always refused to gel.

Did I believe what Pippa had said, and what, apparently, other people were saying about him? Truthfully, I had no idea what to believe.

'I'm so sorry,' I said again. 'I hate this as much as you do. But I couldn't keep it to myself. Secrets like that fester and do more damage than if they'd been shared. Faye…'

But Faye had stopped listening. She was up on her feet, shoving her chair back from the table, gathering up her bag, and heading right for the door. I stared after her, aware that other customers were doing the same. They could go to hell. I didn't care what they'd seen or heard. My daughter was the only one who mattered.

Grabbing my own bag from the chair, I walked up to the counter with as much dignity as I could muster, paid the bill and headed out into the street. I scanned the street, both ways, both sides. But Faye had gone.

THIRTY-ONE
BRIONY

1986

One morning, Alice appeared on the landing as I was coming out of the bathroom.

'I just need a word, Briony,' she said. 'I know you're off to work. It won't take a minute.'

It was Saturday and I was due at Pink's at nine but I'd left plenty of time to get ready and grab a quick breakfast.

'Of course,' I said, wondering what it was that couldn't wait until I was downstairs.

Alice followed me to my room, crossed to the window and perched on the sill, her face serious. 'I've had a bit of bad news. My cousin Pamela passed away yesterday. Her neighbour rang me last night. She was working her way through the list, apparently.' Alice gave a little smile. 'Grim job but someone's got to do it.'

I'd heard the phone ring around ten, and Alice answering.

'Oh no, Alice. I'm so sorry. Were you close?'

'Not really, not since we were children.' Alice smiled sadly.

'But I've got so few relatives left, and those still around are pretty ancient. I'd like to go to the funeral. It's in Worthing.'

'Well then, of course you should go.'

'Thank you, Briony,' Alice said, sounding almost relieved, as if she'd needed my permission. 'It's such a long train journey, so I thought I'd stop over for a couple of nights and catch up with some old friends from where I used to live at the same time. You don't mind, do you?'

I went to the wardrobe, took out my blue puff-sleeved dress and laid it on the bed, along with some clean underwear, then picked up the brush from the dressing table and began brushing my hair, with one eye on the alarm clock.

'Why would I mind? I'll be okay.'

Alice's gaze wandered distractedly about the room before returning to me, her forehead creased with concern. I was puzzled for a moment, until I realised what she was thinking. She was worried about leaving me alone in the house with Jeremy, whose moodiness hadn't improved much, if at all. Alice had noticed – she couldn't have failed to. I was already having misgivings myself but if I kept out of his way as much as possible, I could cope. I had to, for Alice's sake. I couldn't stop her from attending her cousin's funeral and wouldn't have wanted to.

Alice got up from the sill and stood in the middle of the room, her hands clasped together in front of her.

'I was thinking you might like to ask a friend to stay while I'm gone. Samantha, perhaps? Would you like that? It would be company for you. Well, apart from Mr Unsociable.' She raised her eyes and gave a little laugh.

Again, I wondered how much Alice knew about Jeremy and the way he acted with me. He was always careful to keep his snide comments and sneering contempt for when his mother was out of earshot, but she must have picked up on the strained relationship that existed between us. Only a fool could have missed it, and Alice was no fool.

'I'd love to,' I said. 'I'll ask Samantha. Thanks.'

It would be fun to have her to stay. Between the two of us, we could keep the creep at bay. I would have to warn Samantha not to wander about the house half-dressed, especially since Jeremy had hinted that he fancied her. I'd never told her, and was glad I hadn't now. The last thing I needed was Samantha freaking out and turning down Alice's invitation.

I hadn't told her about the argument I'd had with him either, and didn't plan to. I'd already pushed his weird comment about my having 'lost' people out of my mind, and my wild leap to the conclusion that he'd been referring to Molly. Of course he hadn't meant her. He'd been lashing out, saying any old thing that came into his head. My idea that Jeremy was somehow connected to Molly's disappearance had been way off beam. It was only my concern for her safety and my fervent wish to see Jeremy brought down in some way that had made me say that.

It wasn't true, of course, that he didn't know anyone called Molly. He knew the names of my two best friends well enough. But he wasn't giving me an inch, hence the lie.

'Well, that's settled then. I'll leave you to get on,' Alice said, sounding brighter.

She left the room, leaving me to finish getting ready for work whilst marvelling at my godmother's forethought. It was a shade unusual. Normally, Alice blustered through life, taking it day by day and making light of any perceived woe, but now I understood how much she cared for me and I silently thanked my father for posting me to Summerdene like a parcel he couldn't wait to get shot of, whatever his motives at the time.

Far from freaking out, Samantha was ecstatic at the news of her proposed visit. I'd planned to call at her house after work, but I didn't need to because she turned up at the shop halfway through the morning with her mum's shopping list.

'This is brilliant, Bri!' she said, dropping the wire basket to the floor and performing a skip and a jump, perilously close to the teetering displays of Heinz baked beans and Bird's custard powder.

'It's nothing to get that excited about,' I said. 'It'll be a laugh, though.'

I didn't say how grateful I was not to have to spend my evenings – and nights – incarcerated at Summerdene with only Jeremy's dubious company.

'Yes it is! Don't you see what this means?' Samantha did a twirl. I launched myself forward and pulled her away by the elbow from the stacked tins while Mr Pink eyed us from behind the till.

'What? What does it mean?'

'It means we can fix the creep, do something awful to him he'll never, ever forget. This, my dear Briony, is payback time. It's a Heaven-sent opportunity!' Samantha tapped the side of her nose.

'But...' My mind somersaulted, along with my gut.

Whatever fate awaited Jeremy at the hands of Samantha and, by the sound of it, mine too, could only make things worse. I'd said before that Jeremy would get his comeuppance in the end – because I was still naïve enough to believe that was how the world worked, not because of some cock-eyed plan Samantha had cooked up.

'*But* nothing. I don't know what we'll do yet,' she said, 'but we'll come up with something. Something that will make him understand he can't treat you the way he has and get away with it.'

I was already warming to the idea; seeing the fire in Samantha's eyes, I couldn't help it. After all, on my own I was pretty helpless against Jeremy, but the two of us working together, well, that was a different story entirely. Samantha had a point, a very good point...

'I've got to get on,' I whispered. 'There's a queue building up.'

'We'll get together in a day or so and make a plan. Meanwhile, start thinking, *hard*, Bri, and I will, too.' Samantha scooped up her wire basket and skipped off along the aisle.

Make a plan we did, while sitting on cushions of moss beneath the Kissing Tree, the special place where all our great ideas took shape.

The basic idea, the bones of the thing, came from Samantha – of the two of us she was the most daring and probably the most inventive – but I wasn't far behind. We couldn't nail down every last detail because so much depended on the day itself, but we'd make it up as we went along, we said. And we would make it work, whatever; we had to.

I couldn't think about the outcome and how it might impact on me, once Samantha had trundled off home and left me at Jeremy's mercy. It was too big, too unknown. But I would face that when it came to it. My hopes for the success of the plan, and my heightened state of heady excitement in the days leading up to it were enough to carry me through, for now.

THIRTY-TWO

BRIONY

2022

It was five long days since that last disastrous meeting with Faye. I'd kept quiet for a day and a half then, unable to stand the silence between us any longer, I'd tried twice to call her mobile but she refused to take the call. I messaged and got no reply to that either. I drew the line at going round to Candle Street. Painful though it was, I had to respect her wish not to have any contact with me. Neither did I relish the idea of seeing Logan and he definitely wouldn't want to see me if Faye had confronted him with Pippa's story.

I thought about phoning Tony but I knew he would only remind me of his reservations about Logan before he blithely asserted that Faye would sort herself out, and I should leave her to get on with it. He wouldn't understand how guilty I felt at having caused our daughter more heartache, and why I needed to make it right with her. Instead, I walked along to Kestrels one early evening, praying Marcus would be at home. I needed to see a friendly face.

His car was in its usual spot and he answered the door

promptly, greeting me with delighted surprise. I hadn't seen him for over a week; he'd been involved in an induction programme for overseas students starting university and the activities had spilled over into the evenings.

'Sorry to turn up like this,' I said, as he ushered me into the cottage. 'I know you've been busy.'

'I was, but I've got a bit of time now before we're into Freshers' Week. I was about to phone to ask if you fancied dinner out one night, and now here you are.'

We leaned into a friendly but slightly awkward hug in the hallway. When we broke apart, he looked closely at me.

'I see somebody who could do with a drink,' he said, leading me through to the kitchen and opening the fridge.

'You're having your meal and I'm disturbing you,' I eyed the pan of rice and vegetables on the stove.

'I've eaten. I always make enough to last. It saves reinventing the wheel.' Marcus gave me a twinkly smile and handed me a glass of white wine. 'Oh, unless you'd like some? It's passably tasty.'

I smiled. 'I'm sure it is. But no, I'm good, thanks.'

We took our drinks through to the sitting room. The low evening sun bathed the room in soft, golden light and I settled into an armchair and thought again how delightfully cosy the cottage was.

'It seems silly now,' I said, after Marcus had asked me what was wrong and I'd told him about Pippa's disclosure, and how I'd passed this on to Faye.

'She's a grown woman.' I gave a little sigh. 'She's got her own life and I can't expect her to check in with me every five minutes, nor would I want her to.'

Marcus leaned in from his position on the sofa. 'It doesn't sound silly to me. She's blanking you, and that must be upsetting.'

'It is. How can I make her see I was only telling her for her own good? Okay, I made a mistake there. At least, I think I did. But if she's not talking to me or answering my messages, where do I go from here?'

'I think you have to leave her alone, Briony, just for now,' Marcus said kindly. 'Wait for her to come back to you, because she will. You two are close. She won't be able to stay away for long.'

I drank some more wine, already feeling better.

'It might take a while, I guess,' I said, 'but you're right. It's up to Faye, isn't it? She knows where I am and I'm here whenever she needs me, however this thing with Logan turns out. That's my biggest worry, of course. It's not all about me. If he is cheating on her, I don't know how she'll cope. She's so hung up on him.'

'If it does turn out to be true, it's better she finds out now than months down the line,' Marcus said. 'She'll be okay.'

We sat in thoughtful silence for a moment. Then, Marcus smiled regretfully.

'Let-downs are a necessary part of life, are they not?' he said.

'Oh, I'm sorry, Marcus. This is reminding you of Hannah, isn't it?'

'No, not at all. I don't have any feelings left in that direction. I thought you knew that?'

He sounded slightly cross, and I wanted to bite back my question. But I didn't know Marcus that well yet. I wasn't privy to his innermost thoughts. His sharpness had confused me, made me wonder what, or rather who, we were talking about here.

'I'm sorry, I was being insensitive.' I finished my wine, set the glass down on the side table and made to stand up. 'Thanks for listening, and for being the voice of reason. But I should go now.'

'Please don't,' Marcus said quickly. 'Sit down. I'll get you a refill. And, Briony...'

'What?'

'Stop apologising. That's the third time since you got here. And as for being insensitive, I doubt you could if you tried.'

I thought again about my daughter and our conversation in the café, before she upped and left in a huff.

'I don't need to try to be insensitive. The words just fly out of my mouth,' I said gloomily.

Marcus laughed, and so did I. It felt so good to be in his company. I really didn't want to leave, and found myself back in my seat, wondering at my complete lack of resolve and discipline.

I declined Marcus's offer of more wine so he made coffee instead and we sat and talked until the sun dipped below the tree tops and blue shadows crept across the walls.

When I arrived home, I saw a missed call on my phone from Faye. It had come through ten minutes previously. Grabbing the phone from the kitchen table, I returned the call with my heart in my mouth in case I wouldn't like what I was about to hear.

She picked up immediately.

'Oh good, you're there,' she said brightly, as if she hadn't been blanking me at all. Was there an over-brightness to her tone? I may have imagined that.

'Hello to you, too. I was... just outside.' I smiled into the half light. Best not to mention Marcus. I went over and switched on the overhead light, then sat down at the kitchen table.

'Mum, I'm sorry for running out on you at the café,' Faye continued. 'It was childish but you gave me a shock. I did mean to call you back. It was just that...'

'It's okay,' I said.

Faye had come back to me. It was all that mattered. But if

she was waiting for me to apologise for telling her what Pippa
had told me, she'd be disappointed. Mistaken or not, my inten-
tions had been good.

'Yes, well, anyway,' Faye continued. 'I thought I'd come over
tomorrow morning, help with the breakfasts. I could stay for a
while after, if that's cool with you, Mum?'

'Of course it is.' My shoulders sagged with relief, and love
for my daughter. 'What about work, though?'

'It's fine. I'll catch up with that later,' Faye said airily.

'See you in the morning, then.'

A pause, then, 'Yes. Look, Mum, I want to see you and be at
Summerdene but there's one thing. Can we not mention the...
what you told me, the gossip, about Logan? I really don't want
to talk about it.'

'Okay,' I said, feeling my shoulders tense. 'I won't mention it
if that's what you want. But please just tell me, did you speak to
Logan about it? I'm not passing judgement here, Faye. I need to
know if everything's all right, that's all.'

I was entitled to ask, surely. Faye didn't get to call all the
shots, and I had a vested interest in her welfare.

'No, Mum, I didn't. Why would I spoil what we've got for
the sake of a bit of idle village gossip? Whoever you heard it
from must be a nasty troublemaker, that's all I can say, and if
you hear it again, you need to nip it in the bud.'

I wavered on the verge of a retort but pulled it back. Faye
could be right, but I still didn't believe Pippa would have said a
word if she hadn't been convinced there was some truth in the
story.

'See you tomorrow,' I said briskly. 'Sleep tight.'

Faye duly arrived around half past eight, and I was glad Pippa
had the day off. Faye, of course, had no idea she was the source

of the information but I felt easier, knowing the two of them wouldn't be coming face to face today.

Faye and I worked in tandem, replenishing breakfast dishes, making teas and coffees, and chatting to the guests as we went along. It was like old times; we made a good team. By the time the guests had set off on their respective jaunts and we'd cleared up, I'd put the thorny matter of Logan's possible transgression firmly to the back of my mind.

It was a bright, sunny morning but a brisk wind was chasing the clouds across an acid blue sky and it wasn't warm enough to sit in the garden, so we took our coffee and leftover pastries through to the sitting room. We'd no sooner relaxed into casual chat when Faye took out her phone and moved from the armchair to sit beside me on the sofa.

'Look at this, Mum,' she said, scrolling and clicking to reveal a patchwork of pictures.

I saw mountains clothed in exotic greenery beneath cerulean skies, spectacular waterfalls, a table laid for two on a terrace with a fiery sunset in the background, and white sand fringed with palm trees, verging a turquoise sea.

'And this.' Faye scrolled further down, revealing the interior of a hotel room with a panoramic view of beach and sea, and a many-cushioned bed that could sleep five, should there ever be the need.

'Gorgeous,' I said. 'Where is this?'

'St Lucia.'

I laughed. 'We can dream.'

'A dream come true.' Faye grinned. 'We're going, Logan and I. It's all booked.'

She raised her chin, regarding me with something like triumph on her face. I hated to think of it as a *so there* look – that wasn't Faye's style. Or it never used to be. I didn't know what to think now, what to say about this, about any of it, any more.

'I know, it's amazing, isn't it?' she said dreamily, misinterpreting my silence.

'Amazing... It'll be very expensive. Can you afford it?' I hadn't had a chance to check the price but I didn't need to.

'This is the thing, Mum. I said the same, and I told him we should save up and go next year. But Logan said he didn't want to wait, and he's insisting he pays. He wants to treat me to a romantic holiday, and I wasn't to even think of chipping in.'

Really? It sounded too good to be true. But what did I know?

Faye lapsed into pensive silence. Then, 'Logan's not said much about his family, but maybe he gets an allowance or something, to top up what he earns from his writing. The only time I asked about his background, he brushed it off and changed the subject. Like it's some great mystery.' She brightened. 'Not everyone likes sharing stuff like that, do they? He'll tell me in his own time.'

'Well, I hope he does,' I said. 'You two should be talking, not keeping secrets.'

'It's not a *secret*, Mum. He... we just haven't got round to discussing that kind of thing yet. Logan must have his reasons.'

Reasons Faye would obviously like to have known – I could see it in her face. She'd never admit as much to me, though.

I realised I was pouring cold water on her excitement about the holiday. I put my arm around her and gave her shoulder a squeeze, trying to be the mother she deserved.

'Wow, who wouldn't love a trip to St Lucia? You'll have a fab time. Logan must think the world of you.'

First a diamond ring, then a dream holiday. My head spun with suspicion, confusion, and above all, concern for my daughter.

But perhaps there was no need. Perhaps Logan really was the genuine article. Without any real evidence to the contrary, I decided to run with that. I would have a gentle word with Pippa later, warn her not to repeat stories that could cause so much hurt.

I looked out of the window. The trees in the lane were beginning to turn, the tips of the leaves showing red and gold. They were perfectly still; the wind seemed to have dropped.

'Let's walk down to the village,' I said. 'I'll sort out upstairs later. I'll treat you to lunch at the pub.' Then, because I thought I should, I added, 'Perhaps Logan would like to join us?'

'He's busy with work so it'll just be the two of us. Another time, though?' Faye said.

'Another time, yes.'

Later that afternoon, I walked along Back Lane, past the woods, to the farm and climbed over a stile to follow the public footpath that meandered past the backs of the barns and outhouses. I walked as far as the crest of the hill, then leaned on a gate and watched the ragged black shapes of the crows as they dived and swooped above the chocolatey furrows in a distant field. Faye would say I was turning into a proper country yokel, I thought, smiling to myself. Then I corrected myself; Faye wouldn't have a clue what a yokel was, let alone accuse me of turning into one.

As I wandered home, my senses soothed by the landscape and the earthy scent of leaf mould and newly turned soil, I felt my limbs loosen as a quiet peace settled around me. As I reached Summerdene and walked up to the front door, my mobile jangled across the silence.

I pulled it from my pocket, smiling again as Marcus's name came up.

'Hi,' I said, tucking the phone under my chin and inserting my key in the door lock.

I imagined he was calling about our night out. We hadn't actually made arrangements when I'd gone to his house.

'Briony. Hi, it's me.' The words were clipped in a way I didn't recognise.

'Hello, you,' I said, entering the hallway. 'Where did you fancy going for dinner? What night? Any suits me...'

'Ah, I wasn't... Never mind.' I heard Marcus take in breath. 'We need to talk, Briony. I need to talk to you.'

'Do you? Oh, okay.' That was unexpected. I waited.

'Yes.' I sensed Marcus nodding, the jet twists of his curls bobbing. 'I'll pick you up in the car Sunday morning, elevenish, if that's convenient? We'll have coffee out.'

'Yes, sounds good,' I said.

I wanted to know more, of course I did. In fact, I was burning with curiosity, and not a little anxiety. But more wasn't forthcoming, because Marcus had cut the call with a mild thank you and I was left to wonder, and worry, for the next three days.

THIRTY-THREE

BRIONY

1986

'Aren't I sleeping in your room?'

Samantha followed me upstairs, lugging her bulging sports bag, and stood in the doorway as I opened the door to one of the spare bedrooms.

'Why would you when you can have a whole room to yourself? This one's nice. Alice got it all ready for you before she left for the funeral,' I said. 'Don't just stand there. Come in.' I beckoned with a sideways nod.

Samantha stayed right where she was. 'Doughnut! You've not thought this through, have you, Bri?'

She'd lost me now. 'How d'you mean?' I came back out onto the landing.

'We've got to stick together, in case it all goes pear-shaped and something happens in the night. If you-know-who starts prowling about after our guts, we'll be safer together. We can barricade the door if necessary.'

'You're enjoying this,' I said. 'Nothing's going to happen in the night. He won't be prowling anywhere. He'll be... well, you know where he'll be. Besides there's only one bed in my room, and it's mine. And before you suggest topping and tailing, it's not an option. Those feet aren't going anywhere near my face.'

We both looked down at Samantha's feet, in navy leather sandals, at the same time, then burst out laughing.

I supposed it would be safer, as well as more fun, to be in the same room, I conceded, disregarding midnight dramas.

'Okay. Leave it to me.'

I went along the landing, Samantha following, and opened the door to Alice's room. The largest of the five bedrooms, it had a small en suite bathroom, and the double bed had a high, old-fashioned wooden headboard carved with twining roses. I knelt on the floor beside the bed and reached underneath.

'Help me with this,' I said.

'What is it?' Samantha knelt down beside me.

'A folding camp bed,' I puffed, gripping the metal frame and pulling hard.

Samantha pulled with me, and finally the contraption emerged into the light in a plume of dust.

'You're kidding,' Samantha said.

'If you're sleeping in my room, this is the answer. It's antiquated but it's very comfy. So I'm told.'

We lugged the camp bed along to my room, Samantha moaning all the way that it weighed a ton. It took a while and a lot of effort to unfold the metal legs and straighten out the faded green canvas sling attached to the frame, but once we'd set up the thing up, given it a dust with an old petticoat of mine, and dressed it with the bedding from the room she was meant to have slept in, it looked usable.

Samantha plonked herself down on the camp bed, which was only six inches off the floor in its lowest point. 'It's not *too* bad.'

She shuffled from side to side, making the canvas swing, while I prayed she wouldn't move about too much in the night and split the canvas. Given its age, I couldn't vouch for its holding capabilities.

Sleeping arrangements settled, we went downstairs to see what Alice had left us for dinner. I'd told her I would make something, but I don't think she trusted me to rustle up a decent meal; I'd not exactly had a lot of practice.

Jeremy had come back from college around four, looked Samantha up and down in that pervy way of his but had not said a word to her. Now he'd gone out somewhere unspecified, having muttered something to me about being home around six thirty. I'd greeted this news with mixed feelings: Jeremy being out was always preferable to him being in. But tonight, Samantha and I needed him to be in so we could carry out our plan, although I was already beginning to wonder if we'd have the courage to see it through when push came to shove.

'Good old Alice,' Samantha said, as I opened the fridge and found a bowl of green salad, a dish of sliced cold ham and chicken, tomatoes, and a Tupperware box which turned out to contain potato salad, made by Alice, not shop-bought. Further inspection revealed a Pyrex casserole dish. I brought it out and lifted the lid.

'Some sort of mince thing with carrots,' I said. 'We can heat it up tomorrow and do jacket potatoes. Or shall we have this tonight and the salad tomorrow?'

'Let's have the salad tonight,' Samantha said. 'It looks less bother.'

I agreed. I put the casserole dish back in the fridge. Tonight we'd have our hands full with the plan; everything else needed to be kept as simple as possible.

Anxiety was already tugging at my insides. I wasn't the least bit hungry. But we had to eat, and Jeremy would expect a meal as soon as he walked in the door.

'He's in,' hissed Samantha, as we both heard the front door

close five minutes later. 'Shall I lay the table in the dining room, or are we eating out here?'

'Oh, definitely the dining room,' I said, commandeering my lost bravado. 'It is an occasion, after all.'

'The last supper,' Samantha stage-whispered, as Jeremy came into the kitchen, wearing his usual scowl.

'What're you two plotting?' he asked, without humour.

He smelled faintly beery.

'Who says we're plotting anything?' Samantha smiled sweetly and dipped her head coquettishly.

I hid a smile. It wasn't really funny, though. If Samantha was going to play that sort of game, I wasn't sure I'd be able to hold it together. I nudged her and frowned, while Jeremy's back was turned. She just laughed out loud, drawing his attention back to the two of us. Of course, I'd never told Samantha I thought Jeremy fancied her. But Samantha being Samantha, she probably knew anyway.

Jeremy took his place with us at the table, grudgingly, but with obvious relish at the meal set out before him. No 'thank you' but I'd not expected it. I knew he'd never lift a finger in his mother's absence, no more than he did when she was home, but that suited me fine. I'd rather he kept out of the way.

Samantha and I chatted about music and clothes and school – the usual stuff – with Jeremy adding the occasional meaning-less nod or grunt but mostly staying silent. At least Samantha had stopped the pretend flirting, which could have, in my opin-ion, only have led to trouble.

The salad finished, I stood up and collected our plates.

'Ice cream, Jeremy?' I asked, in my best this-is-normal voice.

'That all there is? Didn't she leave anything else?'

'There might be something else in the freezer,' I said, tempering the snap in my voice with a half smile. It wouldn't do to antagonise Jeremy this early. 'I didn't look. I could whip an Angel Delight if you want?'

'Ice cream'll do,' Jeremy said gruffly.

Samantha caught my eye and we exchanged meaningful looks before I trundled off to the kitchen, cut out three portions of Neapolitan ice cream from the box and lobbed them into pudding bowls.

I could hardly eat mine. Samantha, I noticed, had so far eaten everything on her plate and was now scraping the sides of her ice cream bowl. I envied her cool.

'Supposing he goes out again?' Samantha said, a while later, as the two of us dealt with the washing up.

'We talked about that,' I reminded her. 'We'll snaffle him before he leaves, if we can. Otherwise, we'll have to play it by ear. He's already been for a pint, though, if the smell was anything to go by. He looks pretty settled to me.'

The moment the meal was over, Jeremy had kicked off his shabby espadrilles and commandeered the sofa in the sitting room, having flicked the TV on to his programme of choice.

'Yeah, he looks dug in for the night,' Samantha agreed, as we tiptoed along the hall and peered through the half open door of the sitting room. 'So, what time do we...?'

'Soon as poss,' I said. My stomach was already swaying like the canvas on that camp bed. Samantha had chosen that moment to relinquish control of the situation and hand the decision-making to me, which wasn't helping my nerves one bit.

We tiptoed back along the hall. I remembered I still had the key to the old surgery in my pocket, and I put it back in the Blue Bird toffee tin on the kitchen shelf. Before Jeremy returned from college, we'd gone into the surgery and deposited four empty lemonade bottles, refilled with water, a packet of Golden Wonder crisps, a tube of Polo mints and a Crunchie bar. Nobody could accuse us of trying to starve him. There was also a roll of toilet paper and an old galvanised bucket, unearthed from the garden shed.

'Sheer luxury,' Samantha had said, as we'd locked the door behind us. 'Who could ask for more?'

And then we'd giggled, though a trifle nervously.

'Are we really doing this?' I said now. 'Shall we just leave it?'

'Bri! Of course we're doing it! The creep needs teaching a lesson. You're not chickening out now.'

'No, I'm not chickening out,' I said, holding my head high. 'So, go on, then. Do what you gotta do.'

'Right.'

Samantha touched hands with me, ran along the hall and upstairs. She was soon back, carrying an artist's sketchpad and a pencil case. Nodding at me to follow, she walked into the sitting room.

'Jeremy? Can I ask you something? It's a kind of favour, actually,' she said, her voice all sweetness and light.

He swivelled round on the sofa. 'Favour? What sort of favour?'

Samantha went right up to the sofa and leaned on its back. I stayed behind, out of the way.

'Briony told me there used to be a skeleton in the old surgery that your dad used for his doctoring.'

I immediately thought of tom cats and stifled a laugh.

'So? What about it?' Jeremy smiled – sort of smiled – because it was Samantha he was talking to, not me.

'Is it still there?' She leaned further over the sofa back. Immediately, her breasts filled more of her tight sweater than before.

'As far as I know, it is,' Jeremy said.

He knew very well the skeleton was still there, I thought. And he knew how he'd used it to scare me.

'Can I see it then? Only I really need to draw one for my art project, and the one in the school lab got broken. It's not the same, copying it from a book. You can't get the same effect, the shadows and stuff.'

'What, now?'

Jeremy looked disbelieving, as well he might. I crossed my fingers behind my back.

'Please, Jeremy. I won't take long, I promise. The room's locked up, right? Could you come and unlock it for me? Would you mind?'

He sighed, but the corners of his mouth twisted into a secret little smirk. He was clearly enjoying Samantha's attention.

'I don't suppose I'll get any peace until I do.'

He lifted himself off the sofa, pushed past me and trudged to the kitchen.

Samantha and I exchanged smiles. This was where the plan could have fallen down. If he'd simply told us where the key was kept, we'd have had to resort to more desperate measures. But Jeremy's need to be in control ensured we were okay, and a minute later, he was inserting the key in the lock, opening the surgery door and stepping inside. He left the key in the lock, bringing the second phase of the plan to fruition.

I felt Samantha nudge me in the ribs. 'Go!' she yelled.

We surged forwards together, putting our hands on his back and shoving with all our strength. He staggered forwards into the dim void of the room, almost landing on his knees.

'What the friggin' hell…?' we heard.

But we were too quick for him. I'd already pulled the door shut. Samantha turned the key in the lock and we looked at one another, breathing heavily, ecstatic in our triumph.

I stared at the door. 'Oh God. What've we done?'

'Nothing we shouldn't have done yonks ago,' Samantha said. 'Shown that bully he doesn't get to call all the shots, not any longer.'

It was all right for Samantha. She didn't have to live here.

And then I reminded myself I'd had to do something, and I knew I'd never have done it on my own. He wouldn't tell Alice, not without opening several proverbial cans of worms. He wouldn't tell anyone; he'd be too ashamed to admit he'd been tricked and overpowered by two sixteen-year-old girls. Okay, neither was a given, but the chances of Jeremy blabbing, we'd decided, were remarkably slim. There was always a risk that he would take his revenge on me, some time, somehow. But I'd weighed it all up, time and again, and it was a risk I was willing to take.

I was safe, or as safe as I could be.

There was banging, there was shouting, there was swearing, there were threats, there were insults; all of which we'd expected. There were other sounds: knocks and thumps; the crash of metal, by which we guessed he was trying to smash the door lock with a chair or something. Eventually, the shouting died down but the other sounds went on all evening, more spasmodically as the hours drifted by. Samantha and I sat in front of the TV with lemonade and crisps, the sitting room door half open so we'd hear if he should succeed in his quest for freedom.

It was unlikely, we thought. Not impossible, but unlikely. The internal surgery door was thick and solid, like all the doors in Summerdene, the old external door so heavy it would have taken an explosion to make a dent in it. There was always the window, of course. It wouldn't open – it was stuck fast with age, we'd checked that. But he could have smashed it and climbed out. He wouldn't, though, because he'd have had to explain to Alice how it had got broken.

Even if he had got out through the window, it wouldn't have done him any good because I'd fastened the chain on the front door and made sure the back door was locked and bolted. He'd have had to spend the night in the shed with the spiders – plan B – which would have been better than nothing.

We went to bed around eleven, having listened at the door of the surgery, and heard only silence. An ominous silence, I thought, but I didn't say so.

I didn't sleep much. We talked and giggled our way through until gone midnight, when Samantha promptly fell into a deep sleep, leaving me wide awake and worrying. But I must have slept eventually, because the next thing I knew it was 7 a.m. and the rain was hammering the windows.

We'd already decided that one of us should stay home today, to keep guard. But once Samantha was awake, we realised neither of us relished the idea of being in the house alone.

'We'll ring in sick,' Samantha said. 'I'll ring for you and you ring for me. Say it's our mums. Or not, in your case.'

'Thanks for the reminder,' I said.

So Samantha became Alice, and I became Samantha's mother, for the time it took to make two calls to the school secretary, and, although I say so myself, we sounded pretty convincing.

Once we were downstairs, the yelling started up again, and the language got worse, if that was possible. I wasn't sure I could stand it much longer.

'Look on the bright side,' Samantha said, through a mouthful of marmalade toast. 'He hasn't escaped.'

'So far. He's got all day to figure it out.' I suddenly felt full of gloom, as well as a bit scared at what we'd done.

'We just have to hold our nerve, that's all,' Samantha said, and grinned.

And hold our nerve we did – all the following day, and the night that followed. The rain pelted down nonstop so we didn't go out at all – it was probably best we didn't anyway. We played board games, read, listened to the radio, tried on all my clothes, ate our way through the contents of the fridge, and the time passed pleasantly enough. Samantha was all for leaving Jeremy incarcerated for another day but I didn't know exactly when Alice would be home. Okay, it was a long journey from Sussex to Gloucestershire, and even if she turned up today it wouldn't be early.

But at 6 a.m. the next morning, I woke with a start and in a panicky sweat. I couldn't hold out any longer. I woke Samantha, and we crept downstairs. There was no sound from behind the surgery door, no signs of movement at all.

'Oh God, supposing he's dead?' I whispered. 'Supposing we've killed him? Should we go outside and look through the window first?'

'Don't be daft. What's he going to die of? He's got oxygen, hasn't he? The room's not hermetically sealed, you know.'

'Starvation? Dehydration?'

'No chance. Not in that time. If he's got any sense, he'll have realised he was in for the long haul and spun out the rations.'

I wasn't convinced. But Samantha agreed it was time and, cautiously, we unlocked the door and pushed it open.

He appeared to be asleep, wedged full length on the floor between the wall and three of the metal chairs, as if he'd made a makeshift barrier. He wasn't asleep. He sprang to his feet as soon as the door opened, knocking one of the chairs flying, as if he'd been expecting us. I prepared myself mentally for a verbal onslaught, even a physical one. But nothing came. He just stared at us in silence, which I found far more disturbing than if he'd ranted and raged.

'Right, then,' Samantha said. 'You can come out now.'

He didn't move. He blinked, several times. His hair was standing on end; his clothes were rumpled. His shoulders drooped; his hands hung loosely by his sides. He looked subdued, defeated. Almost childlike.

And then he started to walk towards us and, immediately, his haughty demeanour snapped back into place.

'Not so fast,' I said.

'Uh?' He cast me a venomous look.

'The bucket. Bring the bucket. You have to empty it. Nobody else is going to.'

He turned with a heavy sigh and retreated to a corner. Samantha and I stood back from the door as he emerged from the room with the stinking bucket. His face was white, his expression set like stone. He was giving nothing away, yet at the same time, everything. Jeremy was beaten, for however long it lasted.

We watched as he carried the bucket along the hall and up the stairs. His humiliation was complete.

THIRTY-FOUR

LOGAN

2022

Promising her that holiday was a masterstroke. I needed to do something more after I'd sewn the seeds of my betrayal. Oh yes, Faye had been told about that, exactly as I'd planned. You're her mother, you'd never have kept that little nugget to yourself, even if it did take you longer to spill the beans than I'd expected.

I guess it was no surprise that Faye hadn't confronted me about my 'affair' with the redhead with a cleavage like the Grand Canyon. (My messenger's description, not mine; I left the details to her.) It was only 'gossip', after all. But I saw the uncertainty in Faye's eyes. She'd be looking at me, all full of love and devotion, then her gaze would leave my face and hike off into the distance as the doubts rushed in.

One time, she went all quiet on me, refused to speak for practically a whole day. Later, we were in the kitchen and she suddenly stopped slicing mushrooms, put the knife down and looked me in the eye. I reran my prepared speech in my head. I would confess, hold my hands up to my 'crime', say I couldn't help myself because I was weak – no apology. Not that. Then, I would say I wouldn't blame her if she packed her bags and shipped out.

But in the end, she said nothing, just gave me a whisper of a smile and went back to her slicing.

I went out that night. I left the house, no explanation, no nothing, and didn't come home till gone midnight. I've got a mate who was a barman with me at the White Hart and now worked at a remote pub called the Fountain, buried in the hills, where they had regular lock-ins and card nights. So, there was always somewhere I could be, if necessary.

In Faye's eyes, I became a man of mystery, and she took it as part of who I was while I was busily chipping away at the surface of her dreams, piece by piece.

So, the holiday. If she was so madly in love with me she refused to believe I could cheat on her – I was still working on that – then I needed to set her up for a big disappointment some other way.

We sat with the laptop and I guided her towards exotic locations, top end hotels, Faye's eyes growing wider at every click of the mouse. I let her make the final choice, then sent her to the kitchen to make tea, telling her I would go right ahead and complete the booking – my treat. The following day, she booked the two weeks off work, after showing her extreme gratitude the night before.

How the hell did she think I could afford a holiday like that, now I was paying half the rent on the cottage, as well as subsidising my faithful little sidekick? I could barely have managed a budget week on the Costa del Sol, never mind St Lucia.

But the higher I take Faye, the further she has to fall.

I wouldn't say your daughter was gullible, Briony, though if she was a bit, I guess I've got you to thank for that in the way you brought her up. No, it was all to do with love, pure and simple. Or what you women call love, anyway.

And love, Briony, is every woman's downfall in the end.

THIRTY-FIVE

BRIONY

2022

As it happened, my mind was pulled away from Marcus when Faye arrived at Summerdene the next morning and hurried straight to the kitchen with hardly a word. The guests had all finished breakfast and left the dining room, apart from Patrick, a sweet, elderly man travelling alone who liked to linger with the morning paper and a last coffee. Usually we enjoyed a chat but today I left him to it and joined Faye. She was sitting at the table, her face pale and drawn, her eyes dark, as if she hadn't slept.

'Faye? What's wrong?' I sat down beside her.

'I'm okay. I'll give you a hand in a minute.' She gazed sadly at the detritus around us.

'Never mind that. I'll do it later. Talk to me.'

Faye gave a small sigh. 'I don't know that anything's wrong. I expect it's all in my head. That's what Logan said, anyway.'

'When did he say that? Why? Faye, you're obviously not okay. That's why you're here, isn't it?'

I heard Patrick leave the dining room, his soft tread on the stairs. At the same moment, the back door opened and Pippa sidled in. As soon as she saw Faye she coloured up slightly. She was probably thinking about Logan, and what she'd told me. Feeling guilty, perhaps?

'Shall I make a start upstairs?' she asked, directing the question at me with a pointed lift of her eyebrows.

'Please, if you would. Thanks Pippa,' I said.

She went through to the hall, closing the kitchen door behind her.

'So,' I said, turning back to Faye when Pippa was out of earshot. 'What's this about, lovey?'

Faye sighed heavily. 'Logan's been going out and doesn't get back till after I've gone to bed. He doesn't say where he's been. Sometimes he doesn't even tell me he's going out before he leaves.' She looked stricken. 'Mum, supposing it's true and he is seeing someone else? What am I going to do?'

So, Pippa was right all along – or whoever she got the story from was. At least, that's what it sounded like. Okay, as far as I was concerned, Faye and Logan splitting up wouldn't be the worst news I'd ever heard but, after Nick, she'd see it as a disaster, and I couldn't let her know how I felt.

'It may not be that,' I said, trying to sound upbeat. 'There may be some other explanation. How often has he been going out?'

'A couple of times last week. And again last night.'

'What did he say about it? Presumably you've confronted him.'

'Yes, I did, and we had the most awful row. I didn't say I'd heard a rumour about... you know. I just asked him where he went and why he was being so secretive about it.' Faye looks at me, eyes blazing with indignation. 'I'm entitled to ask, aren't I? But he said I was being paranoid and if I didn't trust him there was no hope for us. Oh, Mum, I'm scared. Scared I'm going to lose the best thing that's ever happened to me. I can't bear it.'

Faye gave a little shudder. I put my arm round her, pulling her to me.

'Oh, love...'

'That's not all.' Faye drew back and sat up. 'While we were arguing he said something bad, something about you.'

'Me?' I was puzzled as well as angry now.

'Yes. He said you must have forced Alice to leave you the house in her will. I couldn't believe he'd said such a terrible thing. I don't know where it came from. It was right out of the blue. We hadn't even been talking about you.'

I swallowed hard. I couldn't believe it either.

'You do know that's not true, don't you? I'd not even seen Alice in her later years, let alone have that sort of conversation.'

'Of course I know it's not true, Mum. As if.'

'Good. What else did he say?'

'Nothing else about you. I know he only said that in the heat of the argument, I think. It was like he was throwing anything he could at me, anything that would hurt. I'm sure he didn't mean it about the house. It makes no sense. I don't even remember telling him about Alice and how you came to own Summerdene but I guess I must have.' Faye bit her lower lip, worry in her eyes.

I felt hot. All my doubts and worries about Logan were gathering momentum, coming together as if they were magnetised. I took a slow breath and forced myself to calm down. I had to be the voice of reason here, which wasn't going to be easy but I owed it to Faye to try.

'Right,' I said, tapping a finger on the table. 'Firstly, we don't actually know he's seeing someone else. He could just need a bit of space now and again and that's why he takes off. After all, it has been a whirlwind affair and I know he set the pace but perhaps he's finding it all too much, too soon. Could it be that, do you think?'

'Could be,' Faye said thoughtfully. 'Makes a kind of sense, I suppose.'

'Did you actually accuse him of cheating?'

'No, I didn't. Because I don't know he has, do I? I wanted to wait until I was sure before I blew us apart. But now...'

'Now you're thinking it's the only explanation,' I said.

Of course she was. It was what I was thinking myself. Except Faye was right, we didn't know for certain.

'He said,' Faye continued, her voice wavering, 'we each needed our privacy and he would never question me if I went out without telling him. But that's not true. He asks me where I'm going and what time I'll be back, even if I'm only going to the shops or to see you. I thought his possessiveness was romantic, at first.'

I didn't answer immediately. Cheat or not, that guy had really messed with my daughter's head. He seemed to be pulling her in all directions at once. No wonder she didn't know what to believe any more. I could never forgive him for that.

'What will you do?' I asked gently.

'Nothing. I'll wait and see what happens. I want to trust him, I really do, so I have to give him the benefit of the doubt.'

I brought us back to the second question. 'Why did he pick on me, though? What has my inheritance got to do with Logan? Shouldn't he be pleased I'm well set up, for your sake?'

'I know. I asked him that but he refused to answer. I thought he liked you, Mum. I'm sure he does. It was an off-the-cuff remark, I'm sure. He just wanted to dig the knife in.'

'Well, he dug it in a funny place,' I said. 'If he says anything else like that, you're to tell me, right? I won't be accused of manipulating Alice, not by anybody.'

Faye gave me a half smile. 'If he underestimates you, it'll be his first mistake. Or one of them.'

I got up and switched the kettle on. I could have done with something stronger but coffee would have to suffice.

Faye pushed her chair back and stood up. She looked a little brighter. 'I won't stop. I've got a work meeting at eleven. I'm okay now, or I will be.'

I saw her out. 'Keep me posted, love. Remember, I'm always here if you want to talk. Take care.'

'I will. Thanks, Mum. Sorry to go on. Love you.'

'Love you, too,' I said, closing the door behind her.

As I came back inside, Pippa came downstairs, duster and polish in hand, damp cleaning cloth hanging out of her jeans pocket.

'Faye gone already?'

'Yes, she's got work,' I said.

'All right, is she?' Pippa asked, her head on one side.

'Of course,' I said, and walked briskly away, along the hall.

By the time Sunday morning arrived, my head was so full of Faye and her unhappiness that I'd stopped worrying about Marcus and what it was he wanted to say; I just didn't have the headspace for anything else too taxing. I would find out soon enough, I reasoned.

His face was serious as I got into his car and we gunned out of the gates, into Back Lane, but he seemed to relax by the time we were driving away from the village.

'I thought we'd go to the café in the barn,' he said, offering the first smile of the day.

'Lovely.' I returned the smile, dialling it up a notch, only Marcus was focused on the road and didn't see.

I liked the barn. It was part of a working farm and we'd been there before; the coffee was superb. We didn't talk much on the way but fell into an easy silence while I wondered why Marcus couldn't have told me what this was about over our promised dinner.

I began to feel apprehensive again and was glad when we

were seated inside the echoey barn with mugs of coffee and toasted muffins. 'I didn't have breakfast,' Marcus said, reaching for the dish of apricot jam.

'I did, but it was ages ago.'

I smoothed butter over one half of a muffin. Sunlight strobed through the small windows above us, stencilling pale gold squares of light onto the timbered wall opposite. We sat in our bubble of silence while the somnolent buzz of Sunday morning conversation went on around us. My muffin remained on the plate. Suddenly I wasn't hungry any more.

'You wanted to talk?' I ventured after a while.

Marcus looked at me, his dark eyes sad. 'Yes. I thought it'd be easier on neutral ground.' He gave a humourless little laugh. 'Not sure it is.'

I sipped my coffee and waited.

'Briony, you know I have feelings for you,' Marcus began, 'and I know they aren't reciprocated, and it's fine, I get that. But the truth is I can't go on like this. I can't be with you but *not* with you. I don't want to be just friends, so there we are. I thought I'd be cool with it but I'm not, so I have to find a way to stop.'

I stared at him. My heart jumped around inside me, my lungs wouldn't work. Of course I hadn't forgotten his admission that he had feelings for me, but I'd pushed it to the back of my mind. I'd kept my own feelings for him on a tight leash, never showing them, never letting them develop, or fantasising about what might have been. I may have been divorced from Tony for three years, separated for four, and I'd been on a few dates since then, but I wasn't in the right place to start up a new relationship; I wasn't ready. I didn't want to be in love, and all it entailed. I just wanted to be *me*, to embrace this new phase in my life and see where it led.

Or had I convinced myself of that because I was scared? Scared of starting something that might not end well? Scared of being found lacking in some way – well, let's face it, in many ways. I was beginning to realise the truth of this.

But being scared of love was the same as being scared of life.

I blinked into the dusty sunlight. He was waiting for me to say something. But what? I could hardly perform the swiftest turnabout in history and tell him I felt the same, could I? In any case, my reasons for turning him down in the first place hadn't changed. I couldn't see a future for us. Yes, we got on well when we were together, but we were different in so many ways and Marcus was so young. Well, comparatively speaking.

So, I did what I always did, and made light of it.

'Marcus, as I said before, I'm flattered. But I'm not that wonderful, you know. I've got habits you wouldn't want to witness, believe me. Give it a couple of months and you'd be hotfooting it over the horizon, and quite rightly too.' I gave a little laugh. 'I'd quit while I was ahead if I were you.'

'You don't think I'm serious, do you?' he said. 'You think this is all a big joke. Well, it's not, Briony. I fell in love with you from almost the first moment we met.' He nodded. 'Yep, it took me by surprise, too. Doesn't make it any less true, though.'

'I'm sorry,' I said. 'I didn't mean to sound patronising. It's just that I don't know what to do or say that will make it any better for you.'

'It's okay, you can't help the way you feel any more than I can.'

Marcus reached out and placed his hand over mine, and I longed to lift his hand and press my lips to it. But it was too late. The moment had gone; all our moments had gone, and it was all my fault.

'I'm sorry,' Marcus said, removing his hand. 'I didn't mean to put pressure on you. I can see how it looks, bringing you here, laying my cards on the table, again.' He smiled and raised his eyes.

'Stop saying sorry,' I said. 'You've nothing to be sorry for, and you weren't pressuring me, honestly. I wish... it were different, but for now, well...'

I fell silent. I couldn't change any of this, although I wished with all my heart that I could.

Marcus pushed back his chair and stood up. 'I think it's best we don't see each other any more. Uneven friendships never work.'

'No,' I said quietly. 'You're right, of course.'

Marcus walked to the counter and joined the queue to pay. I had no choice but to stand up and walk to the door while my stupid heart played a song of regret. 'You'll be sorry,' it sang. 'Tell him now. Tell him you love him too. *Tell him.*'

But it was too late.

'I'll be away from the village for a couple of weeks,' Marcus said, as we drove away from the barn.

'Where are you going?' I had no right to ask, but I did anyway.

'A mate of mine is off on a research trip and said I could use his room on campus if I liked. It'll save me the commute.'

And take you away from me. That was clearly what he meant.

I felt rejected, cast off, which was ridiculous, given the circumstances.

We plunged into the shadow of a narrow lane overhung by trees. I twisted in my seat to look at Marcus but his attention was firmly on the road, as it should be. I wanted to tell him to stop the car and talk to me. I wanted to ask him if he really wanted to throw away a perfectly good friendship because of our romantic differences, real or otherwise. I even wanted to ask him if we weren't too far over the hill to let this love malarkey ruin what we already had.

Except we were beyond joking, well beyond it, and I couldn't be so crass as to belittle his feelings. I'd already made that mistake earlier. As for my own emotions, they'd be put right back in the jar where they belonged, with the lid screwed on tight.

We completed the rest of the journey in silence, and all too soon we were back at Summerdene. Marcus stopped the car on the forecourt, keeping the engine running, and I stepped out.

'I'll see you around, no doubt,' I said, forcing a bright smile.

'Yes, see you around.'

How bleak it sounded.

I stepped away from the car, then turned back.

'My daughter calls you "the poet",' I said.

He smiled. 'Nope. Not a single poetic bone in my body. Sorry to disappoint.'

He backed the car out of the gates with a sweep of tyres on gravel, and drove off.

THIRTY-SIX

BRIONY

1986

Jeremy had taken to going for long runs or bike rides every evening after our meal. At least, he said that's what he was doing. I saw him wheel the bike out into the lane sometimes, so I had no reason to disbelieve him, and even less reason to care. When he was at home, he strode about with a permanent look of fury, speaking to no one, his whole body tense as if at any moment a cord would snap and unleash an unstoppable storm.

I felt guilty that Alice had to live with all this, knowing it was because of what I'd done to her son. But I didn't regret it for one second – how could I? He hadn't spoken to me since, unless he had to, which, I decided, was the best possible outcome. He could have wreaked revenge on me in some way, but his mother's presence probably stopped him – unless he was secretly cooking up something for the future. Jeremy was definitely the type to hold a grudge, but there was nothing I could do about that.

One day, I was in my bedroom with the window open when I heard voices drifting up from the garden. Alice was asking

Jeremy if anything was worrying him, and was met with a gruff, 'Nope. Nothing wrong with me.'

I moved closer to the window, leaning my elbows on the sill, and peered down.

'You're not unwell, are you?' I heard, as Alice stood in front of Jeremy, who was reclining in a deckchair.

'I told you, no, Mother. I'm fine,' he said. 'Don't go on.'

The rest of the short conversation was conducted in tones too low for me to hear clearly, but Jeremy's replies were all grunts and monosyllables, and I began to feel sorry for Alice. I knew enough about her by then to know that she would never have entered into that sort of conversation unless she felt she had to.

I had taken to propping a chair under my bedroom door handle at night. I didn't think he would dare to try anything now but it added a layer of extra security, and I couldn't have too much of that. If Alice should come to my room and find her entry barred, I would invent some excuse.

After a week or so, my secret pleasure at having taken revenge on Jeremy began to wane, and I wondered exactly what Samantha and I had achieved, other than to darken the atmosphere in the house. I still had to look at him every day and be reminded of my own drawn-out humiliation at his hands. Was it just wishful thinking that he now saw me as a formidable adversary who wouldn't hesitate to retaliate if he so much as uttered a disparaging comment? Or was he simply biding his time until he could find a way of getting rid of me, which was clearly top of his agenda? I had no idea. Consequently, I worried constantly.

Would it never end?

Then, ten days later, a miracle occurred, and I couldn't wait to tell Samantha about it.

Actually, I did have to wait because she was off school with a cold that was going around. She rang to tell me one

evening, sounding as if she was speaking through several layers
of wet flannel and coughing fit to burst, so I kept my news to
myself. I needed to deliver it face to face for maximum
dramatic effect.

And then, two days later, I woke up with the headache from
hell. Alice took one look at my red eyes and streaming nose,
ordered me back to bed and reappeared shortly afterwards with
aspirin, a warm drink made from lemon and honey, and a hot
water bottle. The bottle made me hotter than ever in my
feverish state and I dropped it over the side of the bed as soon as
Alice had left the room.

I slept fitfully round the clock, then the next morning, I got
out of bed on wobbly legs and inspected my face in the dressing
table mirror. Deciding I didn't look quite such a sight as I had
the day before, and bored out of my mind stuck in my room, I
thought I might venture downstairs and watch TV. As I reached
for my dressing gown from the back of the door, I heard the
front doorbell sound and Alice answering.

'Come in, dear,' I heard her say. 'I expect she'd be pleased
with the company, and you've had this awful bug already, I
understand.'

The voice that replied belonged to Samantha. Moments
later, she thundered up the stairs and flung open my bedroom
door.

'Poor you,' she said, giving me the once-over. 'Bloody awful,
isn't it? I had to kid my mum I was feeling fine before she let me
out. I was *so* bored! I'll be even more bored tomorrow – I'm
going back to school.'

I flung my dressing gown on and tied the belt. 'I know. I've
only been incarcerated for a day and it feels like a life sentence.'

Samantha plonked herself down on the end of my tousled
bed. 'You're such a drama queen, Bri.'

'Takes one to know one.' I let out a hoarse laugh that
dissolved into a rasping cough.

I sat down on the dressing table stool. 'I'm glad you came. I needed to see you. There's been a *development*.'

'Ooh, tell me more.'

Samantha raised herself onto the bed and sat cross-legged. Helping herself to a tissue from my box, she blew noisily into it.

'Are you sure you're fit for school?' I asked, frowning.

'That was the deal. Mum said if I was fit to come out today, I was fit for school. Friday tomorrow, though. Only one day then it's the weekend. Look, never mind all that. What is this *development* of which you speak?'

'He's leaving. The creep's moving in with a mate in Oxford.' Samantha's brows shot up. 'Hard to believe he's got a mate willing to put up with him, or any mates at all, but it's true. He told us over dinner on Monday.'

I had sat at the table with my mouth open, hardly daring to believe I'd be free of Jeremy at long last. Alice had gone awfully quiet.

'I think Alice is wondering how he'll manage,' I said. 'She does everything for him bar wiping his bum.'

'More fool her,' Samantha said, after we'd coughed our way through our laughter. 'Bri, this is amazing. The best news *ever*! So, our little plan worked. Told you it would, didn't I?'

I nodded, giving Samantha her moment of triumph. I wasn't sure we could claim victory exclusively. Maybe Jeremy had been thinking of cutting the apron strings anyway, but I decided we'd helped things along by giving him the push he needed. I definitely believed that, and it was enough to restore some of my self-confidence.

'When's he going?' Samantha asked.

'Not sure. He didn't say, not that I heard, anyway. But he's been sorting stuff out, clothes and that, so it must be soonish.'

I'd seen several carrier bags bulging with Jeremy's discarded clothes, books and general tat, standing outside his bedroom door. Alice had told him to put them in the shed to await the next village jumble sale. The bags were still on the landing as far as I knew. No doubt Alice would lug them downstairs herself at some point, or I would. But that would probably be the last time either of us would wait on him.

I had mixed feelings over Jeremy's impending departure. Whatever he was like, and however blind Alice was to his short-comings, he was her son. He was leaving home, and I was sensitive enough to understand something of how she must be feeling. At the same time, I was in celebratory mood.

'When I'm better we should do something special,' I said. 'Go to Cheltenham, or Gloucester, maybe. Treat ourselves in the shops and have tea out. Go clubbing. Anything, as long as it's away from this village.'

Samantha grinned. 'I'm glad you're taking this in the right spirit, Bri. Yep, we'll do all that, and more. As soon as his skinny arse is out of that door, that's us, out on the razz.'

We fell silent for a moment, a silence only broken by the wheezing sound coming from my chest. I was thinking about Molly, and I could tell Samantha was, too. The three of us would have sat beneath the Kissing Tree, marvelling at how brilliantly we'd dealt with Jeremy, and toasting my freedom from my despised tormentor with bottles of pop.

And then I wondered whether Molly would have taken part in the whole operation or would it, in fact, have still been just Samantha and me? Molly had been on my side, always – outwardly, at least – but she had never dug the verbal spikes in quite so deeply where Jeremy was concerned. Never been quite so scathing about him as Samantha and me.

Molly could sometimes be too soft-hearted for her own good. I'd often thought that.

'I wonder where she is,' I said, biting my lower lip and staring unseeingly out of the window at the pale blue sky. I didn't need to say her name.

'Yeah, I wonder.' Samantha raised herself off the bed and

landed with a thump on the rug. 'Oh well, I guess we'll never know.'

Summerdene felt strange without Jeremy. Strange in a good way, although my state of perpetual watchfulness was proving hard to shake off and I had to keep reminding myself he wasn't going to creep up on me, barefoot, a supercilious expression smeared across his face. My resentment of his bullying ways continued, too, rising up out of nowhere like a malevolent ghost to produce a sickening sensation in my stomach.

It would get better, I knew. It was bound to take time to banish the habits of the past two and a half years. I began to mentally prepare myself for Jeremy's visits because, surely, he would come and see his mother, when it suited him, of course. Then I realised nothing could prepare me for walking into a room and seeing Jeremy there, so I decided to go with my gut and deal with the situation if, and when, it arose.

I didn't blame Alice for what I'd gone through. She knew he overstepped the mark sometimes – the conversation we'd had when she'd apologised if Jeremy had ever said anything out of place bore testament to that – but I was sure she had no idea of how much he'd scared and humiliated me, and enjoyed doing so. I wasn't about to disillusion her.

Alice began to involve me in some of her community activities, which she never had before. I didn't know why she was bothering. I didn't mind helping out but I wasn't short of things to occupy me. I was quite content with school and my somewhat limited social life, and I'd always been happy in my own company and was used to entertaining myself with books and the radio. Maybe Jeremy's leaving had shifted her focus onto me, I didn't know, but it was nice to be asked, and made me feel I was giving something back, however minimal.

One task that fell to me was the typing up of the minutes from the various committees of which Alice was the secretary.

'I don't know why they ask me,' she said one evening, as she prepared for the monthly WI meeting. 'I'm always so busy listening I forget to take the damn notes. But all is not lost!' She produced from her bag a small black device that turned out to be a Dictaphone and, with it, a clutch of mini cassettes. 'Stick one of these in, and I can sit back and let the machine do the talking. Or the listening.'

I exclaimed over this marvel, as was expected, and told her what a great idea it was. I didn't know at that point it would be me typing up the minutes on Alice's ancient Remington.

'You don't mind, do you?' she said, winding a sheet of paper crookedly into the typewriter. 'You'll make a much better job of it than me. It says on the agenda who was at the meeting. You'll soon pick it up.'

I found it a challenge at first. People would talk over one another, nobody ever seemed bothered about sticking to the agenda, and the tiny earpiece kept falling out. Luckily, Alice took a gung-ho approach to her off-loaded secretarial duties, and happily swanned off to the post office to make photocopies of whatever drivel I'd banged out with two fingers on the stiff type-writer keys.

On another occasion Samantha and I spent a giggly after-noon helping to sort jumble at the village hall. We wasted a lot of time holding the various garments up against us to amuse one another and exclaiming over droopy hand-knitted cardigans and corduroy trousers with rubbed knees. We were roped in to help serve the teas and rock cakes at the sale itself, which also turned out to be fun – who'd have thought it? The supply of cheap tea bags diminished fast and by the end we'd topped up the temperamental urn with water so often that the last cups we served had virtually no brown colour to them at all, but nobody complained.

One Sunday morning, I worked alongside Alice and another woman I only knew by sight, planting crocus bulbs in an uninteresting stretch of grass verge. Samantha declined to take part on the grounds that digging might damage her nails, but I found it surprisingly satisfying, making the holes with a dibber thing then dropping in the tiny white bulbs, even though my back ached for ages afterwards, though not as much as Alice's must have done.

Sometimes with Samantha, sometimes alone, I dropped leaflets through doors, manned cake stalls, and stood with a clipboard in the high street, counting the number of lorries that went past. That was okay until a gang of boys from school, including Daniel Wilson, started cat-calling from the other side of the street, and I handed my clipboard to the earnest man wearing a tweed suit, who was in charge of proceedings, claimed a backlog of homework and walked off the job.

I still worked at Pink's on Saturdays, and with a mountain of A level work to get through, I was busy, but never too busy to hang out with Samantha. After school one afternoon, I found her waiting for me at the gate, which was a surprise as I knew her own last lesson had finished at midday. She must have come back for some reason.

Seeing her standing there, her face all alight, made me smile.

'Christ, you took your time,' she said.

'I didn't know you were waiting, did I? I had to get a book from the library. What're you doing here, anyway?'

'Kissing Tree. Now.' Samantha beckoned me to follow her with an illegally varnished fingernail.

She left me no choice but to hurry after her. This had better be important, I thought, as we trekked across the village, along the path and into the woods.

Arriving at the tree, Samantha rounded its trunk and pointed at the bark.

'What am I looking at?' I said tiredly. It had been a gruelling day and I'd been looking forward to the peace of Summerdene and a slice of Alice's ginger cake. Then I saw it. 'Oh.'

New initials had been scored into the bark, fresh and dark: OL ♥ SD

'Who's OL?' I asked, because it was obvious who SD was. Samantha Dean. 'Hang on, it's Ollie, isn't it?'

Samantha had been on a handful of dates with Oliver Ladbury from the Upper Sixth, that I knew of, anyway. She'd pretended she wasn't that keen on him, but he'd been persistent and she'd thought she might as well.

'Right,' I said, peering obediently at the carving, giving it my full attention as Samantha clearly expected. 'Initials on the Kissing Tree. Bit serious, isn't it?'

Samantha coloured up. At least, I thought she did, but the dim light filtering through the overhead branches made it difficult to be sure.

'My initiation,' she said, giving a smug kind of smile. 'My initials on the tree.'

She paused, looking at me, waiting for the penny to drop. It didn't take long.

'Oh my God,' I said, clapping my hands to my mouth. 'It's not just the carving. You've done it, haven't you? You've slept with Oliver Ladbury! Oh, this is priceless!'

Samantha looked miffed. 'That wasn't quite the reaction I was expecting.' Her smile broke. 'You're spot on, though.'

'Oh my God,' I repeated. 'You didn't do it *here*, did you? Out in the open? *Samantha?*'

'No, of course not. We were in his room, Saturday afternoon. His mum and dad were out.'

'Well, that's something,' I said. 'Hang on, if this isn't the scene of the crime, why have we traipsed all this way?'

Samantha flounced her shoulders. 'Not *all this way*. It's only five minutes from school. Okay, maybe ten. I wanted to show you the carving in case you didn't believe me. Anyway, the tree's where we talk about this stuff, you know that.'

'It used to be,' I said, thinking of the missing corner of our triangle. 'Well, I've seen it now.' I skirted the fat tree trunk and leaned against it at the place we usually sat. Samantha followed me.

I gave her a nudge. 'Go on then. What was it like?'

'Okay. Kind of nice... look, I'm not giving you the details now. Another time, maybe. The point is, I'm no longer a virgin. I won't die an old maid.'

I burst into laughter and, after a moment, so did Samantha.

'You got there first. I never doubted you would for a minute,' I said generously.

Out of the three of us, Samantha had been the only one set on losing her virginity as soon as possible. She deserved her moment of triumph.

She looked pleased, then doubtful. 'But we don't know about Molly. She might have done it after she went missing. Or even before.'

We looked at each other, then shook our heads.

'I don't reckon so,' I said.

'Neither do I.' Samantha held her hand out, palm uppermost. 'It's raining. Let's go.'

And so we jogged through the darkening woods to the sound of raindrops pattering on the leaves and each made our way home.

Our lives were changing. *We* were changing. School would be over in a flash and I'd be off to college. Leaving Mistlecombe, leaving Summerdene, and Alice.

I doubted I'd be back.

THIRTY-SEVEN

BRIONY

2022

Marcus's cottage looked lonely, I thought, as I walked past one morning. The curtains were closed on the downstairs windows, the upstairs ones left open but that only seemed to enhance the deserted air. The garden, though, was alive with birds foraging in the hedges and borders. Bees circled the flowers and alighted hungrily on the petals. A squirrel skittered along the side fence, paused, with its nose twitching, then vanished over the edge in a blur of grey. Droppings on the lawn indicated the passing by of a fox or hedgehog.

It was as if the wildlife had taken over Kestrels in its occupier's absence, keeping guard, although I knew the birds, insects and animals were always there.

Unlike Marcus.

I'd grown complacent, I supposed. I'd got used to him being just along the road from me, on hand whenever I felt like a chat, or waiting for me to knock before we set off for a cosy dinner at the White Hart. I felt sad: for Marcus, because I'd somehow managed to cause him heartache without meaning to; for me, because I hadn't trusted my own instincts enough to give our budding relationship a fighting chance.

So what if it all ended in tears? Would that have been so bad? I couldn't run away from everything in case it didn't work out. I'd have no life at all in that case. But knowing this in my heart wasn't enough to convince me I'd been wrong in sending Marcus away. Immersed in campus life, busy with his teaching, he probably hadn't given me another thought. The dragging sense of disappointment I felt whenever he came into my mind would soon disappear.

I walked on past Marcus's cottage and, reaching the end of Back Lane, carried on towards the village centre. But it wasn't shopping I had in mind. My mission today was to do with Pippa.

She'd phoned me three days ago and said she couldn't come to work because she'd caught some sort of virus – she hadn't been specific, and I hadn't asked. Selfishly, I'd been more concerned about coping alone with the workload at Summerdene – even more so since this morning, when her usual arrival time had come and gone and still no sign of my willing helper. She hadn't phoned again, either, nor messaged, but it probably hadn't occurred to her to keep me informed about her return.

Aside from the work issue, I was worried about her. I'd phoned her mobile three times yesterday and got voicemail every time. At the last attempt, I left a message saying I hoped she'd feel better soon. No response to that, either. Pippa lived with her mother so she wasn't alone, but if she was too poorly to look after her little boy, his gran would have her work cut out, caring for both of them. As her employer, I felt some responsibility for the girl, and I was on my way to call on her and see how she was. It was the least I could do.

I'd made a batch of madeleines last night. The small golden cakes were some of Pippa's favourites and I'd made up a box of them to bring with me. I'd entered Pippa's address – number eleven, Blackthorn Street – into my phone, but had memorised it so I didn't need to check as I walked the length of the high street and emerged at the other end, where various lanes wandered away from the main drag towards the outer edges of Mistlecombe. I couldn't remember being in Pippa's actual street before, but had its rough location in mind, and I took the turning beside the petrol station, confident I was in the right vicinity.

A few minutes' walking later, I was about to bring up the map on my phone instead of stubbornly trusting my gut when I spotted the street nameplate, just visible among the over-grown bushes. Actually, I thought, I had been here before, long ago, with Samantha and Molly, although I couldn't remember why. Just hanging out, I expect; wandering the backwaters of the village, talking about boys and trying to outdo each other with the latest gossip from school. It had been one of our favourite pastimes, when we weren't at the Kissing Tree.

The houses in Blackthorn Street were spaced well apart, with large gardens that met one other across stone walls. The houses varied in style and size. Small cottages were neighbours with larger, 1930s houses, and even more substantial Victorian villas. Number eleven, I was surprised to find, was one of the villas. I'd formed a mental picture of Pippa's living arrange-ments and had imagined something much more modest. Standing in front of the house now, I gave myself a stern mental telling-off for making assumptions based on my own prejudice without a shred of evidence.

The house was built of mellow, golden brick, not unlike the colour of Summerdene's stonework. Overgrown trees and shrubs shaded it on both sides, and the front garden was an untamed riot of flowering plants encroaching haphazardly onto a jumble of paving slabs. I walked up to the porched front door – cautiously, because for some reason I'd begun to feel intrusive, turning up at Pippa's home unannounced – and pressed the doorbell.

It was some while before I sensed movement inside, then the door creaked open and I found myself facing a tiny, silver-haired woman, dressed in a long, pleated skirt and floral-patterned blouse. She was surely too old to be Pippa's mother. Maybe she was her gran, or another relative, although Pippa had never mentioned her.

Watery pale blue eyes looked me up and down.

'If you're selling something, it's a "no",' she said sharply. Then, seeming to relent, she added, 'Sorry.'

The door began to close.

'No, wait, please. I'm not selling anything. That's not why I'm here. I've come to ask how Pippa is. I'd like to see her, but only if she's up to it, of course.'

The woman stepped further towards me, her hand clutching the edge of the door. 'There's only me here. My name's Sylvia, and I'm ninety-four, in case you were wonder-ing.' She gave a firm little nod.

I couldn't help smiling. But she'd said there was nobody else here, so...?

I pressed on. 'I'm Briony. I came to see how Pippa was. But if she's out – if everyone's out – I'll leave you in peace.'

'Nobody's out. There's only me, as I said.' Her brow creased deeply as she sank into thought. 'What was the name you said? I don't always hear too well.'

'Pippa.' I groped for the surname. 'Pippa Medhurst. She told me she was unwell...'

'Ah, Pippa, yes.' Sylvia's face cleared. She let go of the door and raised a forefinger. 'I've not seen hide nor hair of her in an age. Why did you think she was still here?'

Still here?

'You do know her then?' I asked, feeling totally confused.

'Pinched-face little thing. Black hair, dyed of course. Tattoo, just here.' Sylvia touched the place just above her collarbone. 'Is that who you mean?'

'Yes, *yes*,' I said, feeling relieved. 'You're not her mother, I take it?' I thought it wise to clear that up, at least.

'*Mother!* Hardly!'

'Of course. I'm sorry. It's just that this is the address she gave me when I took her on to help in my guest house, Summerdene, in Back Lane. She said she lived with her mother, so I assumed this was where she'd still be.'

'Works for you, does she? You have my sympathy.' Laughter bubbled, like a fountain.

I felt suddenly protective of Pippa. 'She's fine. She keeps on top of things. There's a lot to do when you run a B&B.' I smiled. 'How do you know her?'

'I employed her as a domestic help – she was meant to come in Monday to Thursday, mornings, but she lasted less than a month.' The raised finger again. 'I didn't sack her, mind. She was slapdash with a duster, and the bath was never scrubbed properly. She just swished it round with the sponge. I did tell her but it made no odds. But I quite liked having her about, in spite of her shortcomings. I thought I could train her up, eventually...'

'Why did she leave? Did she say?'

I was more than curious now, and annoyed at the waste of my precious time. Why had Pippa given me this address when clearly she'd never lived here, and only worked here for such a short time? I could only assume Sylvia was the employer who Pippa claimed had died. But why would she make up such a terrible lie? Unless it was to get out of providing me with a reference. A bit extreme, in my opinion, even for Pippa. It wasn't as if she'd been sacked – Sylvia had told me that. The whole thing was a mystery I could well do without.

'She never said a dicky bird,' Sylvia said. 'Just shoved a note through the door saying she was leaving and that was the last I heard of her. I haven't bothered to advertise for anyone else. Once bitten, twice shy! There's a cleaning company in Stroud. I ring them when things get mucky. You never get the same person twice but they're usually good. Pricey, though. Isn't everything?'

I nodded in agreement, feeling guilty that Pippa had obviously left Sylvia in the lurch to come and work at Summerdene. Had she now done exactly the same thing to me? If so, as well as being downright rude, leaving jobs on spec when she had a child to support was nothing short of irresponsible, and I was beginning to regret having got involved with her in the first place.

If Pippa had walked out on me, I needed to know.

'I don't suppose you've got an address for her?' I asked. 'Somewhere else in the village, perhaps?' The girl must surely have given Sylvia that kind of information when she'd come to work here.

'Now, I'd have to think about that.' Sylvia cupped her chin. 'Ah, I remember. She'd only just moved to the area, that's right. She told me she was staying somewhere temporarily until she found something suitable. And then she was gone, as I said. So, no, I never had an address for her. She used to turn up on a bike, if that's any clue. It's not, of course.'

'Never mind.' I smiled. 'I don't imagine it would have been easy for Pippa to find somewhere suitable for bringing up a small child. Mistlecombe isn't the cheapest of places. That's probably why she didn't have a permanent address at the time.'

'Child? Pippa hasn't got a child. Not that she ever mentioned, anyway.' Sylvia looked puzzled.

'Oh, well maybe I've got that wrong,' I said, thinking it best to say no more about Pippa's single-mother status. I probably shouldn't have mentioned it in the first place; it wasn't my business to pass on.

Meanwhile, I was no nearer to tracking down my helper. I

ran through what I knew so far, or rather, what I'd pieced together from talking to Sylvia. Living with her mother might well have been a stopgap for Pippa, and she'd intended to move into a place of her own. I'd never gained that impression, but the girl had never been particularly forthcoming with the details of her life, so it was possible.

But in that case, why had she not given me her mother's address instead of this one, the house where I now stood pointlessly on the doorstep, interrogating this rather nice woman?

'I mustn't keep you any longer,' I said. 'You've been very helpful.'

'I doubt that,' Sylvia said, 'but it's been good to talk to you. I hope you find Pippa.' Her tone suggested it might not be worth the trouble.

'And now, I really must leave you in peace.' I remembered the bag I was holding. 'Do you like madeleines, by any chance?' I held up the bag.

Sylvia's face lit up. 'I *do*. I used to make those, and all sorts of cakes. That was when my husband was alive. I don't bother now.'

'Well, then. Have these.' I fished the box out of the bag and handed it to Sylvia. Pippa wasn't getting them now, even if I did manage to track her down.

'How lovely!' Sylvia smiled. 'Thank you.'

'You're welcome.'

I walked to the front gate, turning to wave as Sylvia called, 'Goodbye!' and closed the door.

I was back in the high street in no time, my annoyance quickening my pace at every step. *Damn Pippa!* I'd wasted enough time on her this morning, time that should have been spent cleaning up after my guests. Perhaps I should have asked Sylvia for the name of the cleaning company she used in

Stroud, although it wouldn't be difficult to find, should there be the need. After this morning's little encounter, I wouldn't be surprised if I never clapped eyes on Pippa again.

I stopped outside the shop that sold bikes, scooters and skateboards, and took out my phone to try Pippa one more time. Again, it went straight to voicemail which, considering my mood, was probably a good thing. I hadn't planned what I would say if she'd answered, nor decided how to play this yet. Yes, I was furious with the girl, but at the same time, I needed her. I wasn't ready to go to the trouble of finding help elsewhere, and I couldn't call on Faye too often. Her time was taken up with her own job – and with Logan.

I slipped the phone back into my pocket, and as I looked up, I found myself face to face with the man himself.

'Hi, Briony!' Logan stood before me on the pavement, giving me a wide grin. 'How are you?'

Wrong-footed, I hesitated, while Faye's recent upset flew into my mind. I'd spoken to her twice since then, but only on the phone, not in person. But she'd sounded happy, and in answer to my careful questioning, had assured me the argument with Logan had blown over and all was well. I had no reason to disbelieve her, but I hadn't forgotten Logan's accusation about Summerdene, arrowed at me through my daughter because it was so random and unaccountable.

He must have realised she'd have come straight to me with that little gem. Or perhaps not. Logan had a fiery temperament; that much had become evident. Perhaps, as Faye had asserted, he'd lashed out in the heat of the argument, hadn't meant a word of it and had forgotten he'd said it in the first place. Whatever, here he was, obviously not wanting to avoid me, behaving in his usual slightly over-friendly manner, without any sign of there being anything untoward. I had to run with that.

All this raced through my mind, then I gathered myself. 'Hello, Logan. I'm good, thanks. Except...'

'What is it?' Logan's face showed concern which seemed genuine, though I couldn't be certain.

'I think Pippa's let me down. I don't know for sure, but she called in sick a few days ago and I've not heard from her since. And, stupidly, I don't seem to have an up-to-date address for her.'

I wasn't going to tell him about my visit to Sylvia. It was nothing to do with him.

'Pippa, your domestic help?'

'That's the one,' I said, raising my eyes. I smiled. 'I'm probably jumping the gun. She might just have forgotten to ring me with an update, especially with a kiddie to look after.'

'Kiddie? Pippa's a mum? I didn't know that. Must be hard.'

'It must be,' I agreed. 'She lives with her mother, though – at least I think she does – so she's not without support.'

'What will you do?' Logan asked, his eyes showing more concern for my predicament than perhaps the situation warranted, given our relationship.

I gave a little laugh. 'Wait and see. What else can I do?'

'Well, I'm sure she'll pitch up again in her own good time. I wouldn't worry too much.'

I took a step back from Logan. He seemed to have closed in, invading my personal space, while we'd been talking. I tried hard not to mind, like I tried not to mind a lot of things about Logan, for Faye's sake. It didn't always work.

'Faye not with you?' I asked.

I glanced about, hoping my daughter would appear from a shop and join us. But no.

'She's at home, working. I left her on a Zoom call.' Logan pointed towards the café on the opposite side of the road. 'Can I treat you to a coffee?'

I thought about the work piling up at Summerdene. I'd already been out too long, and I had to pick up the slack created by Pippa's absence. My reason for needing to get home was genuine, but neither did I fancy spending any more one-to-one time with Logan than I had already.

'That's really kind, but I must get back. Loads to do, you know? Another time, maybe.'

'Yep, another time. Nice to have seen you, Briony.' The smile was full-force.

'You too. Well, bye then.'

As I walked off, I glanced over my shoulder and saw that Logan hadn't moved. He was standing facing the bike shop window, hands in pockets. He noticed me looking and gave me a little wave. I waved back, and continued along the street, thinking I could call at the bakery for some scones while I was out – I liked to keep some in the freezer, ready to welcome my incoming arrivals with tea and scones. At least my trip wouldn't have been entirely wasted.

The bakery was on the opposite side of the road. As I hovered on the kerb, waiting for the single-decker bus which served the village to trundle past, I looked back along the street and saw Logan going into the bike shop, as I thought. And then I realised he hadn't entered the shop itself, but had used the door adjacent to it, the door which must lead to the flat above the shop.

What was he doing there? Who was he going to see? His secret lover?

I couldn't help the way my mind was working. Perhaps Logan was a cheat, after all.

I was making it up as I went along now, I realised that, but his behaviour had just seemed odd. When I'd glanced back and seen him standing outside the bike shop, he'd looked... furtive. That was the word that came to mind. And, he hadn't said why he was in the village, but why would he?

I shook my head to force some sense into it. It had been a strange morning altogether. Pippa's 'disappearance' and my encounter with Sylvia had caused my brain to overheat and now I was imagining all sorts, which was stupid. Logan had been perfectly nice to me, and of course he hadn't looked furtive. That was me, making it up again. Maybe he had a friend who lived above the bike shop and his business there was completely innocent. That would be it.

With this simple and plausible explanation firmly in mind, I set off for home, all thoughts of scones forgotten.

THIRTY-EIGHT
BRIONY

The next morning, I slept through the alarm and had to hare downstairs half an hour later than usual to fix breakfast, my hair bundled into a ponytail to disguise its unwashed state. Luckily, none of my current guests – a Norwegian couple, and two female friends from Sutton – appeared in the dining room before nine, so it wasn't a problem, although the buffet looked decidedly slapdash when I'd finally set it out.

It wasn't surprising I'd needed the extra sleep. Yesterday had been manically busy as I struggled to do the work of two people, after having been out for half the morning on a wasted mission. On top of that, I'd had to deal with a blocked kitchen sink. There was no time to ring round for a plumber, let alone wait for them to turn up, so I'd limbo-danced half way into the cupboard, unscrewed the whole caboodle and fished out a lump of suspicious-looking substance from the U-bend, making a mental note to speak to Pippa about being more careful what she put down the plughole, should I ever see her again.

My luck changed, however, when, halfway through the breakfast sitting, the back door opened and she trooped in, looking as fit and healthy as usual, though with her pale complexion, I could never be sure what was usual for her.

'Pippa!' I was so relieved to see her, I forgot yesterday's debacle for the moment. 'How are you feeling?'

The girl had the grace to look a little shamefaced. 'Yep, all good. Sorry, Briony. I had a stomach bug. Couldn't face work.'

'I should think not,' I said, glad she hadn't made it in with a potentially contagious bug. 'If you need to be off for any reason in the future, though, would you let me know what's happening, please? Only I had no idea when you'd be back.'

Or if.

Her hazel eyes widened in genuine surprise, and I found myself shaking my head at her apparent lack of awareness. But she was here now, and I'd have an easier day; I should be grateful for that.

'Yeah, will do.' She shrugged off her denim jacket and slung it over a chair. 'Shall I clear breakfast, or start upstairs?'

'Upstairs, please. I can finish off down here,' I said, then I remembered yesterday's visit to Blackthorn Street.

I didn't have the time or energy for a full and frank 'discussion', which no doubt wouldn't be pleasant. Besides, I didn't want Pippa to know I'd been chasing after her. My conversation with Sylvia would be my secret, for now. On the other hand, I had to say something. It wouldn't be right not to.

'Pippa, before you go,' I said, as she headed for the door, 'I realised I haven't got an address for you. Only I should have one, as your employer. I don't think you ever gave it to me, did you?'

If she knew I was lying rather than being forgetful, I didn't care. She couldn't very well dispute my version of events, having given me an address which had never been hers in the first place.

Her narrow forehead pleated into a puzzled frown. 'Didn't

I?' she said, putting one purple-nailed fingertip to her mouth. 'Oh, right. Tell you what, I'll jot it down for you later.'

She swung through the door, into the hall. She was good, I gave her that. But so was I.

Maybe Pippa's life was a lot more complicated than I'd realised, I thought, as I heard her banging about in the room overhead. She didn't need to tell me the ins and outs of her private life; it wasn't my business. I didn't like being made a fool of, and I hated the way she'd treated Sylvia, but I didn't know what troubles she'd faced in her life, and I resolved to be more sympathetic in future.

It had come on to rain after breakfast. My Norwegian couple had set out, regardless, to continue their exploration of the north Cotswolds, equipped with raincoats and boots. My other two guests, friends who holidayed together once a year while their husbands were on a golfing holiday, sat in the guests' lounge while they waited for a break in the weather.

I popped in and offered them coffee which they were pleased to accept, and then I sat down and joined them, and we chatted for a while. But I still made time to have coffee in the kitchen with Pippa later. I realised I was feeling guilty for half-believing she'd walked out on the job, even though Sylvia's story had given me cause, and I opened a tin of chocolate biscuits gifted to me by a departing guest.

'Ta,' Pippa said, munching on a biscuit. 'These are scrummy.'

Her almost childish delight at the treat struck a chord with me, and I felt an unaccustomed warmth towards her.

'I'll put some of these biscuits in a bag for you,' I said. 'You can take them home for the little one.'

'What?' Pippa gazed at me vacantly. Then, 'Thanks, that'll be great.'

. . .

By lunchtime, the house was back in order, and Pippa rode off on her bike. The rain had stopped, the sullen clouds slinking away over the hills to make way for clear, pale blue skies. After I'd eaten, I wandered around the garden, noting where the worst of the weeds were and the flowers that needed dead-heading.

But that could wait for another day, and I sank onto the slightly damp slats of the bench with a mug of tea and thought fondly of Alice vigorously tending the borders with an ancient hand fork, wearing a floppy cotton hat to keep the sun off. Smiling to myself, I went back indoors and spent the rest of the afternoon curled up on the sofa with a book while the peace of Summerdene wrapped itself around me.

Around seven, as I was preparing an easy supper of quiche and salad, my mobile rang. It was Faye.

'Mum?' I heard, then a kind of stifled sob.

'Faye? Are you okay?'

A sniff, then, 'Yes, well, no, not really. I've lost my diamond ring, the one Logan gave me.'

The ring that had looked suspiciously like an engagement ring, except apparently it was only a 'pre-engagement' ring. *Was there a difference?*

I expressed my dismay and asked Faye when she'd last seen the ring.

'I take it off at night and put it in the drawer in the bedside cabinet. I always do.'

'Does it usually live in its box?' I asked.

'It didn't come with a box. It was in a little cotton bag but I just keep it loose now. I'm ever so careful with it, though, Mum, honestly,' she said, as if she needed to convince me.

'So, you had it last night, then?'

'Well, no, I don't wear it every day. I didn't have it on

yesterday and I don't *think* I wore it the day before, but I can't remember.'

Faye's voice cracked, and at once I knew there was something more to this than a mislaid ring.

Calmly, I pointed out that unless Faye had lost the ring while she was out, which was highly unlikely, it must be in the house and she'd taken it off and put it somewhere different. Or it had fallen down the back of the drawer or something, and it would turn up.

'I've looked and looked,' she said. 'It's just disappeared, and Logan's furious with me for being careless. He keeps reminding me how much it cost, as if the money's the only thing that matters, and...'

Ah, there it was. The real reason for my daughter's distress.

'Oh, Faye,' I said uselessly.

Useless, because I couldn't think of another word to say that wouldn't pitch Faye into deeper misery, although, believe me, those words were saying themselves inside my head, loud and clear.

'It'll be okay,' Faye said, after a moment. 'Logan will calm down eventually and it'll be fine, even if I haven't found the ring by then.'

I couldn't hold back any longer. 'You shouldn't have to wait for him to "calm down", Faye. He should be on your side, always, whatever the circumstances. He must know you haven't been careless. It's not your fault and he's got no right to be angry. Nor to bring up how much the ring cost. Look, why don't you come here? We could have a glass of wine, watch a film. How does that sound?'

Silence, then Faye's voice lowered to a whisper. 'I can't. I've got to go. I'm in the bathroom. I've got to go back down.'

In the bathroom? Since when did Faye have to phone her own mother in secret? I could hit Logan, I really could. Just when I'd decided, yet again, that he was an okay kind of guy, even if I hadn't really taken to him.

An image came to my mind of Logan entering that door next to the bike shop. *Why was he there? What was he hiding?*

'Well, then, I'm coming to you,' I said. 'Make out I was just passing, if you like. Logan doesn't need to know you rang me.'

'No, Mum, don't. I'm okay, really. The ring was special, his gift to me. He's bound to be upset, but it'll all blow over. Gotta go. Love you.'

'Love you,' I said, but she may not have heard me.

I heard the sound of a door clicking open, then Faye cut the call, leaving me clutching my phone as if I wanted to squeeze the life out of it.

THIRTY-NINE
LOGAN

2022

I didn't get as much for that ring as I'd paid for it, but it was a small sacrifice to make, considering the benefits. Give with one hand, take with the other. A simple system, guaranteed to screw the mind, every time.

She's a sticker, I'll say that for your girl, Briony. God knows why. Doesn't want to be seen as a failure, I reckon. Not again, after that other guy – Nick? Rick? – did the dirty on her. She told me all about him one night, after she'd sunk a few bevvies in the pub. You never thought he was good enough for your darling daughter, did you, Briony? She said that, too. But, true to form, she hung right in there. Never wanted to lose face in front of her friends, or you, her darling mother. She didn't want to admit she'd been taken for a mug, I reckon. Same as now.

Anyway, light dawned eventually, and then she finally let go, and her little heart crumpled up until it tore into shreds.

Sound familiar, does it, Briony? If it doesn't, it soon will, believe me.

But time's getting on. I need to draw this thing to a close, pretty soon. It's getting boring now. And bloody expensive, forking out for half the rent on the cottage as well as paying out for the bedsit over the cycle shop. But hey, it's a pretty sound investment, and it's all coming back to me, with interest.

Believe that, too, Briony dearest.

2022

On Sunday morning, Faye surprised me with an early visit, and I was pleased to have her company, as well as her help with breakfast and room tidying, and we had a laugh while we worked. But she wasn't happy, I could see it in her eyes.

Mid-morning, we sat down for coffee in the kitchen, and the reason for her distinct unhappiness became apparent. Logan had gone out on Friday night and not returned till two in the morning. When she'd asked him where he'd been, he'd just said he'd needed a break if that was all right with her, and if it wasn't, she'd have to put up with it. Or words to that effect – Faye wasn't as specific as that, nor as forthright, but I got the gist.

She still hadn't found her ring, either, and clearly she was still upset about that, as well as puzzled.

'I've turned the whole house out, top to bottom, Mum,' she said. 'It's vanished. I wondered if we'd been burgled but Logan said that was ridiculous because there were no signs of a break-in and nothing else is missing. My gold locket from grandma,

Logan's watch, everything else, is still there. So he's right, the ring couldn't have been stolen.'

Not by a burglar, no, I thought, as a dark cloud of suspicion mushroomed inside me.

'Faye...'

She stopped me. 'Mum, I know what you're going to say, but please don't.'

I sighed. Faye was so stubborn, and I felt helpless. I mustn't push her, I'd learned that from experience.

There was more to come, and worse.

'Maybe your holiday will help,' I said. 'You'll both be able to relax and reconnect with each other.' I smiled encouragingly, although a part of me was breaking inside.

Faye looked down at the table. 'That's not happening now.'

'Your holiday to St Lucia?'

She looked up, and smiled sadly. 'Yeah. Logan said we might have to postpone it.'

I was shocked. 'I thought it was all booked and paid for?'

'So did I. It would have been a hell of a lot of money, though, Mum,' Faye said, lifting her chin, as if it wasn't me who'd raised that very point. 'Logan really wanted us to go, and he's dead disappointed, but he lost out on a promotion he was counting on. It went to the boss's nephew or somebody. It's not fair, but it happens. He does okay as he is, but he doesn't net a fortune.'

There was no answer to that. Was this non-promotion really such a disaster? I didn't have a clue how much careers in the gaming industry paid, so couldn't argue. Instead, I showed sympathy to Faye. What else could I do? The last thing she needed was her mother turning against her boyfriend, not to her face, anyway.

'That's a pity,' I said. 'A holiday like that would have cost dream money, you're right.'

'Yes.' Faye was silent for a moment. She'd let half her coffee go cold. 'I suggested we go somewhere else. It doesn't have to be abroad. We could go to the Lake District, or anywhere. It would still be fun.' She smiled, covering her disappointment, though not well enough.

'What did he say to that?' I asked carefully.

Faye flapped a vague hand. 'That he'd think about it. He's not mentioned it since. I guess he's gone off the idea of a holiday, for now. I think he's worried about his future with the company. It's understandable, isn't it?'

I didn't answer.

First, the mystery outings, then the ring, and now the holiday. The holiday that had obviously never been going to happen. Faye knew it; I could see it in her face. And she knew that I knew it, too.

Suddenly, she brightened, and stood up to empty her coffee down the sink.

'It's fine. Logan's brilliant. Okay, he's not perfect, but I'm hardly that, either.' She turned and smiled. 'Don't worry, Mum. It's all good. Maybe you could come to ours for dinner one night? I'll see what Logan says.'

'That would be nice,' I said, thinking that if Faye needed permission to invite her mother for a meal, it wouldn't be nice at all.

'I'm going to London tomorrow.' Faye stood behind the chair she'd vacated, resting her hands on its back. 'I want to catch up in the office and see some friends while I'm there so I'll probably stay at least till Wednesday.'

'Oh, right. I didn't know you were going.'

'Neither did I. I've only just this minute decided.'

'Will Logan want to go with you? He usually does.' I heard the touch of sarcasm in my voice.

'I don't know, but I'll tell him I'm going on my own. I'll be working, and I don't want to have to consider him as well.'

This was good news, and a sign that my daughter was able –

and willing – to be her own person and stand up for herself when necessary. Not that I'd ever doubted it; but sometimes it seemed as if being with Logan had changed her and made her lose some of her spirit.

I smiled. 'Great. Well, you have a good trip and don't work too hard. Come and see me when you're back.'

'I will.' Faye rounded the table and kissed me on the cheek. She glanced at the clock. 'Better go. We're going out for lunch. A pub, somewhere.' She looked at me as if she'd just thought of something. 'Oh, do you want to come with us? I'm sure Logan wouldn't mind.'

'No thanks, lovey. I'm going to have a quiet day here. I've got things to do. I might go for a walk later.'

'Okay!'

Faye swung out of the back door, and was gone, looking a lot more cheerful than when she'd arrived.

I decided to roll with that. Concerned though I was about my daughter, my brain needed a reset if I wasn't to spend the rest of the day embroiled in pointless worry, and after lunch I set out for a walk with no particular destination in mind.

But it seemed as if my mind had its own take on things, and I found myself on the narrow path that led to Mistlecombe Wood, and, eventually, to the Kissing Tree. The gate leaned to one side, its rotting slats suggesting it hadn't moved in a long time, and I entered into the cool quiet of the woods. I followed the old familiar route to the clearing, pushing aside overhanging branches as I went.

Was the tree still there? Maybe it had rotted away by now or been chopped down. But no, there it was. It wasn't as prominent as I remembered; a wilderness of undergrowth and nettles had reduced the clearing to half its former size; some of the tree's thicker, uppermost branches had snapped off, or been sawn off for safety, and the bark clinging to its hefty trunk had dulled and roughened with time, losing its silvery sheen.

I ran my fingers over the knobbly surface of the trunk, tracing the outlines of the carvings that were still visible: the wonky hearts, the crooked arrows, the capital Ls for Love – how unoriginal we were! – and the barely discernible initials. The dark slashes, made by cheap penknives, had weathered into hieroglyphics, as indistinguishable as charcoal on black paper.

Rounding the tree, I kicked away the light covering of beech mast to clear a space and sat down, my back to the trunk, the way we had always had – Samantha, Molly and me. As I inhaled the sharp, sappy scent, listening to the whisperings of the woods and the rhythmic cooing of a wood pigeon, I was sixteen again and there we sat, the three of us, elbow to elbow, high on sugar, our voices spiked by the sheer fact of being young and alive, sharing our dreams, our ambitions, our secrets.

And then the triangle had warped and split because one of us had left, taking her secrets with her.

I thought about how angry and confused Samantha and I had been at Molly's sudden departure. I'd go so far as to say we'd also felt a little bit scared because we didn't know what had happened to Molly, and whether she was okay – we had no way of knowing, no way of finding out. Reliving the feelings of that time drew me back to the present, and my discovery of Molly's swimming costume in the old surgery, the costume I'd first thought was mine.

Since my initial inspection, I'd not given my find much thought, being preoccupied with other things, except on the odd occasion when my hand had encountered the edge of the carrier bag containing the costume and towel while I was ferreting in the drawer for something else. Then, I'd feel a sharp inward tug of air, as if I'd received a light blow to the chest, before I forgot about it again.

As I sat beneath the Kissing Tree where the three of us had

plotted and schemed and worried our brains, mostly over stuff that hadn't mattered at all in the end, suddenly it seemed as if there was an answer to the swimming costume mystery, one I'd known all along. Tilting my head back, I gazed up at the scraps of sky visible through the canopy of leaves. But it wasn't the sky I was seeing, it was Samantha and me, trailing back to Summerdene from the river that Sunday afternoon, having been stood up by Molly after she'd promised to meet us there.

And then the mind picture jumped to my old bedroom, and Samantha and I listening to *Pick of the Pops* on the radio, singing along to our favourite songs, the DJ's voice rising to a crescendo as that week's chart climbed towards number one. The house had been empty apart from the two of us, but I'd heard something above the music, a sound like a door closing. It had given me a sense of unease I'd never truly forgotten.

Sunday afternoon. Sun on the river. Samantha in her swimming costume, showing off to the boys. Then, the kitchen at Summerdene. Ginger cake and orange squash. Molly's mother telling us when we rang that Molly had gone to the river to meet us. She hadn't, but her costume had still ended up in my house.

Finally, I understood. Molly had been at Summerdene that afternoon, so close, but not with us. She'd been in the surgery extension, obviously not alone. And there was only one other person who could have been with her.

FORTY-ONE

BRIONY

I stayed up late, long after I'd heard my guests arriving back with mumbled voices and careful feet on the creaky staircase. Tonight especially, I found the sounds comforting, and was glad I wasn't alone in the house.

Once I'd gone up to bed, I couldn't settle. When I finally fell asleep, I dreamt I was in the old surgery, feeling the pressure on my back from the edge of the reception desk, Jeremy's breath hot on my neck, his hand on my shoulder, tracing a line down my body. I was fighting, and yet I was completely still. As still as death. From the rows of metal chairs, Samantha, Molly, Faye, Logan, Alice and, randomly, Sylvia, watched me. Not moving either. Not speaking. Behind them, in the corner, rictus grin on its face, bones dusted green by the half-light from the window, the skeleton stood.

I don't often remember dreams, but this one stayed fresh and sharp when I woke in a sweaty tussle of bedclothes at daybreak, the dawn chorus filtering through the open top window.

I went downstairs, made myself a cup of tea and brought it

back to bed. I made myself stay there until a reasonable time but I was too wired for more sleep. My thoughts returned to Faye. Wanting to hear her voice, I reached for my phone to call her but it was too early, so I messaged instead, wishing her a good trip to London. She answered in minutes with a thumbs-up emoji, saying she planned to catch the ten-fifteen train from Stroud and she hoped I had a nice day.

I prepared breakfast and presided over the dining room almost on automatic pilot. Pippa arrived in time to help with the clearing up, and I chatted to my guests and asked what they planned to do today. One couple were going to Blenheim Palace, and I told them I'd been, and how impressive it was. That day with Marcus seemed so very long ago, and my heart skittered as I thought of him so close by – I knew he was back as I'd seen the car – and yet so far away he might as well have been on another planet.

But I couldn't afford to dwell on what might have been, not today. I had other concerns.

Around eleven, I went upstairs to find Pippa, who was dusting one of the guest bedrooms.

'I have to go out for a while,' I said. 'You'll be okay, won't you?'

I'd left her in the house before, and it was never a problem; she seemed puzzled that I'd asked.

'Yeah, of course. I'll finish off upstairs then run the vac around the hall. It could do with a go.'

'Yes, please. The laundry van's due any minute. The dirty stuff's by the back door,' I said. 'And help yourself to coffee and biscuits.' Not that she needed telling. 'Oh, and remember to lock the back door if you go before I get back. I'm not sure how long I'll be.'

Not too long, I hoped, but it was best to cover all eventualities.

'Yep, will do.' Pippa gave me a funny look and resumed her dusting.

I hesitated over taking the car, usually preferring to walk to the village, but in the end I decided to drive to save time.

I arrived in Candle Street in twelve minutes. The road was narrow and cluttered with parked vehicles. I squeezed into a space and sat for a few minutes, gazing across at number nineteen, Faye and Logan's cottage, with its incongruously modern front door and wooden slatted window blinds, thinking how strange it was that I hadn't been here before – I'd never actually been invited; my visits were always proposed for some future time which never happened. I'd had no reason to turn up unannounced.

Until now.

The houses in Candle Street were terraced and fronted directly onto the pavement. I got out of the car before my nerve gave out, marched up to the front door of number nineteen and pressed the bell. He might be out, of course. Part of me was already hoping he was. But then the door swung open, and Logan did a double-take when he saw me standing there.

'Briony! Good to see you again, so soon.' He couldn't hide his irritation, but his expression swiftly turned to one of polite regret. 'You've missed Faye, I'm afraid. She's gone to London.'

'I know,' I said. 'It's you I've come to see. Can I come in?'

'Of course.' He smiled, held the door back and I stepped inside the tiny hallway. 'Would you like some coffee? Tea?'

'No, thanks.' I walked into the small sitting room on the left, without being invited. 'I'll just say what I've got to say, then go.'

My brusque tone clearly annoyed him; it was written all

over his face. I didn't care what he thought of me. This wasn't a
social call.

He followed me into the room, dropped into an armchair
and waved nonchalantly towards the other. I sat.

'What's this about? Only you don't look too happy,' Logan
said, his tone edging towards sarcastic.

It was to my advantage, I thought, that he'd dropped his
slightly ingratiating manner. It meant I didn't have to fight my
instincts and remind myself that this was the man my daughter
had chosen as her partner, and I should behave accordingly. I
couldn't pretend any longer.

Sorry, Faye.

I took a deep breath. 'No, I'm not happy. Not at all. It's
about Faye that I'm here. You're playing her, reeling her in.
You're all over her one minute, turning on her the next, messing
her around so she doesn't know where she is, and I won't have
her treated like that. That's what I came to say. That's not love,
Logan, it's the worst kind of control.'

He reared up in his seat. 'What're you talking about? How
dare you come here and accuse me of not treating Faye properly? It's *nonsense*!'

His protestation sounded so fake I almost laughed.

'I'm not stupid, Logan, and neither is my daughter. She may
be in love with you, or thinks she is, but she'll see you for what
you are, sooner or later, as I have.'

Logan rubbed a hand across the top of his head. 'Look, I
don't know where you're getting this rubbish from, but let's just
calm down, shall we?' He modulated his voice, but it took him
some effort.

I wasn't finished; I'd only just begun. 'The ring, Logan. The
diamond ring you gave her, with all kinds of promises, no doubt.
You blamed her for losing it and you were angry with her for
being careless, which she wasn't. She was *so* upset. You must
have realised that?'

'Oh, so that's what this is about? The bloody ring.' Logan pointed a finger at me. 'That ring cost me over two grand. Of *course* I was annoyed she'd lost it. Couldn't expect otherwise, could she?'

Lost it. Right. I decided not to pursue that one any further. One look at Logan's face told me it wouldn't get me anywhere.

'Then you promised her a dream holiday when you had no intention of taking her,' I said, moving on. 'Faye's not a gold-digger and you should know that. She doesn't expect to be whisked off to the Caribbean, or wherever. But you lied and told her it was all arranged, let her book time off work, and then you let her down with a load of excuses.'

I was partly guessing now – I didn't know exactly what had taken place between the two of them because Faye hadn't told me. But my gut instinct told me that Logan had never even booked that holiday, never mind paid for it.

'I couldn't afford it,' he said belligerently. 'She was the one who chose it.'

He was twisting things now, putting the blame on Faye.

'You misled her, Logan, you know you did, and that's unfor-givable.'

He shrugged but said nothing.

I considered raising the subject of his rumoured infidelity, but as Faye's stance on that was to dismiss it as idle gossip and there was no real evidence, I decided not to challenge him directly.

But I could allude to it in a roundabout way to test his reaction.

'Good relationships are based on mutual trust, Logan. You shouldn't have secrets. They're harmful.'

'Secrets? What secrets?' His voice was scornful.

'You've been going out, staying out late and not saying where you've been. Faye rationalises it because that's how she is. But that doesn't mean she likes it.'

'Nobody's asking her to like it,' Logan snarled.

I ignored him and pressed on.

'The day we met in the village, I saw you going into the flat above the bike shop. You thought I hadn't seen, but I had. Who lives there? Who were you going to see?'

Logan shook his head slowly. 'Who says I was going to see anybody? You've got a vivid imagination, Briony. I'll say that for you.'

'If you've got nothing to hide, you won't mind telling me why you were there, will you?'

'That's none of your business. It's nobody's business but mine where I go and who I see. Anyway, Faye won't be best pleased you came to warn me off, I can tell you that.'

He had a point about Faye. It went through my mind that I could lose her altogether over this. But I'd deal with that if it came to it. I didn't regret coming here – I couldn't – because everything I'd heard so far only underlined the truth about Logan, what kind of a man he really was.

He got to his feet. I stood up, too. We faced each other across the small space. He went to speak again but I beat him to it.

'As soon as Faye's back I'm getting her out of here, away from you. You won't break her, Logan, and you won't break me.'

'I wouldn't be so sure about that.'

His mouth twisted into a sneer. I felt pinpricks on the back of my neck, like a series of tiny electrical shocks. I'd seen that exact expression before.

The backs of my knees began to itch. Unable to resist, I reached down and scratched at one of them beneath my cotton skirt. And that was when I noticed that Logan was barefoot.

Long, pale feet. Toes liberally coated with fine, dark hair, like rows of creepy little furry creatures, nestled together. I stared and stared at those feet, until I sensed Logan's eyes on me, and I looked up.

'*My God.*' I breathed the words rather than speaking them.

I met his cold grey gaze, and all my moments of recognition, my brain's underlying insistence that there was something I should know about this man, suddenly added up and made a truth.

'I know who you are. You're... *his* son. Your father was Jeremy Church.'

Logan clapped his hands slowly, several times.

'What took you so long, Briony?' He grinned unpleasantly. 'But, hey, it's been fun watching you try and work it out. Yep, poor old Jeremy was my real father, apparently.'

Apparently? If there was any doubt in Logan's mind, there definitely wasn't in mine. I felt shaky and sick from the shock revelation. I didn't know what to say next, what to do.

Logan was Jeremy's son.

Their names weren't the same – Logan's surname was Worth, not Church, but that would be because of the adoption – and the physical resemblance wasn't a perfect match. But the more I looked at this man, the more I saw my old tormentor, and the more my brain re-enacted my long-buried, but never forgotten, teenage fears and anxieties.

I swallowed away the constriction in my throat; my voice came, but sounded strange, different, to my ears.

'Let's get back to the point, shall we? What do you get out of ruining my daughter's life? *Trying* to ruin it, I should say. What's she ever done to you?'

'Nothing. It's a simple concept – take Faye down and I take you down with her. That's how it works, doesn't it?'

'*Me?* What have you got against me? You don't even know me!' I spat the words, unable to believe what I was hearing.

'You spread lies about Jeremy when you lived at Summerdene before. You made out he was some kind of monster. Turned the whole damn village against him, I shouldn't wonder. He couldn't wait to tell me all about it.'

'That's *not* how it was, Logan. For the record, he treated me abominably, and I had every right to say what I liked about him. But it's ancient history. I was *sixteen*, for God's sake! Anyway, why do you care, all of a sudden?'

Logan held up a hand, the palm facing me. 'Give me a minute and it'll all start to make sense.'

'*What* will?' I was on fire with anger and frustration. The backs of my knees itched like fury. I reached down and scratched angrily at them.

He perched on the arm of the chair as if we were having a neighbourly chat.

'You and your girly friends sat around that bloody tree, calling Jeremy all sorts, making fun of him. Making out he was some sort of pervert. Okay, he resented you for cosying up to Alice, but he never did anything to hurt you. Whatever he said, it was only in fun. It was just banter. Only you were too sensitive and took it personally.'

I sat down. My legs wouldn't hold me any longer. My head whirled with all I was expected to take in as an unstoppable tide of questions began to roll forwards. Logan carried on talking, oblivious to my discomfort. But of course, he didn't care about that, no more than his father had.

'He heard you, so don't deny it, Briony. He followed you into the woods and heard it all,' he said, answering one of my unspoken questions.

I'd always suspected we were followed, more than once. Jeremy had hidden from us on the riverbank, so why not in the woods as well?

'What you didn't know,' Logan continued, 'was that one of you didn't go along with all the bad-mouthing. She just acted like she did. And that was because she had a secret, the biggest secret you'd never have guessed at.'

'No,' I said, shaking my head firmly. 'It was nothing like that. This is wrong.'

We hadn't held back on our opinion of Jeremy, it was true. Turning him into the worst kind of joke had helped me put it all into perspective. But we were the three witches, or The Three Musketeers, depending on what day it was – we were united in our revulsion for Jeremy. Logan must have misinterpreted what he'd been told and twisted the story. Or Jeremy had falsified events to suit himself, which was more like it.

Samantha, Molly and I used to share secrets all the time but it was schoolgirl stuff, and not that secret anyway. I wondered if Jeremy had heard us talking about boys and sex, and put some sort of spin on it. Was that all it was? Had he heard Samantha say she wanted to be the first to lose her virginity, and been deluded enough to believe he was in with a chance? He'd fancied Samantha, I'd always known it, but if he'd imagined she was thinking about him in those terms, he couldn't have been more wrong.

I couldn't think what else it could be but there was no more time to try and make sense of it because Logan was talking again. He sat forward on the arm of the chair, his upper body thrust aggressively towards me.

'It wasn't just poisonous chitchat either, was it? You and your little mate decided to play a game. A dangerous game. Enjoy that, did you? Humiliating my father?'

I felt a rush of guilt for the first time. I knew exactly what he meant. But I'd been desperate; I'd had to do *something*, and, actually, the whole thing had been Samantha's idea...

Logan broke into my thoughts. 'Actions have consequences, Briony. Your vendetta against Jeremy had serious consequences, for me. What you did back then affected my whole life. Didn't know that, did you?'

His life? What did that mean?

I pressed on, regardless.

'Vendetta's a bit strong,' I said. 'And actually, you have *no idea* what Jeremy did to me. No idea at all, and I doubt he's filled you in on that. But how could any of it affect you? You didn't even exist. Logan, this is getting ridiculous now.' I stood up. 'I don't know what planet you're on but I've heard enough. I'm going now. But remember what I said about Faye...'

'Ah yes, precious little Faye.' His voice was scathing. 'Let's not forget about *her*.'

'Stop it!' I said. 'Just shut up.'

I walked across the room and stepped into the hall. Logan followed me.

'Shut up? That's not very ladylike, is it?'

I couldn't be bothered to argue with this madman any more, or try and make sense of any of this. All I could think about now was intercepting Faye's arrival home and getting her safely back to Summerdene.

But there was one question I had to ask.

'If all that... *anger* has been festering inside you for so long, why did you suddenly decide to come looking for me with all this revenge-by-proxy nonsense?'

Logan shook his head. 'No, you don't get it. I didn't know about any of it, not until quite recently.' He glanced past me, avoiding my gaze, as if finally some kind of emotion had been triggered. 'I was adopted, as I'm sure Faye told you. Jeremy Church was my biological father, except nobody thought to tell him, until I found out his name, tracked him down, and got the whole story from him. And that is *why*, Briony, it was all your fault. If you hadn't made him out to be the bad guy, he might have had a say in where I ended up, and my life would have turned out a whole lot differently. Instead, he was kept in the dark.'

'Wait a minute,' I said, not fully understanding. 'You're saying that if Jeremy had been named as your father, you might not have been put up for adoption? If so, it's a pretty wild theory. Your birth mother would have had the biggest say, I imagine. You might still have been adopted, even if Jeremy had known about you.'

'*Might*, Briony.' Logan's eyes blazed. He took a step nearer to me. 'That's the key. He told me the girl suddenly refused to have any more to do with him, let alone tell him she was pregnant.'

'But it's all conjecture, isn't it?' I was still confused, although now I knew a little of how Logan's mind worked, it was obvious he believed what he wanted to believe, and nobody could persuade him otherwise.

Just like Jeremy.

'Not really. When you think about it, it makes perfect sense. Explains everything,' Logan said.

'Does it?' *Explains what, exactly?* There was still something I wasn't getting.

'So why come after me now?' I asked. 'Because, honestly, I have no idea where this is all leading. And, even if any of it's even halfway true, there's nothing I can do about it. I can't rewrite history.'

'That's where you're wrong, Briony. That's exactly what you *can* do. I had a bloody awful childhood. My adoptive parents, if you could call them that, didn't give a shit about me – I won't go into detail, but just so you know. Say Jeremy had been told he was about to become a daddy, might he not have stepped up to the plate and taken responsibility for me? Because that's what he told me he would have done. And then, years down the line, when Alice penned her last will and testament, with her son already gone, would she not have left all her worldly goods, including Summerdene, to me, her only grandchild and not to you, the cuckoo in the nest, who had no connection to the family whatsoever? Of course she would. No doubt about it.'

. . .

The cuckoo in the nest. Jeremy's words came straight from Logan's mouth.

And, *Summerdene.* Right. We were finally getting to the crux of the matter. It explained Logan's remark about my inheritance when he and Faye were arguing. It hadn't been a random, meaningless attack at all.

'This is crazy, Logan!' I stared at him. 'Like I said, it's all conjecture. You have no idea what would have happened if Jeremy had been named as your father. You didn't know Alice and you can't possibly guess at what she might have done. You've fabricated the story to suit your own ends, that's what it sounds like to me.'

Logan shook his head. 'If it wasn't for you, Briony, I'd have been set up for life. I *deserved* that, and I still do.'

I couldn't speak. This man's innate sense of entitlement was off the scale, as well as his loose grip on reality. The whole thing was a work of fiction, maybe not the bit about Logan's adoptive parents but definitely the rest of it. I was pretty sure that Jeremy wouldn't have wanted to know he'd fathered a child. The Jeremy I knew would have run a mile. A thousand miles. For a moment, I felt sympathy for Logan. If Jeremy had fed him those lies, made out he was the kind of man he could never be, I couldn't help but feel a little sorry for him.

But how did I know Logan wasn't making it up, and Jeremy had said no such thing? It seemed all too likely.

And then there was the girl, Logan's birth mother. I'd not had a chance to think about her. Who was she? Somebody from the village? Somebody he'd met in Oxford, a fellow student with her whole life ahead of her, who'd got pregnant at the wrong time? A married woman, even, who'd had to keep the whole thing secret? I thought about asking Logan if he knew who she was, but it hardly mattered now. Whoever it was had clearly been taken in by Jeremy's fake charm, and more fool her.

Actually, no. I shouldn't say that. Jeremy could turn on the charm and come across as totally plausible when it suited him. As could his son.

I drew in a long, deep breath. It became a violent shudder. Noticing, Logan smirked. He heeled a hand against the wall.

'So there you have it. Your past has jumped up and hit you in the face, like it always does in the end. The thing is, Briony, what are you going to do about it?'

'Nothing. I don't owe you a thing, Logan, although you seem to have taken it into your head that I do.'

I reached for the door handle. I had to be out of here, now. Away from this fantasist.

Logan quickly reached above me and held the door shut.

'Not so fast. I'll tell you exactly what you're going to do, Briony. You're going to give me two hundred and fifty thousand pounds. That's right, a quarter of a mill, and that's letting you off lightly.'

I would have laughed if I wasn't so appalled.

'As if I'm going to do that,' I spat. 'Now let me out of here.'

Logan kept his hand on the door, pinning me with a look that was way past threatening.

'Oh, you'll pay. You'll pay up if you want to keep your pretty daughter safe. And don't take too long about it.'

If I didn't give him the money, money I didn't even have, he would harm Faye. Or somebody would. That was the bottom line. I understood him all too clearly now.

My blood ran cold.

I couldn't let him see what this was doing to me. I couldn't let him see how scared I was, not for myself but for Faye. But I probably wasn't that good an actor.

I lifted my chin, meeting his gaze. 'You're living in a dream world. I haven't got that sort of money anyway.'

'Raise it on Summerdene. Sell it if you have to.'

'I'll go to the police. Blackmail's a crime.'

'Gotta prove it first. Who's to say this conversation ever took place?'

Logan let go of the door and I almost fell through it, my feet landing heavily on the pavement. I looked around. The street was still as quiet as the grave. Nobody to see; nobody to wonder. I jogged to my car.

Moments later, I was away. It wasn't until I was almost home that I realised my face was wet with tears.

FORTY-TWO
BRIONY

Somehow I made it through the village, and home. I drove through the gates of Summerdene and onto the gravelled forecourt, a little unsteadily, took out my phone and fired off a misspelt text to Faye asking about her arrangements for coming home.

The guests' cars were gone and I slumped over the steering wheel in relief; I craved the peace and quiet of an empty house like never before. I needed to process what had happened this morning and sort my head out before I was fit to be seen in public.

But it seemed there was no reprieve – Pippa's bike was still there, leaning drunkenly against the hedge. The clock on the dashboard told me it was twenty minutes past the girl's normal leaving time. She usually left on time because of her little boy, and I wished today hadn't been an exception. I found a packet of tissues in the glove compartment and used one to dab my face. My body felt three times its usual weight as I heaved myself out of the car, half-staggered to the front door and keyed in the code. Pippa was at the end of the hall as I entered, bundling the vacuum into the cupboard. She turned when she heard me. If she'd noticed I'd been crying she didn't say anything.

'Hi, Briony.' She shut the cupboard door with a bang. 'All done. The laundry bloke turned up. He said to tell you the prices are going up next week and to watch out for the email about it.'

'Okay. Thanks, Pippa. You'd better get going. It's past your time,' I said, my voice dull with the thickness in my throat.

'Yeah, but I thought I'd better wait for you. You might have a problem. Here, look.'

She pointed at the floor. I couldn't see anything at first; the kitchen door was closed and the light in the hall was dim.

'There's water on the floor,' Pippa said. 'See?'

She sounded a little impatient, which wasn't like her, but she obviously wanted to be off home. I peered down and saw what she meant; the wooden floor was definitely wet.

'I reckon it's coming from in there.' Pippa jabbed a thumb at the internal door to the old surgery. 'The water's right outside it. Don't see where else it could've come from. I hung on to tell you in case you didn't spot it.'

In my frazzled state, I definitely wouldn't have noticed a drop of water on the floor. But actually, it was more than a drop, and unless water had seeped up through the floorboards, which was near impossible, or come from above – equally impossible – it must have come from under the surgery door.

I sighed. 'It doesn't seem to be getting any worse. I'll clear it up and see what happens. Thank you for waiting for me.'

'S'okay. Hadn't you better have a look in there? Could be a worse flood inside if a pipe's burst or something.'

Reluctantly, I visualised the inside of the surgery. There was a hand basin in the inner room, so there were water pipes. Very old pipes, probably rusty. If one of those had finally given out, it would need sorting without delay. I would have thought the water had been turned off years ago, but maybe the surgery didn't have a supply separate from the main house.

'I'll check. I'll just fetch the key. You needn't wait. Your little one will be wondering where you've got to.'

Please, just go, Pippa.

A leaky pipe, inconvenient though it would be, was the very least of my problems. Why today of all days?

I went to the kitchen, taking off my shoulder bag and hooking it over a chair as I passed, and fetched the surgery door key from the drawer, where I'd put it for safekeeping after I'd located it before. Pippa hadn't moved. Maybe she didn't trust me to sort out the problem on my own, but I didn't know what use she could be. This could be a job for a professional.

Still, it was good of her to wait. I slid the key into the lock and the door creaked open. The same smell hit me as before: dusty, damp, faintly chemical, but as the room was never aired, it wasn't surprising the smell still lingered. Some weeks ago, I had hacked the greenery away from the outside of the window and given it a perfunctory clean, but the foliage had since recommenced its insidious journey across the glass and the light was filtered to a greenish haze.

I stepped inside and peered at the floor area around the door. There was one small patch of wet close to the door, but that was all. I went through the interconnecting door to the former consulting room and checked the basin. Its surface was bone-dry, as were the pipes beneath it when I ran my finger along them. I fiddled with the taps but they wouldn't turn. No leakage could have come from anywhere in here, and in any case, the whole floor was perfectly dry.

'It's okay,' I called to Pippa, who was still waiting outside the door. 'No flood or anything in here. It's just one of those mystery things. I might get someone in to take a look at some point...'

The surgery door closed. Had it swung shut in the draught?

There were no draughts, not that I could feel. I went to the door and twisted the doorknob impatiently. If I didn't sit down soon with a cup of tea or, better still, lie down, my head would explode. For some reason, the door wasn't opening. Like everything else in this part of the house, it had hardly been used for years. I twisted it forcefully and pushed, using the little strength I had left, but the door still wouldn't open.

'Pippa? Open the door, will you? Give it a yank, it's got stuck.'

No reply.

And then I realised I'd heard something a moment ago, a sound that could have been the key turning in the lock. Surely the girl hadn't locked the door, thinking I'd already come out? Of course she hadn't; she could hardly have missed me.

'Pippa? Are you there?'

Where was the stupid girl? Seeds of panic were flourishing in my gut. My head throbbed from the traumas of the morning. I didn't need anything else to go wrong.

Still no answer. I shouted again, louder, and banged my fist on the wooden panel of the door, several times. It was a thick door but Pippa couldn't have failed to hear me.

'Pippa! I can't get out. Please open the door.'

This time I heard sounds. I put my ear to the door. Footsteps. I could have cried with relief. Pippa must have wandered off, and now she was back.

'Sorry about that,' a muffled voice said. 'Just had to...'

'Will you please hurry up!' I ordered, noticing the panic in my voice. 'Just unlock this bloody door!'

'Ah, now, that might not be so simple,' Pippa said.

And then she laughed. She actually laughed.

I stepped back from the door and took a deep breath, telling myself this was my house and everything was under my control. Even the plumbing, which hadn't failed at all. At least, not today. I remembered now seeing my big enamel jug standing beside the sink when I'd gone to fetch the key. It usually lived on the top shelf. I hadn't questioned it then. Now I didn't need to. Pippa must have used it to pour water onto the floor and tricked me into coming in here. Whatever crazy game she was playing, it had to stop.

'Pippa, this isn't funny,' I said, more quietly, but still loud enough for her to hear. 'I've got things to do. I haven't got time to muck around. Get this door open.'

A moment's silence, then I heard: 'Don't like it, do you? Being stuck in there with no way out. Horrible, isn't it? So now you know how it feels. Or you will do in a few hours' time.'

A few hours? How many hours, exactly? What was the girl trying to do to me, and why? I dredged my shattered thoughts for answers, but after this morning's encounter with Logan, they weren't exactly co-operating.

Except, certain things were beginning to line up...

So now you know how it feels.

It sounded like payback, comparing how I felt about being locked in the old surgery with somebody else's experience. And that somebody else could only be one person. But how did Pippa know about him, and what happened more than thirty years ago?

No, it was impossible. In my current mental state, I was imagining things; putting two and two together and making five, as Alice used to say, and yet...

Jeremy and Logan.

Jeremy and Logan... and Pippa.

My mind raced, my head spun, as the third link forged itself to the chain. I'd had one shock today when I'd discovered who Logan really was. I wasn't sure I could take another.

I pressed my palms to the door and shouted.

'Pippa? Are you still there? Look, I don't know what you think you're doing but this won't end well, and I'm not talking about myself here.'

'You have to give him what he wants, Briony. You have to. It's only fair.' Pippa's voice came through loud and clear.

'Logan. That's who you mean, isn't it?' I said. 'He's black-mailing me, Pippa. I don't know what it's got to do with you, but you don't want to get mixed up in something nasty like that. You need to steer clear of that man. Do you hear me? Think about your mum, and little Rory. Think about them and do the right thing. Let me out of here and we'll say no more about it.'

I had to play to her better nature. Pippa might act the part of the tough cookie, but she was young, and clearly more impressionable than I'd realised. And she was a mother.

'It'll be all right. I'll protect you from Logan, if I have to,' I said.

I had no idea how I was going to do that, any more than I could protect myself. But if I could only get out of here, the rest would follow. Everything would be fine, in the end.

'I don't need *protecting* from Logan,' Pippa said, laughing. 'He's okay, and so am I. I can think for myself, Briony. What you stole from him, well... you deserve everything that's coming to you.'

So, Logan must have met Pippa – in the pub, around the village, wherever – enticed her into his web and fed her the same ridiculous theories he'd fed me. Theories he truly believed, and she'd fallen for every word. But why get involved? Unless he was paying her, which I supposed must be the case. I still couldn't imagine she'd take the risk. It didn't stack up, somehow.

I sank against the wall beside the door, thinking hard.

It had only been a matter of hours since Logan had demanded money from me; he must have been in touch with Pippa as soon as I'd left and updated her on my visit. Had they planned my incarceration between them? Had Pippa come up with the idea on her own, or had she been following instruc-tions? Maybe Logan had put the fear of God into her and threatened her if she didn't do as she was told. Knowing him, it was entirely possible. Yet, somehow, I didn't have the impression Pippa was scared of him. She sounded almost pleased to be a part of this, as if she was enjoying every moment.

I remembered her telling me about Logan's cheating on Faye with a full-figured redhead, ostensibly because she was concerned for Faye. But if she was on Team Logan, why say anything against him? It didn't make any sense. Clearly I was missing something. Forcing my unwilling mind back to this morning's debacle in Candle Street, I recalled Logan's words: *Take Faye down and I take you down with her.*

Logan might possibly have been seeing somebody, but my instinct told me it wasn't true. There had been no affair. It was all part of the same twisted plot to break my daughter's heart, and her spirit.

Tears sprang to my eyes again as I thought of my lovely girl, and how she'd been used to get at me. Faye, typically, would only be concerned for me when I told her the story, not for herself. I smudged the tears away with the back of my hand. I couldn't fall apart now; there was too much at stake.

I was about to yell at Pippa again and demand to be released when her voice sailed through the door, as bright as if this was an ordinary day.

'I'll be off now. Mustn't be too late home. See ya!'

I heard footsteps, and then the faint click of the front door closing.

FORTY-THREE

BRIONY

2022

I stepped back from the door in disbelief. What did the girl think she was playing at, locking me up inside my own house? Okay, I had imprisoned Jeremy in here, with Samantha's help, but, for God's sake, that was over thirty years ago!

I thought about Logan, and the grudge he'd carried all his life because his adoption had been an unhappy experience, the grudge that had mushroomed into mammoth proportions when he'd traced his birth father – Jeremy – and hung on every word he'd said, every lie he'd told and, through an intensely convoluted route, had finally found somebody to blame for his misfortune: me.

Logan was only thirty-five; with luck, he had a lifetime ahead to set the world on fire and make his own money. His adoption had clearly not ruined his life completely, since he'd gone on to get himself educated and trained in his chosen field. Gaming, I'd read, was the fastest growing of the entertainment industries, offering plenty of opportunity.

So, why? Why all this? I couldn't understand it, and yet,

when I thought about Jeremy, and how he'd taken against me, the girl who'd landed at Summerdene through no fault of her own, and become Alice's protégée almost by default, I saw the similarities in the pair of them. The way their minds worked, the way everything had to be on their terms, and how they twisted everything out of shape until it caused untold damage to everyone around them and, eventually, to themselves.

The sins of the fathers.

I wondered how long Pippa planned on keeping me imprisoned. Samantha and I had left Jeremy in here for a day and two whole nights, but we had at least provided water and snacks. Hopefully, as I had been given nothing, Pippa wasn't planning to match this and would come back soon and let me out. Teaching me a lesson, as she and Logan saw it, was all part of the master plan – Logan's plan – to exert his power and to extort money from me. Pippa was just being dragged along in his wake. If she thought she was getting a share of the quarter of a million I was supposedly parting with, she was even more stupid than I'd thought.

I went back to the door and put my ear against it. The house was ominously silent. It was unlikely any of the guests would return before late afternoon at the earliest. If by any chance I was still stuck in here, I could draw their attention to my plight, tell them the door had slammed accidentally, and rely on them to get me out. If the key was still in the lock, there'd be no problem. If not, they'd figure it out somehow.

But it was a small comfort to realise I might be in here for another six hours at least, with no water, no food, no toilet facilities, nothing at all except the clothes I stood up in, and I sensed the beginnings of panic.

I shook the door handle violently. It wouldn't budge, as I'd known it wouldn't. I crossed to the window, reached up and heaved on the two metal handles securing the casement, but of course, it wouldn't open; it never had. The remaining lopsided waiting room chair might hold my weight if I used it to climb up. I might be able to smash the glass with the old black telephone or the rotary card holder, but even if I managed that, the window was too high for me to exit easily, and the thought of snagging myself on lethal jagged glass put paid to that idea. Too risky by far.

No, I'd just have to wait it out.

There was a chilly dampness in the air, and I was only wearing a thin skirt and a T-shirt. The backs of my knees were sore where I'd scratched at the eczema, and the mouldy, disinfectant smell in the room was making me feel nauseous. I wandered around the waiting room area, my arms wrapped around myself, then went through the open connecting door to the consulting room. It felt even colder in here, and I was about to come out again when my eyes alighted on the cork noticeboard propped in the corner, where I'd found the bag containing the towel and swimming costume amongst the other rubbish.

Molly's costume, which was still in my bedroom drawer.

That Sunday afternoon, while Samantha and I had been listening to the radio in my room after our wasted trip to the river, Molly had been in the house, too, hiding out in the surgery with Jeremy – I'd worked that out before, although I'd never been certain until now.

I recalled the gist of Logan's words – was that really only a few hours ago?

One of the three of you didn't go along with badmouthing Jeremy as much as the other two... because she had a secret...

He hadn't meant Samantha at all.

He'd meant Molly.

Time stood still. I sat on the floor beneath the window, hugging my knees. I almost felt that if I looked up now, I would see, not the stained ceiling of the old surgery, but the spreading branches of the beech tree – the Kissing Tree – its bright green leaves quivering gently in the breeze against the blue backdrop of the sky. And our little trio of friendship, forged forever by hopes and dreams and fears and pent-up excitement for the unknown future. Unbreakable. Or so I'd thought.

It was forever summer.

And we were forever sixteen.

The chill in the atmosphere made its insidious way into my bones, but still I sat there, enmeshed in the past. There were questions I wanted to ask, except there was nobody to ask them of. Had Molly been in love with Jeremy? I supposed she must have been – or he'd talked her into believing she was. I couldn't bring myself to think she'd have slept with him if she didn't have feelings for him, and there would have been no reason for them to hide out in the surgery, other than for sex. Had Jeremy felt anything for Molly apart from lust and the need to control?

I dragged myself back to the present, and my predicament. I'd already decided that, if Pippa didn't relent and come back and let me out, my B&B guests would help. But supposing I didn't hear them come in? Or I shouted and banged, and they didn't hear me? Would they settle down for the night, thinking I'd gone out for the evening, leaving me to stew? I'd be in the dark; the strip lights didn't work. I couldn't even think about the morning, and my guests making their way down to find no breakfast and their host missing.

Damn Pippa! Stupid girl!

Stretching my legs out straight in front of me, I took several long, deep breaths – working myself into a panic wouldn't help – and posted my mind back to the past again. Deliberately blocking Jeremy from my thoughts, I latched onto happier memories of my past life in Mistlecombe: school; my job at Pink's; my friendships with Samantha and Molly.

The three of us had spent much of our free time waiting

around for buses and trains to lift us out of our boring little village and deliver us to the delights of Cheltenham, Stroud and Gloucester. Sometimes, because of a late bus or missed train, we'd arrive at our destination with time only for a quick tour of the shops or an hour in a disco before we'd have to turn around and head home again. But we didn't care; we'd been together, and we'd had fun.

I smiled, recalling the time Samantha left her shopping on the bus home – a skirt and jumper from Tammy Girl – and despite it being late afternoon, she made Molly and I wait with her at the bus stop until the same bus had completed its circuit of the surrounding villages and arrived back so she could reclaim it.

But my reminiscing could only sustain me for so long, and when I opened my eyes – I hadn't realised I'd closed them – the full impact of what was happening now hit me afresh. How long had I been stuck in here? I had no watch on me and no phone – it was in my bag, in the kitchen – but the light from the window above me had shifted, and now brightened a different part of the room. Several hours, clearly. It felt like days.

Feeling the sensations of panic again, I got up from the floor and re-examined the window. I'd have to smash my way out, risky or not. There was nothing else for it. I stooped down and inspected the defunct black phone, but with the receiver and the wires attached, it would be awkward to handle, especially while I was balancing on the chair. The rotary card holder might be better. I picked it up from the floor. It was heavy enough to do the job, although again, difficult to hold. Perhaps if I used both hands...

I heard the muffled ping of the front doorbell. Perhaps it was one of the guests, having forgotten the door code. It rang again. I dropped the card holder and scooted to the surgery door, but there was nothing I could do about it. Maybe if I banged on the window, whoever was at the front of the house would hear me. I rushed across, my fist raised, ready to attack the glass. But then I heard footsteps. They were inside the house, faint, then growing louder as they approached. I raced back to the door.

'Who is it? Who's there?' I yelled, my mouth an inch from the door. Then, when there was no reply, 'Pippa? Is that you?'

'Briony? Briony, where are you?'

Not Pippa. *Marcus*.

'Here! I'm in here!' I thumped hard on the door. 'In the surgery!'

His voice came from inches away. 'Can't you get out?'

I wanted to laugh. 'Does it look like it? Can you unlock the door? Is the key in the lock?'

'Nope. No key here.'

Oh God.

'Don't worry. I'll kick the door down.'

'No, you can't. It's too solid. You'll do yourself an injury. Look around. Look for the key. That daft girl might not have taken it with her.'

'What daft girl? How did you get in there?'

Now I did laugh. 'I'll explain later. Check the kitchen.'

'Okay, hang on.'

Footsteps receded. He seemed to have been gone an age, and then: 'Found it. At least, I think... Yes, this is the one...'

The lock clicked. The door opened, and I fell into Marcus's arms.

FORTY-FOUR

BRIONY

I clung to Marcus, and he held me while I cried hot tears of relief, but they were short lived. I was free, and I was fine. There was nothing to cry about. I peeled away from him. He pressed a tissue into my hand and led me to the kitchen, filled the kettle and switched it on.

'Somebody could do with a cup of tea, I think.'

He smiled. I'd missed that smile, so much. It almost broke me. I dropped into a chair.

'Why are you here? How did you know I...?'

He didn't answer immediately. He brought two mugs of tea to the table and sat down opposite me, his eyes not leaving my face. I realised then that finding me locked in the surgery had shaken him. And I'd only been thinking about myself.

'I'd just got home. I was getting out of my car as you went by in yours. You seemed upset.'

'I didn't notice you,' I said. As if I'd have noticed anybody on that journey home, even if they'd been standing in the middle of the road. 'How could you see I was upset from where you were?'

'It's a narrow road. You slowed down as you passed my gate,

enough for me to see you were crying. I told myself it was none of my business and I went indoors, but I couldn't stop thinking about you. I was going to phone to ask if you were okay, but then I thought it would be better to come and see for myself. I rang the bell twice and looked through the front window and there was no sign of you, so I thought I'd better let myself in.'

'But that's... oh God, Marcus...'

I could find no more words. It seemed like some sort of miracle that Marcus had come. I didn't believe in miracles; apparently they existed.

'I've got to tell you off, though. Can't let it go.' He grinned, widening his eyes.

'Oh? What for?'

'For not changing the bloody key code on the front door often enough. How long has it been? Come on, Mrs Harrington. Fess up.'

'I forgot,' I said, lifting my chin in mock defiance.

'Hmm, well, I'll let you off, this once. Given the circumstances.' Marcus drank some of his tea. 'So now, are you going to tell me all about it?'

'I didn't expect to inherit Summerdene. I'd never even thought about who Alice might leave it to. Hearing it from the solicitor was the biggest shock of my life.'

We'd moved from the kitchen to the sitting room. I'd made more tea and brought it through, with a Victoria sponge from the village bakery. Then I'd told Marcus the whole story, the story as I knew it – composed mostly of facts and fleshed out with reasonable assumptions and educated guesswork.

'You don't have to convince me,' he said, smiling ruefully. 'Logan has no rights, and no hold over you. When someone's adopted, they're no longer part of the original family. They can't dip in and out when they feel like it.'

'I know. But Logan's take on the world isn't the same as other people's. Neither was Jeremy's. They're takers and users, the pair of them. And delusional. Or were, in Jeremy's case. I'd say they were psychotic, only that would imply it's not their fault, and right now I can't get on board with that idea.'

'You should go to the police, Briony,' Marcus said. 'Logan threatened to hurt Faye if you didn't give him the money, didn't he?'

'He wasn't specific, but that's what he implied. It was clear to me what he meant. There's no proof of blackmail, Marcus. It was a private conversation, nothing written down, no record, no witnesses. What would be the point?'

'All the same, you should report it,' Marcus said. 'It's up to you, of course. But I wouldn't leave it too long if you decide to go to the police. I'll go with you, if you want.'

'That's sweet of you,' I said.

But my mind was on Faye, my number one priority. I'd sent her a text when I'd arrived home from Candle Street, asking her to let me know when she would be back, and on which train. My phone was on the arm of my chair, no message indicator showing. I picked it up and checked to see if she'd read my message; she hadn't. That wasn't unusual for Faye, if she was busy working, or with friends. Usually it was nothing to worry about, except now I really needed to know her plans. I had to be at that station to collect her and bring her back to Summerdene before she set foot in Candle Street. I wasn't sure yet how I was going to explain why, or how much I would tell her at first. I only knew I had to get to her before Logan did.

My phone pinged and I scooped it up. There was a reply from Faye.

'Home Wednesday, prob lunchtime. Don't know what train yet.' Then two question marks and a puzzled-face emoji.

Wednesday; two days away. But that was fine. I could use the respite.

I quickly scrolled to her number and pressed the call button. She answered straight away.

'Mum? What's going on?' I heard the clatter of a busy café, or pub, in the background.

'Lovey, I can't explain it all now but I have to meet you off that train and you have to come home to Summerdene with me, before you go anywhere else, or do anything else. Sorry I'm sounding weird but you'll understand when I tell you all about it.'

'All about what? You're worrying me now. Is it to do with Logan? Is he okay?' I could hear the frown in her voice.

I hesitated. 'Logan's okay. But please do this, for me, Faye. If by any chance you're early and I'm not there, wait at the station. Please, promise you will. It's very important.'

Faye promised, and I believed her. And then, I realised the first thing she'd do was to phone Logan. Stupidly, I hadn't factored that in at all.

'Faye, listen,' I said. 'If Logan tells you to go straight home to him, don't take any notice. It may not be safe for you to be there. You have to trust me on this. *Faye?*'

'Yes, Mum, whatever you say.' She thought I'd lost the plot, that was obvious. Either that or I was grossly exaggerating some little incident. 'But, Mum, Logan's not going to be telling me anything because he's blocked me. I haven't been able to speak to him since I phoned him from the train on Monday morning. When I say "blocked" I mean that's what it looks like. He'll have broken his phone or something. He wouldn't have done it on purpose.'

Wouldn't he?

My heart went out to my girl. At the same time, I felt unutterably thankful at this turn of events.

'See you Wednesday,' I breathed. 'Don't forget to text the train time.'

Unwillingly, I ended the call. I had to leave her wondering. I couldn't possibly go into it all until we were face to face.

'Okay?' Marcus asked gently.

I found a smile. 'No, but I will be.'

The afternoon wore on. Sensing my need for some normality, Marcus talked about the university, and I talked about my B&B guests, and somehow another hour and a half passed. The sun moved around the room, lighting it from different angles. It didn't seem like my room any more, the room I had lovingly brought back to life, the objects within it carefully curated to create a pleasant haven. It seemed like a stranger's room, in a stranger's house. But it was only my mind playing tricks, I knew that.

Around five thirty, I heard the front door open and close. Through the partly open door, I saw the thirty-something couple from Room One heading upstairs. They'd probably go out again later for dinner. The other guests, two energetic and sweetly talkative elderly sisters, would be in soon. The single room was empty this week.

'I don't want to leave you, not like this,' Marcus said.

I assured him I'd be fine, and believed I would. But, oh, how I wanted him to stay, at least for a while longer! I had no idea when I'd see him again. Or even if I would. He may have had enough of me by now; I wouldn't blame him for that.

My eyes filled. I rubbed them impatiently. It was tiredness, that was all. It had been one hell of a day.

'No,' Marcus said firmly. 'I'm not leaving you, so no arguments.'

I smiled. 'I haven't got the strength to argue.'

We watched the news on TV, not talking much. And then I realised I felt hungry for the first time that day, and Marcus definitely needed to eat if he was staying, so we ordered in pizzas. We ate them in front of the TV, straight from the boxes, and drank lager from cans. The food and drink, and Marcus's presence, helped soothe my anxieties and gradually I felt my mood lift. We talked a little more about what had happened, and Marcus had just touched again on the subject of the police with his usual sensitivity when we heard the front door open.

The sisters had arrived back at the same time as the pizza delivery guy, and I hadn't heard any of the guests going out again. I got up from my chair and went out to the hall, Marcus following.

'You're out then,' Pippa said, closing the door behind her and planting herself squarely in front of me. 'Could've saved myself the trip.'

I'd almost forgotten about Pippa, or, at least, temporarily wiped her from my mind. Now, the sight of her set my nerve ends on fire and I only just managed to stop myself from hitting her as adrenaline fuelled my limbs.

I balled my hands into fists by my sides.

'You finally decided to let me out, did you? I'm guessing that's why you're here.'

Her skinny shoulders lifted up and down in a shrug. 'Wasn't going to, at first. Thought I'd better, in case the B&B lot got all excited and called the police, or you died or something. Didn't need that sort of bother.'

'No, I don't suppose you did.' I gave a hollow laugh. 'How could you, Pippa? How *could* you do that to me? Why get mixed up with a man like Logan Worth? Couldn't you see how he was using you, the same as he did Faye? The same he does everyone? You had a nice little job here. I repeat *had*. By the sound of it, your life in this village wasn't exactly tragic. You've got your mother, and your son... *Why*, Pippa?'

I ran out of steam. And, truth to tell, I realised I didn't care why she'd done those things. I just wanted her to understand the full impact of her actions, and then I wanted her gone, out of my range, out of my life.

She adopted a casual stance, her weight on one leg, hand on hip, and stared at me in astonishment.

'Ha, you still haven't worked it out, have you, Briony?'

'Oh, believe me, I've worked out one heck of a lot today, Pippa, and more fool me for not seeing it before. You're not in charge you know, Pippa. *He* is. Logan Worth. He'll dump you when you're no longer any use to him, if he hasn't already. Money's not everything, you know. Stupid girl.'

'Don't call me stupid!' Pippa flared up, her pale face pinking up. 'And don't keep calling him Logan *Worth*!'

'Why not? It's his name, isn't it?'

Pippa pointed a finger at me. 'Ha, that's one thing you haven't worked out, then. That's funny.'

I glanced round at Marcus, who was standing on guard just behind my right shoulder.

'What *is* his name, then?' I shot at Pippa.

'Medhurst. Logan Medhurst. Worth's a made-up name.'

'*Medhurst?* But that's *your* name...? Unless that's made up as well.' Nothing would surprise me now. Or so I thought.

'Oh, that's real all right. I'm Logan's sister. Not blood related. I was adopted into the same crummy family. Got screwed up by them, same as he did. He looked out for me, always did. Still does. So, I owe him, see? Logan's my big brother, and he's all I've got.'

She stared at me, wide-eyed, challenging, forthright.

My reactions – my emotions – went into freefall. I'd not understood the half of it, had I? Not even a fraction. There was more, I could tell, and I needed to hear it.

'So, you were adopted, and your birth mother was...?'

'No fucking clue who she was,' Pippa said. 'Nor my old man. Not that it's any of your business.'

'You fed me a pack of lies,' I said. 'You don't live in the

village with your mother. And you don't have a child, either, do you?'

'Me? Have a kid? Do me a favour.' Pippa laughed without humour.

I felt faint. I wanted to sit down. But we were still in the hall, and I wasn't letting Pippa any further into my house; she'd crossed the threshold for the last time. Marcus cleared his throat pointedly, and I looked round. Coming down the stairs were the two sisters, the young couple behind them. I didn't know how much they'd heard, but they looked decidedly awkward. They gave me tight little smiles as they reached the bottom of the stairs. Marcus and I automatically moved aside. Thankfully, Pippa did the same.

'Have nice evenings,' I said, faking brightness, as they disappeared through the front door.

For one manic moment, I wondered if they'd gone for good, and I'd end up giving them refunds and returning all their belongings to them by courier. But this was life, real life, and I doubted any of them would be fazed by a little altercation. They didn't seem the types to let rip on Trip Advisor, either.

'They'll be fine,' Marcus said quietly.

I nodded, and turned my attention back to Pippa, who had stayed close to the wall and now subsided against it, her mouth drooping in a sulk. She looked like a child made to stand in the naughty corner, and I felt my heart soften; I couldn't help it. But as she pushed away from the wall to face me again, I saw only hardness and defiance.

I thought about the questions she had asked me about Summerdene during our coffee morning 'chats'. They were nothing to do with the house's aesthetic appeal, I knew now, but because she'd been primed to pump me for information – anything I might let slip about how I came to be Alice's heir, any little snippet which would back up Logan and Jeremy's twisted narrative. She'd been wasting her time, of course. I'd never have given her any personal information of that nature, even if there had been any to give.

And then there was the time I'd found her in my sitting room when she'd had no reason to be there. The cupboard door had been ajar. Maybe she'd been told to look for documents or letters, anything related to Summerdene and my inheritance that could be used against me. Only I'd interrupted her search, which would have been futile anyway. When I'd drawn her away, she'd asked me questions about Alice, random questions that had no context.

She'd looked tired and jaded that day, I'd thought. I wouldn't have been surprised if Logan had used his controlling ways to coerce her into the actions she'd taken. No doubt, he'd been behind her applying for the job in the first place...

A thought hit me: the flyer – the bit of paper that had come through the letter box late one evening, advertising Pippa's services; it hadn't been delivered to any house other than mine, I'd swear to it. And then, my postcard in the post office window had vanished. Logan, with Pippa in tow, following his instructions, had been responsible for both incidences. I couldn't know for sure, and I wasn't going to demean myself by asking, but I sensed in my bones I was right.

Marcus stepped forward to stand by my side. He'd left the confrontation to me so far, understanding that this was something I needed to do myself. Now, perhaps sensing my uncertainty as to what came next, he spoke for the first time.

'I think it's time you left, Pippa. Obviously you're not going to apologise to Briony for everything you've put her through, so you may as well go.'

He looked at me for confirmation. I nodded.

I thought of something else.

'Where will you go *to*, exactly, Pippa? You never did give me your address, did you?'

Lax as I had been where my employee was concerned, I'd

never chased her up on that. Obviously she didn't live with her mother, and in fact had no connection to Mistlecombe at all; another pack of lies I'd been told. She wasn't living at Candle Street, either. But I had a good idea where she did live.

Pippa confirmed it without hesitation. She had no need to hide it from me now.

'I've gotta flat, well, more of a studio. Over the bike shop in the high street. Logan got it for me,' she said, with a *so-there* sort of nod.

In other words, Briony, he's not all bad. That's what she was telling me, wasn't it?

I stepped past her opened the door wide, and she went through it.

'Goodbye, Pippa,' I said firmly.

Other than a grunt, I got no reply. I didn't expect or want one.

'Would you like me to stay the night?' Marcus said, as we lolled in front the TV neither of us was watching. 'I could kip down on the sofa, no problem,' he added, in case I misconstrued his offer.

'No, there's no need. I'll be fine,' I said, truthfully, whilst imagining how marvellous it would be to come down in the morning and find Marcus here.

But I wouldn't impose any further. There was no reason, and I felt safe now. Besides, I'd already given my guests enough to talk about for one day.

'Well, if you're sure.' He sounded disappointed, although I might have been wrong about that.

'I am, but thank you for the offer. And I'll change the entry code tonight, once everyone's in. I won't forget.'

'I'll be along to check.'

'D'you mean that?' I asked quietly.

'Yes. But only if you want me to.'

'Please,' I said. Then: 'I've missed you, Marcus, and I'm sorry, for...'

For letting him walk away. For not believing. For not trusting my own stupid heart. But he knew, without my saying the words.

He knew.

His dark, dark eyes softened, and looked right into mine. 'I'll ring the doorbell then, shall I?'

'No need. I'll text you the new code tonight.'

Marcus left soon after. We hugged on the doorstep, and I thanked him again for coming to my rescue.

'You're welcome,' he said. 'Don't make a habit of it, though.'

As we laughed softly, our arms went around each other and, somehow, although I don't think either of us meant it to happen – or maybe we did, I don't know – we kissed, and for me it felt like coming home.

FORTY-FIVE

BRIONY

At 2.45 p.m. on Wednesday, I swung the car into the car park alongside Stroud's pretty Victorian train station, relieved that I'd made it on time. It had been touch and go at one point, when a bus ground to a halt in front of me to let about a hundred schoolchildren board – well, maybe ten or so – and the narrowness of the road meant I couldn't safely overtake. Then I'd been forced into another lengthy standstill while a flock of sheep were driven from one field to another across the road, their hooves skittering on the tarmac.

Faye's train was coming in on time, in another eight minutes. I knew that because I'd texted her several times during her journey and she'd answered every time, with patience and good humour, which couldn't have been easy when she had no idea why I was making all this fuss.

I got out of the car, paid for my parking, then sat back inside, resisting the urge to hover near the station exit, not wanting to alarm Faye too much. She knew where to find me.

What to say? How much to say? How to even begin?

These questions, and more, rampaged around my brain and were still in motion, unresolved, when Faye flung her bag on the back seat, climbed into the passenger seat and kissed me on the cheek.

'I'm sorry about all the drama,' I said, breaking a smile. 'You're not going to like what I've got to tell you, but we'll deal with it together, and it'll be okay in the end.'

Faye cast me a perplexed look, and I realised how cryptic I must have sounded, and that I was talking to her as if she was six years old.

I started the engine. 'Can we just get home, to Summerdene, and I'll explain then. Is that okay?'

Faye flounced in her seat, reminding me of her teenage self.

'God, no, it's not okay. You tell me I can't go home, to my home, to my boyfriend, and I've got to wait to find out why? I want to see him, Mum. I need to find out why we've lost phone contact. And what was that about not being safe? You couldn't have been serious, surely?'

I sighed and switched off the engine. Of course, she didn't want to wait. I'd already pitched her into a state of anxiety and she needed to know what was going on without further delay.

Faye leaned into my shoulder. 'I'm *so* sorry, Mum. It's all my fault. If I hadn't got involved with him in the first place, you wouldn't have to go through all that.' Her voice was full of anguish.

I'd given her the bare bones of the saga, as much as she needed to know for now.

'No, darling. Please don't ever think that. Logan's a conman and a manipulator, and very good at it, and if it hadn't been through you, no doubt he'd have found some other way to get to me.'

I couldn't speak any more; the more I unpacked the story, the more it seemed there was to unpack. We would talk again later. Meanwhile, I'd overstayed my welcome in the station car park. I switched on the engine and headed for home.

'I'll need to fetch my stuff from Candle Street,' Faye said, coming into the kitchen.

She'd been in her bedroom for almost an hour. I hadn't gone up to see if she was okay. We'd talked some more over mugs of tea when we'd got home, then she'd disappeared upstairs. Clearly, she needed the time alone. Her eyes were pink-rimmed when she reappeared, but that was only to be expected. I'd given her a lot to take in all at once, and we weren't even done with the details yet.

While Faye was upstairs, I'd sat alone in the kitchen, wondering how I was going to fix this. It had to be me; nobody else could do it for me. The house's silence, broken only by the faint click-click as the hands moved round the clock, pressed softly around me, as if it was a tangible thing. My thoughts circled, fell back like ball bearings in a pinball machine as the trajectory was lost, circled again, until, finally, the circle broke, and they began travelling forwards in a straight line. I was getting somewhere. Whether that somewhere was where I should be, I had no idea, but I had to try.

'What are we going to do, Mum?' Faye dropped into a chair opposite me. She sounded subdued, defeated.

I found a smile. 'Let me think about it some more, then I'll let you know. It'll be all right. You'll see.'

Which of us I was trying to convince more, I didn't know.

Marcus rang later to ask if I wanted him to come along. I'd texted him earlier to let him know Faye was safely home. I told him no, I was fine, but I needed to talk to him tomorrow if he could spare the time and he promised to call around ten, before he went to work. Hopefully, I'd have things straighter in my mind by then.

Marcus duly appeared the following day, and I left Faye to finish off the guests' breakfast while he and I talked in the sitting room. Then, after Marcus had left, the guests had gone out and Faye was upstairs, out of earshot, I rang Logan.

Thankfully, he answered straight away. He may have blocked Faye, but I wasn't among his contacts, and I'd obtained his number from Faye.

He didn't seem surprised to find it was me.

'Ah, Briony. I was wondering when I'd hear from you.'

I heard the arrogance in his voice, and bristled. But I needed to stay calm and emotionless, and only say what was absolutely necessary. As he obviously would, too, since he couldn't be certain if anyone was listening in.

'Come over to Summerdene tomorrow, about midday. There'll be something for you,' I said, mustering my best commanding tone, which, in fact, I found easy. I was in charge now, and Logan had better understand that.

'Can't you come to me?' he said.

'No. It has to be here. It suits me best.'

'It'll be just you? Nobody else?'

'Just me. Nobody else will be in.'

'They'd better not be,' snapped Logan, dropping the casual conversation vibe. He moderated his tone. 'Right, I'll see you tomorrow, then.' He cut the call.

FORTY-SIX

BRIONY

I opened the front door to Logan, noting the absence of his car, which meant he'd arrived on foot. He marched straight in, glancing left and right, opening the door to the guests' sitting room, then striding along the passage to the kitchen and peering out of the window, into the garden.

'There's no one else in?'

'No. I told you there wouldn't be. I'm not stupid.'

'What about upstairs? Faye? The holidaymakers?'

'Faye's still in London. The guests have all gone out for the day. Go up and check if you like.'

But he seemed satisfied, and followed as I led the way to the sitting room, pulling the door behind me but leaving a six-inch gap; that should be enough. Declining my offer of a seat, Logan walked across and stood with his back to the window.

'Phone.' He held out his hand. 'Your phone. Give it to me.'

I looked at him as if I was surprised he'd asked. Wriggling my phone from the pocket of my jeans, I switched it off and handed it to him. He examined it, then put it down on the coffee table between us.

'Let's get down to business, then, shall we?' he said.

I nodded. 'That's what we're here for. But, as I said before, I don't have that kind of money to hand.'

'Wait a minute. You said you had something for me. I told you I wouldn't wait. You know what'll happen if you cross me.'

'Nobody's crossing anyone,' I said evenly. 'This is what I propose. I'll give you something on account today, to show my intention, and the rest when the money's released on the house. These things don't happen overnight, you know.'

'You'd better not be messing me about. So, how much am I getting now?'

Logan took a step towards me. I automatically took a step back.

'Before we get to that,' I said, 'if you leave here today with, shall we say, a down payment, you have to promise not to harm my daughter in any way at all. You'll leave Faye alone, and you'll stop harassing me.'

'I *said*, how much? I'm not promising anything until I've seen the colour of your money.'

I went to the unit, the one with the shelves above and the cupboard below. The cupboard door was slightly open, as I'd left it. I took a box from one of the shelves, brought it back and placed it on the coffee table, next to my phone. It was a long black velvet box, with the name of a jeweller inscribed in gold on the lid.

'What's this?' Logan snarled.

I opened the box to reveal a necklace on a bed of white silk. The fine gold chain was studded with white gems, interspersed with brilliant blue, and at its central point hung a pendant comprising a sizeable deep red stone surrounded by smaller white ones.

'Diamonds, sapphires, and a ruby. It belonged to Alice, my godmother. She left it to me amongst her effects. She inherited it from her grandmother. It dates from the 1920s. It was worth twenty thousand back in the eighties, a lot more now. These vintage pieces command top prices. Take it, and sell it. Put it into auction, whatever.'

'Those stones real?' Logan cast me a cynical look. 'How do I know it's genuine?'

The necklace gleamed from its box, subtly, expensively, as if to advertise its own credentials. I was fond of it because of its association with Alice, though I doubted I'd ever have occasion to wear it. She used to wear it at Christmas, I remembered. She hadn't been a one for jewellery as a rule, and the only other pieces among her effects were her wedding ring – a thin, gold band – a string of fake pearls and an old-fashioned cameo brooch.

'You don't, unless you're an expert,' I said. 'You'll have to take my word for it. Look, Logan, I know what's at stake here. I'm hardly likely to con you, am I?'

'How the fuck do I know what you'd do, Briony?'

I faced him, locking my gaze to his. 'You made demands from me. I'm now meeting those demands, except it's not happening all at once. You intimated you would harm my daughter if I didn't pay you a quarter of a million pounds. That's what you said, isn't it?'

'Oh yes, make no mistake about that. Your Faye's a stunner. Wouldn't it be a pity if that pretty face got, shall we say, *spoilt*? Believe me, Briony, this is no bluff. I know people, I can make things happen. If you want her to stay in one piece, you have to play the game. *My* game.'

He reached down and picked the necklace up out of the box, holding it up to the light, twisting it this way and that. It sparkled obligingly.

'Right.' He dropped the necklace back in its box and snapped the lid shut. 'If I take this now, you'll pay me the money on top.'

It wasn't a question. 'As soon as I can raise the funds, yes.

The broker said it would be quick, once the survey on the house was done.'

Logan scanned the room, apparently enmeshed in thought. My heart was thundering like racehorses' hooves. I wondered if he could hear it. Eventually, he spoke again.

'This house is worth nine hundred thousand, easily. If I take this little trinket as a down payment, I want four hundred thousand. In cash.'

'*Four hundred thousand?* It was two hundred and fifty a minute ago!'

'That's the deal. It's not even half what the place'll fetch. My final offer. Take it or leave it,' Logan said coolly.

'And if I take it, Faye won't get hurt and you'll leave us both alone?'

'Said so, didn't I?'

I sank onto the sofa. My legs wouldn't hold me up any longer. 'Doesn't look as if I've got any choice, does it? Okay. We have a deal.'

'Sensible lady.' Logan smirked, picked up the jewellery box and slid it into his pocket. 'I'll be in touch, mind. I'll be waiting. But no more phone calls, and you'll act normal and keep schtum if you don't want Faye coming to harm.'

'Obviously,' I said, daring to sound a little sarcastic.

'Come to me when you've got something to tell me. Just you, on your own. Got it?'

'Got it,' I said.

And then I felt a whisper of air as the door opened fully behind me.

'Oh, she'll have something to tell you. In fact, why don't we get that out of the way, right now?' Marcus said.

FORTY-SEVEN
BRIONY

Logan spun round and glared at Marcus. 'Oh look, it's the boyfriend. Well, well.'

I got to my feet. Logan turned his gaze to me. *'What've you done?'*

Logan took a step towards Marcus, who'd entered the room and was now standing beside me. I could see Logan weighing up the situation, noting that Marcus was a good head taller than him, broader in the shoulder, better equipped, physically, in every way. Logan began to walk towards the door. Marcus headed him off.

'You leave here only when I tell you to,' he said. 'Briony. Show him.'

Logan looked from one of us to the other, confused, his anger building almost visibly. For the first time I felt a little scared, but I followed Marcus's instructions. I crossed to the small table in the corner which held an oversized table lamp, slid my hand beneath its gold-coloured shade and detached Faye's mobile phone from its sticky tape. I held it up between my finger and thumb for Logan to see, its recording light still showing.

'It'll all be on here. A mobile phone recording is admissible evidence in a court of law.'

Logan puffed out air. 'One little phone with a dodgy recording? I don't think so.'

'It'll be clear enough,' I said, 'but there's a backup.' I went to the cupboard below the shelves, opened the door fully and took out Alice's Dictaphone, a pre-digital relic she'd used to record the minutes of her various committees for me to type up. I'd found it in the box of junk in the landing cupboard. Amazingly, it still worked – I'd tested it out. I pressed the switch now and the cassette stopped whirring.

'Here's another,' I said, holding the machine up.

'*Christ!*' Logan spun round on his heel, spun back, probably cursing himself for having agreed to come to Summerdene in the first place rather than have me go to him.

Which, of course, would never have worked. I still didn't know why he hadn't insisted we meet at his house, or on neutral ground, but Marcus probably had the right idea about that.

'He thought he'd won and you were about to pay up. He didn't want to jeopardise that, so he agreed to your terms. That, and him being short of a brain cell or two,' he'd said.

Marcus stepped forward again. 'And just in case you were thinking two recordings aren't enough, how about this one?'

He held up his own phone and thumbed an icon. Logan appeared on the screen, with me at the edge, its audio loud and clear. Once Marcus had left his hiding place in the old surgery, all he'd had to do was stand beside the half-open sitting room door and hold his phone to the gap. Risky, yes, but we'd envisaged Logan being so intent on his negotiations with me, he wouldn't have thought to keep watch on the door. We were right.

Logan's face turned white with rage. He lurched towards Marcus and tried to grab the phone from his hand, but Marcus lifted it high out of his reach, then turned swiftly and shoved

Logan, hard, with his shoulder. He staggered backwards, cracking his elbow on the doorframe.

'*Shit!*' He rubbed his elbow. A blob of spittle escaped the corner of his mouth.

'If you want a fight, you've got one,' Marcus said evenly.

Comparing the two men, it would be obvious to anyone, even Logan, who would win, hands down.

Logan looked at each of us in turn, venom in his gaze, then pushed past Marcus and made his way to the front door. I jumped as I heard it slam. My lungs pumped with the effort it took to breathe. My brain might have registered victory; my body had a way to go before it caught up.

Marcus went to the window and peered out, presumably to check that Logan had left, and then he came to me and held me loosely, his arms around my waist.

'Okay?'

'Yes, I'm all right. I can't believe we pulled it off. Do you think it's really over and Faye's safe? He won't hurt her now, will he?'

'He'd be an idiot if he did, knowing what we've got on him,' Marcus said.

A tiny wave of fear broke inside me. I knew Marcus couldn't tell me irrevocably that the nightmare was over – neither of us could know that for absolute certain – but I had to remain positive.

I detached myself from his embrace. 'All the same, it would be best if Faye was away from the village, at least for the time being. I'll speak to her when she comes back. I should ring her now. Logan will be well clear.'

I picked up my mobile and rang the landline at Kestrels, Marcus's cottage. Having driven off in her car well before Logan was due at Summerdene, Faye would have taken the long way round to Candle Street to avoid passing him. Then, having collected her belongings, she would have returned by the same circuitous route and let herself into Kestrels to wait until she heard from me, as we'd arranged.

I made the call; Faye would be home in a few minutes.

Marcus and I went to the kitchen and began preparing lunch together.

'He's still got your necklace,' Marcus said suddenly. 'He didn't put it back.'

I laughed. 'Nope. He took it. I was quite fond of it because it was Alice's but it was a small price to pay to be free of him.'

'Not that small. How many thousands did you tell him it was worth?'

'I can't remember now. He might get a hundred quid for it on a good day.'

'A *hundred*...?'

'The stones aren't real, they're paste. In other words, buffed up glass. It's 1960s, not 1920s. Possibly foreign.'

Marcus slapped a hand to his forehead, and laughed. 'I didn't know. I thought it was the real McCoy.'

'That makes two of you,' I said, grinning.

Marcus stayed for lunch then went home, sensing correctly that I needed a little time alone with Faye.

'Did you manage to get all your stuff?' I asked her, after we'd talked some more about Logan and all that had happened.

I'd seen her bulging bags in the hall, so I knew she'd had no trouble getting into the house.

'Yeah, I think so. Bound to be a few bits left. I had to be really quick in case he showed up.'

'I know,' I said, feeling guilty for having placed Faye in another, possibly dangerous, situation. 'I'm sorry.'

'It's cool. Anyway, while I was there, I had a look through the drawer where Logan keeps his papers and stuff. I thought there might be something that would be useful to know, about his background and how much of what he said was true, anything like that. There was an envelope with his birth certificate, his passport and his adoption papers. I had a quick look, there were no surprises. But there was a letter written to Logan himself by a social worker. I didn't have time to read it properly but it looked interesting so I photocopied it on his printer.

'A letter...?'

'Yes, hang on.'

Faye nipped along the hall and I heard the zip of one of her bags opening. She returned with a piece of paper and placed it on the table in front of us, flattening out the creases with her hand. We read it together, silently. The address at the top was of a Midlands social services department, then:

22 April 1987

Dear Logan

I thought it might be helpful if I wrote something down about your birth parents and how you came to be adopted.

You were born at North Manchester General Hospital on 5 March 1987 at 4.27 a.m. weighing 6 lbs 12 oz.

Your birth mother's name was Molly Jones. She was 17 years old, still at school, living with her parents in the small village of Mistlecombe, Gloucestershire. She was petite and pretty, with sandy hair, and freckles. She was popular at school and enjoyed spending time with her friends. Molly had a younger sister, Sharron. Her father, Ralph, was a pharmacist, her mother, Dulcie, was a housewife.

At the time, an illegitimate birth was often viewed as shameful and the subject of possibly hurtful gossip. Given your birth mother's young age, her parents believed it best for her to leave the village, and she was sent to Manchester to stay with her aunt and uncle. Later, the rest of the family also moved to Manchester.

While she was pregnant, Molly thought long and hard about whether to have the baby adopted. As a schoolgirl, even with parental support it would have been difficult for her to bring up a child, and she wanted you to have the best life possible with all the advantages she did not feel able to give you. The decision to have you adopted was not made lightly by any means, but circumstances at the time convinced Molly that it would give you the best chance in life.

Molly had never told your birth father about the pregnancy, neither had she told anyone who he was, including her own parents. As you know, he is not named on your birth certificate.

It was not until after your birth, around a month prior to the date of this letter, that Molly changed her mind and decided to reveal the name of your birth father to you. She asked me to do this through this letter. She felt it would be unfair to withhold this information from you for perpetuity.

Your birth father's name was Jeremy Church, also living at the time in Mistlecombe with his mother, Alice Church. He was around 22 years of age, and thought to be a student. His father, Edward, had died around five years before. He was a doctor, the village's GP.

When you were born, Molly took you home and cared for you for three weeks. You were then fostered with a Manchester family, and later adopted by Kathleen and Joseph Medhurst, who were living in Bedfordshire at the time. I expect your parents have shown you the paperwork relating to the Adoption Order. Kathleen and Joseph had no natural children of their own and were very happy to make you part of their family.

I hope that what I have written will help you understand how you came to live with your parents. Perhaps, after you have read this letter, you should discuss it with them, as they will be able to help you sort out anything that seems unclear.

With all good wishes for the future.

Denise Weller
Social Worker

'Molly was one of your friends, wasn't she?' Faye asked. 'Did you know about this, Mum?'

'No, I didn't. Not all of it, anyway. Molly and Samantha were my best mates, until Molly and her family suddenly left the village. I was checking out the old surgery a while ago and I found something of Molly's – her swimming costume. I couldn't think how it had got there, until I cast my mind back and started piecing all the memories together, and then I realised Jeremy must have been her secret boyfriend. Samantha and I had no idea at the time, and I don't imagine anyone else did either. Perhaps he insisted it was kept secret. He was twenty-one, she was a sixteen-year-old school girl, so that would figure. Maybe the secrecy made it more thrilling for her. It certainly would for him; he was that type. It didn't necessarily follow that she'd got pregnant by him but I suspected she had.' I pointed at the letter. 'Now we know for certain.'

I felt so sad for Molly. Giving up her baby must have been heartbreaking, whatever the circumstances. I wondered if she'd already broken up with Jeremy before she knew she was pregnant. His moods had been mercurial – I'd had cause to notice them more than most. Had his bouts of silent anger been connected to Molly? He'd definitely become weirder than ever after she'd left the village, I remember that. Although that would suppose he'd had feelings for her. Unless it was all about control, which was more likely, I thought.

'Have you ever looked her up online, Mum? Tried to find her?' Faye asked.

'I did once. I looked for Samantha, too. I didn't find either of them, but they'd have changed their last names if they got married.'

'Well, it was ages ago. They could be anywhere,' Faye said, leaning her elbows on the table and cupping her chin.

She made it sound as if my teenage years were virtually pre-war. I had to smile.

My mind rewound to the night of the school disco, when Molly had sloped off somewhere afterwards, leaving Samantha standing at the gate. She never did tell us where she'd gone, or who with. And then there was the mystery of her not showing up at the river that Sunday afternoon – a mystery no longer. It hadn't been long after that she had suddenly left the village.

I could see it all now. Molly had gone without saying a word to Samantha and me, her best friends, not only because she was ashamed of getting pregnant, but because of who the father was. And, because she didn't want him knowing either, which I found perfectly understandable, she'd followed her parents' wishes and moved from Mistlecombe, away from gossip and prying eyes, to deal with her situation in the way she felt best.

Molly Jones was Logan's mother. The final piece of the puzzle slotted quietly into place.

FORTY-EIGHT
BRIONY

A few days later, Faye and I had a heart to heart. It was half past ten and I'd just gone to bed when Faye tapped on the door, came in and sat down on the side of the bed. She wanted to talk, I could tell. I wasn't surprised. Everything that had happened with Logan must have affected her deeply, and would for some time. She must have so many questions, about herself as well as Logan.

I propped myself up on the pillows and waited.

'I really loved him, Mum,' Faye began. 'Doesn't that count for something? I keep thinking it must mean there's some good in him, somewhere. Or have I got that wrong as well?'

She smiled, but even by the low light of the bedside lamp I could see the glint of tears.

'No, I'm sure you haven't got it wrong. If that's what you truly feel, then that's how it is. Whatever Logan did, whatever faults Logan has, there'll be some good inside him, even if he doesn't let it show. You fell in love with that deeper version of him, and that makes it real.'

'Do you really believe that?' Faye eyed me closely, searching.

'I do. Logan's not truly evil, just wholly misguided. He's damaged, Faye. Damaged by whatever life has thrown at him. Some would come out the other side unscathed; others, like Logan, can't accept and move on. But he will, in time.'

'I do hope so,' Faye said. 'I don't wish him any harm. Oh, I did, when he was threatening you, but not now. Is that okay?'

I smiled. 'Of course it's okay. I feel the same.'

Faye nodded. She looked peaceful. I hope she was feeling that inside, after my thin attempt at reassurance. I wasn't quite ready to forgive Logan for the trauma he'd put me through. Faye was already a step ahead of me, and that was fine.

We were silent for a moment, then Faye reached into the pocket of the grey hoodie she wore over her pyjamas and took out her phone.

'I've got something to show you, Mum.' She clicked onto Facebook and scrolled.

'Oh?' I said, sitting up straighter.

The screen was still. Faye angled it towards me. 'Look. Could this be her? Is that Molly?'

I glanced at the screen briefly, not looking properly. I wasn't prepared for this. 'I don't...'

'Sorry, Mum. I kept thinking about her, and I know you said you'd looked and hadn't found her, but I thought it wouldn't do any harm if I...' Faye gave her head a little shake and shuffled closer to me so that we were side by side. 'Did Molly have a middle name?'

'Middle name?' I said dully, still not able to bring myself to look at the screen. I thought for a moment. 'Yes, she did. I think it was Frances. In fact I'm sure it was. Molly Frances Jones.'

'Okay, right...' Faye sounded businesslike now. 'She may have married – this Molly has – but it looks like she's using her single name for her business: "Molly F Jones Clothes for Kiddies". And look, if you click on the website...' Faye clicked and a colourful page appeared. 'Her bio says she was born and raised in a rural Cotswold village in Gloucestershire, moved to the Midlands, is married to someone called Mike and has two grown-up daughters. It's all there, Mum. It *has* to be her.'

I could sense Faye's excitement; I wasn't sure I shared it. Not yet. This was so left field I was finding it hard to infuse my brain with any kind of sense.

'Give me that.' Faye handed me her phone. I looked. The website page was, as you'd expect, full of shots of children wearing the clothes on offer, but beneath the company logo was a small, square picture of a petite woman in a floral dress, leaning against a tree.

I looked harder. I blinked. I clicked back to Facebook, revealing a better, full-face photo. The pixie cut was gone, in its place a shoulder length layered style, fairer and less sandy than I remembered. I couldn't detect any freckles but makeup would have disguised them. But those green eyes, her face shape, her slightly pointy chin, and something in the way she held herself told me this was indeed my one-time best friend.

And then I saw, probably for the first time, something of Logan in his mother's expression, something that had obviously been there all along only I had, understandably, failed to recognise it.

'It's her,' I said, almost to myself.

'So now you know she's okay, Mum. It says she married and had children. She looks happy, wouldn't you say?' Faye looked at me, awaiting approval for her discovery.

Now I was able to give it.

I hugged her. 'Thank you, lovey. She's fine and that's all I wanted to know.'

'Will you get in touch?' Faye asked hesitantly, as if she already knew the answer.

'No. She left all those years ago, left her life behind, and I understand that. She could have found me had she wanted to. Best to leave her alone.' I smiled. 'It's as it should be.'

. . .

On Friday, Faye went to Brighton to stay with Tony and his wife for the weekend. She planned to head to London for a few days after that, and then return to Summerdene. I wasn't sure she'd want to come back to Mistlecombe after all that had happened, but apparently I needed 'somebody to keep an eye on me'. I had to smile at how our statuses had reversed.

I had spoken to my ex-husband briefly, telling him his instincts had been correct, and Logan wasn't who, or what, Faye had thought he was, but I felt it was her call if she wanted her father to know the whole story, and I left it to her to decide. In truth, I rather hoped she'd let him think it was a straightforward break-up situation, and she just needed time out to recover. Tony didn't need to know anything more, and I really didn't want to have that conversation with him.

I drove Faye to Stroud station and waved her off with a cheery smile and a heart as heavy as lead. My initial euphoria had worn off and I'd begun to question whether I really was free of Logan and his crazy, manipulative ways. Surely, it couldn't be that easy. I'd lain awake for a good part of last night, alert to every little creak and thump, despite having fixed the chain on the front door and the double bolts on the back, and checking both, twice, before I'd come up to bed.

But I didn't have time to lie on the sofa in a decline; I had work to do.

My first task was to replace Pippa, and I decided to take Sylvia's lead and use a cleaning company. I found one in Stroud, which might have been the same one Sylvia used, and arranged for somebody to come in three times a week. With Faye's help, I could manage the rest of the time.

Marcus had offered to help with breakfast at weekends, and on the days he didn't have to be at the university early. I only put up a token resistance before I gratefully accepted. If I hadn't, I suspected he'd have turned up anyway. We still had some talking to do, Marcus and I, but the time would come, for that; the right time. Meanwhile, all I wanted was normality, and peace of mind, if such a thing was possible.

I threw myself into my domestic tasks of necessity as the agency wouldn't be sending anyone until next week, and also because keeping busy helped my mental state, and I discovered a new energy as I raced around with the vacuum, stripped beds and scrubbed bathrooms.

It was almost three o'clock when I realised I hadn't had lunch, so I sawed up half a French stick and stuck it on a plate with a wedge of cheddar and two pickled onions. It was while I was demolishing my slapdash version of a ploughman's lunch that the doorbell rang. I levered myself off the kitchen chair and trotted to the front door, catching a glimpse of myself in the hall mirror as I passed. My hair had half fallen out of its ponytail, my face was red where I'd sweated off my make-up and my pink shirt was spotted with dirty water from my cleaning efforts.

It was Marcus at the door. Of course it was.

'You don't need to ring the bell, I said before.' I gathered my hair back into its elastic band. 'Just use the code, or come round the back.'

'I wasn't sure if I should,' he said, as he came into the hall. 'Anyway, I still don't know the new code. You didn't send it to me.'

'Didn't I? Could be just as well. We get some funny types round here.'

We laughed, me a little awkwardly. I was still at the stage where a little warning of Marcus's appearance would be useful.

'I'll give you the code,' I said, leading the way to the kitchen. 'If I can remember what I changed it to.'

'Ah, sorry. You're having lunch.' Marcus eyed my plate and its surround of crumbs. 'Or is it early tea?'

'You tell me. Would you like a beer? Or a cup of tea?'

'I'm good, thanks. Briony...?'

Marcus sat down at the table and I regained my own seat, praying that whatever was coming wasn't anything I wasn't going to like. My nerves couldn't take any more bad news.

It was the opposite.

'I stopped off at Candle Street on the way home,' Marcus said, his eyes soft with kindness. 'He's gone.'

He paused while this plum of information found its target.

'Logan's gone?' I swallowed the constriction in my throat. 'Gone, *how*? How d'you know?'

'The blinds were down and there were extra bags of rubbish on the pavement, next to the bin. I looked in them. There were packets of food, toiletries, books, all kinds of things. I looked through the letter box and I could tell the place was empty. The man next door came out. Sergeant major type. He must have seen me looking and thought I was up to no good.' Marcus smiled. 'I explained I'd come to call on a mate but he didn't seem to be at home. The neighbour said the man who'd been renting the house had got into a taxi with his bags, early yesterday morning. He'd told him he was leaving the village for good when he came out to see what was going on. Thumbs up for nosy neighbours, eh?'

My mouth had dried. No words came.

'I thought you should know as soon as possible. Briony? Are you okay?'

'Yes, I'm fine.' I gathered myself. 'If Logan's left the village, he must have given up on me. That's what it means, doesn't it?'

'I say it was pretty certain,' Marcus said. 'There's something else. The neighbour said there was already somebody already in the cab, a girl. One of those Goth types, that was how he described her. Close enough, I thought.'

'Pippa...'

'Must have been.'

'You'd think after everything, she'd have wanted to cut loose from her brother,' I said thoughtfully. 'She wasn't all bad, just misguided.'

Marcus rubbed his hands together. He wasn't going to let me be anything but pragmatic over the Medhursts' departure. 'You're shot of the pair of them, that's all that matters. How about I take you out tonight, a nice dinner somewhere?'

'I'd like that,' I said, and then I had another thought. 'Instead of going out, would you like to come here, and I'll cook?' I chuckled. 'That's a promise, not a threat, by the way.'

Marcus pretended to be considering this. 'Go on, then. I'll risk it.'

I reached across and whacked him playfully on the arm. Then, almost without realising it, I was on my feet, Marcus had stood up, too, his arms went around me and we kissed.

After much thought and several changes of mind, I settled on the homely option for dinner: cottage pie. Easily prepared in advance, hard to mess up – unless I left it in the oven too long, which for me was always a possibility. Or it was, when I used to make it for Tony.

Overcooked and therefore dry, too much mashed potato, or too little, the wrong herbs... all of which was said with patient indulgence at my shortcomings, yet the barbs showed through. And they hurt, they really did. Metallic rods of pain that were fed into the furnace along with a thousand others and emerged as one huge, red-hot ball of disappointment and failure.

Thankfully, I'd managed to shake off this pointless round of negativity by the time Marcus arrived at seven and presented me with a bedraggled but sweet-smelling, riotously colourful bunch of flowers from his garden, the damp stalks tied with rough brown string.

'I didn't have any ribbon.'

'Who needs it?' I said. Then, half to myself: 'Oven! Oven!' as the timer pinged.

At least I'd remembered to set the damn thing. I took the perfectly browned pie from the oven, then poked a fork into the vegetables in the steamer.

'Nearly done,' I said.

'Briony...'

I turned. Marcus was standing close beside me. 'Yes...?'

He took both my hands in his. I was wearing my hedgehog-patterned oven gloves but, honestly, I didn't think he even noticed.

'How do you feel about me, Briony? Truly? I was going to suggest we talk properly, later, but really, it's all I – *we* – need to know, isn't it?'

And so I told him. I told him all the reasons I'd pushed my feelings aside, pushing him aside in the process, and as I heard the words coming out of my mouth, they sounded as insubstantial and as transient as the steam rising from the pan on the stove. Except for that one word 'love' which hung in the air between us, as real, as solid, as immoveable as a house.

'Have I answered the question?' I asked eventually, when Marcus's lips had peeled away from mine.

'That'll do,' he said, smiling into my eyes.

The cottage pie was perfect. The vegetables had turned to mush.

A bit like my heart, really.

FORTY-NINE
BRIONY

Eight months later

Summerdene is sold now, to Stuart and Freddie, a mid-fifties couple making the move from London. As they walked around the house on their second visit, they spoke about parties, and having friends and family to stay. They were full of ideas on décor and will make the house even more beautiful than it is already.

I had only the slightest qualms about selling, and they were soon overcome. I'd never truly envisaged Summerdene as my forever home. Living in it was fun – well, mostly – but I didn't feel an emotional attachment to it. It had been my home, twice, and that was enough. Logan was right about one thing: the house would have gone to Jeremy had he not been struck down by that tragic illness. I'm still sad about the way it ended for him; always will be, despite everything.

As for my stint as a B&B host, I'd enjoyed that, too. But it's hard work, and relentless, if you don't have people to take over while you take time out. I would never rely on Faye, even though she'd have willingly stepped in. It wouldn't have been fair on her. Besides, teaching was always my first love; I guess I always knew deep inside that I'd return to it.

Summerdene is in safe hands. It will be lived in and loved, and that would make Alice happy. I owe her that.

I had the old surgery demolished before I put the house up for sale. It felt right to restore it to its original perfect proportions before it changed hands. It was the least I could do, a kind of recompense for my having received such a gift. The former internal door to the extension has been blocked up and a shallow cupboard fitted in its place, cleverly disguising the door frame. It's as if the surgery never existed. I like to believe Alice would have approved of that, too.

Faye has moved back to London. She's living in a different area from before but still has her friends, and the job she enjoys. She's determined to stay single for the foreseeable – so she says. But my daughter does like to have a boyfriend around, and I feel it won't be long before she meets somebody else, hopefully somebody who will love her properly and see her for the wonderful girl she is.

That is my wish for her.

I never saw or heard from Logan again. Perhaps he high-tailed it back to Hertfordshire, or dragged his sense of entitlement and his innate, festering resentment against the world and everyone in it to cause havoc somewhere else. I'll never know, nor do I want to. But I hope he finds a way to quell the anger inside him and find contentment in whatever lies ahead. His future happiness is in his own hands.

Something totally unexpected happened before I left Mistlecombe. I'd just accepted the offer on the house and was feeling restless, so I baked a batch of madeleines. I'd wound down the B&B business and had no guests; I didn't know who was going to eat the cakes apart from me, so I packed some into a box and took them round to Sylvia in Blackthorn Street. She asked me in, made tea and we got talking.

Fortunately, she didn't ask me if I'd found Pippa. I expect she'd forgotten why I'd called on her before, and I was glad; I didn't want to talk about Pippa, or any of that. But Sylvia had remembered I lived at Summerdene.

'You wouldn't remember the house from years back,' she said, as we sat in her cosy, overstuffed sitting room.

I explained how I'd come to live there with Alice when I was a teenager, not mentioning Jeremy.

'Alice Church was your godmother! Fancy that. Oh yes, I knew Alice. Everyone in the village did. Lovely lady, did a lot for charity. I was sorry when I heard she'd passed on.' Sylvia tilted her silver head sideways. 'Of course, *he* went years before, Doctor Edward – we called him that. You wouldn't have known him, I don't suppose?' Sylvia said this with a note of cautiousness in her voice, which puzzled me.

'No. I knew he was the village GP of course.'

Sylvia harrumphed, lifting her chin. '*Was* being the operative word.' She held up a bony finger. 'Don't mind me. Shouldn't have said anything.'

I was intrigued. I had to ask what she meant. She shook her head slowly, then: 'Well, it's all in the past so I don't suppose there's any harm in you knowing. He was struck off, you see. Not allowed to practise any more,' she added, in case I'd misunderstood.

'Struck off? No, that can't be right.'

Sylvia must be confusing Edward with another doctor, at a different time, perhaps.

'I'm afraid it is. It was *said* he touched a young girl, in a place he shouldn't have, if you know what I mean. While he was examining her for something else. I never knew if it was true or not, but there's no smoke without fire. There was a dreadful to-do, all supposed to be kept under wraps but these things get about, you know? Anyway, the next thing we knew, Doctor Edward was removed from his post and we all had to traipse to the next village to get seen to. Most inconvenient, it was.'

I was in shock. I'd never heard a thing about this before, not even a whisper. But Alice was hardly likely to tell me.

'What about Alice, his wife? It must have been a dreadful time for her.'

'Oh, it was, dear. But Alice wasn't one for hiding away. She let it be known she knew nothing about what her husband had done, and most of the village believed her. Then she just held her head up and carried on. *He*, Doctor Edward, moved out of Summerdene, to a cottage not far from here. Kept his head down, as one would, and gradually the village got tired of talking about it all, Alice took her rightful place in the community, and that was that.'

Sylvia leaned towards me with a worried frown. 'I did right to tell you, didn't I?'

'Yes, it's fine,' I said, after a pause. 'I had no idea, but thank you for telling me.'

Having said a final goodbye to Sylvia, I walked slowly home, my mind clouded with thought. His father's actions must have had an impact on Jeremy, as well as Alice. But I couldn't bring myself to blame father-son genetics for the way Jeremy treated me, not entirely. Life is never that simple, is it? And there is such a thing as free will.

What I'd heard probably explained why the old surgery was kept locked up and forgotten, and possibly why Alice never invited people to Summerdene; the committees she served on and the local groups she belonged to always met at somebody else's house. I hadn't questioned it at the time, but I'd thought about it later, and wondered. Maybe Alice thought people wouldn't want to come to Summerdene because of its connection to their erstwhile GP. And perhaps her involvement in village activities and her outward willingness to dive in and help wherever help was needed were her way of giving back a little of what her husband had taken away. Whatever the truth of it, I felt sad for her, and admired her bravery.

But it's all in the past. The many happy memories I have of Mistlecombe and Summerdene are safe, the rest discarded, mostly. That's the way it should be.

I live in Cheltenham now, renting a maisonette in a pretty Georgian terrace until I decide where I want to put down roots. I thought about moving back to Brighton, but although I love my home town, it would have felt like a backward step. Meanwhile, Cheltenham suits me fine. I'm teaching at a junior school, a maternity leave cover post, and enjoying it.

Wonderful and surprising though it still seems to me, I have Marcus. He gave up Kestrels and is sharing a house with a fellow academic, close to the university, although he spends more time at my place than his own. Where the two us are headed I don't know, but it's an adventure, and I'm not worrying about the future.

It can take care of itself.

A LETTER FROM THE AUTHOR

Dear readers,

Thank you so much for reading *Her Best Friend's Secret*. I hope you enjoyed following Briony's story.

If you would like to hear about my new releases and bonus content, you can sign up for my newsletter!

www.stormpublishing.co/deirdre-palmer

If you enjoyed this book, I'd really appreciate it if you could leave a review. Even a short review can go a long way towards helping readers discover my books for the first time. Thank you so much!

Inheritance, especially when it's unexpected and substantial, can trigger all kinds of emotions and complications, not only for the recipient. It's something within everyone's experience, either personally, or from stories in the press and television programmes. This was my starting point when I was trying to think of a premise for *Her Best Friend's Secret*.

I only had a vague idea as to how the story would play out until I'd started writing and got to know my characters and how they behaved. I don't plot in detail in advance – I admire writers who can, but it just doesn't work for me. Characters are easy – at least I find they are. Briony, a divorcee in need of a recharge in her life, came to me fully-formed, as did Jeremy. I loved writing him! The beautiful old Cotswold house came easily too, and in my mind I saw the abandoned doctor's surgery attached to it. I had no idea how I was going to bring it into the story; I only knew it was there and I had no idea why! But it served its purpose, in the end.

Thanks again for reading the book. I love to hear from readers, so do get in touch if you'd like to.

Deirdre

facebook.com/deirdre.palmer.735
x.com/DLPalmer_Writer
instagram.com/deirdrewrites

ACKNOWLEDGMENTS

As always, a heartfelt thank you to the dedicated and talented team at Storm, particularly to Kathryn Taussig for taking me on in the first place. Special thanks to my brilliant editor Kate Smith, for her wisdom and guidance in making this book the best it could be. Thanks also to my family, and to my dearest friends, writerly and otherwise, for their cheerful and unfailing encouragement while this book was in the making. I'm indebted to you all.